Titles by Mark Greaney

The Gray Man

On Target

Ballistic

Dead Eye

Back Blast

Gunmetal Gray

Agent in Place

Mission Critical

One Minute Out

Relentless

Sierra Six

Red Metal

(with LtCol H. Ripley Rawlings IV, USMC)

Praise for Mark Greaney and the Gray Man novels

"Greaney keeps this vengeance story red-lined and blistering . . . Writing as smooth as stainless steel and a hero as mean as razor wire . . . *The Gray Man* glitters like a blade in an alley."

—David Stone, *New York Times* bestselling author

"Hard, fast, and unflinching—exactly what a thriller should be."

—Lee Child, #1 *New York Times* bestselling author

"The story is so propulsive, the murders so explosive, that flipping the pages feels like playing the ultimate video game."

—*The New York Times*

"A high-octane thriller that doesn't pause for more than a second . . . Greaney has a good understanding of weapons and tactics . . . and he uses that to enliven his storytelling, including lots of the kinds of details that action junkies love." —*Chicago Sun-Times*

"Never has an assassin been rendered so real yet so deadly. Strikes with the impact of a bullet to the chest . . . A debut not to be missed."

—James Rollins, *New York Times* bestselling author

"Take fictional spy Jason Bourne, pump him up with Red Bull and meth, shake vigorously—and you've got the recipe for Court Gentry . . . Such a souped-up, efficient killing machine, Bourne's a piker by comparison."

—*The Memphis Commercial Appeal*

"Court is endearing in his perseverance even as his schemes are undermined by sympathetic victims, misleading information, outright lies, poor planning, betrayal, conflicting agendas, and simple bad luck . . . An action-filled yet touching story of a man whose reason has long ago been subsumed by his work ethic." —*Publishers Weekly*

THE GRAY MAN

MARK GREANEY

BERKLEY / NEW YORK

BERKLEY
An imprint of Penguin Random House LLC
penguinrandomhouse.com

ISBN: 9780593547588

The Library of Congress has catalogued the first Berkley trade paperback edition of this book as follows:

Greaney, Mark.
The gray man / Mark Greaney.
pages cm.—(A gray man novel; 1)
ISBN 978-0-425-27638-9 (paperback)
1. Assassins—Fiction. I. Title.
PS3607.R4285G73 2014
813'.6—dc23
2014012552

Jove premium edition / October 2009
Berkley trade paperback edition / September 2014
Second Berkley trade paperback edition / September 2021
Berkley movie tie-in trade paperback edition / July 2022

Printed in the United States of America
1 3 5 7 9 10 8 6 4 2

Book design by Laura K. Corless

This is a work of fiction. Names, characters, places, and incidents either are the product of the author's imagination or are used fictitiously, and any resemblance to actual persons, living or dead, business establishments, events, or locales is entirely coincidental.

For Edward F. Greaney Jr.
and Kathleen Cleghorn Greaney

Mom and Dad, I miss you both

ACKNOWLEDGMENTS

I would like to thank James Yeager and his brilliant cadre of trainers at Tactical Response Inc. in Camden, Tennessee, for getting me up to speed on rifles, pistols, immediate-action medical, and team tactics, and most especially for having the decency to put me out after setting me on fire. God bless you; America is a safer place because of all you and your students do. Now go lay down some hate.

Many thanks also go to James Rollins, Devin Greaney, Karen Ott Mayer, John and Carrie Echols, Mike Cowan, Greg Jones, April Adams, Nichole Geer-Roberts, Stephanie and Abbie Stovall, and Jenny Kraft. Writers appreciate readers, and I appreciate you all.

My agent, Scott Miller at Trident Media Group, and my editor, Tom Colgan at Berkley, also receive my deep and eternal gratitude. This was fun, guys. How 'bout we do it again sometime?

MarkGreaneyBooks.com

PROLOGUE

A flash of light in the distant morning sky captured the attention of the Land Rover's blood-soaked driver. Polarized Oakleys shielded his eyes from the brunt of the sun's rays; still, he squinted through his windshield's glare, desperate to identify the burning aircraft that now spun and hurtled towards earth, a smoldering comet's tail of black smoke left hanging above it.

It was a helicopter, a large Army Chinook, and horrific though the situation must have been for those on board, the driver of the Land Rover breathed a subdued sigh of relief. His extraction transport was to be a Russian-built KA-32T, crewed by Polish mercenaries and flown in from over the border in Turkey. The driver found the dying Chinook regrettable but preferable to a dying KA-32T.

He watched the chopper spin in its uncontrolled descent, staining the blue sky directly in front of him with burning fuel.

He turned the Land Rover hard to the right and accelerated

eastward. The blood-soaked driver wanted to get as far away from here as fast as possible. As much as he wished there was something he could do for the Americans on board the Chinook, he knew their fate was out of his hands.

And he had his own problems. For five hours he'd raced across the flatlands of western Iraq, fleeing the dirty work he'd left behind, and now he was less than twenty minutes from his exfiltration. A shot-down chopper meant that in minutes this place would be crawling with armed fighters, defiling bodies, shooting assault rifles into the air, and jumping around like fucking morons.

It was a party the bloodstained driver would not mind missing, lest he himself become a party favor.

The Chinook sank off to his left and disappeared behind a brown ridge in the distance.

The driver fixed his eyes on the road ahead. *Not my problem,* he told himself. He was not trained to search and to rescue, he was not trained to give aid, and he certainly was not trained to negotiate for hostages.

He was trained to kill. He'd done so back over the border in Syria, and now it was time to get out of the kill zone.

As his Rover accelerated through the haze and dust at over one hundred kilometers an hour, he began a dialogue with himself. His inner voice wanted to turn back, to race to the Chinook's crash site to check for survivors. His outer voice, on the other hand, was more pragmatic.

"Keep moving, Gentry, just keep moving. Those dudes are fucked. Nothing you can do about it."

Gentry's spoken words were sensible, but his inner monologue just would not shut up.

ONE

The first gunmen arriving at the crash site were not Al Qaeda and had nothing to do with the shoot down. They were four local boys with old wooden-stocked Kalashnikovs who'd held a sloppy morning roadblock a hundred meters from where the chopper impacted with the city street. The boys pushed through the growing phalanx of onlookers, the shopkeepers and the street kids who dove for cover when the twin-rotor helicopter hurtled down among them, and the taxi drivers who swerved off the road to avoid the American craft. The four young gunmen approached the scene warily but without a shred of tactical skill. A loud snap from the raging fire, a single handgun round cooking off in the heat, sent them all to cover. After a moment's hesitation, their heads popped back up, they aimed their rifles, and then emptied their barking and bucking guns into the twisted metal machine.

A man in a blackened American military uniform crawled from

the wreckage and received two dozen rounds from the boys' weapons. The soldier's struggle ceased as soon as the first bullets raked across his back.

Braver now after the adrenaline rush of killing a man in front of the crowd of shouting civilians, the boys broke cover and moved closer to the wreckage. They reloaded their rifles and raised them to shoot at the burning bodies of the flight crew in the cockpit. But before they could open fire, three vehicles raced up from behind: pickup trucks full of armed Arabian foreigners.

Al Qaeda.

The local kids wisely backed away from the aircraft, stood back with the civilians, and chanted a devotional to God as the masked men fanned out in the road around the wreckage.

The broken corpses of two more soldiers fell clear from the rear of the Chinook, and these were the first images of the scene caught by the three-man Al Jazeera camera crew that jumped from truck three.

Just under a mile away, Gentry pulled off the road, turned into a dry streambed, and forced the Land Rover as deep as possible into the tall brown river grasses. He climbed out of the truck and raced to the tailgate, swung a pack onto his back, and hefted a long camel-colored case by its carry handle.

As he moved away from the vehicle, he noticed the drying blood all over his loose-fitting local clothing for the first time. The blood was not his own, but there was no mystery to the stain.

He knew whose blood it was.

Thirty seconds later, he crested the little ridge by the streambed and crawled forward as quickly as possible while pushing his gear in front of him. When Gentry felt suitably invisible in the sand and reeds, he pulled a pair of binoculars from the pack and brought them to his eyes, centered on the plume of black smoke rising in the distance.

His taut jaw muscles flexed.

The Chinook had come to rest on a street in the town of al Ba'aj, and already a mob had descended on the debris. Gentry's binoculars were not powerful enough to provide much detail, so he rolled onto his side and unsnapped the camel-colored case.

Inside was a Barrett M107, a fifty-caliber rifle that fired shells half the size of beer bottles and dispatched the heavy bullets with a muzzle velocity of nearly nine football fields a second.

Gentry did not load the gun, only aimed the rifle at the crash site to use the powerful optics mounted to it. Through the sixteen-power glass he could see the fire, the pickup trucks, the unarmed civilians, and the armed gunmen.

Some were unmasked. Local thugs.

Others wore black masks or wrapped keffiyeh to cover their faces. This would be the Al Qaeda contingent. The foreign fucks. Here to kill Americans and collaborators and to take advantage of the instability in the region.

A glint of metal rose into the air and swung down. A sword hacking at a figure on the ground. Even through the powerful sniper scope Gentry could not tell if the prostrate man had been dead or alive when the blade slashed into him.

His jaw tightened again. Gentry was not an American soldier himself, never had been. But he *was* an American. And although he had neither responsibility for nor relationship with the U.S. military, he'd seen years of images on television of carnage just like that which was happening before him, and it both sickened and angered him to the very limits of his considerable self-control.

The men around the aircraft began to undulate as one. In the glare from the heat pouring out of the arid earth between his overwatch and the crash site, it took him a moment to grasp what was happening, but soon he recognized the inevitable outpouring of gleeful emotion from the butchers around the downed helicopter.

The bastards were dancing over the bodies.

Gentry unwrapped his finger from the trigger guard of the huge Barrett and let his fingertip stroke the smooth trigger. His laser range finder told him the distance, and a small group of canvas tents between himself and the dance party flapped in the breeze and gave him an idea of the windage.

But he knew better than to fire the Barrett. If he charged the weapon and pulled the trigger, he would kill a couple of shitheads, yes, but the area would turn so hot in an instant with news of a sniper in the sector that every postpubescent male with a gun and a mobile phone would be on his ass before he made it to within five miles of his extraction. Gentry's exfiltration would be called off, and he would have to make his own way out of the kill zone.

No, Gentry told himself. A meager measure of payback would be righteous, but it would set off a bigger shit storm than he was prepared to deal with.

Gentry was not a gambler. He was a private assassin, a hired gun, a contract operator. He could frag a half dozen of these pricks as fast as he could lace his boots, but he knew such retribution would not be worth the cost.

He spat a mixture of saliva and sand on the ground in front of him and turned to put the huge Barrett back in its case.

The camera crew from Al Jazeera had been smuggled over the border from Syria a week earlier with the sole purpose of chronicling an Al

Qaeda victory in northern Iraq. The videographer, the audio technician, and the reporter/producer had been moved along an AQ route, had slept in AQ safe houses alongside the AQ cell, and they'd filmed the launch of the missile, the impact with the Chinook, and the resulting fireball in the sky.

Now they recorded the ritualistic decapitation of an already dead American soldier. A middle-aged man with handwritten name tape affixed to his body armor that read, "Phillips—Mississippi National Guard." Not one of the camera crew spoke English, but they all agreed they had clearly just recorded the destruction of an elite unit of CIA commandos.

The customary praise of Allah began with the dancing of the fighters and the firing of the weapons into the air. Although the AQ cell numbered only sixteen, there were over thirty armed men now in step with one another in front of the smoldering metal hulk in the street. The videographer focused his lens on a moqtar, a local chieftain, dancing in the center of the festivities. Framing him perfectly in front of the wreckage, his flowing white dishdasha contrasting magnificently with the black smoke billowing up behind him. The moqtar bounced on one foot over the decapitated American, his right hand above him swinging a bloody scimitar into the air.

This was the money shot. The videographer smiled and did his best to remain professional, careful to not follow along with the rhythm and dance in celebration of the majesty of Allah to which he and his camera now bore witness.

The moqtar shouted into the air with the rest. "Allahu Akhbar!" *God is greater!* He hopped in euphoria with the masked foreigners, his thick facial hair opened to reveal a toothy smile as he looked down at the burnt and bloody piece of dead American meat lying in the street below him.

The crew from Al Jazeera shouted in ecstasy as well. And the videographer filmed it all with a steady hand.

He was a pro; his subject remained centered, his camera did not tremble or flinch.

Not until the moment when the moqtar's head snapped to the side, burst open like a pressed grape, and sinew, blood, and bone spewed violently in all directions.

Then the camera flinched.

Gentry just couldn't help himself.

He fired round after round at the armed men in the crowd, and all the while he cussed aloud at his lack of discipline, because he knew he was throwing his own timetable, his entire operation out the window. Not that he could hear his own curses. Even with his earplugs, the report of the Barrett was deafening as he sent huge projectiles downrange, one after another, the blowback from the rifle's muzzle break propelling sand and debris from the ground around him up and into his face and arms.

As he paused to snap a second heavy magazine into the rifle, he took stock of his situation. From a tradecraft perspective, this was the single dumbest move he could have made, virtually shouting to the insurgents around him that their mortal enemy was here in their midst.

But damn if it did not *feel* like the right thing to do. He resecured the big rifle in the crook of his shoulder, already throbbing from the recoil, sighted on the downed chopper site, and resumed his righteous payback. Through the big scope he saw body parts spin through the air as another huge bullet found the midsection of a masked gunman.

This was simple revenge, nothing more. Gentry knew his actions altered little in the scope of things, apart from changing a few sons of bitches from solids into liquids. His body continued firing into the now-scattering murderers, but his mind was already worrying about his immediate future. He wouldn't even try for the LZ now. Another chopper in the area would be a target too good for the angry AQ survivors to ignore. No, Gentry decided, he would go to ground: find a drainage culvert or a little wadi, cover himself in dirt and debris, lie all day in the heat, and ignore hunger and bug bites and his need to piss.

It was going to suck.

Still, he reasoned as he slammed the third and final magazine into the smoking rifle, his poor decision did serve some benefit. A half dozen dead shitheads *are*, after all, a half dozen dead shitheads.

TWO

Four minutes after the sniper's last volley, one of the Al Qaeda survivors warily leaned his head out the doorway of the tire repair shop where he had taken cover. After a few moments, each second giving him increased confidence that his head would remain affixed to his neck, the thirty-six-year-old Yemeni stepped fully into the street. Soon he was followed by others and stood with his compatriots around the carnage. He counted seven dead, made this tabulation by determining the number of lower appendages lying twisted in the bloody muck and dividing by two, because there were so few identifiable heads and trunks remaining on the corpses.

Five of the dead were his AQ brethren, including the senior man in the cell and his top lieutenant. Two others were locals.

The Chinook continued to smolder off to his left. He walked towards it, passing men hiding behind cars and garbage cans, their pupils dilated from shock. One local had lost control of his bowels in terror; now he lay soiled and writhing on the pavement like a madman.

"Get up, fool!" shouted the masked Yemeni. He kicked the man in the side and continued on to the helicopter. Four more of his colleagues were behind one of their pickup trucks, standing with the Al Jazeera film crew. The videographer was smoking with a hand that trembled as if from advanced-stage Parkinson's. His camera hung down at his side.

"Get everyone alive into the trucks. We'll find the sniper." He looked out to the expanse of fields, dry hillocks, and roadways off to the south. A dust cloud hung over a rise nearly a mile away.

"There!" The Yemeni pointed.

"We . . . we are going out there?" asked the Al Jazeera audio technician.

"Inshallah." If Allah wills it.

Just then a local boy called out to the AQ contingent, asking them to come and look. The boy had taken cover in a tea stand, not fifteen meters from the crumpled nose cone of the chopper. The Yemeni and two of his men stepped over a bloody torso held together only by a torn black tunic. This had been the Jordanian, their leader. There was a splatter path of blood from where he'd fallen to the outer walls and window of the tea stand, all but repainting the establishment in crimson.

"What is it, boy?" shouted the Yemeni in an angry rush.

The kid spoke through gasps as he hyperventilated. Still, he answered, "I found something."

The Yemeni and his two men followed the boy into the little café, stepped through the blood, looked around a fallen table and back behind the counter. There, on the floor with his back to the wall, sat a young American soldier. His eyes were open and blinking rapidly.

Cradled in his arms was a second infidel. This man was black and appeared either unconscious or dead. There were no weapons apparent.

The Yemeni smiled and patted the boy on the shoulder. He turned and shouted to those outside. "Bring the truck!"

A dozen minutes later the three AQ pickups split at a crossroads. Nine men headed to the south in two trucks. They worked their mobile phones for local help to assist them as they went to scour the landscape for the lone sniper. The Yemeni and two other AQ drove the two wounded American prisoners to a safe house in nearby Hatra. There the Yemeni would call his leadership to see how best to exploit his newfound bounty.

The Yemeni was behind the wheel, a young Syrian rode in the passenger seat, and an Egyptian guarded the near-catatonic soldier and his dying partner in the bed of the truck.

Twenty-year-old Ricky Bayliss had recovered some from the shock of the crash. He knew this because the dull throbbing in his broken shin bone had turned into molten-hot jolts of pain. He looked down to his leg and could see only torn and scorched BDU pants and a boot that hung obscenely off to the right. Beyond this boot lay the other soldier. Bayliss didn't know the black GI, but his name tape identified him as Cleveland. Cleveland was unconscious. Bayliss would have presumed him dead except his chest heaved a bit under his body armor. In a moment of instinct and adrenaline, Ricky had dragged the man free of the wreck as he crawled into a shop next to the crash, only to be discovered by wide-eyed Iraqi kids a minute later.

He thought for a moment about his friends who had died in the Chinook and felt a sadness muted by disbelief. The sadness dissipated quickly as he looked up at the man sitting above him in the truck bed. Ricky's dead friends were the lucky bastards. *He* was the unfortunate one. He and Cleveland, if the dude ever woke up, were going to get their goddamn heads chopped off on TV.

The terrorist looked down at Bayliss and put his tennis shoe on the young man's shattered leg. He pressed down slowly with a wild grin that exposed teeth broken like fangs.

Ricky screamed.

The truck sped down the road, crested a rise just outside of al Ba'aj, and then quickly slowed before a roadblock at the edge of town, a standard local insurgency setup. A heavy chain wrapped to two posts hung low across the dusty pavement. Two militiamen were visible. One sat lazily on a plastic chair, his head leaning back against the wall of a grammar school's playground. The other stood by one end of the chain, next to his resting partner. A Kalashnikov hung over his back, muzzle down, and there was a plate of hummus and flatbread in his hands, food hanging off his beard. An old goat herder urged his pitiful flock along the sidewalk on the far side of the roadblock.

The Al Qaeda man cursed the weak resolve of the insurgency here in northwestern Iraq. Two lazy men were all they could muster for a checkpoint? With such idiocy the Sunnis might as well just hand over control to the Kurds and the Yejezi.

The Yemeni slowed his truck, rolled down the window, and shouted to the standing Iraqi, "Open this gate, fool! There is a sniper to the south!"

The militiaman put down his lunch. He walked purposefully towards the pickup truck in the middle of the road. He put a hand up to his ear as if he did not hear the Yemeni's shout.

"Open the gate, or I will—"

The Yemeni's head swiveled away from the insurgent nearing his truck and to the one seated against the wall. The seated man's head had slumped over to the side, and it hung there. An instant later, the body rolled forward and fell out of the chair and onto the ground. It was clear the militiaman was dead, his neck snapped at a lower cervical vertebra.

The gunman in the back of the truck noticed this as well. He stood quickly in the bed, sensing a threat but confused by the situation. Like his new leader in the driver's seat, he looked back to the local man in the road.

The bearded militiaman approaching the truck raised his right arm in front of him. A black pistol appeared from the sleeve of his flowing robe.

Two quick shots, not a moment's hesitation between them, dropped the Egyptian in the truck bed.

Bayliss lay on his back, looking up at the scorching noontime sun. He felt the vehicle slow and stop, heard the shouting from the driver, the impossibly rapid gunshots, and watched the masked man above him fall straight down dead.

He heard another volley of pistol rounds cracking around him, heard glass shatter, a brief cry in Arabic, and then all was still.

Ricky thrashed and shrieked, frantic to get the bloody corpse off of him. His struggle ended when the dead terrorist was lifted away, out of the truck bed, and dumped onto the street. A bearded man dressed in a gray dishdasha grabbed Ricky by his body armor and pulled him up and into a seated position.

The brutal sun blurred Bayliss's view of the stranger's face.

"Can you walk?"

Ricky thought it some sort of shock-induced vision. The man had spoken English with an American accent. The stranger repeated himself in a shout. "Hey! Kid! You with me? Can you walk?"

Slowly Bayliss spoke back to the vision. "My . . . my leg's broken, and this dude is hurt bad."

The stranger examined Ricky's injured leg and diagnosed, "Tib-fib fracture. You'll live." Then he put his hand on the unconscious man's neck and delivered a grim prognosis. "Not a chance."

He looked around quickly. Still, the young Mississippian could not see the man's face.

The stranger said, "Leave him back here. We'll do what we can for him, but I need you to get up in the passenger seat. Wrap this around your face."

The bearded man pulled the keffiyeh head wrap from the neck of the dead terrorist and handed it to Bayliss.

"I can't walk on this leg—"

"Suck it up. We've got to go. I'll grab my gear. Move!" The stranger turned and ran down into a shaded alleyway. Bayliss dropped his Kevlar helmet in the cab, wrapped the headdress into place, climbed out of the bed and onto his good leg. Excruciating pain jolted from his right shin to his brain. The street was filling with civilians of all ages, keeping their distance, watching as if an audience to a violent play.

Bayliss hopped to the passenger door, opened it, and a masked Arab in a black dress shirt fell out into the street. There was a single bullet wound above his left eye. A second terrorist lay slumped over the steering wheel. Bloody foam dripped from his lips with his soft wheezes. Ricky had just shut his door when the American stranger opened the driver's side, pulled the man out, and let him drop to the asphalt. He drew his pistol again and, without so much as a glance, fired one round into the man in the street. He then turned his attention to the pickup, tossed in a brown gear bag, an AK-47, and an M4 rifle. He climbed behind the wheel, and the truck lurched forward and over the lowered chain of the roadblock.

Ricky spoke softly, his brain still trying to catch up with the action around him. "We've got to go back. There might be others alive."

"There aren't. You're it."

"How do you know?"

"I know."

Ricky hesitated, then said, "Because you were with the sniper team that fragged those dudes at the crash site?"

"Maybe."

For nearly a minute they drove in silence. Bayliss looked ahead through the windshield at the mountains, then down at his shaking hands. Soon the young soldier turned his attention to the driver.

Immediately the stranger barked, "Don't look at my face."

Bayliss obeyed, turning back to the road ahead. He asked, "You're American?"

"That's right."

"Special Forces?"

"No."

"Navy? You're a SEAL?"

"No."

"Force Recon?"

"Nope."

"I get it. You're like in the CIA or something."

"No."

Bayliss started to look back to the bearded man but caught himself. He asked, "Then what?"

"Just passing through."

"Just passing through? Are you fucking kidding?"

"No more questions."

They drove a full kilometer before Ricky asked, "What's the plan?"

"No plan."

"You don't have a plan? Then what are we doing? Where are we going?"

"I *had* a plan, but bringing you along wasn't part of it, so don't start bitching about me making this shit up as I go."

Bayliss was quiet for a moment. Then he said, "Roger that. Plans are overrated."

After another minute of driving, Bayliss snuck a glance to the speedometer and saw they were moving over the bad gravel road at nearly sixty miles an hour.

The private asked, "You got any morphine in your bag? My leg is hurtin' bad."

"Sorry, kid. I need you alert. You're going to have to drive."

"Drive?"

"When we get into the hills, we'll pull over. I'll get out, and you two will go on alone."

"What about you? We've got an FOB in Tal Afar. It's where we were heading when we were hit. We can go there." The forward operating base would be spartan and isolated, but it would be well-equipped for holding off attackers and a hell of a lot more secure than a pickup truck on an open road.

"*You* can. I can't."

"Why not?"

"Long story. No questions, soldier. Remember?"

"Bro, what are you worried about? They'd give you a medal or some shit for this."

"They'd give me some shit."

They entered the foothills of the Sinjar Mountains minutes later.

The stranger pulled the pickup over to the side of the road and into a dusty grove of date palms. He climbed out, pulled the M4 and his bag with him, and then helped the soldier into place behind the wheel. Bayliss grunted and groaned with pain.

Next the stranger checked on the soldier in the truck bed.

"Dead." He said it without emotion. Hurriedly he removed Cleveland's Interceptor body armor and uniform and left him in the cab of the truck in his brown boxers and T-shirt. Bayliss bristled at the treatment of the dead soldier but said nothing. This man, this . . . whatever the hell he was, survived out here in bandit country through expediency, not sentiment.

The stranger threw the gear on the ground next to the trunk of a date palm. He said, "You're gonna have to use your left leg for the brake and the gas."

"Hooah, sir."

"Your FOB is due north, fifteen klicks. Keep that AK in your lap, mags next to you. Stay low-pro if you can."

"What's low-pro?"

"Low profile. Don't speed, don't stand out, keep that keffiyeh over your face."

"Roger that."

"But if you can't avoid contact, shoot at anything you don't like, you got it? Get your mind around that, kid. You're gonna have to get nasty to survive the next half hour."

"Yes, sir. What about you?"

"I'm already nasty."

Private Ricky Bayliss winced along with the drumbeat of pain in his leg. He looked ahead, not at the man on his left. "Whoever you are . . . thanks."

"Thank me by getting the fuck home and forgetting my face."

"Roger that." He shook his head and grunted. "Just passing through."

Bayliss left the grove and pulled back onto the road. He looked in the rearview mirror for a last glimpse of the stranger, but the heat's haze and the dust kicked up by the truck's tires obstructed the view behind.

THREE

On London's Bayswater Road, a six-story commercial building over-looks the bucolic anomaly in the center of the city that is Hyde Park and Kensington Gardens. Comprising a large suite on the top floor of the white building are the offices of Cheltenham Security Services, a private firm that contracts executive protection officers, facility guard personnel, and strategic intelligence services for British and other western European corporations working abroad. CSS was conceived, founded, and run on a daily basis by a sixty-eight-year-old Englishman named Sir Donald Fitzroy.

Fitzroy had spent the early part of Wednesday hard at work, but now he forced himself to push that task out of his mind. He took a moment to clear his thoughts, drummed his corpulent fingers on his ornate partners desk. He did not have time for the man waiting politely outside with his secretary—there was a pressing matter that required his complete focus—but he could hardly turn his visitor away. Fitzroy's crisis of the moment would just have to wait.

The young man had called an hour before and told Sir Donald's secretary he needed to speak with Mr. Fitzroy about a most urgent matter. Such calls were a regular occurrence at the office of CSS. What was irregular about this call, and the reason Fitzroy could hardly ask the emphatic young man to return another day, was the fact his visitor was in the employ of LaurentGroup, a mammoth French conglomerate that ran shipping, trucking, engineering, and port facilities for the oil, gas, and mineral industries throughout Europe, Asia, Africa, and South America. They were Fitzroy's largest customer, and for this reason alone he would not send the man off with apologies, no matter what other matters pressed.

Fitzroy's firm ran site security at LaurentGroup's corporate offices in Belgium, the Netherlands, and the UK, but as large as was Fitzroy's contract with Laurent as compared to CSS's other corporate accounts, Sir Donald knew it was no more than a drop in the bucket as far as the mammoth corporation's total annual security budget. It was well known in protection circles that LaurentGroup ran their own security departments in a decentralized fashion, hiring locals to do most of the heavy lifting in the eighty-odd nations where the corporation owned property. This might mean something as innocuous as vetting secretaries at an office in Kuala Lumpur, but it also included the nefarious, like having a recalcitrant dockworker's legs broken in Bombay, or a problematic union rally broken up in Gdansk.

And surely, from time to time, executives at Laurent's Paris home office required a problem to go away in a more permanent fashion, and Fitzroy knew they had men on call for that, as well.

There was a dirty underbelly to most multinational corporations that worked in regions of the world with more thugs than cops, with more hungry people who wanted to work than educated people who wanted to organize and bring about reform. Yes, most MNCs used methods that would never make the topic list of the chairmen's briefing or a budget line in the annual financial report, but LaurentGroup was known as an especially heavy-handed company when it came to third-world assets and resources.

And this did not hurt the stock price at all.

Donald Fitzroy forced his worry about the other affair from his head, thumbed the intercom button, and asked his secretary to escort the visitor in.

Fitzroy first noticed the handsome young man's suit. This was a local custom in London. Identify the tailor, and know the man. It was a Huntsman, a Savile Row shop that Sir Donald recognized, and it told Fitzroy much about his guest. Sir Donald was a Norton & Sons man himself, dapper but a tad less businessy. Still, he appreciated the young man's style. With a quick and practiced glance, the Englishman determined his visitor to be a barrister, well-educated, and American, though respectful of customs and manners here in the United Kingdom.

"Don't tell me, Mr. Lloyd. Allow me to guess," Fitzroy called out as he crossed his office with a gracious smile. "Law school here somewhere? King's College, I suspect. Perhaps after university back home in the States. I'm going to venture to guess Yale, but I will have to hear you speak first."

The young man grinned and offered a well-manicured hand with a firm grip. "King's College it was, sir, but I graduated from Princeton back home."

They shook hands, and Fitzroy ushered the man to a sitting area at the front of his office. "Yes, I hear it now. Princeton."

As Fitzroy sat in a chair across the coffee table from his guest, Lloyd said, "Impressive, Sir Donald. I suppose you learned all about sizing people up in your former profession."

Fitzroy raised his bushy white brows as he poured coffee for both men from a silver service on the table. "There was an article about me. A year or two ago in the *Economist.* You may have picked up a few tidbits about my career with the Crown."

Lloyd nodded, sipped. "Guilty as charged. Your thirty years in MI-5. Most spent in Ulster during the Troubles. Then a change of vocation to corporate security. I'm sure that flattering article helped with your business."

"Quite so," Fitzroy said through a well-practiced smile.

"And I must also confess that I'm pretty sure I've never met an honest-to-goodness knight."

Now Fitzroy laughed aloud. "It's a title that my ex-wife still mocks to our circle of friends. She likes to point out that it is an honorific of gentility, not nobility, and since I am clearly neither, she finds the designation particularly ill-suited." Fitzroy said this with no bitterness, only good-natured self-deprecation.

Lloyd chuckled politely.

"I normally conduct business with Mr. Stanley in your London office. What do you do at LaurentGroup, Mr. Lloyd?"

Lloyd set his cup down in the saucer. "Please forgive my abruptness in requesting a meeting with you, and please also forgive the abruptness with which I come to the point."

"Not at all, young man. Unlike many Englishmen, especially of my generation, I respect the acumen of the American businessman. Endless tea and cakes have hurt British productivity, there's little doubt. So just let me have it with both barrels, as you Yanks like to say." Fitzroy sipped his coffee.

The young American leaned forward. “My rush has less to do with me being American, more to do with the critical nature of my firm’s need.”

“I hope I can be of service.”

“I’m certain of it. I am here to discuss an event that took place twenty hours ago in Al Hasakah.”

Fitzroy cocked his thick head and smiled. “You’ve got me there, lad. Must admit I don’t recognize the name.”

“It’s in eastern Syria, Mr. Fitzroy.”

Donald Fitzroy’s practiced smile faltered, and he said nothing. Slowly he lowered his cup to his saucer and placed it on the table in front of him.

Lloyd said, “Again, I apologize for the way I am rushing this along, but time is not merely crucial in this matter, it is virtually nonexistent.”

“I am listening.” The Englishman’s warm smile of ten seconds ago was dead and buried now.

“Around eight o’clock local time last evening, an assassin took the life of Dr. Isaac Abubaker. He was, you might know, the Nigerian minister of energy.”

Fitzroy spoke with a tone markedly less friendly than before. “Curious. Any idea what the Nigerian minister of energy was doing in eastern Syria? The only energy to be mined there is the fervency of the Jihadists who congregate before sneaking into Iraq to fuel the conflict.”

Lloyd smiled. “The good doctor was a Muslim of radical thought. He may have been in the area to offer some material support for the cause. I am not here to defend the man’s actions. I am concerned only about his assassin. As it happens, the killer survived, escaped into Iraq.”

“How unfortunate.”

“Not for the assassin. The killer was good. He was better than good. He was the best. He was the one they call the Gray Man.”

Fitzroy crossed his legs and leaned back. "A myth."

"Not a myth. A man. A man of great skill, but ultimately a man of flesh and blood."

"Why are you here?" Fitzroy's voice held none of the paternal charm of their earlier conversation.

"I am here because you are his handler."

"His what?"

"His handler. You vet his contracts, supply his logistical needs, assist him with intelligence, collect from the payers, and forward compensation to his bank accounts."

"Where did you hear this nonsense?"

"Sir Donald, had I the time, I would offer you every courtesy you deserve, we could verbally fence, and I would feint and you would parry and we'd both strut around the room until one of our swords scored a killing strike. Unfortunately, sir, I am under a tremendous pressure, which forces me to dispense with the customary pleasantries." He sipped his coffee again and made a little face at the bitterness of the brew. "I *know* the assassin was the one called the Gray Man, and I know you run him. You can ask me how I know this, but I will just lie, and our relationship in the next few hours depends upon our ability to speak frankly."

"Go on."

"As I said, the Gray Man crossed into Iraq but missed his extraction, because he foolishly engaged a superior insurgent force in a firefight. He killed or wounded ten men or more. Saved an American National Guardsman and recovered the body of another. And now he is on the run."

"How do you know the Gray Man was the assassin of Dr. Abubaker?"

"There is no one else in the world who would be sent on that mission, because there is no one else in the world who could pull off that hit."

"And yet, you say, he made a foolish mistake."

"More evidence I am right. The Gray Man was once an operative for the U.S. government. Something went wrong, he was targeted by the CIA, and he went into hiding from his former masters. His soured relationship with Langley notwithstanding, the Gray Man is still very much an American patriot. He could not ignore a helicopter crash and eleven dead Americans without finding a measure of retribution."

"That is your proof?"

Lloyd smoothed the drape of his suit coat. "It has been known by us for some time that the Gray Man had accepted a contract for the Abubaker hit. When the good doctor died as a result of foul play, there was no need to speculate as to the identity of his killer."

"I'm sorry, Mr. Lloyd. I am an old man; you will have to connect the dots for me. What are you doing in my office?"

"My company is prepared to offer you a threefold increase in contracts if you will only assist us in the neutralization of the Gray Man. Without going into unnecessary detail, the president of Nigeria is asking us to help him bring justice down on his brother's killer."

"Why LaurentGroup?"

"That would involve unnecessary detail."

"You will find it to be quite necessary if this discussion is to continue."

FOUR

Lloyd hesitated. Nodded slowly. "Very well. Two reasons. One, my firm has a powerful and far-reaching security apparatus, and the president thinks we have the means at our disposal to handle this situation for him. We've done other little odd jobs for the Nigerians in the past, you understand." With a wave of his hand Lloyd added, "Good customer service."

Fitzroy's eyebrows rose and touched.

"And two, Julius Abubaker feels he has some leverage over us. We have a large contract pending signature. It was on his desk when your man killed his brother. The president leaves office in less than a week. He's given us until then to avenge his brother's murder."

"What sort of a contract do you have pending his approval?"

"The sort that we cannot afford to lose. Did you know, Sir Donald, that Nigeria not only produces an abundance of oil, but they also produce an overabundance of natural gas? This gas is completely squandered, bubbles up at their oil wells and drifts into the atmosphere to the tune of thirty billion tons a year. A complete waste of energy and profit."

"And LaurentGroup wants the gas?"

"Certainly not. The gas is a natural resource that belongs to the good people of Nigeria. But we alone have the technology to cap their wells, pipe the liquefied gas to port in Lagos, transport it to refineries in our dual-hulled, temperature-controlled tankers, and refine it for the Nigerians. We've spent four years and over three hundred million dollars on R & D for this project. We've built ships, we've retrofitted shipyards to build more ships, we've negotiated land rights for the pipeline."

"All without a contract to export the product? Sounds like LaurentGroup needs new lawyers," Fitzroy quipped.

Lloyd, a LaurentGroup lawyer, bristled. "We *had* a contract with Abubaker. His people found a loophole. We fixed the unfortunate error and needed only the wave of his pen over the document to seal the deal and begin operations. And then your man killed his brother."

"I still don't see the connection."

"The connection, if you will pardon my language, is that President Abubaker is a prick."

Fitzroy noticed something in the young solicitor's agitation.

"I think I have it. Your office was at fault for the loophole in the contract. Your masters have sent you on this errand to fix your cock-up."

Lloyd took off his thin glasses and rubbed the bridge of his nose slowly.

"A minuscule oversight that wouldn't justify five seconds' consternation in any courtroom in the civilized world."

"But you are dealing with the most corrupt nation on earth."

"Third most corrupt, actually, but your point is valid," said Lloyd.

He pressed a fresh smile into his lips just after a taste of coffee. "Abubaker is threatening to sign the operation over to our competitor, a firm that did not even bid on the job. Our competitor would take a decade to arrive at our present level of infrastructure assets and engineering know-how, and Nigeria would lose billions of dollars in profits in the intervening years."

"As would LaurentGroup."

"Admittedly, we are not a social services department within the Nigerian government. Our own self-interest propels us; I just make mention of the dual benefit to the poor wretches of Nigeria who will lose out if I don't find and kill the Gray Man."

"If those poor wretches remain poor wretches after the billions annually in oil wealth that already pour into Nigeria, I don't imagine a few gas lines would much improve their lot in life."

Lloyd shrugged. "Perhaps we are straying from the subject at hand."

"What about the payer of the contract? Why doesn't the president go after him? The Gray Man is, if your intelligence is correct, only the triggerman."

Lloyd smiled without humor. "As you well know, the payer of the contract was killed in a plane crash months ago. The Gray Man could have and should have kept the money he'd already been wired and forgotten the job. But your assassin continued on his mission. Seemed to think he was doing something noble."

"What about me? If you think I am involved with coordinating Isaac Abubaker's death, why not take me out, as well?"

"We know that the payer of the contract acted through a cutout. That cutout, in turn, had a cutout, who had a cutout who negotiated with you. President Julius Abubaker doesn't have the attention span for such intrigue. He wants the head of his brother's killer brought to him. That's all."

"When you say he wants a head . . . I presume you are speaking figuratively."

"Would that I were, Sir Donald. No, the president has dispatched a man from his personal staff to my office in order to verify that my mission has been accomplished. This man tells me he's to put the Gray Man's head in an ice chest and deliver it to his leader in the diplomatic pouch. Goddamned savages." The last part Lloyd seemed to say to himself.

"Is there not some other way you can bribe President Abubaker?" asked Fitzroy. He knew how third-world public sector contracts often worked.

Lloyd looked to a spot on the wall. His eyes grew distant, older than his visage. "Oh, we already bribed him, Mr. Fitzroy. Cash, whores, drugs, homes, boats. He's an insatiable son of a bitch. We've given the moon and the stars for the Lagos contract. Even so, he's now negotiating with our competitor. Bringing him the head of his brother's assassin is the one thing we can do for him that no one else can, and it is therefore the one thing that he is holding over us."

"If Abubaker's such a despot, why is he leaving power willingly?"

Lloyd waved a hand in the air as if the answer were obvious. "He's already an obscenely rich man. He's raped his country. Now it's time to enjoy the afterglow of his act."

"And that's why you are here."

"As simple as that, Mr. Fitzroy. Again, I am sorry for the discourtesy of my intrusion, but I am sure the work we will offer Cheltenham Security will more than make up for the loss of one assassin, even a very good one."

Fitzroy said, "Mr. Lloyd, I employ chaps who are . . . very base. They respond well to loyalty and trust and a sense of honor. Often it is misplaced, but it drives them on nonetheless. If I give up the life of a man, my best man, in order to win some lucrative contracts, it would hardly serve my best interests."

"On the contrary. This hit man of yours is a product like any other. This sort of product has a short shelf life. Six months, a year, certainly not more than three. And then he will be dead or incapacitated. Worthless to you as a generator of revenue. What I offer you will fill your coffers for the life of your firm."

"I don't sacrifice my men for business."

A slight pause. "I understand. I will speak with Paris. Maybe I can sweeten the pot."

"The flavor of the stew doesn't enter into it. It is the stew itself I don't fancy."

Lloyd leaned closer. There was a faint trace of menace in his voice. "If I can't sweeten the pot, I will be forced to stir it. I *need* your assassin terminated. I'd like to use a carrot. But I am prepared to use a stick."

"I suggest you go carefully, lad. I don't like the direction this discussion is veering."

The two men stared at one another for several seconds.

Lloyd said, "I know you have an extraction team on the way to pick up the Gray Man tonight. I want you to order your men to terminate him. A single phone call and a financial incentive should take care of this matter quickly and cleanly."

Fitzroy's eyes narrowed. "Where on earth did you hear that?"

"I'm not at liberty to disclose my intelligence sources."

"You're bluffing. You know nothing."

Lloyd smiled. "I'll give you a quick taste of what I know, and then you decide if this is all a bluff. I suspect I know more about your boy than you do. Your killer's real name is Courtland Gentry, goes by Court. He is thirty-six years old. American, his father ran a SWAT school near

Tallahassee, Florida, where Gentry grew up. The boy trained with tactical officers on a daily basis. He was instructing SWAT teams in close quarters battle techniques by the time he was sixteen. When he was eighteen, he fell in with a bad crowd in Miami, worked for a Colombian gang for a while, was arrested in Key West for the shooting death of three Cuban drug dealers up in Fort Lauderdale.

"A CIA big shot who had trained at Court's father's shoot house snatched the kid out of prison, sent him to work in a secret division within the Operations Directorate. He worked covert ops around the world for a few years, black bag jobs mostly, until 9/11, when he was placed in the Special Activities Division, working in an agency irregular rendition task force. Officially known as Special Detachment Golf Sierra, it became affectionately known, to those few who knew about it at all, as the Goon Squad."

"Surely you are making this up."

Lloyd ignored him and continued. "It was an ad hoc, special sanction tactical team, made up of what we call in the business, high-speed, low-drag operators. The very best of the very best. Not James Bond types. No, with these guys there was considerably more emphasis on the dagger and less on the cloak. For a few years they were the CIA's best wet unit. They killed the ones we couldn't render, they killed the ones from whom we did not expect to be able to extract much useful information, and they killed the ones whose deaths would sow the most fear in the hearts and minds of the terrorists.

"And then four years ago it went bad. Some say politics was involved; others are convinced Gentry screwed up an op and outlived his usefulness. Still others insist he turned dirty. For whatever reason, a burn notice went out on him. Then a shoot-on-sight directive. He was targeted by his former colleagues in the Special Activities Division. Gentry did not go quietly; he killed some Golf Sierra teammates intent on killing him and then went underground, off the grid. Spent time in Peru, Bangladesh, Russia, who knows where else. Within six months he was out of money. Went into the private sector, working for you, doing what he does best. Head shots and sliced throats. Sniper rifles and switchblades."

There was a soft knock at the door to the office. Fitzroy's secretary leaned in. "I'm sorry, sir. You have a call." She shut the door behind her.

Fitzroy stood, and Lloyd followed. The young American said, "I can wait outside."

"No need. Our business is done."

"You would be making a big mistake by sending me away. I need you to have your extraction team terminate the Gray Man. If you don't feel the offer I have extended is sufficient, I will make a few calls and see what I can do. What I can*not* do, Mr. Fitzroy, is return to my employers without this matter resolved."

Fitzroy had had enough. "Your company has misjudged. They can't bribe me as they would some tin pot African dictator."

A severe look came into the eyes of the young American. "Then I extend my apologies." They shook hands, but the friendly gesture did not reach up to their cold eyes. As Lloyd walked towards the door, he detoured to the left and stepped over to a framed copy of the *Economist* article hanging on the wall. The title read, "Former Spymaster turns Corporate Security Tycoon." Lloyd pointed to it and turned back to the older Englishman.

"Great article. Lots of information."

He then regarded a photo on the wall of a younger Fitzroy with his wife and teenage son. "Your son has two daughters now, does he not? Lives here in London, a town house in Sussex Gardens, if I remember correctly from the *Economist*."

"That was not in the *Economist* article."

"Wasn't it?" Lloyd shrugged. "Must have picked that up somewhere else. Good day, Sir Donald. We'll be in touch. You may expect a package within the hour."

He turned and disappeared through the door.

Fitzroy stood alone in his office for a moment.

Sir Donald did not scare easily, but he felt the unmistakable chill of fear.

FIVE

Two hours before dawn and already the abandoned airfield was sweltering hot. The hulking Lockheed L-100 positioned at the end of the runway idled with its lights off so as not to be detected from a distance, but the flight crew sat in their seats and their hands twitched near the throttle. The propellers blew dry dust and sharp sand into the wind-worn faces and parched throats of the five men standing on the tarmac at the foot of the aircraft's lowered ramp. All eyes were fixed to the south, out past the little shack of a terminal, out past the chain-link fence, and out into the infinite darkness of western Iraq.

The five men stood within feet of one another, but normal communication was impossible. Even at idle, the aircraft's Allison four-blade engines filled the air with a steady hum that shook the earth. Without the Harris Falcon short-distance radios and the throat mikes, the men's words would have been lost like the landscape beyond the reach of their night vision goggles.

Markham fingered the Heckler & Koch submachine gun hanging off his chest with his left hand and pressed the radio transmit button on his load-bearing vest with his right. “He’s late.”

Perini bit on the end of the tube hanging over his shoulder, sucked warm water from the half-empty bladder in his backpack. He spat most of it onto the sand-strewn airstrip in front of his boots. His Mossberg shotgun dangled unslung from his right hand. “If this mo-fo is supposed to be such hot shit, how come he can’t make his exfil on time?”

“He’s the shit all right. If the Gray Man is late, he has a good reason,” said Dulin, hands on his hips and his squat-barreled submachine gun horizontal on his chest. “Stay sharp; it’s just a short op. We pick him up, babysit him over the border, and then forget we ever saw the bastard.”

“The Gray Man,” McVee said with a degree of reverence. “He’s the guy who killed Milosevic. Snuck into a UN jail and poisoned the son of a bitch.” His MP5 submachine gun hung from a sling, the fat silencer pointing straight down at the tarmac. He propped his elbow on the butt of the squat weapon.

Perini said, “Nah, bro. You got it backwards. He killed the guy who killed Milosevic. Milosevic was going to name names. UN officials who helped him with the genocide in Bosnia and Kosovo. The UN sent a hitter in to poison old Slobo, and the Gray Man killed the hitter, after the fact.” He swigged and spat another mouthful of warm water. “The Gray Man is one bad son of a bitch. He don’t care, he don’t scare.”

Markham reiterated his earlier decree. “He’s fucking late, is what he is.”

Dulin looked at his watch. “Fitzroy said we might have to wait, and we might have to fight. Every hajji for fifty klicks is hunting Gray Man’s ass.”

Barnes had been silent, but now he spoke up. “I heard he did that job in Kiev." He paced, farthest from the ramp of the aircraft, sweeping the dark with the three-power night vision scope on his M4 assault rifle.

"Bullshit," said Dulin, and two of the others immediately agreed.

But McVee sided with Barnes. "That's what I heard. The Gray dude did that shit solo."

Markham said, "No way. Kiev was not a one-man op. It was a twelve-man A-team at the very least."

Barnes shook his head in the dark. "Heard it was one gunner. Heard it was the Gray Man."

Markham replied, "I don't believe in magic."

Just then there was a simultaneous crackle in the earpieces of the five men. Dulin held a hand up to silence his team, pressed the talk button on his chest rig. "Repeat last transmission."

Another crackle. Then another. Finally, disjointed words popped through the static. "Thirty seconds . . . move . . . pursuit!" The voice was unrecognizable, but clearly the message was urgent.

"Is that him?" asked Barnes.

No one could say.

Again a burst of life from the comms, clearer now. They looked towards the open gate at the front of the little airfield. "I'm coming hard! Hold your fire!"

Dulin replied into the comm. "Your signal is intermittent. Say again your location?"

A pop of static. " . . . Northwest."

Just then they heard a crash to the north and a honking horn. Everyone had been looking to the south. They turned their heads and gun barrels north to the sound of the noise and saw a civilian pickup truck, one headlight dead and black, smash through the fence and bounce out of the sand and onto the tarmac. The truck was moving at an incredible clip, directly towards the L-100.

The voice came over the comms again. "I've got company!"

Just then, headlights appeared along a wide track behind the wildly bouncing vehicle. First two sets, then four, then more.

Dulin assessed the situation for one second. Then he called out to his crew over the engine's whine, "Up the ramp!"

All five were aboard, and the L-100 was already rolling down the runway when an armed man in dirty gear and body armor sprinted up the back ramp. McVee grabbed the "package's" gloved hand and pulled him up the steep incline, and Markham slammed his hand on the hydraulic lift lever to close the ramp. Dulin gave a command to the pilots on the cabin intercom, and the four turboprop engines gunned for takeoff.

With the ramp sealed shut, the package dropped onto his kneepads in the middle of the bare cabin. His M4 rifle was slung over a general issue chest harness missing most of its ammunition and a brown Nomex tunic torn in several places. The man's face was covered with goggles, smeared greasepaint, and sweat. He pulled his helmet off, dropped it to the floor of the cabin, already inclining during its takeoff rotation. Steam poured from a sopping mat of thick brown hair, and his beard dripped perspiration like a leaky faucet.

Dulin lifted the Gray Man from the floor and put him on the bench along the cabin's skin. He secured him to the bench with a belt and sat next to him.

"You hurt?" he asked.

The man shook his head.

"Let me help you get your gear off." Dulin shouted over the engines.

"I'll keep it on."

"Suit yourself. Just a forty-minute flight. Once in Turkey, we'll go to a safe house, and tomorrow night Fitzroy will have instructions for you. We'll watch your back till then."

"I appreciate it," said the filthy man through labored breaths. His eyes stayed on the floor as he spoke. His arms draped over the top of the black rifle hanging from his neck.

The other four men had strapped themselves into the red mesh bench lining the side of the fuselage. They all stared at the package, trying without success to reconcile the average-looking operator next to them with his superhuman reputation.

The Gray Man and Dulin sat by a pallet of gear strapped with webbing to the middle of the deck.

Dulin said, "I'm going to call Fitzroy, let him know we're wheels up. I'll grab you some water and be back in a second." He then turned and climbed the steeply ascending aircraft to the front of the cabin. He pulled out his satellite phone as he walked.

It was just after three in the morning in London, and on the sixth floor of a whitewashed office building on London's Bayswater Road, an aging man in a wrinkled pinstripe suit drummed his fingers on his desk. His face white, perspiration ran down his fleshy neck and soaked his Egyptian broadcloth oxford. Donald Fitzroy tried to relax himself, to remove the obvious worry from his voice.

The satellite phone chirped again.

He looked again, for the twentieth time, to the framed photograph on his desk. His son, now forty, sitting on a hammock on a beach, his beautiful wife beside him. Twins, both girls, one in each parent's lap. Smiles all around.

Fitzroy looked away from the framed photo and towards a sheaf of loose photographs in his thick hands. These shots he had also given twenty looks. It was the same four, the same family, though the twins were slightly older now.

It was typical surveillance quality: the family at a park, the twins at their school near Grosvenor Square, the daughter-in-law pushing a shopping cart through the market. Fitzroy detected from the angles and the proximity to their subjects that the photographer was sending a message that he could have easily walked up to the four and put a hand on each of them.

Lloyd's implication was clear: Fitzroy's family could be gotten to at any time.

The sat phone chirped a third time.

Fitzroy exhaled fully, threw the photos to the floor, and grabbed the nagging device.

"Standstill. How copy, Fullcourt?"

"Five by five, Standstill," said Dulin. He pressed his ear tight into the earpiece of the satellite phone to drown out the engine's roar. "How do you copy?"

"Loud and clear. Report your status."

"Standstill, Fullcourt. We have the package and have exfiltrated the target location."

"Understood. What's the status of your package?"

"Looks like shit, sir, but he says he's good to go."

"Understood. Wait one," Fitzroy said.

Dulin rubbed a gloved hand over his face and looked to the back of the cargo airplane at his four operators. His gaze then centered on the Gray Man, sitting at the end of the bench. Goggles, a beard, and greasepaint hid his face. Still, Dulin could tell the man was exhausted. His back rested against the wall of the fuselage, and both arms hung over his M4. His eyes stared into the distance. Dulin's crew was on Gray's right, all geared up in a nearly uniform manner but segregated from the package by a few feet of bench.

Thirty seconds later, Donald Fitzroy came back on the line. "Fullcourt, this is Standstill. There has been a change in the operation. You and your men will, of course, be remunerated accordingly."

Dulin sat up straighter. His brow furrowed. "Roger that, Standstill. Go ahead with the update to the op specs."

"I need the delivery of the package canceled."

Dulin's head cocked. "Negative, Standstill. We can't return to the airfield. It's crawling with opposition and—"

"That's not what I mean, Fullcourt. I need you to . . . destroy the package."

A pause. "Standstill, Fullcourt. Repeat your last?"

The tone of voice over the sat phone changed. It was less detached. More human. "I have a . . . a situation here, Fullcourt."

Dulin said, his own voice losing the clipped cadence of radio protocol, "Yeah, I guess you do."

"I want him terminated."

Dulin's head was propped in his gloved hand. His fingers began strumming on the side of his face. "You sure about this? He's one of your guys."

"I know that."

"*I'm* one of your guys."

"It's complicated, lad. Not how I normally do business."

"This isn't right."

"As I said, you all will be compensated for this deviance from the original operation."

Dulin's eyes stayed on the package as he asked, "How much?"

Five minutes later, Dulin looked towards his men while reaching for his radio's selector switch on his chest rig. He turned the dial a few clicks.

"Don't say anything. Just nod if you copy." Barnes, McVee, Perini, and Markham all looked up and around. Their eyes found Dulin up at the bulkhead and they nodded as one. Unaware, the Gray Man stared blankly at the pallet of equipment in front of him.

"Listen up. Standstill has ordered us to waste the package." Across the thirty feet of open space in the well-lit cabin Dulin saw the stunned reaction on his men's faces. He shrugged, "Don't ask me, boys. I just work here."

The four men on the bench with the package looked to him, saw him to be closest to the ramp, strapped in, with his M4 rifle on his chest and his bearded face gazing at the floor of the cabin.

They looked back to their team leader and nodded slowly as one.

SIX

Court Gentry sat alone near the closed ramp of the aircraft, listened to the engines whine, and tried to catch his breath, to get control of his emotions. His ass was on a mesh bench in the back of an L-100-30, but his mind was back down below, in the dark, in the sand.

In the shit.

The operator closest on his right got up and moved around the pallet, sat down on the bench facing him. Idly Gentry glanced to his right, noticed the extraction team's leader adjusting his gear. He began to look to the other guys, but his head returned to the man at the bulkhead.

Something wasn't right.

The team leader's back was ramrod straight, and he had an intense expression on his face, though he wasn't looking at anything in particular. His MP5 was across his chest; he adjusted the glove on his right hand.

And his mouth was moving. He was transmitting into his close quarters radio, giving orders to his men.

Gentry looked down at his own Harris Falcon radio set. He had been on the same channel as the rest of the team, but now he could not hear the transmission.

Strange.

Court turned to the three men next to him on the bench. From their posture, from their facial expressions, Gentry determined that, just like their leader, they weren't decompressing after the tension of the extraction from the hot zone. No, they moved and looked like they were about to go *into* action. Gentry had spent sixteen years in covert operations, studied faces and evaluated threats for a living. He knew what an operator looked like when the fight was over, and he knew what an operator looked like when the fight was about to begin.

Surreptitiously he unhooked the strap securing him to the bench and swiveled in his seat to face the men around him.

Dulin was up at the bulkhead; he was no longer transmitting. He just stared at Gentry.

"What's up?" shouted Gentry above the engine's roar.

Dulin stood slowly.

Court shouted again across the noisy cabin, "Whatever you're thinking about doing, you need to just—"

Markham turned quickly on the bench, spun towards the Gray Man, his pistol already rising in front of him. Gentry pushed off the wall under the bench with his sandy boots and launched himself across the cabin, tried to put his body behind the pallet of gear lashed to the floor.

The fight was on. The fact that Court didn't know why the fuck his rescuers had turned on him was a nonissue. He did not waste a single brain cell pondering the turn of events.

Court Gentry was a killer of men.

These were men.

And that's all there was to it.

Markham got a shot off with his Sig Sauer handgun but missed high. Before Gentry disappeared behind the cargo, he saw Markham and Barnes quickly unhooking their bench harnesses.

McVee was the only man on Gentry's left as the Gray Man crouched behind the pallet and faced the cockpit doors, thirty feet away. Dulin was up by the bulkhead wall near the doors, and the other three operators were ahead and to his right. Court knew that if he put down the man to his left, he would eliminate one of their fields of fire, so he rolled onto his left shoulder, emerged from behind the pallet with his M4 raised, and fired a long burst at the operator. The man's goggled face slammed back against the wall, and his HK dropped away from his fingertips.

McVee fell back on the bench, dead.

Gentry had killed him, and he had no idea why.

Immediately every man in the back of the L-100 began firing his weapon; four guns poured metal-jacketed lead at Gentry's position.

Court tucked tight down behind the equipment cache as the fuselage wall behind him began to scream, whistling as the holes made by a dozen rifle rounds allowed pressurized air to race out of the aircraft. The flight crew in the front of the cargo plane could not hear the shriek from the compromised skin, but they obviously heard the gunfire behind them, because they put their L-100 into a nosedive to drop to thicker air in order to lower the pressure differential and, hopefully, keep their aircraft from tearing to pieces.

The nosedive created a seemingly weightless environment for

Gentry and his four remaining would-be assassins. Court's body rose away from the relative safety of the pallet and rolled in a pair of reverse summersaults, finally landing on the ceiling of the cabin and scooting along its back to the rear ramp, which was now the highest point of the cargo compartment.

Two of the gunmen lifted into the air as well, firing above them at their target.

Gentry felt a pair of nine-millimeter slugs from an MP5 stitch across the armor plate in his tactical vest. The force of the impact knocked him off balance for an instant, but from his position completely upside down, he saw one of the operators had not unhooked his bench harness, and he kicked frantically in the air, strapped to the wall to Gentry's right.

The man was a sitting duck.

Gentry shot Perini in the head with his M4. His body went limp, his arms and legs danced with the weightlessness of the plane's rapid descent.

For the next ten seconds the four men still alive in the cabin spun through the air like socks in a dryer. The team leader, Dulin, was below the others. He had managed to grab hold of some webbing on the forward bulkhead and hook his arm securely through it, and now he tried to aim his submachine gun at Gentry thirty feet above him. But Markham and Barnes bumped into Gentry as they all swirled through the air, completely out of control. Buttstocks, boots, and fists flew each time a target moved too close to engage with a rifle.

Though the men had a sense of weightlessness, they were, in fact, hurtling towards earth, dropping through the sky at maximum velocity. Only there was an airplane surrounding them and dropping as well, so they could see no reference points to prove to them that they were falling like stones.

In the chaos, the screaming and the confusion of losing hold of terra firma, Court spun backwards again, and his hand slipped from the grip of his rifle, and its sling slipped over his head. The weapon twisted out of reach. He drew his Glock-19 pistol, raised to fire without sighting, but he felt the sting of a bullet as it tore into his right thigh. The impact kicked his leg back like a hammer's blow. He ignored the injury, and his feet found purchase again on the rear ramp. He looked up, which was now straight down, and found Dulin in his sights. The extraction team's leader had one arm wrapped in the bulkhead webbing, and he held his submachine gun over his head with the other, pointed up towards the Gray Man. Court fired six quick rounds and saw the operator's body react as the bullets slammed into Dulin's groin and lower torso.

Gentry next turned to get a bead on Barnes and Markham, his final two targets, but McVee's dead body sailed across his field of fire. Just then the pilot apparently decided he'd seen enough sand in his windscreen, and he pulled quickly out of his dive. All passengers in the back, the dead and the living alike, now dropped through the air, slammed hard into the steel flooring of the transport, and rolled like bowling balls towards the front bulkhead of the aircraft. Court's pistol flew free of his hand on impact, and he bounced forward, the sting from the gunshot wound in his thigh burning with each jolt.

Court rolled towards the netting on the front bulkhead as the plane leveled, almost got a handhold, but the pilot put the L-100 back into a climb. Gentry's momentum pushed him forward for a while, but as the cargo floor became a steep incline, passing forty-five degrees now, he lost the last of his inertia, and his fingertips just barely managed to tickle the nylon webbing next to Dulin's motionless form.

Then the Gray Man went backwards. He rocked back on his heels first and fell down, then slid, then rolled, and finally Court went airborne halfway down the length of the cabin. The pain in his thigh was compounded when he landed on his hip at the rear of the plane, but this pain paled in comparison to the excruciating crush of Markham's body as he slammed into Court's chest. Markham faced the other direction and was even more stunned than Gentry by the violent impact, so the Gray Man easily got his arms around the operator's head. With a merciless twist, Markham's neck snapped, wrecking his spinal cord and killing him instantly.

The dead operator wore his rifle around his neck on a one-point sling, essentially a necklace with an automatic assault weapon dangling as its charm. Court tried to remove it, but the sling was caught on the operator's load-bearing vest. Court pulled the gun up to the dead man's shoulder, tried to quickly sight on the last remaining extraction team member, who was using the legs of the long bench as a ladder to climb up the cabin to the forward bulkhead loadmaster's galley.

Court pulled the trigger, but the weapon clicked empty. He fumbled around Markham's chest rig for another magazine and slammed it into the MP5's magazine well. He readied to fire at his target just as the man disappeared into the galley. The plane leveled off again, and Court's gravity returned to normal. He stayed low behind the pallet towards the rear hatch, waiting for Barnes to peek back around the door.

Without warning, Gentry heard a loud noise and felt the rear cargo ramp behind him move. The wind roared.

Barnes had activated the ramp from the front of the cabin. A second later, the aircraft began another steep climb.

As Court scrambled to grab on to the netting over the pallet on the floor in front of him, Barnes appeared near the bulkhead. The dark-clad operator had slung a parachute rig onto his back. Apparently he figured this plane had taken all the damage it could, or perhaps he worried the pilots were dead from stray gunfire. Barnes held the bulkhead webbing with all his might and fired burst after burst in Gentry's direction, one-handed, with his M4 as the ramp opened fully behind the Gray Man.

Court reached behind him with his free hand and stripped the gun off Markham's neck just before the dead man rolled out of the plane and into the darkness. The pilot continued his climb, and soon McVee's body slid past Gentry and out into the night. Perini's body was lashed into his seat, and Dulin's corpse was still secured in the bulkhead webbing.

Gentry and Barnes were the only two left alive.

Court held on to the submachine gun with his right hand, and his left hand squeezed the net on the pallet. His glove had twisted on his fingers, and he knew he could not hold on much longer. His boots kicked at the deck of the plane to try to find purchase as the climb angle grew steeper and steeper.

He was seconds away from falling backwards down the ramp.

But Gentry had one last chance. He lifted Markham's rifle and fired a long burst over the pallet at Barnes, hitting him squarely on his chest plate, slamming his head back against the bulkhead hard enough to knock him out cold. The aircraft's incline was forty-five degrees now, and the wounded Barnes lost his hold of the webbing, dropped to his knees, and rolled down the length of the plane towards the rear hatch.

This was Gentry's ride off the damaged aircraft and he did not want to miss it. As the incapacitated operator bounded past, Court let go of the pallet and pushed off the floor with his boots and kneepads. Gentry leapt to his right and grabbed hold of the unconscious man by the parachute harness, and they sailed together out the open hatch and into the night sky.

Gentry hooked his arms around Barnes and crossed his legs behind his back. The L-100 disappeared above them, and soon the roar of the engines was replaced by the howl of the wind.

Court grunted and screamed with the effort of holding on as tightly as possible. He did not dare reach for the ripcord of the chute. If he lost his tenuous hold, he would never find it again in the black night sky. He was reasonably sure this rig would have a CYPRES automatic activation device that would pop the reserve at seven hundred fifty feet if its occupant was still in free fall.

Gentry and his would-be killer tumbled end over end through the cold blackness.

One of Court's hands found a good hold on the parachute's shoulder strap, so he released the other hand to find a similar grip. Just as he let go, he heard a one-tone beep that lasted less than a second.

Then the reserve chute deployed.

Court held on with one hand. This parachute was not meant for two people, one of whom was kicking and yanking, desperate to get a firmer grip, so the men fell too fast and spun around like a whirligig.

This continued for just a few seconds before Gentry began to vomit from the vertigo. He did not have far to fall, but his nausea had already turned to dry heaves before they slammed together on the ground.

Court's impact was muted by landing squarely on the man in the chute. He checked on the other operator. He'd landed hard, face-first, with Gentry on his back. Court found no pulse.

Once on terra firma, Gentry got control of his heaving stomach, grabbed his thigh and writhed in pain for a moment, and then recovered enough to sit up. The first hues of morning were glowing to his left, showing him the way east.

Now that he had his bearings, he took stock of his surroundings. He was on flat ground, at the bottom of a gentle valley. There was a brook close enough to hear and goats bleating in the distance. The dead operator lay broken, the reserve chute flapping behind him in a cool, predawn breeze. Court searched the man's gear and found a medical blow-out bag on Barnes's hip.

He sat down on the grass and did his best to treat his wound in the dark. He assumed he had a long walk to reach the border and wanted to patch his injured leg so it could stand the trek. It was a clean wound, in and out, no major vascular or orthopedic damage, nothing much to worry about if you treated it early and well and did not mind days or weeks of throbbing discomfort. Gentry puked bile once more, his body and his mind just catching up to the chaos of the past five minutes.

Then he stood and slowly began walking north towards Turkey.

SEVEN

Fitzroy sat across from Lloyd on the couch in his office. Even as the older man listened to the other end of the satellite connection, his angry eyes did not flicker away from the young lawyer.

"I see," said Fitzroy into the phone. "Thank you." He terminated the call and placed the phone gently on the table in front of him.

Lloyd stared back, hopeful.

Fitzroy broke the staring contest with a gaze to the carpet. "It seems they are all dead."

"Who's dead?" asked Lloyd, the tint of optimism ever growing in his voice.

"Everyone but the flight crew. I am told there was a bit of a dustup in the aircraft. Courtland did not go down easily; no surprise there. The pilot found two of my men's bodies in the back, no sign of the other four. Blood on the floor, walls, and ceiling, over fifty bullet holes in the fuselage."

"My firm will compensate you for the damages." Lloyd said it matter-of-factly. He cleared his throat. "But they did not find Gentry's body? Could he have survived?"

"It appears not. There was a lot of gear lost, the plane flew for miles with its rear cargo door open, and among the unaccounted-for items is a parachute, but there's no reason to assume—"

Lloyd interrupted. "If our target is missing out the rear of an airplane along with a parachute, I can hardly convince the Nigerians the job is done."

"He was outnumbered five to one against a tier-one crew, all ex–Canadian Special Forces. Clearly I have fulfilled my end of our bargain. I ask you to now kindly carry out yours. Stop your threats to my family."

Lloyd waved a dismissive hand in the air. "Abubaker wants proof. He demanded Gentry's head in an ice chest."

"Dammit, man!" said Fitzroy. "I did as I was told!" Fitzroy was angry, but he was no longer fearful for his son's family. Shortly before Lloyd arrived, Sir Donald had called his son, had him collect his wife and children, and rush to St. Pancras Station in time to make the morning's second Eurostar train to France. At this very moment they should be settling into the family's summer villa just south of the Normandy beaches. Fitzroy felt confident Lloyd's men would not find them there.

"Yes, you did do as you were told. And you will continue to do so. I have a very quiet but very ominous Nigerian back in my office who will not leave with my assurances only. I will need for you to ascertain the flight path of the pilots, and I'll need to send a team to investigate—"

The phone on Fitzroy's desk chirped with a distinctive ring of two short bleats. Sir Donald spun his head to it and then back up to Lloyd.

"It's him," said Lloyd, responding to Fitzroy's obvious shock.

"That's his ring."

"Then answer it, and activate the speaker function."

Fitzroy crossed the room and pressed a button on the console on his desk. "Cheltenham Security." The voice that came through the line was distant. The words came out between labored breaths. "You call that a rescue?"

"It's good to hear your voice. What happened?"

Lloyd quickly pulled a notebook from his briefcase.

"I was going to ask you the same thing."

"Are you hurt?"

"I'll live. No thanks to the extraction squad you sent to pick me up."

Fitzroy looked to Lloyd. The young American scribbled something on his notepad and held it up. *Nigeria.* "Son. I heard from the flight crew about the melee. These were not regular employees of mine. Just a mercenary unit I had used once before. I was rushed to get a team together after the Polish pulled out."

"Because of what happened in Iraq?"

"Yes. That whole sector has become a no-go zone after your little demonstration yesterday. The Polish refused to go in. The men I sent instead let me know they'd do anything for money, despite the risks. Clearly someone got to them, bought them off."

"Who?"

"My sources tell me Julius Abubaker, the Nigerian president, is after your head."

"How does he know I was the one who waxed his brother?"

"Your reputation, no doubt. You have reached the status where some jobs are so difficult or high-profile that they just *have* to be you."

"Shit," said the voice through the line.

Fitzroy asked, "Where are you? I'll send another team to pick you up."

"Hell *no*, you won't."

"Look, Court, I can help you. Abubaker leaves office in a few days. He will leave with unimaginable wealth, but his power and his reach will be lessened once he is a civilian. The danger to you will soon pass. Let me bring you in, watch over you until then."

"I can lie low on my own. Call me when you get more intel on the men after me. Don't try to find me. You won't."

And with that, the connection died.

Lloyd clapped. "Well played, Sir Donald. Quite a performance. Your man didn't suspect you at all."

"He trusts me," Fitzroy said angrily. "For four years he's had every reason in the world to think I was his friend."

The American lawyer ignored Sir Donald's anger and asked, "Where will he go?"

Sir Donald sat back on the couch and ran his hands over his bald head. He looked up quickly. "A double! You want a head in an ice chest? I will bloody well get you a head in an ice chest! How the hell will Abubaker know the difference?"

Lloyd just shook his head. "Weeks ago, before the president demanded we kill him, he asked us for all the intelligence we had on the Gray Man. I happened to have photos, dental records, a complete history, et cetera. I sent that to him, thinking the son of a bitch would just kill Gentry himself before the hit on his brother was carried out. Abubaker knows your man's face. We can't use a body double or, as you suggest, a head double."

Fitzroy cocked his head slowly. "How the bloody hell did you come by this information?"

Lloyd regarded the question for a long moment. He picked at a piece of lint on the knee of his pants. "Before I moved to Paris to join Laurent, the Gray Man and I worked together."

"You're CIA?"

"Ex. Definitely ex. There's no money in patriotism, I'm afraid."

"And there *is* money in hunting down patriots? Threatening to hurt children?"

"Good money, as it happens. The world is a funny place. I copied personnel files when I was with the agency. I planned to use them as a bargaining chip if they ever came after me. It's just serendipity that these documents have proven useful in my current position." Lloyd stood and began pacing Fitzroy's office. "I need to know where Gentry is now, where he's going, what he normally does when he goes into hiding."

"When he goes into hiding, he simply vanishes. You can kiss your natural gas good-bye. The Gray Man will not turn up on anyone's radar again for months."

"Unacceptable. I need you to give me something, something about Gentry I don't already know. When he worked for us, he was a machine. No friends, no family that he gave a damn about. No lover stuck away for those long nights after a job. His SAD file is about the most boring read imaginable. No vices, no weakness. He's older now; surely he's made associates of a personal nature, developed tendencies that will help us figure out his next step. I'm sure you can tell me something, no matter how trivial, that I can use to flush him out."

Fitzroy smiled a little. He sensed the desperation in his young adversary.

He said, "Nothing. Nothing at all. We communicate via untraceable sat phone and e-mail. If he has a home or a girl or a family hidden away, I wouldn't know where to tell you to look."

Lloyd walked over to the window behind Fitzroy's desk. The Englishman remained on the sofa and watched the uninvited guest pace the office as if Fitzroy himself were the visitor and Lloyd was the proprietor of Cheltenham Services.

Suddenly the American spun around. "You can offer him a job! An easy job for big money. Surely he won't turn down a high-paying milk run. You send him on a new mission, and I'll have a team there to ambush him."

"Bloody hell, you think he's survived out there this long by being a fool? He has no interest in earning wages at the moment. He's busy blending into his surroundings. You had one shot to take him out, and you made a mess of it. Go back to your office and lick your wounds; leave me and my family alone!"

Fitzroy noticed a nervous twitch in Lloyd's face. It was replaced, slowly, by a smile.

"Well, if you won't help me use Gentry's weakness to flush him out, I will be forced to use yours." He pulled his phone from his pocket and smiled at Don Fitzroy as he spoke into it. "Pick up Phillip Fitzroy and family. They're at their summer cottage in Normandy. Take them to Château Laurent."

Fitzroy rose to his feet, "You bloody wanker!"

"Guilty as charged." Lloyd's tone mocked the Englishman. "My associates will hold your son and his family at a secluded property LaurentGroup owns in Normandy. They will be well taken care of until this matter is resolved. You will contact the Gray Man and give him their location, tell him the Nigerians are holding your only child, his adoring wife, and their darling little kiddies there. Tell him those black savages promise to rape dear Mommy and slaughter the rest of the clan in three days unless you give up your assassin's location."

"What good will that do?"

"I know Gentry. He is loyal like a fucking puppy. Even though he's been kicked around a few times, he will defend his master to the death."

"He won't."

"He will. He'll take it upon himself to save the day. He'll understand the police are useless, and he will move heaven and earth to get to France.

"You see, Sir Donnie, Court Gentry's compass never has pointed true north. He's a hit man, for God's sake. But all his operations, both with the CIA as well as in his private practice, have been against those he deems worthy of extrajudicial execution. Terrorists, Mafia dons, drug dealers, all manner of nefarious ne'er-do-wells. Court is a killer, but he thinks himself to be a righter of wrongs, an instrument of justice. *This* is his flaw. And this flaw will be his downfall."

Fitzroy knew the same about Court Gentry. Lloyd's logic was sound. Still, the older man tried to appeal to the young solicitor. "You needn't involve my family. I will do as you say. I've already shown you that. You don't have to hold them for me to tell Gentry they are held."

Lloyd waved a hand in the air, striking down Sir Donald's offer. "We will take good care of them. If you try to trick me, some sort of double cross, then I will need leverage against you, won't I?"

Fitzroy stood and crossed the room towards Lloyd, slowly and with menace. Although he was easily thirty years older than the American lawyer, the former MI-5 man possessed a larger frame. Lloyd took a step back and called out, "Mr. Leary and Mr. O'Neil! Would you step in, please?"

Fitzroy had given his secretary the day off; he was all alone in his workplace. But Lloyd had brought associates. Two athletic-looking men entered the office and stood by the door. One was redheaded and fair-skinned, on the downside of forty, with a simple business suit that bulged at the hip with the impression of a gun's butt. The second man was older, near fifty, with salt-and-pepper hair cut in a military high and tight, and his jacket hung loose enough on his body to hold an arsenal tucked away from view inside.

Fitzroy knew muscle goons when he saw them.

Lloyd said, "Irish Republicans. Your old enemies, though I shouldn't think we'll give them much to do. You and I will be seeing a lot of each other in the next few days. There is no reason our relationship should be anything less than cordial."

Claire Fitzroy had just turned eight years old the previous summer. It was the end of November now, and she and her twin sister Kate had expected to stay in London throughout the wet, gray, and chilling autumn without a break from the routine. Up each weekday morning early for the walk to her primary school on North Audrey Street, out of class and into thrice-weekly piano practice for Claire and vocal lessons for Kate. Weekends spent with Mummy in the shops or Daddy at home or on the football pitch. Each fortnight one of the girls would have a friend over for a slumber party and, as the dreary London skies of fall morphed into the drier but drearier skies of winter, all Claire's dreams would turn to Christmas.

Christmas was always spent in France at her father's holiday cottage in Bayeux, just across the channel in Normandy. Claire preferred Normandy to London, fancied a future for herself on a farm. So it had been a great moment of surprise and adventure when the headmaster of her school stepped into the girls' class Thursday morning, just after roll, to call Claire and Kate out and back to the office. "Bring your schoolbooks, ladies, please. Lovely. Sorry for the intrusion, Mrs. Wheeling. Do carry on."

Father was in the office, and he took each girl by the hand and led them out to a waiting taxi. Daddy had a Jaguar and Mummy drove a Saab, so the girls could not imagine where they were going in a taxicab. Mummy sat in the vast backseat, and she, like Daddy, was serious and distant.

"Girls, we're off on a little holiday. Down to Normandy, taking the Eurostar. No, of course nothing's wrong, don't be daft."

On the train the girls barely sat in their seats. Mummy and Daddy stayed huddled together talking, leaving Claire and Kate to run amok up and down the car. Claire heard Daddy ring Grandpa Don on his mobile. He began speaking quietly but angrily, a voice she had never heard him use with Grandpa Don. She stopped following her sister as they attempted to hop down the complete length of the car on one leg. She looked to her father, his worried face, the biting tone of his voice, words impossible to hear but impossible to interpret as anything other than anger.

Daddy snapped the phone shut and spoke to Mummy.

The only time young Claire had ever seen her daddy so visibly upset was when he yelled at a worker fixing the sink in their town house after he'd said something to Mummy that made her face turn red as a strawberry.

Claire began to cry, but she did not let it show.

Claire and her family left the Eurostar in Lille and took another train west to Normandy. By noon they were in their cottage. Kate helped Mum in the kitchen wash fresh corn for dinner. Claire sat on her bed upstairs and looked out to the drive below, to her father. He marched up and down the gravel speaking into his mobile. Occasionally he rested a hand on the picket fence along the garden.

Her father's anger and consternation twisted her tiny insides into knots.

Her sister was downstairs, unaware and unworried, but Claire considered Kate the less mature of the two eight-year-old twins.

Finally Daddy put his phone in his pocket, shivered against the chill in the air, and turned to walk back up the drive. He'd not gotten more than a few steps when two brown cars pulled in behind him. He turned back to the cars as men began pouring out. Claire counted six in all, big men, leather jackets of different colors and styles. The first man to Daddy smiled and stuck out a hand, and Daddy shook it.

The other men filed around her father, up the drive and towards the cottage. Daddy looked to the men as they passed, and for an instant Claire saw his expression. It was first confusion, and then it was terror, and young Claire leapt to her feet in her little room.

And when the six men, all as one, reached into their coats and drew big black and silver guns, eight-year-old Claire Fitzroy screamed.

EIGHT

Kurt Riegel was fifty-two years old, and as tall, blond, and broad as his Germanic name implied. He had joined LaurentGroup just out of the German Bundeswehr, seventeen years prior, worked his way up from associate director of security in the Hamburg branch office, through a half dozen third-world foreign postings, each dingier and more dangerous than the last, and now he sat firmly ensconced in the Paris home office as vice president of Security Risk Management Operations. It was a long title, a fancy heading that belied a simple explanation of his job.

Riegel was the man one called if one needed something bad to happen. Off-the-books projects, black arts, human resource problems that required a visit from the heavies. Black bag, sneak-and-peek burglary squads, corporate espionage teams, media disinformation experts. Even hit men. When Riegel's agents came to your office, it either meant they were there to help you clean up a difficult problem, or you yourself were the difficult problem someone had sent them to clean up.

Leading the "Department of Malicious Measures" virtually assured Riegel would climb no higher up the corporate ladder. No one wanted the chief head knocker out in the daylight, running the show. But Riegel did not mind the glass ceiling above him. On the contrary, he saw his position as virtually a tenured one, as he had erected a security dynasty around himself. In his four years as VP of SRMO, his agents had eliminated three political candidates in Africa, three human rights leaders in Asia, a Colombian general, two investigative journalists, and nearly twenty LaurentGroup employees who, for one reason or another, failed to tow the firm's heavy line. Only one man at LaurentGroup knew of all the operations; Riegel compartmentalized those below him well, and those above him in the corporation knew enough of his tactics to recognize that they really didn't want to know any more.

Problems arose, Riegel was called, problems disappeared, and Riegel was quietly appreciated.

This made Kurt Riegel an extremely powerful man indeed.

The big German's teak-paneled office in the Paris HQ suited him well. It was, like Riegel himself, large and blond and strongly built but quiet and discreet, tucked near Competitive Intelligence and IT in LaurentGroup campus's southern wing. Along his office walls hung over a dozen hunting trophies. There was a taxidermist in Montmartre who virtually made a living on Kurt's African safaris and Canadian expeditions. Rhino, lion, moose, and elk all stared vacantly from their perches high on the walls around the room.

It was also here where he did his daily calisthenics every afternoon at five. He was nearly to his one hundredth sweat-inducing knee bend when his outside line chirped. Several lines he could ignore until he finished his set, but this was the encrypted number, the hotline, and he'd awaited this call for most of the day.

He grabbed a towel, walked to his desk, and turned on his speakerphone.

"Riegel."

"Good afternoon, Mr. Riegel. This is Lloyd, from Legal."

Riegel sipped from a bottle of vitamin-infused water as he sat down on the edge of his desk.

"Lloyd from Legal. What can I do for you?" Riegel's voice was powerful, like the artillery officer he once was.

"I was told you would be expecting my call."

"I was contacted by the chief executive officer, no less. Marc Laurent himself told me to drop everything and focus all my efforts on a project you will have for me. He also told me to supply you with some muscle and a communications specialist. I hope the technician and the team of Belarusian paramilitaries I sent have been helpful to your situation."

"Yes, thank you for that. The tech is here with me. The muscle is down in France at the moment, and they are doing as they are told," said Lloyd.

"Good. This is the first time Marc Laurent himself has called and asked me to pay special attention to an operation. I am intrigued. What kind of mess have you boys over in Legal gotten yourselves into?"

"Yes. Well, this matter needs to be cleared up quickly, for the good of the company."

"Then let's not waste another moment. What else can I provide other than the team I have sent?"

Lloyd paused. Then he said, "Well, I hate to shock you with this, but I urgently need a man killed."

Riegel said nothing.

"Are you there?"

"I am waiting for you to say something shocking."

"I take it you have done this sort of thing before?"

"Here in Risk Management Operations we like to say that every problem can be dealt with one of two ways. A problem can be tolerated, or a problem can be terminated. If a problem can be tolerated, Mr. Lloyd, my phone does not ring."

Lloyd asked, "Are you familiar at all with the Lagos Natural Gas contract?"

Riegel answered immediately. "I suspected this would be in reference to the Nigerian fiasco. Rumor has it some fool attorney over there in Legal forgot to proofread a contract, and the Nigerians are backing out of a ten-billion-dollar deal we have already put two hundred million into. I had a feeling I would be contacted on the matter."

"Yes, well, it's a little more complicated than that."

"Doesn't sound so complicated. I just need the offending attorney's address. We'll make it look like suicide. The stupid bastard should be enough of a good company man to go ahead and kill himself, but you can't expect that kind of loyalty from a lawyer. No offense, Lloyd from Legal."

"No! No, Riegel, you've got it wrong. We need someone else killed."

Riegel cleared his throat. "Go on, then."

Lloyd told the VP of Security Risk Management Ops of the assassination of Isaac Abubaker, the president's refusal to sign the repaired contract without proof of his brother's killer's own death.

Kurt snorted. "We climb into bed with these dictators, and then we act surprised when they grab us by the nuts." Riegel's English was flawless, idiomatic American. He sat down behind his desk, grabbed a pen, and pulled a notepad across the leather blotter to him. "So we need to ID the hit man and dispose of him?" asked Riegel.

"He has already been identified."

"You just need him eliminated? I was expecting something more complicated than this after Mr. Laurent's phone call."

"Yes, well, this assassin is no slouch."

"The trouble with private killers is all in the identification. If you know who he is, I'll have him found and dead within twenty-four hours."

"That would be ideal."

"I mean, unless we're talking about the Gray Man. He's a couple of cuts above the rest."

Lloyd said nothing.

After the American's long hesitation, Riegel said, "Ach, so! We *are* talking about the Gray Man, aren't we?"

"Is that going to be a problem?"

It was Riegel's turn to pause. Finally he said, "Certainly a complication . . . but not a problem. He is extremely good at keeping a low profile, hence his moniker. He'll be hard to find, but the good news is he will have no reason to expect we are coming after him."

Lloyd remained silent yet again.

"Or will he?"

"I arranged an attempt on his life last night. It failed. He survived."

"How many men did he kill?"

"Five."

"Idiot."

"Mr. Riegel, the Gray Man is clearly no idiot. His history shows us—"

"*He* is not the idiot! *You* are the idiot! A damn lawyer who tries to orchestrate a hit on the greatest alpha killer in the world. Some poorly planned, cobbled-together, hurriedly executed disaster of an operation, no doubt! You should have come to me immediately. Now he will be on guard, expecting whoever it was who organized the attempt on his life will just try again."

"I am no idiot, Riegel. I have his handler in my custody. I have persuaded him to help us locate Gentry."

"Who's Gentry?"

"Courtland Gentry is the Gray Man."

Riegel sat up as erect and broad and square as the desk in front of him. "How is it you know his identity?"

"I am not at liberty to say."

"Who's his handler?" Riegel did not like being the one on the receiving end of such information inside LaurentGroup. He had his own intelligence network for that. That some shit American barrister was passing this intel around like it was common knowledge made Riegel ball his fists in anger.

"His handler's name is Don Fitzroy. He's a Brit, has a straight operation here in London, even does some work for us occasion—"

Riegel's balled fists closed together tighter. "Tell me, Lloyd from Legal, that you have not *kidnapped* Sir Donald Fitzroy!"

"I have. And I have his son and his son's family held at a Laurent-Group property in Normandy."

Riegel dropped his huge shoulders and put his head in his hands. After several seconds he looked to his speakerphone. "I have been notified, in no uncertain terms, that *you* are in charge of this operation. I am to provide you men, matériel, intelligence, and any advice I have."

"That's correct."

"Then why don't I start with some advice?"

"Excellent."

"My advice, Lloyd from Legal, is to apologize to Sir Donald for the gross misunderstanding, release him and his family, retire to your home, put a gun in your mouth, and pull the goddamn trigger! Crossing Fitzroy was a huge mistake."

"You can dispense with the advice then and just supply me with more men. Right now I don't know where the Gray Man is, but I do know where he will go. Fitzroy will send him to Normandy. He'll be traveling overland, east to west. I don't know his starting point yet, but if you give me enough support, I'll send them everywhere across Europe to hunt him down as he gets closer.

"Why will he go to Normandy? To rescue Fitzroy's family?"

"Exactly. He will be told Nigerians have kidnapped them and are holding them until Fitzroy turns him over. He will take it upon himself to rectify the problem."

Riegel drummed on his desk. "I agree with your assessment. He does have a reputation as a paladin, and he won't trust the French authorities."

"Precisely. I just need from you a surveillance team and a kill team. Right now your crew from Minsk is guarding his family in France, but I'd like Gentry dead before he gets to Normandy, as time is of the essence."

"This is the Gray Man. You need more than this."

"What do you suggest? I mean, other than me killing myself."

Riegel looked up to the far wall of his office. The head and shoulders of a wild boar stared back at him. Slowly Kurt nodded to himself. "To get this done in the time allowed, you'll need a hundred watchers."

"You can get me a hundred surveillance experts?"

"Pavement artists, we call them."

"Whatever. You can provide that?"

"Of course. And you will need a dozen teams of hunter-killers, spread out and placed all along each possible route, coordinated by a central command center, each with an incentive to be the unit that finds and kills the target."

Lloyd's voice showed his astonishment at the scale of the undertaking Riegel proposed. "A dozen teams?"

"Not company men, of course. Too many chances for comebacks on LaurentGroup. Not local talent, either. Local boys would be known to local police, and that would compromise the hunt. No, we need foreign operators from parts unknown, as you Americans like to say. Hard men, Lloyd from Legal, if you get my meaning. Hard men who do hard jobs when no other solution can be found."

"You are speaking of mercenaries."

"Absolutely not. The Gray Man has either dodged or dispatched every gang of hired hit men sent after him in the past. No, to be certain, we will need established field units. Government hit teams."

"I don't understand. Whose government?"

"We have branch offices in eighty nations. I have good relationships with the internal security chiefs in dozens of third-world countries. These men run stables of operators in their countries to keep their citizens and their countries' enemies in check."

Riegel paused while he thought through his plan. "Yes, I will contact my government counterparts in offices in the third world, hard places where I am likely to find hard men without the faintest shred of scruples. I will contact these men and, within half a day of this very moment, there will be a dozen corporate jets flying back from these armpit countries. Each jet will be packed tight with the baddest boys and the biggest guns, and each team will be tasked with the same mission. They will all be vying for the chance to kill the Gray Man."

"Like a contest?"

"Exactly."

"Incredible."

"We've done it before. Admittedly on a smaller scale, but we've had cause in the past to bring in multiple teams to vie for a single objective."

"But I don't understand. Why would these governments help us?"

"Not the governments themselves. The intelligence agencies. Can you imagine what a bounty of twenty million dollars added to the coffers of the secret police in the nation of, shall we say, Albania, would do to the security and stability of the state? Or to the Ugandan Army? Indonesia's Directorate of Internal Intelligence? These organizations work independently of their heads of state from time to time, when it suits the purposes of the organization or its leaders. I know which countries' internal security apparatus will sanction their men to kill for cash; I have no doubt of it."

There was a pause before Lloyd responded. "I get it. These intelligence agencies won't worry about American retribution. They will know the CIA won't hunt down the killers of the Gray Man."

"Lloyd, the victorious team will probably tell the CIA themselves, seek bounty from the Americans, as well. Langley has been after the Gray Man for years. He killed four of their own, you know."

"Yes, I know. I like your plan, Riegel. But can we do this quietly? I mean, without negative impact on LaurentGroup?"

"My office maintains shell corporations for deniability's sake. We'll use LaurentGroup aircrews in planes flying under the shells to infiltrate the kill squads and their weapons onto the Continent. It will be expensive, but Marc Laurent has instructed me to succeed by any means necessary."

Riegel's connections to the upper levels of the company couldn't be denied, but Lloyd's political instincts demanded that he reassert his position. "I remain in charge of the operation. I will coordinate the movements of the watchers and the shooters. You just get me this manpower."

"Agreed. I'll arrange our little contest, get everyone on station, but I will let you guide the teams. Keep me posted on the progress, and don't hesitate to seek out my counsel. I am a hunter, Lloyd. Hunting the Gray Man on the streets of Europe will be the greatest expedition of my career." He paused. "I just wish you didn't fuck with Fitzroy."

"Leave him to me."

"Oh, I have every intention of doing just that. Sir Donald and his family are your problem, not mine."

"No problem at all."

NINE

Gentry allowed himself to admit that his fortunes seemed to be changing. After limping northward towards the Turkish border for less than an hour, he was picked up by a patrol of local Kurdish police. The Kurds in northern Iraq love Americans, especially American soldiers, and from his tattered uniform and injuries, they presumed him to be an American Special Forces operator. Court did nothing to dissuade them of this assumption. They drove him into Mosul and cleaned him up and rebandaged his leg wound in a clinic built by the U.S. government. Within seven hours of dropping from the ass of an airplane without a parachute on his back, the American assassin found himself dressed in pressed slacks and a linen shirt, boarding a commercial aircraft bound for Tbilisi, Georgia.

The improvement in his circumstances was not due entirely to luck. One of Court's fallback plans involved him finding his own way out of Iraq, and to prepare himself for this eventuality, he'd sewn a forged passport, forged visas for Georgia and Turkey, cash, and other necessary documents into the legs of his pants.

No, Gentry benefited from a little luck from time to time, but he did not rely on it. He was nothing if not a man prepared.

After passing through Georgian customs with a Canadian passport identifying himself as Martin Baldwin, freelance journalist, he bought a ticket to Prague, Czech Republic. The five-hour flight was nearly empty, and Court landed at Ruzyne Airport just after ten in the evening.

He knew Prague like the back of his hand. He'd worked a job here once and often used the neighboring suburbs as a place to hide out.

After a cab and a metro ride, he walked through the cobblestone streets of the Stare Mesto District, then checked into a tiny attic hotel room a quarter mile from the Vltava River. After a long, soaking shower, he had just sat down to redress his thigh when the satellite phone in his new backpack began to beep.

Court checked it, saw that Fitzroy was calling, and continued to work on the gunshot wound. He'd talk to Don in the morning.

Gentry was understandably pissed about the extraction team turning on him.

He didn't even entertain the possibility that Sir Donald himself had ordered his men to kill him. No, he was angry because Fitzroy's operation was obviously compromised to the degree that the Nigerians were able to infiltrate a mission in progress and almost succeed in turning his rescuers into his executioners. Fitzroy had been strongly against Court going through with the hit on Abubaker after the death of the paymaster, and now Gentry wondered if Fitzroy had put together a half-assed support structure for the op as a way to show his disapproval.

Fitzroy's organized support structure was called the Network, and the Network was Gentry's only lifeline in the field. It was made up of legitimate doctors who would patch up a wounded man, no questions asked, legitimate cargo pilots who would take a stowaway on board without looking over the gear on his back, legitimate printers who could alter documents. The list went on and on, grew over time. Gentry used the Network as little as possible, much less than the other men in Fitzroy's stable. The Gray Man was, after all, a high-speed, low-drag operator. But everyone who works in Gentry's arduous profession needs a little help from time to time, and Court was no different.

Gentry had worked for Fitzroy for four years, beginning within a few months of the night the CIA indicated that they no longer required the services of their most experienced and successful man hunter. Court thought back to the night. The indication of their dissatisfaction was followed immediately by a bomb in his car, a hit squad in his apartment, and an international arrest warrant processed from the Justice Department, distributed through Interpol to every law enforcement agency on the planet.

At that time, Gentry was desperate for work to fund his life in hiding from the U.S. government, so he contacted Sir Donald Fitzroy. The Englishman ran a seemingly aboveboard security business, but Gentry had had dealings with the black side of Cheltenham Security Services when performing hits and renditions with the CIA's Special Activities Division, so it was a natural place for the recently unemployed gunman to seek work.

Since then, he had become something of a star in the world of private operators. Although virtually no one knew his real name, or the fact that he worked for Fitzroy, the Gray Man had become a legend amongst covert operators across the Western world.

As with any legend, many of the details were enhanced, enriched, or wholly fabricated. One of the details of the myth of the Gray Man that *was* true, however, was his personal ethic to only accept contracts against targets that he felt had earned the punishment of extrajudicial execution. This was entirely novel in the world of killers for hire, and though it enhanced his reputation, it also caused him to be extremely choosy about his operations.

Gentry took the toughest of the tough ops, went into bandit country alone, faced legions of enemies, and built a reputation and a bank account that was unrivaled in his admittedly low-profile industry. In four years he had satisfactorily performed twelve operations against terrorists and terrorist paymasters, white slavery profiteers, drug and illegal weapons runners, and Russian Mafia kingpins. Rumor had it he'd already made more money than he could ever need, so the inference was that he did what he did for the purpose of righting wrongs, protecting the weak, making the world a better place through the muzzle of his gun.

The myth was a fantasy, not reality, but unlike most fantasies, the man at the center of this one *did* exist. His motivations were complex, not the comic-book stimuli that had been ascribed to him, but at his core he did consider himself one of the good guys.

No, he didn't need the money, nor did he have a death wish. Court Gentry was the Gray Man simply because he believed there existed bad men in this world who truly needed to die.

Lloyd and his two Northern Irish henchmen put Fitzroy into a LaurentGroup limousine and motored through the city in a driving rain. There was no conversation. Fitzroy sat quietly, holding his hat in his hands between his knees, looking out the window into the rainy night like a beaten man. Lloyd worked his mobile phone, making and taking call after call, constantly checking in with Riegel, who was contacting men all over the globe to set their rushed plan into motion.

The limo arrived at LaurentGroup's UK subsidiary just after one in the morning. The French corporation's local office was housed in a three-building campus in Fulham. Lloyd, his men, and their cargo rolled through the front gates, past two rings of guards and guns, and down a road towards a single-story structure alongside a helipad.

"This will be home for a while, Sir Donald. I apologize if it's not up to the standards of that to which you are accustomed, but at least you won't go wanting for company. My men and I will not leave your side until we get everything settled and we can take you back to Bayswater Road and put you right back where we found you with a pat on your bald head."

Fitzroy said nothing. He followed the entourage through the rain into the building and down a long hallway. He passed two more men in suits standing in a little kitchen, and he immediately identified them as plainclothes security officers. For a moment Fitzroy had a flicker of hope, and it showed on his face.

Lloyd read his thoughts. "Sorry, Sir Donald. These are not your boys. A couple of heavies from our Edinburgh office. These Scotsmen hold allegiance to me, not you."

Fitzroy continued down the hall. He mumbled, "I know a thousand chaps like that. Those blokes hold no allegiance. They're in it for the money, and they will turn on you if the price is right."

Lloyd waved a card key over a reader alongside the last door in the hall. "Well, then, lucky for me I pay so well."

It was a large conference room, with an oak table and high-backed chairs, the walls lined with flat screen monitors, computers, and a big LCD display showing a map of western Europe.

Lloyd said, "Why don't you take the head of the table? Considering your knighthood, I apologize we couldn't arrange something round for you. I'm afraid oval was the best we could manage." The American chuckled at his own joke.

The two Scottish security men took places near the door, and the Northern Irishmen found corners in which to stand. A thin black man in a chestnut brown suit entered and sat at the table with a bottle of water in front of him.

"Mr. Felix works for President Abubaker," Lloyd explained. It was far short of an introduction. "He's here to verify we kill the Gray Man."

Mr. Felix nodded to Fitzroy from across the table.

Lloyd conferred with a young man with a ponytail and a nose ring whose thickly rimmed glasses reflected the light from the computers on the desk in front of him. He looked up to Lloyd and whispered.

Lloyd turned to Sir Donald. "Everything is on schedule. This man will be in charge of all communication between the watchers, the hunters, and myself. We will call him the Tech."

The young man stood and proffered a hand politely, as if he had no idea he was being introduced to a kidnapping victim.

Fitzroy turned away.

Just then the Tech took a call in his headset. He spoke softly to Lloyd in a British accent.

Lloyd replied, "Perfect. Get assets there immediately. Pin down his location."

Lloyd smiled at Fitzroy. "It was time I had a little luck. Gentry was spotted in Tbilisi, boarding a plane to Prague. The flight has already landed, so we can't tail him from the airport, but we have men checking the hotels. Hopefully, we'll have a hit team there waiting for him when he gets up in the morning."

An hour later Lloyd sat at the table opposite Fitzroy. The lights were dimmed, and the Tech placed a backlight behind the American. A camera on the ceiling spun under motor power to face him. A monitor displayed a silhouette of Lloyd so obscured that the young attorney had to lift his arm in the air in a wave to be sure he was looking at himself in real time.

Next, one by one, LCD screens along the wall across the table came to life. At the bottom of each screen were a title and the local time. Gaborone, Botswana, was first online. Four men sat in a conference room similar to the one in England. They were backlit and in silhouette, similar to Lloyd. Then Jakarta, Indonesia, came up. This time, there were six dark figures sitting shoulder to shoulder at a table and looking at a monitor. Then Tripoli, Libya. A minute later Caracas, Venezuela; Pretoria, South Africa; and Riyadh, Saudi Arabia, all illuminated simultaneously. Within the next five minutes the feeds from Albania, Sri Lanka, Kazakhstan, and Bolivia were up and running. Freetown, Liberia, took another minute for the Tech to patch through. Finally the transmission from South Korea appeared. A single Asian man sat alone at a desk.

These were the government kill teams Kurt Riegel had arranged for the hunt. Riegel had already spoken to the head of each team's agency, so he declined speaking to the operators directly. That was Lloyd's job. As Riegel had said, he was just helping with arrangements and consultation.

Before the audio came online, Lloyd called across the room to the Tech, "Where are the rest of the Koreans?"

The Tech checked a paper on his desk quickly. "They just sent one guy. Don't guess it will matter. All in all, there are over fifty men total on the twelve teams."

The Tech next assured Lloyd his voice would be altered with both hardware and software to make it completely unrecognizable.

After a final moment for the Tech to check the audio link with the translators sitting off camera in each location that needed them, Lloyd cleared his throat, his silhouette brought a hand to his mouth and then lowered it.

"Gentlemen, I know you have been briefed in general about the mission we have for you. It's very simple, really. I need a man found, but that is not your problem. I have nearly one hundred pavement artists either on call or already on the job combing the area of operations at this very moment. Once found, I will need this man neutralized. *This* will be your objective." The image in the monitors at the twelve remote locations changed. A color photo of a clean-shaven Court Gentry in a sport coat and wire-rimmed glasses appeared on the screen. Lloyd had taken it from a forged passport in his CIA file. "This is the Gray Man, Court Gentry. The photograph before you is five years old. I am afraid I do not know how he might have changed his appearance. Don't let his normalcy fool you. He was the best scalp hunter who ever worked for the CIA."

Someone mumbled something in Spanish. Lloyd understood only one word: "Milosevic."

"Yes, I thought some of you may already know this man by his reputation. Rumors abound regarding his operations. Some say he killed Milosevic, some say he did not. Some say he was responsible for the events in Kiev last year . . . Most reasonable minds recognize that to be impossible. Nevertheless, I know enough about specific jobs that he has carried out, both working for the U.S. government as well as his private work, to assure you Mr. Gentry is the most formidable singleton operator you will ever encounter."

A new disembodied voice spoke. "Looks like a faggot." From the accent, Lloyd immediately turned his attention to the South African feed.

Lloyd's altered voice reverberated through the speakers. "He will be the faggot who walks right up to you and slips an ice pick between your ribs, pops your lung, and stands above you while you choke to death on your own blood." There was anger in the American lawyer's voice. "You kill him, and then you can tell me what a fucking joke he is. Until you kill him, you keep your goddamn juvenile comments to yourself."

The South African feed fell silent.

Lloyd continued, still glaring at the silhouettes in Pretoria. "The Gray Man is trained in long-distance sniping, in close quarters battle, in edged weapons, Krav Maga, the martial art used by Israeli Special Forces. He can kill with a long gun, a short gun, or no gun at all. He can take you out from a mile away, or you can die with his breath in your ear. He has extensive training in explosive ordnance and even poisons. There was a rumor going around the CIA that once in Lahore, Pakistan, he used a blowgun to take down a target in a restaurant, while he went unnoticed by the target's security detail." Lloyd paused for effect. "Gentry was at the next table. Kept right on eating his meal as the target dropped dead.

"As soon as we finish here, you will all board aircraft. We will send a dozen teams in a dozen planes to a dozen airports along the route we expect Gentry to take across Europe in the next forty-eight hours. I will oversee and coordinate the activities from here, and I will pass on any intelligence I may be able to obtain. Each team that takes part in the hunt and survives will be paid one million dollars plus any expenses incurred. The team that kills Gentry will be paid a bonus of twenty million dollars."

"What's America going to do if we kill him?" asked a man with a booming African voice.

Lloyd turned to the Liberian feed, but he was not certain. "This has been addressed by the leaders of your organizations. This man is already marked for death by the U.S. government. There is shoot-on-sight sanction at the CIA. He has no friends, no close family. No one on this earth will cry for him when he dies."

Next someone spoke in an Asian language. When he finished, a translator asked, "Where is he now?"

"He flew to Prague last night. I have our agents asking around at hotels for him, but there is no way to know if he is still there."

"Which team is being sent to Prague?" someone asked.

"The Albanians. They are closest."

"That's hardly fair!" shouted a South African.

Lloyd, in silhouette, took off his glasses and rubbed the bridge of his nose. "No offense to the Albanians, but I don't think the first team he encounters will be the one that gets him."

There was grumbling on the Albanian feed, but it was quickly extinguished with hisses.

"We will kill Gentry in the next two days, yes. But we will likely do it through attrition. Many of you may die." He paused a beat, a half-hearted attempt to act like he gave a shit. "That said, we don't know that the Albanians will get the first crack at him. He may well have moved west by the time your plane lands. If that is the case, if we do pick up his trail past Prague, we will put you back on your plane, and you will take up a new ambush point closer to the final destination. There is no clear advantage to being farthest east, I assure everyone."

Lloyd sat up straighter in his chair. His silhouette appeared thin but athletic. "Let me finish by saying this. Do what it takes to get the job done. I could not possibly care less about collateral damage. If you can't stomach a few dead kids or dead pensioners or dead puppy dogs, then don't get on my goddamn airplane. Your job is to kill Court Gentry. Do that, and you will make millions for your organization and garner the thanks of the Central Intelligence Agency. Fail, and you will most likely die by his hand. You would be well served to avoid worrying about anything else.

"Any questions?"

There were none.

"Then, gentlemen . . . game on."

At four fifteen in the morning a LaurentGroup security officer from the firm's massive truck farm in Brno, Czech Republic, showed Gentry's photo to a sleepy hotel desk clerk at a narrow four-story inn in the Stare Mesto, the old town of Prague. The old man behind the hotel counter looked at the photo for a long time, said he could not be sure, but upon taking payment of five hundred crowns from the beady-eyed stranger, he changed his tone. He was certain the clean-shaven man in the picture and the bearded tourist in his attic room were one and the same.

The surveillance agent called Lloyd immediately. He was an employee of LaurentGroup, and Lloyd was under strict orders to keep company people away from any direct action, so Lloyd instructed him to go home.

"A team is on the way," Lloyd said.

"If you need him dead, I'll do it for one hundred thousand crowns."

Lloyd chuckled into the phone. "No, you won't."

"Are you saying I can't handle—"

"Yes. That's exactly what I'm saying."

"Fucking Americky prick."

"I'm the fucking Americky prick who just saved your worthless Czech life. Go home. Forget. You will receive a bonus for your good work."

"I hate Americans."

Lloyd laughed out loud as the line went dead.

TEN

Gentry awoke at five in the morning. The bullet wound in his thigh stung and throbbed; it had been anything but a good night's rest. He sat up slowly and painfully, leaned forward to stretch his lower back and hamstrings, stood, and tilted hard to each side. He wanted to spend the day moving. He had not yet decided on a destination, but he knew the sooner he left the hotel, the better.

After a quick trip to the bathroom to relieve himself and check the dressing on his leg, he dressed in the same clothing as the night before. He then looked out the window for signs of surveillance. Finding nothing amiss, he descended the stairs and left the building at twenty-five minutes past the hour.

He had created a mental to-do list for the day. One, go to his local cache here in Prague and retrieve a small handgun. He would not be doing any more flying; the plane trips of the last twenty-four hours were an anomaly in his life, because Court hated to be unarmed. He only boarded commercial aircraft as a last resort, had flown no more than a dozen times in the past four years. Now, as he walked unarmed through the darkened and deserted cobblestone streets of Prague, he felt naked. The only consolation to his martial needs was a small Spyderco folding knife in his waistband that he'd bought off a Kurdish policeman. It was better than nothing but inferior to any sort of firearm.

After hitting his cache he'd need to get out of town: pay cash for a cheap motorcycle and just buzz on out of Prague. Maybe spend a week or so moving from village to village in the Czech Republic or Slovakia. He hoped this would keep him safe until the Nigerian president left office and, hopefully, left him in peace.

No one could disappear more quickly or cleanly than the thirty-six-year-old American.

As Court walked towards the subway, he decided to place one more important item at the front of his to-do list. He smelled fresh coffee wafting from a little café just opening. And at that moment he felt he needed coffee as much as he needed a gun.

He was wrong.

A dense fog filled the dark street in front of the café, and it began to rain just as Court climbed up a pair of steps and entered the tiny eatery. It was just five thirty; he had the impression he was the first customer of the day. Court knew enough Czech to extend a greeting to the young girl behind the counter. He pointed to a steaming urn of coffee and a large pastry, watched the pale-skinned girl pour a foam cup full of rich black brew and place his breakfast in a bag.

Just then the doorbell dinged behind him. He glanced back to see three men enter, close umbrellas, and shake fresh rain from their coats. They looked local, but Court could not be sure. The first man glanced up at him as Gentry took his purchases over to a tiny stand with milk and sugar to dress his coffee.

Court looked at a glass-covered flyer promoting a poetry reading that hung on the wall, gazed idly at the window at his right, towards the dark and rainy street.

A few seconds later, he was out in the elements, ignoring the cold morning shower and walking towards the metro station at Mustek. There were no other pedestrians around; the cold and the rain and the early hour saw to that. Court did not mind the frigid air; he appreciated its ability to inject life into his tired muscles and still-fatigued brain. A few delivery trucks were about, and Gentry looked into the wet windshields of each as they passed. He found the entrance to the metro and descended the steep stairs. His still-tired eyes adjusted slowly to the harsh electric lighting around him, the cold, white tile reflecting the illumination from above.

He followed signs down a winding tunnel towards the trains. Another escalator took him deeper below the sleepy city, and another turn took him even farther into the brightly lit bowels of the metro station.

Shortly before a right turn in the passage, he passed a garbage can. In it he dropped his untouched coffee and his bag of pastry. Then he made the right turn, took two more steps, and stopped.

He flexed his muscles quickly. His arms, back, legs, neck, even his jaw tensed.

Then he reached into his waistband for his folding knife. He retrieved it and flicked it open, the maneuver executed in an impossible blur of speed and proficiency.

He spun around, took a single step back the way he came, leapt into the air to cover as much ground as quickly as possible, and plunged the three-inch blade hilt-deep into the throat of the first man following him.

The man was thick and hard and tall and broad. His meaty right hand grasped a stainless steel automatic pistol. Gentry grabbed the wrist of the gun hand and held the muzzle down and away, lest the dying man's spasms cause the weapon to fire.

Court took no time to look into the square-jawed man's eyes; had he done so, he would have seen shock and confusion long before the onset of panic or pain. Instead, the Gray Man pushed the man backwards to the tunnel's corner, slammed him into the second would-be assassin, and caught this man as he was rounding the turn and pulling his gun. Court held the knife's grip with his right hand. It was still stuck in the first man's throat, and he used it to push the first into the second, used his other hand now to fight for the handgun in the first's dying grip. The gun would not come free. Court could now see the third man behind the second's falling form, and the third's gun was rising to fire.

Gentry ducked his head into the chest of the man with the knife sunk into his throat, pushed forward over the goon falling back to the floor, and advanced quickly towards the last in line.

An ear-splitting gunshot rocked the tiled tunnel, the cacophonous explosion amplified by the low ceiling and narrow corridor. Gentry felt the bullet slam into the back of the bloody man in his arms. A second round barked and punched into Court's dance partner. Still the American pushed the man backwards, finally shoving him as hard as possible. As the operator's bloody body was flung at the third man, Gentry pulled his knife out of the throat and made a final reach for the pistol in the beefy right hand. He managed to hold on to the knife, but the corpse slammed into the third operator with his dead hand still firmly clutching the gun.

Now Gentry stood between two living assassins, both armed, each less than ten feet from him. Behind Court was the armed man on the ground. Surely by now he was rolling around to get a shot off.

And in front of Court was the standing man, now shoving his blood-spewing partner out of his way to resight his weapon on his target. Court flicked his knife so that he was holding the blade and quickly threw it overhand at the standing gunman. The blade struck perfectly, buried itself in the man's left eye socket. Blood erupted, and the operator dropped his gun to bring both hands to the knife. He fell to his knees.

Gentry did not look to the threat behind him. Instead, he dove forward, both arms outstretched, desperate to get his hands on a firearm. Just before he hit the ground, another gunshot cracked through the passage. He did not feel an impact, assumed the operator behind had aimed at his back but missed due to his leap to the ground.

Court slammed into the cold tile floor, slid forward, and lifted the third gunman's pistol. The man with the knife in his eye was on his knees now, dying but not yet dead, screaming bloody murder. Gentry rolled onto his back next to him and turned to fire back at the last enemy still in the fight. This man had a half chance to shoot but hesitated; Court was alongside his partner.

The Gray Man, however, did not hesitate. From his prone position he poured round after round between his splayed legs into the armed man and watched him spin and die.

When Court was certain the only man alive was the hit man next to him with the knife in his eye, he placed the barrel of the gun to the wounded man's temple and pulled the trigger without hesitation.

The American stood over the bodies of three men sprawled in the bright, white corridor. Blood splatters stained the wall, and pools grew from the corpses at his feet. His ears rang, and his thigh wound stung and throbbed.

They had compromised themselves back at the coffee shop. He'd pegged them as operators in just over one second as they came through the door and he noticed the unmistakable flicker of recognition in the first man's face as he met Gentry's glance.

After identifying the threat these three men posed, Court had watched them in the reflection of the handbill of the poetry reading, in the reflection of the café's windows, out on the street in the windshields of the few passing vehicles. In the stairway down to the metro, he sensed them closing. They closed further in the tunnel, and by the last turn before the trains, he knew the time had come to act.

Court had been faster, better-trained, colder-hearted, but as he stood over the three bodies, he knew good and goddamn well there was only one reason they were now slaughtered meat and his racing pulse continued to pump blood through him.

Dumb fucking luck.

These assassins just decided to stop in for coffee before taking position outside of his hotel, and Court just happened to be at the café when they got there.

Everything else just fell into place after that.

Court was lucky.

He knew it was good to be lucky. But he also knew his luck could turn in an instant. Luck was fleeting, arbitrary, fickle.

Court scavenged the bodies quickly and without a shred of remorse. He knew the morning's first commuters would be rounding the corner either towards or away from the trains in moments. Less than thirty seconds after the last gunshot, the Gray Man had collected a Czech-made CZ pistol and a small wad of euros and crowns.

One minute after that, he was back at street level and wearing a canvas jacket taken from one of the men. The blood on his dark brown pants was concealed by the morning's shower. Through the mist he walked, purposefully but without haste, towards a bus stop near the Charles Bridge. A slight limp in his gait, but nothing else differentiated him from the ever-increasing throngs of people on the street, each beginning their workday commute.

Fitzroy had been offered a small room with a cot to rest, but he refused on principle. Instead, he dozed fitfully in the conference room in a high-backed executive chair. Around his slumped form, the Tech moved from terminal to terminal, and Lloyd made call after call on his mobile. The security men stood both inside and outside the door throughout the night.

Sir Donald awoke at six thirty and was just sipping black coffee when the Tech called across the room to Lloyd. "Sir. The Albanians are not checking in."

Lloyd had been sitting in a chair across from Fitzroy, drinking coffee and staring at a map of Prague. He looked up at his man, shrugged his shoulders, and pursed his lips. "Hard to do when you're dead."

The Tech remained hopeful. "We have no way of knowing—"

Lloyd wasn't listening. He spoke mostly to himself. "One down. Eleven to go. That didn't take long."

Fitzroy smiled behind his coffee cup, and Lloyd noticed this. He rose to his feet, circled the mahogany table, and kneeled in front of Sir Donald. In a soft voice he said, "You and I may seem like adversaries, but we have the same goal here. If you are secretly celebrating the Gray Man's victory, remember that as he gets closer to his target, the stakes will rise. The quicker he is put in the dirt, the better it is for you, your son, your daughter-in-law, and your precious little granddaughters."

Sir Donald's smile faded.

Over an hour later, Fitzroy's satellite phone chirped. Lloyd and his men immediately went into silent mode. Sir Donald pushed the speakerphone button just after the third ring.

"Court? I have been trying to reach you. How are you?"

"What the hell is going on?"

"What do you mean?"

"Another kill squad just tried to zap me."

"You're joking."

"Do I joke?"

"Admittedly not. Who were they?"

"I'm pretty fucking sure they were not Nigerians. Three white dudes. Looked Central European. Didn't have time to pull IDs. If they were any good, they wouldn't have been carrying them, anyway."

"Abubaker must still be using hired hands. No surprise, considering his deep pockets. Are you injured in any way?"

"Yeah, I am, but not by these clowns. I took a bullet to my thigh in the plane yesterday morning."

"You've been shot?"

"No big deal."

Lloyd reached quickly for a notepad and jotted this information down.

"Son, there has been a complication."

"Complication? I've had to take down eight guys in the last twenty-eight hours because of some breach in your Network. You're damn right there's been a complication!"

"The Nigerians know I am your handler."

The satellite connection went quiet for a moment. Finally Gentry said, "Shit, Don. How did that happen?"

"Like I said . . . a complication."

"Then you are in just as much danger as me. It's just a matter of time before they come for you, too." There was concern in the younger man's voice.

"They already have."

A pause. "What's happened?"

"They have my family. My son and my daughter-in-law, my two grandchildren."

"The twins," Court said softly.

"Yes. They are holding them in France, telling me I must give you up, or they will kill them. Thirty minutes ago they gave me forty-eight hours to produce you, dead or alive. They have teams hunting for you, but they want me to give them intel on your whereabouts."

"Which you already have, apparently."

"No, son. I haven't said a word. You were compromised in Iraq somehow, yes, but a Nigerian agent saw you board the plane in Tbilisi. I've told them nothing, and I don't intend to."

"But your son's family."

"I don't turn on my men. You are family, too."

Fitzroy's face was twisted into a pained expression of disgust at his words, but Lloyd's eyes widened appreciatively at the elder Englishman's two-faced ability to simultaneously cajole and betray his top killer. Fitzroy was playing whatever remaining heartstrings his assassin possessed like a virtuoso.

Lloyd knew Gentry's file like the back of his hand. He knew what would come next.

"Where are they holding them?"

"A château in Normandy, France, north of the town of Bayeux."

"Forty-eight hours?"

"Minus thirty minutes. Eight a.m. on Sunday morning is the

deadline. They say they have assets in the French National Police; any hint of an operation against their location will result in a massacre."

"Yeah. The cops will be useless. I've got a better chance going solo."

"Court, I don't know what you are thinking, but it is too dangerous for you to try any sort of—"

"Don, I need you to trust me. Best thing I can do is get there and clean this shit up myself. I need you to get me all the intel you can about their force structure, don't give up any info on me, and I will get your family back."

"How?"

"Somehow."

This time it was Sir Donald's turn to pause. He rubbed his thick fingers in his eyes and said slowly, "I would be forever in your debt, lad."

"One thing at a time, boss." The line went dead.

Lloyd punched his fists into the air in victory.

Fitzroy turned to Lloyd and said, "I'll get you the scalp you are after. But you have to adhere to your end of the bargain."

"Sir Donald, nothing will make me happier than calling off my men and leaving you and your family alone."

ELEVEN

Court Gentry had worked as a private operator for four years. Before that was Golf Sierra, AKA the Goon Squad, and previous to this he ran singleton ops for the CIA. A few steely-eyed agency operatives notwithstanding, Gentry had spent the majority of adult life alone. To be sure, when he was in deep cover, he developed the relationships necessary to conduct his missions, but these interactions were fleeting and based on a bed of lies.

His was a life lived out in the cold.

There had been but one episode in the last sixteen years when Court was not an assassin, not a spy, not a shadowy figure moving into and out of the landscape. Two years earlier, for just under two months, Fitzroy had employed the Gray Man in a capacity completely unique to anything else on his résumé. Court took a post in Close Personal Protection, bodyguard work, to watch over Sir Donald's two granddaughters.

Their father, Sir Donald's son, was a successful London real estate developer. He did not follow in his father's footsteps into the shadowy realm of intelligence; he was an honest businessman, played by the rules. Still, Phillip Fitzroy managed to run afoul of some Pakistani underworld types, something to do with his firm's lobbying against a municipal proposal that would have allowed more uncertified and unqualified labor on his construction sites. Phillip Fitzroy logically argued that it was best for everyone in London if only well-trained workers built apartment dwellings and shopping centers, but the Pakistani mob had been extorting from the undocumented populace for years, and they decided that if more immigrants had higher-paying jobs, they could squeeze out from them a few quid more.

It began with threatening phone calls. Phillip was to back off, quit the lobbying campaign. A fake pipe bomb in the mailbox was found by Elise Fitzroy, Phillip's wife. Scotland Yard opened an investigation; dour-faced detectives rubbed their chins and promised to be vigilant. Phillip continued his fight against the labor law, more threats came, and the Yard put a car with a narcoleptic officer in front of their Sussex Gardens townhome.

Elise was cleaning out six-year-old Kate's school backpack one afternoon while the girls watched television. She pulled a folded page out of an outside pouch, thinking it to be a note sent home from Mrs. Beasley. She opened it. Handwritten scrabble. Large capital letters.

"Any time we want them, we can have them. Lay off, Phil."

Elise hysterically called Phillip, Phillip called Sir Donald no less frantic, and seven hours later Sir Donald arrived at the door with an American in tow.

The Yank was neither big nor small, he was quiet, and he made little eye contact. Elise thought he was in his late twenties; Phil put him near forty. He wore jeans and a small backpack that never left his shoulder and an oversized sweater under which Phillip assumed was stashed God knows what manner of obscene apparatus for doing harm to his fellow man.

Sir Donald sat with Elise and Phillip in the drawing room while the man waited in the hall. He explained to the worried parents that this man's name was Jim, just Jim, and he was quite possibly the best in the world at that which he did.

"What, exactly, is that, Dad?" asked Phillip.

"Let's just say you're better off with him than you'd be were your whole street lined with cars filled to bursting with bobbies. That's no exaggeration."

"Doesn't look like much, Dad."

"That's part of the job. He's low-profile."

"What the bloody hell do we do with him, Dad?"

"Throw him a sandwich a couple of times a day, keep the coffeepot hot in the kitchen, and forget he's here."

But Elise refused to treat the man as an inanimate object. She was polite and found him to respond in kind. He never looked at her; this she insisted when her husband asked. "He looks out the window to the street, out the window to the back garden, at the door to the twins' room. Never *at* me. You and he have that in common, Phillip; you should get on brilliantly."

The introduction of an additional man to the Fitzroy household inevitably caused friction between husband and wife.

Claire and Kate took to Jim. They mimicked his American accent, and he was good-natured about it. He drove them to school each day in the Saab while Elise rode along. Young Kate teased him once about being a bad driver, and he surprised mother and daughters with a burst of laughter, admitting he usually traveled by trains or rode a motorcycle. Within a second his face rehardened, and his eyes returned to the mirrors and the road ahead.

For almost two months he was at the girls' sides every moment they were awake, and he was on a cot in the hallway by their door while they slept. The only moment of excitement in the eight weeks came one Sunday on the way to the market when a car accident blocked the road. As soon as traffic stopped, Jim bumped the car up onto the pavement. He opened his sport coat, and Elise saw the butt of a handgun nestled under his arm. He drove down the pavement with his left hand, through a scrambling crowd, while his right hand curled around the pistol in its shoulder holster. Ten seconds later they were in the clear. He said not a word to the passengers, like it was just another normal Sunday jaunt out for milk and cakes. Mum and her girls stared at him wide-eyed for the rest of the drive.

And then one morning he was gone. The quilt was left folded on the cot, the pillow laid on top. It was in the papers that the Pakistani mobsters had been arrested by the dour-faced men at Scotland Yard, the danger had passed, and Sir Donald had sent his Yank away.

Phillip and Elise breathed an incredible sigh of relief that the threat was no more, and the ridiculous law had been defeated.

But the little girls cried when their father told them Uncle Jim had to go back to America and, no, he was not likely to return.

Court bought a motorcycle less than an hour after he closed his call with Fitzroy. It was an '86 Honda CM450 with a decent enough engine and tires that looked like they could make it for a few days of heavy use.

The seller was a local boy who worked at a petrol station alongside the road in Seberov, just southeast of Prague. No paperwork, just a cash transaction, a few hundred crowns extra for a helmet and a map, and Court was on the road.

He hadn't hesitated a moment since hanging up the phone with Don. Court knew there was a day or so of travel ahead of him if he was to go to Normandy. He could work on a plan while on the move and check in with Fitzroy en route. No, there was no time to sit on a park bench here, six hundred miles away, and contemplate.

After buying the bike, he stopped at his cache in a long-term rental unit four miles south of the city center. He no longer had a key for the door, so he merely picked the lock. He could recite the credit card number used to pay the monthly rent if he had been questioned, but in fact there was no one around. He'd established the cache nearly three years earlier, had only been back once, and now the small, unlit room was dusty and moldy and cold. It was eight feet square, empty except for four duffel bags stacked one on top of the other, each wrapped in a white garbage bag covered in dust. The cache contained pistols, rifles, ammo, clothing, and vacuum-packed food and medical supplies. He tossed the CZ he'd picked up in the gunfight in the metro into one of the bags and retrieved a small Walther P99 Compact pistol and two extra magazines. The weapon was clean and well-lubricated, but still he checked the ammunition and the operation of the slide and the striker. He ignored the rest of his guns. He knew he could hardly cross the border into the European Union with an arsenal on his back.

The handgun would just have to do.

Next he ripped open a medical kit, dropped his pants, and sat on the cold, dirty floor. The scratching of a rat in the aluminum walls let him know just how unsanitary these conditions were. He examined his day-old injury with a professional fascination. Court had never before been shot, but he'd picked up dozens of other injuries in his work. His leg throbbed like a bitch, but he'd been hurt worse from burns, broken bones, a chunk of shrapnel in his neck. It came with the job.

He poured a generous splash of iodine on the entrance and exit wounds. He tore open packages of bandages and antiseptic cream, redressed his injury as well as possible in the low light, and then crumpled all his supplies back into a small bag and shoved it into his pocket. In his second duffel he found cold weather gear. He changed out of his light clothing into thick corduroys, a grease-stained brown cotton shirt, and a thick canvas jacket. A pair of work gloves went on his hands, and they warmed his fingers instantly. Leather hiking boots. A black watch cap that could be pulled down as a ski mask was positioned on his head. He zipped up all his cases, left them as he'd found them, closed the door, and climbed back on his bike.

Minutes later he found himself at a crossroads south of the city. A few hours west was the German border, then the French border, then Normandy.

He blew out a sigh masked by his engine's rumble. Steam from his exhalation poured through the microfiber ski mask covering his mouth.

If it were only that easy.

No, he had to make a few crucial pit stops along the way. Gentry needed to pick up some matériel before he arrived in Normandy. He knew where to get what he needed, but he also knew it would involve an extra half day on the road.

For one, Court needed a new "escape," new forged identity papers. He still had the passport he'd used to get into the Czech Republic, and he knew it would get him around in Central Europe, where they did not have all their immigration processes computerized and integrated, but he'd already been burned once under the legend Martin Baldwin, Canadian freelance journalist. Only a hopeless optimist or a damn fool would try to use it to get into the European Union, and Gentry was neither. But more than entrée to the EU, he needed an escape solid enough to get him out of Europe when the shooting stopped. He knew that after he did what he had to do in Normandy, he would need to disappear somewhere far away, and clean identity papers would be the easiest way to achieve this end.

Court knew a man in Hungary who could provide him with documentation quickly. With well-made docs, he could cross quickly and efficiently into the EU and, should he have to produce papers for any reason along the way, he could safely do so. And then, once he'd finished his operation, he'd be able to dump all his guns and gear, hop on a plane to South America or the South Pacific, or fucking Antarctica if the heat on him remained as hot as it had been the last two days.

There'd be no time to run around and buy dirty docs after Normandy, and no way to quickly get off the Continent without them.

A cold November wind blew from the west as Gentry turned onto the E65, the highway that would take him past Brno, into Slovakia, around Bratislava, and then south to the Hungarian border. From there it would be a quick trip down to Budapest. Six hours' travel time, factoring in a couple of quick stops for gas and two poorly guarded borders.

As he opened the throttle and leaned into the cold wind, he forced himself to think about the next forty-eight hours. It was grim contemplation, but necessary, and a hell of a lot better than dwelling on the past forty-eight.

TWELVE

Gentry entered the capital of Hungary at three in the afternoon. Rain clouds hung low and gray white, just tickling the rounded green tips of the hills of Buda on the west side of the Danube River that bisected the city of four million. Court had last visited Budapest four years earlier on his first job for Fitzroy, a simple domestic op against a Serbian hit man who'd put a bomb in a local restaurant to kill a mob gunrunner but in so doing also took out an American man's brother. The surviving brother had money and ties to the underworld, so it was a simple thing for him to connect with Fitzroy and hire a triggerman. And it was a simple thing for Fitzroy to send his newest asset to Budapest to find the offending Serb in a dockside bar, fill him with drink, then slip a knife into his spine and let his lifeless form slip silently into the black waters of the Danube.

Gentry also knew Budapest from before, back in his time with the agency. He'd been in and out of the city once every couple of years for nearly a decade, tailing diplomats, running sneak-and-peeks against shady Russian businessmen in the mansions of Buda or the hotels in Pest. He'd once chased off a Tajik assassin targeting the local CIA chief of station because there was no one else handy to deal with the matter.

In Court's work in the city he'd had multiple run-ins with a local fraudster named Laszlo Szabo. Szabo was an amoral, devious scumbag; he'd do anything for anyone waving a big enough wad of crumpled Hungarian forints in his face. His specialty was forgery, buying and selling identity papers and modifying them for whoever needed their identity changed on the fly. He'd helped a dozen wanted Serb war criminals flee Central Europe just ahead of the International Court of Justice and had made a shitload of money cleaning up the dirty loose ends of that war and others. Then in 2004 he ran afoul of Gentry himself when he agreed to create papers for a Chechen terrorist who'd slipped out of Grozny and the Russians' grasp and into Budapest on his way farther west. Court and his Goon Squad caught up with the Chechen in a warehouse Laszlo owned in the suburbs. It had gone loud, and in the melee a tub of Szabo's photographic chemicals had blown up, killing the terrorist. Court and his team had to disappear before the fire trucks arrived, leaving Laszlo to slip away. Immediately thereafter, Court was sent after bigger fish, but he remembered Szabo, kept tabs on the forger, just in case someday he needed his services. Court normally used documentation assets from Sir Donald Fitzroy's Network, but it was nice to know there was also a man in Budapest who could, for the right price, turn him into anyone he wanted to be, at least on paper.

Laszlo Szabo was an irredeemable piece of shit. Court knew this beyond a shadow of a doubt. But Court also knew Szabo *was* damn good at his work.

It was three thirty by the time Court had filled his gas tank, bought a gyro and lemonade at a little Turkish stand on Andrassy Street, and parked his bike a block away from Laszlo's lair in Pest, just a kilometer or so from the shores of the Danube. Icy sheets of cold rain poured down, but Gentry did nothing to shield himself from the weather. His muscles were tiring from the already long day; the rain soaked his hair and his beard and his clothes, but it also kept him alert.

The door to Laszlo's building was a deception. A rusty iron plate on hinges sunken in a stone building on Eotvos Utka Street, it was covered with yellowed and torn handbills and stood no more than five feet high. It looked like no one had passed through since the Second World War, but Court had just finished his soggy meal of lamb chunks and cucumber sauce folded into a pita when the door creaked open and disgorged two thin black men. Somalis, Court guessed. In Europe illegally, obviously, since no one who had access to legitimate papers would have need to come see Laszlo. Court knew how easy it was for Africans and Middle Easterners to immigrate legally to the Continent these days. The two knuckleheads walking past him in the rain somehow didn't qualify for the near-universal rubber stamp entry, which indicated to Gentry that these were some seriously shady fuckers.

In a moment of perspective, the Gray Man realized there were few people on earth more wanted than he, so Court allowed he was, by definition, likely a shadier fucker than either of these two Somalis.

Gentry banged on the little iron door with an open left hand. His right hovered above the Walther pistol in his waistband and hidden under his wet jacket. There was no answer after a minute and a further knock. Finally Court found a little plastic intercom button tucked into the upper left corner of the doorway. "Szabo? I need your help. I can pay."

A tinny response through the intercom. "References?" His accent was unmistakably Hungarian, but his English was good. The tone of his voice was sheer boredom. A clerk in a paint store. Court was just the next of a long line of customers reaching the counter to inquire about goods.

"I'm one of Donald Fitzroy's men." Though Szabo was not a Network asset, he would certainly know of Sir Donald.

A pause just long enough for Court to worry ended with a buzz and the sound of remote-controlled door locks clicking open. Court pushed in the iron door warily, knelt, and entered a dark hall behind it, followed a pinprick of light fifty feet on. The light was another doorway, and through it Court found a large workshop, part science lab, part library, and part photo studio. Laszlo was there, sitting at a desk against the wall. He turned to face his visitor.

Szabo wore his gray hair long over his shoulders. His clothes were Hungarian drab, black jeans and a polyester shirt open halfway down to expose his rail-thin chest. He was sixty, but an East bloc sixty, which looked eighty in the face but thirty in the physique. A life of physicality, a life of hardship. He appeared to Court something like an aging rock star who still fancied himself a catch.

He stared at Court for a long time. "A familiar face," he said. "Without the beard and the rainwater, perhaps I would know you?"

Court knew Szabo had never seen his face. He'd worn a balaclava mask when he took down Szabo's lair with the Goon Squad in 2004, plus it had been dark and the action quick and confusing.

"Don't believe so," said Gentry, looking around the room for security threats. Wires hung off the walls like ivy, tables and shelves of equipment and boxes and books, locked file cabinets along the wall, a full-sized photography studio in the corner with a camera on a tripod facing a chair on a riser.

"An American. Thirty-five years old. Height five eleven, weight one seventy. You don't carry yourself like a soldier or a cop, which is good." Court remembered fragments from the man's dossier. Szabo had been trained by the Soviets in electronic surveillance and forgery and other nonlethal black arts, he'd been used to spy on his own people by the Russians, but he had played for both teams, giving Moscow information on his countrymen while providing well-off Hungarians with escapes to get them through the Iron Curtain.

His marginal and conditional and halfhearted help of his own people had proven to be just enough to keep a knife out of his chest after the fall of the Soviet Union, though Gentry remembered reading that Laszlo had been no stranger to getting his ass kicked in retaliation for his association with Moscow.

"I'm just a man who needs some of your product. In a hurry," Court said.

Laszlo stood up and reached for a cane leaning against the desk. He leaned heavily on it as he crossed the room to his visitor. Court noted the Hungarian's slumped body and severe limp. This injury had developed since he last saw him five years ago.

After an eternity, Szabo arrived in front of Court, leaned well into his personal space. Put a hand up to the American's chin and turned his head left and right.

"What sort of product?"

"A passport. Clean, not fake. I need it now. I'll pay for the extra trouble."

Laszlo nodded. "How is Norris?"

"Norris?"

"Sir Donald Fitzroy's son, of course."

"You mean Phillip."

"Yes. Does Sir Donald still have the summer place in Brighton?"

"I wouldn't know."

"Neither would I, to be honest," Szabo allowed with a sheepish shrug.

Court said, "I understand your need to establish my bona fides, but I am in a rush."

Szabo nodded, hobbled to a little bench, one of a dozen in the room and each in front of a different table or desk covered with computers, microscopes, papers, cameras, and other gear. "Fitzroy has his own network. His own facilitators of documentation. Why would you be slumming with Laszlo?"

"I need someone good. And someone quick. Everyone knows you're the best."

The Hungarian nodded. "Maybe that's just flattery, but you are exactly right. Laszlo *is* the best." He relaxed. "I'll do a great job for you; maybe you can speak to Fitzroy about the service. Put in a good word for Laszlo, you understand."

Court knew to loathe men who referred to themselves in the third person. But he also knew to be polite when in need. "You get me out of here with clean papers in under an hour, and I will do just that."

Szabo seemed pleased. He nodded. "I recently came into possession of a consignment of Belgian passports. New serial numbers, not reported stolen. Perfectly legitimate."

Court shook his head emphatically. "No. Two-thirds of the stolen passports on the market are Belgian. They are guaranteed extra scrutiny. I need something less obvious."

"An informed customer. I respect that." Laszlo stood, leaned on his cane, and made his way to another desk. He strummed his fingers on a little notebook full of pencil scratches. Then he looked up. "Yes. I suppose you could pass as a Kiwi. I've had a few New Zealand passports for a long time. Most of my clients these days are Africans or Arabs . . . Can't pull off a Kiwi, needless to say. Like I said, these books have been around a while, but Laszlo can doctor the serial number when I put in your information without tainting the hologram. No way it can be traced back to a missing lot."

"Fine."

Szabo sat back down and blew out a sigh that showed Gentry the movement was tiring and uncomfortable for him. "Five thousand euros."

Gentry nodded, pulled the money from his pack, showed it to Laszlo, but did not hand it over.

"What about your appearance? I can photograph you as you are, or we can create something more professional."

"I'd like to clean up first."

"I've got a shower. A razor. A suit coat and tie that should fit you. You ready yourself while Laszlo works on the papers."

Court walked down a hall and sniffed his way to a bathroom that reeked with body odor and mildew. The shower was equipped with soap and razors and shears, all laid out for operators and illegal immigrants and criminals who needed to camouflage their nastiness for a few minutes in order to pose for a photograph intended to portray them to cops and border control agents as little Lord Fauntleroys. For the first time in three months Gentry shaved his beard. He'd laid his Walther on the little shelf with the shampoo and the razors. It was covered with lather by the time he finished.

Gentry cleaned up his shavings. He saw each brown hair as DNA evidence, so he spent more time collecting his beard than he had cutting it off.

He looked at himself in the mirror while he combed his brown hair to the right in a wet part that would disappear when it dried. He was aging in the face, the creases of sun and wind and life itself deepening into his skin. He could tell he'd lost weight since he'd begun the Syrian operation, and soft bags of discoloration hung under his eyes.

When he was twenty-six, he'd once gone four days without sleep. He'd been tracking an enemy agent in Moscow and was following him to a dacha in the country, when Court's piece of shit two-door Lada broke down in the snow. The Gray Man had to stay on the move overland to keep from freezing to death.

Now, at thirty-six, he feared he looked much worse after four days of work than he did back then when his extraction team pulled him, half-frozen, out of the ice and into a helicopter.

After he dried off, he pulled his rain-soaked pants back on. He was careful to keep the soggy bandage in place on his leg. He cinched his belt and climbed into his boots and socks. He dressed in a white dress shirt Laszlo had left out for him that was too small for his neck, tied the cheap tie with it carefully, a big knot covering the open collar. A blue jacket that felt like cardboard bunched at his shoulders. He didn't even try to button it. Court slid his pistol onto his hip, tossed the extra mags and his multi-tool in his pocket, and went back into Laszlo's lab.

Szabo sat in a wheelchair at a drafting table, leaning over an open passport with a razor. He looked up at his customer for a long moment. "Quite a metamorphosis."

"Yeah."

"Sit for the picture, please." There was a small plastic chair on a riser in front of a blue background hanging from the ceiling. A digital camera on a tripod was connected to a computer on a desk a few feet away.

Court stepped up on the hollow wooden riser and sat in the chair. He fumbled with his coat and tie while Szabo rolled the wheelchair into position behind the camera. "We need to think of a name for the passport. A good Kiwi name."

"It's up to you. Whatever is fine."

The camera flashed, and Gentry began to stand.

"A couple more, please."

He sat back down.

"I have a name for you. Don't know if you will like it."

"Anything is—"

"It's flashy. Dramatic. Mysterious."

"Well, I don't think I need—"

"Why don't we call you Gray Man?"

Gentry stared blankly into the camera as it flashed in his face.

Shit.

Szabo glared at him.

Gentry began to stand.

He felt movement in his seat. He had shifted his weight to his feet, but his heels felt like they were dropping. Before he could react, his arms flew up to his sides, his borrowed coat bunched up higher on his neck, and his knees raised in front of his eyes. He was falling backwards, the plastic chair sliding back with him. The light around him vanished, and he dropped into darkness, finally landing on his side, his fall cushioned by something soft and wet.

The impact, though cushioned by padding, still knocked the wind from his lungs. Reactively he leapt to his feet, pulled the pistol from his hip, and spun in all directions to both engage any threats and get his bearings.

It was a brick-lined pit, a cistern of some sort. Looking up, he saw he'd fallen twelve feet or so from where the riser had opened up to swallow him. Before he could reach for it, the chair raised into the air, its leg held with a thin chain. It clanged back over the edge of the riser and disappeared. A Plexiglas trapdoor closed above him, sealing him into the dank container.

Slowly, Szabo leaned over the side, looked down through the plastic at his captive, and smiled.

"You've got to be kidding me!" shouted Gentry in utter frustration.

"I presume you are armed. Beasts like you usually are. You might want to think before firing a weapon in there." Szabo used the tip of his cane to tap the clear lid over the hole. "Two inches of hardened Plexiglas; you'll be dodging your own ricochets." He then tapped his forehead with a bony finger. "Don't be stupid."

"I don't have time for this, Szabo!"

"On the contrary. A little time is all you have left." Szabo backed away from view.

THIRTEEN

Gentry ripped off the jacket, the tie, the shirt, and looked around the pit. It was a seven-foot-wide circle, seemed to be some sort of old sewage well. A cylindrical wall of stone around him too sheer and slick with mildew to climb. The mattresses on which he'd fallen were smelly and rotting. There was a drainage problem to be sure. He looked under the mats and discovered an old iron water pipe. He wrapped his hand around it and found it to be hot. Budapest's thermal baths were a tourist draw; this pipe likely pumped hot springwater from one location to another. Water pushed through it, dripping and steaming a little where it disappeared into the wall.

Court looked up and around. This would be a particularly awful place to die.

Ten minutes later, Szabo returned. He stood over Court and smiled.

Gentry said, "Whatever you are planning on doing—"

"I remember you. You thought I'd forget? Two thousand four. Central Intelligence Agency super special A team."

Court knew Szabo had not seen his face in the operation in '04. Still, he shouted, "That's right, and my field team knows where I am right now."

"Pathetic. You aren't with the agency anymore."

"Where did you hear that?"

The sixty-year-old Hungarian disappeared for a minute. He returned above the pit, placed a sheet of paper facedown on the glass six feet above his prisoner's head.

Gentry looked up at his own face, an old head shot taken by the CIA for some dirty documentation. Above the photo were the words, "Wanted for questioning by Interpol." It was just a photo and a description. His name was not given.

"American government men sat in a car outside in the street, seven days a week, for an entire year after you, shall we say, *resigned* your position with the agency. They actually thought you'd come to Laszlo for help. Their presence was bad for business, Mr. Gray Man."

"Szabo. This is serious. Look, I know you. I know you'll let me buy my way back up. Just name your price. I can call a man and get money wired—"

"Sir Donald can't purchase your path to safety. I don't want his money."

Gentry looked up at the man above him. His voice lowered. "I'd hate to hurt a cripple."

"You were the one who crippled me!"

"What are you talking about?"

"You shot up my darkroom. You thought I'd forget?"

"I didn't shoot *you*."

"No, you were shooting at the Chechen, hit a container of ammonium persulfate. Knocked the powder into a bath of aluminum water and . . . bang! The Chechen is dripping off the ceiling, and poor, helpless Laszlo is burned, the nerves of his lower body damaged from inhaling the toxic fumes."

Shit. Court shrugged. "Whose fault is that? You were helping a terrorist enter the West. The CIA should have sent me back to finish you."

"Maybe they should have, but I've since made friends with the good men of the Central Intelligence Agency. After the FBI came to talk to me, the agency came. They were the ones who told me you were the leader of the group that blew up my warehouse and ruined my legs. Believe it or not, these days, the local CIA station and Laszlo have a reasonably good working relationship."

"Why wouldn't I believe that? You always did play all sides."

"I think our relationship will get even better now that I've called them and told them I have you locked away. They are on their way here to pick you up right now."

The muscles in Court's face twitched. "Tell me you did not do that."

"I did. I am going to trade you to the CIA in exchange for a little détente. Our relationship is not so good that me handing over their number one target won't make Laszlo's life easier."

"How long until they are here?"

"Under two hours. The station chief is ordering up a helicopter full of heavies from Vienna to take you into custody. I told him your reputation was overrated; old frail Laszlo captured you by himself, after all, but he was undeterred. You warrant a big operation just to carry you away. You will just have to amuse yourself in the meantime while you—"

"Laszlo, you need to listen very carefully to me."

"Ha! Look at him shake. Look at the Gray Man shake like a little—"

"They aren't sending a team to haul me away. They'll send a wet team. There's a shoot-on-sight directive against me. And when they come here to wax my ass, don't expect them to just walk away and leave a witness behind. That's not how these guys operate."

Laszlo cocked his head, seemed to think this over, then said, "They won't hurt me. The CIA needs me."

"They only needed you until you made that phone call, you dumb son of a bitch!"

Szabo's nerves began to show. He shouted, "Enough talk! If you think the grim reaper is on the way for you, maybe you should spend the next few minutes asking your God for forgiveness for your sins."

"You, too."

Laszlo Szabo's wrinkled and confused face disappeared from the glass above Court.

Sir Donald Fitzroy's mobile rang at three. Lloyd pushed the speaker button, though the call had not come from Gentry's satellite phone.

"Cheltenham Security."

"Good afternoon, Sir Donald. I am calling in regards to an important business matter."

"Do I know you?"

"Our paths have not crossed, I don't believe. You may call me Igor."

Fitzroy was short with the caller. There was more than enough on his plate to where he felt no need to be polite to some heavily accented solicitor. "And you may call me not interested. I am busy. If you have legitimate business, you can bloody well contact my secretary and make an appointment."

"Yes . . . well, the Gray Man seems to think he represents legitimate business to you. He told me to call, is insisting you will pay handsomely for his safe return."

"The Gray Man is with you?"

"Indeed."

"Which team are you with?"

"Which team? I am my own team, sir."

Fitzroy and Lloyd looked at one another. Lloyd pushed the mute button. "I don't think this is one of our hunters."

Sir Donald tapped the button to allow the caller to hear him. "Let me talk to him."

"I'm afraid that won't be possible at the moment."

Lloyd hit the mute button again. He turned to the Tech at the bank of computers on the wall. The young man said, "The call originated in Budapest, the Pest side. He's got some misdirection software on it. I'll try and get it pinned down."

Lloyd looked up at the large map on the wall monitor. "What's Court doing in Budapest, for fuck's sake?"

Fitzroy ignored him and hit the speaker box in the middle of the table, releasing the mute yet again.

"I . . . I may be very interested in accommodating you, Igor. I just need assurance that my man is, in fact, in your care."

"No trust in this world, that's what's wrong. Very well, Sir Donald. Give me a moment. I don't move as quickly as I used to." There was shuffling through the speakers for nearly a minute. Then finally, "Go ahead, Mr. Fitzroy, you may speak."

"Lad? Is that you?"

Gentry's voice, distant or muffled by something: "He called the agency. A kill squad will be here in less than ninety minutes, Don! I'm in—"

There was more scratching and shuffling over the speakers. Then the accented voice came back on the line. "You have one hour, Sir Donald. Wire five hundred thousand euros, and I will have your boy spirited away in plenty of time to avert a counteroffer from a competitor. Here's the account number. Do you have a pen?"

A minute later, the call was disconnected. Both Fitzroy and Lloyd looked to the Tech. The young Brit with the nose ring shook his head.

"Budapest, Sixth District. That much we know. But I couldn't pinpoint it closer. There are a quarter million phones in the Sixth District. He could have called from any one of them."

Lloyd was annoyed but in too much hurry to show it. He turned to his captive. "Who does he know in Budapest?"

Fitzroy rubbed his forehead and shrugged.

"Think, damn you! Who would Gentry go see there?"

Sir Donald lifted his head quickly. "Szabo! Not in my Network, you see; an old counterfeiter, used to work for the Reds back in—"

Lloyd interrupted. "Got an address?"

"I can get it."

"My closest kill team is in Vienna, a hundred miles away. No way we can have them there in that time frame. We'll have to pay Szabo off to keep Gentry out of the CIA's hands."

Fitzroy shook his head. "Forget it. Szabo is a snake. If he called the CIA, he did it to curry favor with them. He just called me because Gentry told him I'd pay for his release. Laszlo Szabo will take my money and still give him up to the CIA. He'll fuck me over long before he'll fuck them over."

"Will the CIA take Gentry in or kill him?"

"Irrelevant. If they kill him, they'll cover their tracks. The body won't turn up for weeks, if ever. Abubaker won't sign just because we *tell* him Gentry's on ice. You'll kill my family just the same as if Gentry survived."

"Then we have less than an hour to get killers to Szabo's location and do the job before the agency boys get there."

Gentry's neck was sore from staring up at the plastic ceiling above him. He heard noises near the opening, so he yelled out, "How are you going to get me out of here before the agency assets come to kill us both?"

Szabo's wrinkled face appeared above. "Once I have Sir Donald's money, the only one leaving here will be me."

"Fitzroy will kill you for double-crossing him."

"Ha. I still have friends in the East. I have been looking for a way out. A half-million euros will be just about enough for a new start."

"Look," Court implored, "there's more at stake here than you know. A family has been kidnapped. Two little girls have been taken, eight-year-old twins. They will be murdered if I don't get to France in time to stop it. You let me out of here, and I swear you'll get your money. You'll get whatever you—"

"Two little girls?"

"Yes."

"Murdered?"

"Not if I can get—"

Laszlo laughed cruelly. "You've obviously mistaken me for a man with a soul. The Russians had it surgically removed thirty-five years ago. I really could not possibly care less." He disappeared from Gentry's view.

Lloyd called Riegel, reached him in his teak-paneled Paris office. The German answered before the first ring ended. The American asked, "Do you have assets in Budapest?"

"I have assets everywhere."

"Tier-one assassins?"

"No. Just a few pavement artists. I could arrange some low-class triggermen, I suppose, but why? Haven't I provided you with enough alpha killers in the past twelve hours? Surely the Gray Man hasn't chewed through them all yet!" His tone mocked the young lawyer.

"We sent the teams to the west. Gentry went south, to Hungary, apparently to get a passport to use to flee Europe after he's finished in Normandy."

"Prudent. Optimistic, but prudent."

"Yeah, well, it didn't work out so well for him. The forger in Budapest double-crossed him. Locked him up. He just called Sir Donald to demand ransom."

"Let me guess. Laszlo Szabo?"

"How did you know?"

"Let's just say you can't mention 'Budapest' and 'double-cross' in the same sentence without Szabo's name coming up."

"Can you get some men to his address in Pest?"

"Of course. Is it just Laszlo or does he have security?"

"It's more complicated than that. Szabo also turned Court in to the CIA. They have a team racing to the location now. Supposedly they are an hour out."

Riegel sighed, resignation now in his voice. "He falls into CIA hands, and the Lagos contract is history. If they take him, we won't be able to prove to Abubaker if he's dead or alive by Sunday."

"Then we can't let that happen. Right?"

"You want to send a team to shoot it out with American intelligence? Are you insane?"

"The CIA will think they're men working for Gentry or working for the kidnapper. If your guys are any good, they won't hang around to explain their motivation."

Riegel thought a moment. When he finally spoke, it sounded to Lloyd as if the German was formulating the plan as the words left his mouth. "The Indonesian hit team is in the air at this moment. They are heading to Frankfurt, but they should be over south Central Europe right about now. Maybe we can divert them, get them on the ground and into the city in the next hour. We'll be cutting it razor close, but it's our only chance."

"Are they any good?"

"Yes. They are Kopassus, Group Four. The best shooters Jakarta has to offer. Let me get to work."

Captain Bernard Kilzer checked the altitude on the radio altimeter. It was a Wolfsburg model he was not entirely familiar with, as this plane was rented and not his normal craft. He was flying west-northwest at 37,000 feet. The Bombardier Challenger 605 was state-of-the-art, fly-by-wire technology. His duties and responsibilities as a pilot were great, but at this point, seven hours into his nine-hour flight from New Delhi to Frankfurt, there was little for him and his copilot to do other than stay awake, monitor the onboard systems, and scan the afternoon skies.

The two pilots had been flying, nearly nonstop, for sixteen hours. Their route had originated in Jakarta, Indonesia, at two a.m. local time. They'd flown west, stopped for fuel in New Delhi, and then immediately returned to the sky.

Normally, Captain Kilzer and his copilot, First Officer Lee, flew corporate heads around Southeast Asia. They also transported

LaurentGroup scientists, critical IT personnel, anyone who was needed in any one of fifteen corporate facilities from the southern tip of Japan to the eastern edge of India.

In addition to these work-related trips, Kilzer and Lee also ferried executives and their wives on island-hopping vacations or to lavish parties in Brunei with the sultan himself. He'd once even shuttled company clients and Philippine call girls to a secluded tropical isle populated by French chefs and Swedish masseuses for a week of indolent debauchery.

Kilzer had flown all manner of LaurentGroup employees, but he'd never transported a group like the one he was hauling now.

Behind him in the cabin were six men. Indonesians, they looked to be young military types, but they wore civilian clothing. The cargo hold of the Challenger was full of green canvas rucksacks. The men kept quiet for the most part. On Kilzer's trips out of the cockpit to the lavatory he'd glanced into the twenty-eight-foot cabin and had seen darkness perforated by penlights, some men poring over maps while others slept.

They seemed a disciplined group, heading out on some important mission, and Kilzer did not have a clue why he'd been tasked with ferrying them.

The bald-headed thirty-eight-year-old German pilot reached behind himself to retrieve his lunch box. The multifunction display flashed. His copilot said, "Ground-to-air call coming through for you from the home office on the secure link."

"Roger." Kilzer turned away from his meal and flipped a switch on the center console to send the impending transmission into his ears alone.

"November Delta Three Zero Whiskey, over?"

"This is Riegel speaking, do you read me?"

Kilzer knew Riegel was the VP of security operations for the entire corporation. The German was known as an incredibly tough bastard. Suddenly Kilzer had a better idea about the mission of the fit young men in the cabin behind him. "Loud and clear, Mr. Riegel. How can I help you, sir?"

"How close are you to Budapest?"

"Just a moment." Kilzer looked to the copilot, an Asian with a British accent. "It's Riegel. Wants to know how far we are from Budapest."

First Officer Lee checked his flight's location on the navigation management system. He typed into the keypad on his left and in a few seconds responded. "We are one hundred seven kilometers south-southeast and twelve kilometers above."

Kilzer relayed the information, and Riegel said, "We have a change in plans. I need you to land there as soon as possible."

Kilzer felt the sting of sweat on the back of his neck. He did not feel good about disappointing the chief of security ops. "I am sorry, sir, that is not possible. We haven't filed a flight plan for Hungary. We will have serious problems with immigration and security."

"Don't tell me what is possible. Put the airplane on the ground, distribute to the Indonesians their gear, and then get out of there."

Captain Kilzer did not back down immediately. "How are we supposed to get out of there? We'll be thrown in jail if we land without authorization, if we—"

"Declare an emergency. Surely you can find a reason to land the plane wherever you want. If you get detained for questioning, I'll pay your way out. We can smooth things over with the Hungarians after the fact. That's not your concern. Just make sure the Indonesians are off the plane before you taxi to the tarmac."

"There is too much security at Budapest Ferihegy. They will surround the aircraft, and we will—"

"Then don't land there. Find a little regional airport nearby, land the plane, and let loose the men in the back. Do I make myself clear?"

The captain frantically flipped through pages on his multifunction display. He scrolled through electronic charts of all the region's airports.

"Tokol is forty minutes' driving time from the city center. Its runway is long enough."

"Too far! I need the Indonesians in the city center in under an hour!"

Kilzer kept looking. "There is Budaörs. It is half the drive time, but the runway is not paved, and it is too short."

"How short?"

"This aircraft with this load requires one thousand meters on a paved runway in perfect conditons. Budaörs is one thousand meters exactly, but there is heavy rain and, as I said, it is unpaved. It will be like mud!"

"Then you should have no problems slowing down before you run out of runway. Land the plane!"

"You are demanding a crash landing, sir! It will be very unsafe."

"If you want to be safe from me, Captain, you will land that plane in Budaörs. Am I clear?"

Kilzer gritted his teeth.

Riegel said, "I'll have a coach and a driver there to pick them up."

"Sir, I need to stress again, this will create an incident."

"Let me worry about that."

"Roger, sir."

Kilzer disconnected the call. He squeezed his hands on his control column in frustration.

The copilot asked, "What's going on?"

"Apparently, Lee, you and I are about to help Indonesia invade Hungary."

The first officer turned white. "Riegel is an asshole."

"*Ja,*" said Kilzer. He then flipped a few switches on his center console, took the jet off autopilot, and slowly pushed the controls forward. He spoke into his headset. "Mayday, mayday, mayday. November Delta Three Zero Whiskey—"

FOURTEEN

For the next hour, Laszlo Szabo used his computer every fifteen minutes to check the numbered Swiss account he'd given Fitzroy. Between his frequent log-ons he packed a suitcase full of essential items for a permanent road trip, called a local car service, and ordered a limo to wait out front at four thirty, destination the Budapest Ferihegy airport. He bought a ticket to Moscow, first-class, and then called an acquaintance in the Russian capital to arrange pickup from the airport there.

Even with all this activity, he still limped over to the riser and looked down through the glass every now and then to check on his prize. The Gray Man sat shirtless on the mattresses in the cold pit, his back against the slimy wall and his eyes fixed ahead.

Laszlo thought nothing about leaving the young man to die; thought nothing of taking a half million euros from Sir Donald the

Fat and then reneging on the deal; thought nothing of the ridiculous assertion that the lives of some poor, pitiful schoolgirls hung in the balance of his quickly orchestrated scheme. He'd not been born a sociopath, but he'd learned his way, executed the tenets of the disorder as precisely and with the same attention to detail as he counterfeited passports.

It was no lie when he said it was the Russians who'd removed his soul. He'd lived so long as an informer, had worked with local resistance to help dissidents escape out of the country, and then passed on to the Soviets their routes to the West. He'd played both sides in so many games over so many years that, to Laszlo, there remained no longer any right and wrong, only paths to his own benefit and obstacles to negotiate.

At the one-hour mark, he checked his account. The money had not yet been wired. He called Fitzroy to learn there had been a delay at his bank. He needed just a few more minutes; the funds were en route. Laszlo smelled a rat, swore he would go put a few bullets into the Gray Man's head himself if the money didn't come soon, then conversely warned Sir Donald that the CIA would bleed every detail of Cheltenham Security Service's real operation out of its top killer, and Fitzroy's own head would be on the chopping block within a day or two of Szabo handing over the man in his pit to the Americans.

Finally, Laszlo granted fifteen minutes more to the convincing Englishman, checked on his prisoner in the hole, and then phoned the driver waiting outside and told him he'd be delayed but to keep the engine running.

Szabo had been cutting it close all his life. If the CIA killers arrived before he left, he'd likely be killed. If they did not, he'd have his new start in Russia.

Captain Bernard Kilzer turned his head slowly to First Officer Lee. The action made the perspiration on his forehead run into his eyes. Lee looked back to his captain and blinked his own sweat away.

Both men's faces were chalk white.

The Bombardier Challenger stood still in the mud. Out the windscreen both pilots could see only grass and fence obscured by a heavy rain shower. They had used every centimeter of the runway given them, then an additional eighty meters of soggy open field. There was no more.

Kilzer's heart pounded, and his blood boiled. Riegel had forced them into this situation, a situation that had come within three seconds' flying time of ending very, very badly, and even though it had not terminated in a ball of fire and an insurance payout to his wife, the German captain had every expectation he would be spending some time as a guest of the Hungarian penal system.

Still, they had survived. This aircraft had been equipped with anti-skid carbon brakes and a "Gravel Kit," deflectors placed around the tricycle gear to keep runway debris from destroying the plane upon landing. Still, Kilzer and Lee both knew their rented Challenger would not be flying out of Hungary under its own power. The gear and engines were surely damaged, and it would take some serious towing equipment to pull this twenty-million-dollar aircraft out of the sucking mud pit where it now sat.

After a few more seconds to recover from the stress and fatigue of the landing, Kilzer shut down all systems, standard procedure for a fire on board. Now the only sound was the pelting rain against the aircraft's skin and windows.

In his mayday message to Budaörs Airport's control tower, he'd claimed he smelled smoke in the cockpit. Had he more time to come up with something, no doubt he and Lee could have conceived a ruse that would have been more verifiable. But from the time he'd gotten the call from Riegel to this moment, only thirty-five minutes had passed; in the interim, his wits were fully occupied as he dropped his jet from four hundred knots and seven miles in the air to a standstill beyond the far edge of a rain-soaked, too-short, unpaved runway at an unfamiliar airport.

He'd done damn well, and he knew it. He even thought, in the moment of buoyant optimism that came from the adrenaline high following the landing, that he might just manage to talk his way out of jail time if he could keep his winning streak going a few minutes more. But this pipe dream faded as a movement out the windscreen jolted him back to reality. A black van smashed through the fence directly in front of him. The six Indonesians appeared from around the starboard side of the Bombardier, pulling rucksacks retrieved from the cargo hold. Hurriedly they clambered into the vehicle. While Captain Kilzer and First Officer Lee sat silently and stared at the activity in front of their cockpit, the black van backed through the mud and grass from whence it came, skidded in the rainwater on a road on the other side, and then sped off into the storm.

That dramatic event, Kilzer knew, would not have gone unnoticed by the control tower behind him. And that dramatic event, Kilzer knew, would land both him and Lee behind bars until that asshole Riegel could buy them out.

And it occurred to Kilzer as he placed his hat on his head and left the airplane, the rain whipping into his face and his ears assaulted with the shrieking sound of approaching sirens, that Mr. Riegel would certainly have other messes to attend to before the day was through, so he and Lee should prepare themselves to be forgotten about for some time to come.

The wire transfer appeared in Szabo's account as he was furiously making a third call to Fitzroy. The CIA was due to arrive within ten minutes, he'd cut it way too close, but now the money was received, and he could leave. He hung up the phone as Fitzroy answered. Next he checked back in on the Gray Man one final time, bade him adieu and bon chance, finished packing his suitcase, and then hobbled out of his studio/laboratory/workshop, shuffling down the hall as quickly as his paralytic body would allow.

He was almost to the door when the phone rang. Thinking it was the CIA station chief giving him an update on the progress of the operators on the way, he decided to answer. They wouldn't have called if they were moments away.

He lifted the phone off the hook. "I have fulfilled my side of the bargain. It is time for you to fulfill yours," said Fitzroy.

"I am impressed, Sir Donald. My phones are scrambled, how did you—"

"I have my ways, Laszlo. Now, free the Gray Man before they come for him!"

The sweat already dripping down the sixty-year-old Hungarian's back turned ice-cold. Fitzroy knew who he was. Szabo realized he'd be watching his back for the wily Englishman for the rest of his life.

"I will release your boy immediately."

"You wouldn't be talking out of both sides of your mouth, would you? Playing a game with myself and the CIA."

"You have my word as a gentleman."

"Very well, Laszlo. Enjoy the money." The line went dead.

Szabo thought about taking a final step up on the riser, one more glance into the pit, but he decided against it. He hurriedly limped back down the hall, suitcase in hand.

He stepped to the small iron door, but it flew inwards as he reached for it. Bright lights shone into the Hungarian's eyes, though it was dark and raining outside. In shock he leapt back, tripped over his bad leg, and fell onto his back. Squinting the lights away, he saw a team of men dressed in black, hooded faces, a half dozen gunmen with short-barreled weapons held to eye level. Protruding from each rifle was a powerful flashlight. The first man to him dropped onto a black kneepad. He lifted Szabo by the neck.

"Going somewhere?" He spoke softly in English. It was the CIA. Szabo could barely see eyes behind the operator's goggles.

"I . . . I was waiting for you. Just putting the bag in the car, you see. I'll be heading out after you boys finish."

"Sure. Where's the subject?"

Szabo was helped back to his feet. All the men in the narrow hall kept their weapons trained ahead.

"He's in the front room, at the end of the hall. Step up on the riser and look down. He's twelve feet down in the cistern, covered with a thick sheet of—"

"Show us." Szabo read the man's voice. There would be no negotiation. He turned and hobbled back up the hallway with the American paramilitaries.

Inside the low-lit room the leader of the SAD unit positioned his five men against the walls and stepped to the riser slowly. Laszlo urged him on, told him there was nothing to be afraid of, managed to drop the station chief's name no less than three times as a way to let the CIA gunmen know he was "one of them." Finally, the heavily armed and armored leader stepped up on the riser and peered warily over into the glass.

Laszlo called out, still trying to curry favor. "He probably has a gun, but he can't use it while the lid is shut. He'd have to be quite a dancer to dodge a ricochet in that little space. Your boss promised Laszlo he'd be taken care of. Maybe I should call him and you can all have a talk so you see everything Laszlo's done for your side. Laszlo the Loyal, he calls me."

The tac team leader leaned over farther. Then farther. He took a knee over the Plexiglas. Turned slowly around, back to Szabo. "What the fuck is this?"

Laszlo did not understand. "What do you mean? It's the Gray Man, all wrapped in a nice bow for my friends at the CIA—"

"Did you kill him?" asked the American operative, standing up now and turning to face the Hungarian.

"Of course not. Why do you ask me this?" Quickly the master forger hobbled on his cane towards the riser to see what was wrong.

Court had not sat as idly for the past seventy minutes as Szabo had presumed. As soon as the Hungarian left him alone, he'd pulled his necklace over his head, stripped off the thin leather to reveal a wire saw. He used this to cut away at the exposed water pipe below the mattresses. He'd cut it down in two places to where a few more passes of the wire's teeth would open the pipe and fill the cistern with hot springwater in a matter of minutes.

Once this was done, Gentry pulled his pistol, ejected the round from the chamber, and retrieved the spare mags from his pants.

Using his waterproof boots for a collection bin and the pliers on his multi-tool, he'd pulled each cartridge apart, poured the potassium nitrate–based gunpowder in the boot. When he had the powder from thirty of the thirty-one bullets he carried on his body collected, he disassembled one of his magazines, removed the spring, reattached the plate, filled it tight with gunpowder from his boot, and then placed the follower at the top, packing the explosive agent tighter in the metal magazine. Court used the magazine spring to bind the follower securely in place.

Laszlo checked in on him from time to time. The old cripple made so much noise climbing up on the wooden riser it was no trick for the Gray Man to stuff his arts-and-crafts project below a rotten mattress in time to avoid detection.

Next Gentry took off a sock, filled it with the empty cartridges, because the powder would not ignite without help from the primer each cartridge contained. He crammed the powder-filled magazine in the sock and lashed everything together tight with his bootlace.

In his fist he held it. It was a big, heavy sock and roughly the power equivalent of a hand grenade.

Gentry feverishly ripped several lengths of fabric from a mattress, tied them together to make a thin strand about ten feet long. He reloaded his Walther pistol with his one remaining round, left the magazine well empty, and tied the gun with more mattress strands to where the muzzle of the three-and-a-half-inch barrel was placed point-blank at the sock full of primers and explosive. The long strand he tied to the pistol's trigger.

Finally, Gentry took off his pants. He tied the legs tight at the ankles and then again at the crotch. This created two chambers filled with air. They wouldn't stay watertight for long, but long enough for Court's needs. He used his last shoelace to tie the grenade to the pants. He sat with the pants draped over his legs so Laszlo would not easily notice he wasn't still wearing them.

Lastly, he pulled wads of soggy foam from a mattress to use as earplugs when the time was right.

Satisfied with his preparations, Court waited.

Soon Szabo leaned over and said good-bye, then disappeared. This was the Gray Man's cue. Frantically, the American cut the water pipe. Within a minute the cistern had filled more than knee-deep with water as hot as a bath. Court stood and held the grenade with the pistol affixed to it and the pants with the air chambers, all in his hands.

He stood there in his underwear and waited for the water to rise.

Within three minutes he floated up with the water and the mattresses, treading in place. After six minutes, the cistern was filled nearly to the top. He fought panic; he knew there was no guarantee his contraption would work or, even if it did, that it would be powerful enough to blow open the trapdoor.

When the water was three inches from the Plexiglas ceiling, Court forced himself to hyperventilate in the little space. He filled his lungs to capacity and then ducked down below the surface, positioned the floating bomb at one of the hinges. He pushed a mattress between himself and his bomb, then he swam down to the bottom of the cistern, one hand holding the line of mattress fabric that led to the pistol's trigger and the other hand wrapped around the water pipe to hold him at depth. Looking up to make sure everything was in place, he saw his contraption had floated away from the hinge. Quickly, with depleting air reserves, he shot up to the top. Now there was no air here left to breathe. He fought the mattress to the side, repositioned the bomb, and struggled again to the bottom. The day-old gunshot wound in his right thigh burned with the flexion of his muscles. Panic, frantic exertion, and oxygen depletion all seemed to compete with one another to squeeze on his heart and crush it tight deep inside his body.

Finally he reached the water pipe and took hold. He looked back up and saw his device was in place.

Shortly before he pulled the cord, he saw a dark figure step onto the riser and kneel down, then turn back to face someone in the room.

The team leader said, "He must be dead. This hole is filled with—"

With a muted pop, the black-clad operator lifted into the air. The Plexiglas burst below his feet, white water sprayed in all directions, pieces of sharp plastic tore into the ceiling above. The operator crashed to the left of the riser, a tidal wave of warm water sloshing over him.

The other armed men dived for cover. Szabo fell on his back in the middle of the room.

The leader was alive. He scrambled to his knees and retrained his weapon on the riser to his left.

"Jesus! All elements, stand fast!" he shouted, his eardrums ringing from the explosion.

Just then, small men in civilian attire and rifles held high poured into the room from the hallway, and gunfire erupted all around.

Laszlo Szabo was the first to die.

FIFTEEN

Even with his ersatz plugs, Court's ears screamed from the pressure of the blast. He pushed off with his feet at the bottom of the cistern and shot to the surface. He had no idea who was waiting above for him. The CIA? Laszlo back for a last check on him? Ultimately, it didn't matter; he needed air.

He'd built momentum on the way up, so when his head broke the surface of the water, he shoved open the plastic door. Both hinges were broken off, and the Plexiglas was cracked through. He sucked in a huge breath of air and scrambled over the side, rolling off the riser and down to the floor, enveloped in a wave of the warm water. He found himself along the wall in the back corner of the room. All around was the sound of close gunfire and shouting men, but Court could see no one around the platform's edge. He rolled to his knees, into a low crouch, and bolted towards the back hallway, his wet feet slapping the linoleum. He didn't take time to look back. Whatever was going down in this room, Gentry had no intention of getting in the middle of it with no firearm and no idea who the players were.

The doorjamb to the hallway splintered with a burst of submachine gun fire just a step in front of Gentry's face. He ran right at it, through the overpressure of the supersonic ammo and the flying splinters, down into the dark hall and to the bathroom where he'd shaved an hour and a half earlier. He ducked in quickly for his backpack and threw it over a shoulder.

Wearing only his underwear and a bandage on his thigh, he sprinted into a small bedroom at the end of the hall. Over the low twin bed was a window with a thin wire grating. He shattered the glass with a metal end table, lifted the mattress and pushed it over the windowsill to cover any remaining shards, then rolled out over it into a small courtyard. A door to the building behind Laszlo's was locked, so Court ran to the far corner of the courtyard. He used iron security bars over a first-story window to climb his way to a second-story balcony where, after four or five tentative kicks from his left heel, he finally shattered a glass window.

Loud snaps of gunfire continued below and behind him. He took care to avoid the broken glass left in the pane as he stepped through the window, but as he climbed into the apartment, he cut both his feet stepping in on the carpet. He cried out in pain, fell to his knees, and cut them, too.

Crab-walking through the small bedroom, he finally stood, hobbled into the bathroom, and rifled through the medicine cabinet. A few seconds later, he sat on the toilet and dressed his fresh injuries. His right foot was okay, a little jab that he poured antiseptic into and wrapped with toilet paper. The ball of his left foot was much worse. It was a relatively deep puncture. He washed it quickly and cinched a hand towel tight around it to stanch the bleeding. It needed stitches but, Court knew, he wouldn't be getting stitches any time soon.

Similar to his feet, his left knee was okay, but his right was badly injured. With a wince he pulled a shard of glass from his skin, an unlucky barb at the end hooked on his flesh as he removed it. Blood ran down to the floor.

"Fuck," he groaned as he cleaned and dressed the gash as best he could.

Three minutes later, he realized the shooting had died down across the courtyard. He heard sirens, shouting, a baby crying in the next apartment, woken from its nap by the activity.

He'd thought the apartment was empty, but when he walked into the living room, still just in his wet boxers but now with wrapped feet and knees, he found an elderly lady sitting alone on a couch. She looked at him with eyes unafraid, bright and piercing and blue. He put a hand out to calm her but lowered it slowly.

"I won't hurt you," he said, but he doubted she understood. He mimicked pulling on pants, and she slowly pointed to a room down the hall. There he found men's clothes. A dead husband, maybe? No, a son away at work. He found blue coveralls and climbed into them, and heavy steel-toed boots that were too big but serviceable with two pairs of white socks.

Gentry thanked the lady with a bow and a smile. She nodded back slowly. He pulled a wad of euros from his backpack and laid them on a table. The old woman said something he did not understand, and with another bow, he was out the door to the second-floor hallway.

Injured, unarmed, with neither means of transportation nor the documents he came all the way to Budapest to acquire, Court Gentry stepped outside and into a steady rain. He looked down to his watch. It was five in the afternoon, eight and one-half hours since beginning his journey. He seemed so much farther away now than when he started.

At LaurentGroup's London office, Lloyd and Fitzroy waited for the news of the Indonesians. It came after four p.m., but not from the team itself. Sir Donald's phone rang. It was Gentry.

"Cheltenham."

"It's me."

Fitzroy had to compose himself before speaking. Finally he said, "Thank God! You've gotten clear of Szabo?"

"Yeah. Just."

"What happened?"

"Not sure. Sounded like an SAD field team showed up, Szabo must have had some personal security, and it went loud."

Lloyd and Fitzroy stared at one another.

"Uh . . . Right. Understood. How are you?"

"Surviving."

"Where are you now?"

"Still in Budapest." Both Lloyd and Fitzroy looked over to the Tech. His head leaned over a computer terminal, but he bobbed it up and down, confirming the truthfulness of the target by pinpointing the cell tower the phone was using.

"What now?" asked Fitzroy. The question was as much to the American on his right as it was to the American on the other end of the line.

"I head west. Everything's still on track. Do you have any more information for me?"

"Umm, yes. The men you met this morning in Prague were Albanians. Simple mercenaries. Hired by Nigerian Secret Service."

"They've probably contracted a new team by now. Any idea what I'm up against?"

"Hard to say, son. I'm working on it."

"What do you know about the enemy force structure around your family?"

"Four or five Nigerian secret police types. Not tier-one gunmen by any stretch, though they have my family scared witless."

"As I get closer, I'll need the exact location."

"Aye. You'll be there by tomorrow morning?"

"No. I have a stop to make first."

"Not another dangerous detour, I hope."

"No. This one is on the way."

Fitzroy hesitated, then said, "Right. Anything else you need from me?"

"Anything *else*? What have you given me so far? Look, you are my handler. *Handle* something. I need to know if I am going to run into any more goons along my route. I need to know how the fucking Nigerians found out my name. Found out about you. There is something very screwed up here, and I need as much of it figured out as possible before I get to Normandy."

"I understand. I am working on it."

"Have you had any more contact with the kidnappers?"

"Sporadically. They think I'm turning over every rock to find you. I'm calling everyone along my Network. Just to make it look good, you know."

"Keep it up. I'll stay away from the Network. Call me if you learn anything." The line went dead.

Within two minutes Fitzroy and Lloyd had more of an explanation about what had happened. Riegel called, and between the three of them, they managed to put the pieces together. The six Indonesians had been completely wiped out. All dead. The CIA had torched the building to cover their tracks. It was unknown if the agency had taken casualties. Szabo was dead, and Gentry had used another of his nine lives but had gotten free.

"So where is he now?" asked Riegel.

"Heading west from Budapest."

"Via train, car, motorcycle?"

"We don't know. He called us from a cell phone. He'd apparently pulled it off a passerby, dumped it just after he hung up."

"Anything else to report?" asked Kurt Riegel.

Lloyd barked into the phone angrily, "*You* report to *me*, Riegel! What happened to your shit hot Indonesian Kopassus commandos? I thought you said Gentry would be no match for them."

"Gentry didn't kill them. CIA paramilitaries did. Look, Lloyd, we knew the Gray Man would have some resiliency; my plan all along was for one or two teams to knock him off balance, get him reactive instead of proactive. That way, he'll stumble into the next team unprepared."

Lloyd said, "We have ten more teams lying in wait for him. I want him dead before the night is through."

"Then we agree on something." Riegel rang off.

Lloyd then turned his attention to the Englishman. A pained expression flashed on the older man's face.

"What is it?"

Fitzroy's anguish was unrelenting.

"What's wrong?"

"I believe he told me something. He didn't mean to tell me, but I sussed it out."

Lloyd sat up. The few wrinkles in his pinstripe suit smoothed out with the movement. "What? What did he tell you?"

"I know where he's going."

The young American attorney's face slowly widened into a smile. "Excellent!" He reached for his mobile phone. "Where?"

"There's a catch. This place he's going, only three blokes have ever known about it. One of those blokes is dead, one of those blokes is the Gray Man, and one of those blokes is me. I'll tell you where, but if your little reality show contest doesn't destroy him there, he's going to know I've set him up. Your chaps miss him this time, and it's game over."

"Let me worry about that. Tell me where he's going."

"Graubünden."

"Where the fuck is that?"

SIXTEEN

Song Park Kim had sat motionless in a meditative state while airborne, but his eyes opened, awake and alert, upon touchdown at Charles de Gaulle Airport. The only passenger of the Falcon 50 executive jet, his small, rough hands rested on his knees, and his eyes remained hidden behind stylish sunglasses. His perfectly tailored pinstripe suit fit his environment precisely. The cabin was appointed for executive travel, and he appeared to be a youngish but otherwise unremarkable Asian executive.

The Falcon taxied off the runway, down and off the taxiway, past a long row of parked corporate jets, finally turning into an open hangar door. A waiting limousine, still wet from the drizzle of the gray evening, idled in the middle of the hangar. A driver stood alongside.

As soon as the jet came to a complete stop and the turbines slowed, the copilot made his way back to the seven-seat cabin carrying a nylon gym bag. He sat in front of Song Park Kim and lowered the bag onto a mahogany table between them.

Kim said nothing.

"I was told to give you this upon touchdown. Immigration has been dealt with. No customs problems. There is a car waiting for you."

A curt nod, nearly imperceptible, from the short-haired Korean.

"Enjoy Paris, sir," said the copilot. He stood and retreated to the cockpit. The small partition closed behind him.

Alone, Song Park unzipped the bag. Pulled out a Heckler & Koch MP7A1 machine pistol. He ignored the telescoping stock and held the weapon like a handgun out in front of him, looking through the gun's simple sight system.

Two long, thin magazines, each filled with twenty 4.6x30mm hollow-point cartridges, were attached to one another by means of a nylon cinch.

He replaced the weapon into the bag.

Next he pulled out a mobile phone and an earpiece. He tucked the earpiece in place on the side of his head and turned it on. The phone he also turned on before slipping it into his coat pocket. A handheld GPS receiver went into another pocket. More MP7 magazines, a suppressor, and a change of clothes remained in the bag untouched.

A black-handled, black-bladed folding knife emerged from the bag, and he slipped this into his pocket.

Two minutes later he sat in the limousine. The driver looked straight ahead as Kim said, "City center."

The limo rolled forward towards the hangar doors.

Kim was South Korean, an assassin with the National Intelligence Service.

He was their best. Five wet jobs inside North Korea, most of them with no support whatsoever, had built a legend for him in his unit. Seven more operations in China against North Korean sanction's violators, two in Russia against purveyors of nuclear secrets, and a few hits on fellow South Koreans in need of permanent attitude adjustments vis-à-vis their nefarious northern neighbors had made Song Park Kim, at thirty-two, the obvious choice when his leaders were asked to furnish a killer to send to Paris to hunt a killer in exchange for cold, hard cash.

Kim did not voice opinions on his assignments. Working alone, he had no one to voice them to, but were his thoughts solicited, he would have said this mission smelled rotten to the core. Twenty million dollars for the head of the Gray Man, a former CIA operative who, he'd heard through the grapevine, had not deserved the sellout he had gotten from his masters. The twenty million was being offered by some European corporation. This was nothing like the nationalistic operations Kim worked throughout his career.

Still, Kim knew he was an instrument of South Korea's domestic and foreign policy, his counsel had not been sought, and those whose judgment was valued had decided he should come here to Paris, settle in, wait for a call giving him the Gray Man's whereabouts, and then pour hot bullets into the poor bastard's back.

Graubünden is an eastern canton of Switzerland, tucked into a little niche near where the southwestern Austrian border concaves. It is known as the canton of a hundred and fifty valleys, and one of these valleys runs east to west in an area called the Lower Engadine. There the tiny village of Guarda rests atop the sharp ledge of a steep hill high above the valley floor, just miles from both the Austrian and Italian borders. There is only one sheer, winding road up to the little village, and it connects the one-room, whistle-stop train station below to the half-timbered houses above, a laborious forty-minute hike.

There are almost no cars in the village, and farm animals greatly outnumber the human residents. Narrow cobblestone roads wind steeply up and between the white buildings, alongside water troughs and fenced gardens. The town ends abruptly, and the steep hill resumes, a meadow that rises to a thick pine forest that itself gives way to rocky cliffs that loom above the town that surveys the valley floor below and all who pass or approach.

The villagers understand German but among themselves speak Romansch, a language spoken by barely 1 percent of the seven and a half million Swiss, and virtually no one else on earth.

At four a.m., a few snow flurries swirled around the little road that led from the valley floor up to Guarda. A lone man, dressed in thick jeans, a heavy coat, and a black knit cap, limped up the steep, winding switchback. A small backpack hung off his shoulders.

Ten hours earlier, minutes after speaking with Don Fitzroy from a pink cell phone he'd snatched from the open purse of a staggeringly drunk female university student meandering alone on the sidewalk, Gentry found an outdoor clothing store in Budapest and purchased a full wardrobe, new from the bottom of his leather boots to the top of his black knit cap. Within an hour of leaving Szabo's building, he was boarding a bus at Népliget Bus Terminal for the Hungarian border town of Hegyeshalom.

He climbed out of the bus a half mile from the border, walked north out of the village into a field, and turned left.

There was no moon; he had a tactical flashlight in his pack but did not use it. Instead, he stumbled to the west, walked a mile on his cut feet, could feel the sting and the warm blood squish in his socks and between his cold toes.

Finally, just before eight in the evening, he crossed a field full of modern windmills and found himself in the Austrian border town of Nickelsdorf.

He had made it into the European Union.

It was another mile walk—a limp, really, with the gunshot wound to the thigh and the injured feet and knees—before he found the road. He walked west with his thumb out for a few minutes. A trucker pulled over, but he was heading north and could not help. A second driver and then a third were also heading in the wrong direction.

At a quarter past nine, he was picked up by a Swiss businessman heading all the way to Zurich. Court told him his name was Jim. The businessman wanted to practice his English, and Court obliged. They talked about their lives and families on the trip across Austria. Court's story was 100 percent bullshit, but he was a pro. He sold the tale of the messy divorce back in Virginia, the lifelong desire to visit Europe, the mugging in Budapest that cost him his belongings, and his good fortune to still have his wallet and cash and passport and a friend in eastern Switzerland who could put him up until he caught his plane back home the following week.

As they drove through the night and talked, Court kept part of his focus on the side mirror, nonchalantly making sure he'd not been followed. He also, between the BS stories of places he'd never been and people he'd created out of whole cloth, kept in mind his task at hand. He tried to get his head around the events still to come in the next thirty hours.

It was a Friday night, traffic on the A1 was heavy, but the businessman's Audi was sleek and fast. They skirted to the north of Salzburg.

Court offered to drive, and the Swiss businessman caught a couple of hours of sleep.

The Audi turned onto the Engadiner-Bundesstrasse and crossed the northeastern border of Switzerland at three a.m. There was no customs control at the Swiss border, though Switzerland was not officially a member of the EU. The Swiss driver pulled into an all-night rest stop, insisting Jim simply must try Swiss beer and give his honest opinion. Court did so, gushed over the body and color and texture, threw in a few other accolades he'd once overheard in a Munich biergarten in reference to German brews, and this convinced the now-smitten businessman to take Jim directly to his destination instead of dropping him off once their paths diverged.

They took the 180 south and then the 27 west through a valley, though in the overcast night they could see nothing on either side of their headlights. Finally in the burg of Lavin, Gentry picked a half-timbered house just off the main road and claimed it as his destination. Actually, by climbing out of the warm Audi here, Court was left with a two-mile walk in the snow, but, he decided, should there be trouble waiting at his real objective, there was no reason for this nice fellow to suffer for his good deed.

"Thanks for the lift. *Auf Wiedersehen.*" Court climbed out of the car and shook the gentleman's hand through the window. He stood in the road as he waved good night.

As the taillights of the Audi rounded a corner in the distance, the Gray Man turned in the opposite direction and began walking westward through a gentle snowfall.

He trudged along purposefully, but he was bone tired. The adrenaline that, along with his discipline, had moved him forward without pause for the past twenty hours had now given out, and all that remained was the discipline. He needed rest and hoped to find a few hours of it up the steep road in Guarda.

By four ten, the snowfall had picked up. Court was up the hill and in the village now. He saw not a single soul, though there were still some lights on in the little hotel. The lights of the homes of the villagers were all extinguished, the shepherds and the blacksmiths and the innkeepers and the pensioners were sound asleep for a few hours more. He continued on, still climbing higher through the village, past ancient stone water troughs for the sheep flocks that moved through the hamlet's pedestrian-only streets, past the tiny gardens surrounded by tiny fences in front of the tiny homes, until he broke out the other end of town and climbed higher up the steep hill along a dirt path. The evening's snow settled on earlier accumulation, and it nearly blanketed the hillside, though even in the moonless night Gentry could see patches of darkness, bare spots on the prominence that had yet to accept the cover of the white powder.

After climbing through the white meadows for three hundred yards above Guarda, Gentry clicked on his small tactical flashlight. Behind him was sheer pastureland, but he was now entering a pine forest, and the snow swirling though the trees and the black night made the road invisible ahead of him. The light helped. He pressed forward another hundred yards and found his destination in the woods, a tiny shack.

It stood thirty yards from the road, which continued on and up through disused private property. There was no reason anyone else would pass by, and no reason, if someone did, that they would look hard to their right through the forest and notice the simple structure. A huge, rusty padlock hung uninvitingly on the front door, the three windows around the one-room shack were boarded from the inside, and the surrounding pines grew unfettered nearly to the edges of the building.

Gentry walked through the trees and circled the building with his tac light. At the back of the cabin stood a utility shed, also heavily padlocked, and he checked this and found it secure. Continuing around the structure, he scanned the walls, the wooden slats on the roof, and finally the front door. He took off his gloves, ran his fingers around the door's edges slowly, and in the top right corner he found it. A wooden toothpick jabbed flush with the frame. Had the door been opened, this telltale would have dropped to the ground and given the Gray Man the tipoff that his cabin had been compromised by visitors.

Satisfying himself that the location was secure, Court next turned his back to the front door, took thirty measured steps away into the pines, pushing through the needled branches. At thirty paces, he shifted five yards to his right and knelt down.

The key was buried in a metal coffee tin, just six inches or so below the pine mulch and frozen dirt. He dug it out with a flat rock. After retrieving the key, he returned to the cabin and opened the lock.

The interior air was dry and stale and every bit as cold as outside the door. There was a knee-high coal furnace in a corner, but Gentry ignored it. Instead, he lit a lantern on a card table in the center of the room, its dim glow the only warmth to be had.

A shelf on the wall held cases of military rations, meals ready to eat, and the thirty-six-year-old American tore into the first MRE he could grab as soon as he came out of the restroom with the chemical toilet. He ate hard crackers and cookies, wolfed them down as he sat alone at the card table.

He finished his meal in ninety seconds. Next he stood and pushed the squat coal furnace out of the corner and lifted the loose floorboards below it.

Placing the tactical light in his mouth, he climbed down a wooden ladder exposed with the removal of the floorboards, into a dirt-walled basement six feet high and ten feet square. When he turned from the ladder, he faced three chest-high stacks of black cases, each case the size of a very large toolbox. This took up nearly half the room in the underground cellar, and a metal workbench filled the space to his right. There was only room to climb up and down the ladder and move sufficiently to manipulate the cases. Court hefted the first container off the first stack, dropped it heavily on the table, and flicked open the latch.

Early that morning, when Court told Fitzroy he would rescue his family, he immediately decided to go to Guarda, Switzerland, to his massive weapons cache hidden in the forest. He had a half dozen other stores around the continent, but nothing like Guarda.

Guarda was the mother lode.

The heavy metal.

The first case housed a black Swiss Brügger & Thomet MP9 submachine gun. He pulled it out of its foam bed and snapped a loaded magazine into the mag well, affixed the sling to its buttstock, and lifted it over his head to push it outside the trapdoor onto the floor above him. Another case held a sub-load, a nylon and canvas rig full of loaded magazines for the weapon that would strap both to his thigh and his utility belt. He tossed this through the hole above him as well.

For the next five minutes Court went through case after case. Into a huge duffel he stuffed all manner of small arms and explosives. Into a smaller bag he placed a black tactical suit, a face mask, ballistic eyewear, a small surveillance scanner that would allow him to pick up short-distance communication, and a pair of binoculars.

Finally, just before five a.m., Gentry climbed out of the basement, following behind the two duffels he pushed out in front of him. He left the entrance to the basement cache open. He drank from a half-frozen water bottle, washed down a couple of mild painkillers for his thigh, used the chemical toilet a second time, and pulled a sleeping bag from a shelf. He rolled it out on the floor, unlocked the latch of the front door, prepared the cabin's defenses a bit, and then climbed inside his bedding. He set the alarm on his watch to seven thirty. A couple hours' sleep would have to be enough to get him through another long day.

They came for him just after five. The minivan slid to a stop at the bottom of the hill. To the passengers, it seemed as if the driver had been out of control on the slick streets for virtually the entire two-and-a-half-hour drive from Zurich. The driver's lack of skill in such conditions was understandable. There was black ice on the road, and the visibility was next to nil at times. Plus these Middle Easterners' orders were to get to the blinking dot on their GPS as fast as possible, and the Tech was calling them on the satellite phone every ten minutes for an update.

There were five of them, Libyan external security officers from the Jamahiriya Security Organization, a fire team from the best of Qaddafi's men. All ex-army commandos, each knew his Skorpion SA Vz 61 machine pistol like a trusted friend. The leader was forty-one, stern-faced and bearded, dressed in civilian adventure travel attire like the rest of his team. He sat in the passenger seat, incessantly barked admonitions at the commando behind the wheel, unforgiving of the man, though all knew the driver was more accustomed to negotiating desert dunes in an armored jeep than he was icy mountain switchbacks in a minivan.

Still, they made it to Guarda in good time and parked their vehicle in the lot by the train station at the bottom of the valley. The driver lifted the hood and quickly removed the distributor rotor and threw it into his gym bag, thereby rendering the vehicle useless until he returned. They then found the little road up the hill, spread their formation as wide as possible across it, and began their ascent on foot.

Each man carried his little Skorpion in a gym bag with its stock folded, and a backup pistol in a shoulder holster. Different operators carried grenades and breaching charges as well. They all wore knit caps, heavy cotton pants, and the same black parkas, an expensive name brand associated with professional athletes.

Also in their gym bags were night vision goggles; they remained stowed for now.

The five Libyans climbed the steep, winding road to the village in the dark. They moved quickly and efficiently. Any passerby would know from their near uniformity and the severe facial expressions bobbing up and down in the vapor of their exhalations that they were up to no good. But no locals walked the hillside road at five thirty in the morning in a snowstorm, so the Libyans arrived undetected into the cobblestone streets of the Swiss hamlet.

Each operator also had a small handheld radio attached to his belt and connected to an earpiece. With a single command from their leader, they separated on the western edge of Guarda, continued individually to the east, each through a different little pedestrian passageway. This tactic ensured that anyone looking out their window would only see one of the men. If an alarm was raised and the villagers began to talk about strangers, they all might well think they saw the same individual.

On the far end of the town the kill squad re-formed like a biologic entity, detached cells rejoining in a petri dish. The leader consulted his GPS and turned to the left at an unpaved track that continued from the ledge on which the tiny hamlet was situated, up the hillside and into the forest, only visible in the distance after they donned their night observation devices.

The leader updated the team from the information on his GPS. "Four hundred meters."

The snow had picked up even more; the swirling bands of flakes had turned to thickening sheets of falling white. The Libyans had seen snow before, during training in Lebanon or on other missions in Europe, but their bodies were wholly unaccustomed to this cold. Forty-eight hours earlier, this very team of operators had sat in a Tripoli apartment working with an electronic surveillance detachment to try to locate the source of a ham radio broadcast emanating from the city that had made comments critical of Colonel Qaddafi. It had been nearly one hundred degrees in that cramped room, so the cold of the eastern Swiss valley was a shock to their systems indeed.

They almost passed the shack. Only the GPS coordinates provided by the Tech had saved them hours of wandering through the woods. By now their Skorpions were out of the gym bags, the bags were hanging from their backs, the weapons' folding stocks were deployed, and the guns were raised to the low ready position, stocks pressed against shoulders and sights just below the sightline of their night vision goggles. Each man took a careful position around the cabin. They reported in one by one.

The leader was first. "One in position, ten meters from the front door. No movement. The windows are shuttered."

"Two is with One."

"Three on west side. One window. Shuttered."

"Four at east side. One window. Shuttered."

"Five at back. No windows, but there is a utility shed alongside the main building. A secure padlock on the outside. Nothing else back here."

The leader said, "Five, stay at the back. Find cover and be ready. Three and Four, come to the front. We will enter as a team."

"Understood."

Gentry slept dreamless in his sleeping bag next to the hole in the floorboards that led to the earthen basement. The pain meds had dulled the ache in his thigh and given him the respite needed to relax. His sleep was deep, restful.

Brief.

The leader retrieved a fragmentation grenade from his belt. He pulled the pin and moved slowly to the front door with his hand on the spoon. Two was in front and preparing a breaching charge when he noticed the door was not completely shut. He turned to his leader and motioned to the crack in the door.

The leader nodded, turned to the two men behind him, and whispered, "It's open. Get ready."

Number Two pushed the door open quickly and knelt down so that other weapons could train on any targets inside. It was completely dark at first; even the night vision equipment could not make out the features inside.

One lobbed the grenade into the room underhanded. Two, Three, and Four stepped to the edges of the cabin to avoid the blast. The grenade left the leader's hand and disappeared into the dark, but the sound of the missile's impact with a hard surface came too early. As the leader made to turn away from the door, the grenade reappeared in his night vision goggles, bounced out of the cabin, and landed in the snow in front of the door.

Fortunately for the Libyans, all four saw the sputtering grenade in time. They dove for cover, either to the snowy ground or around the edges of the cabin. The explosion whited out the goggles of the three men facing in the weapon's direction, and a fourth man was hit in the elbow and knocked down by a small piece of shrapnel. Collecting himself quickly, the leader ripped his now-useless goggles from his eyes, returned to the edge of the door, and entered, firing into the dark. Number Two and then Three followed, but within two seconds the leader's shout made the others stop dead in their tracks.

"Mantrap!"

SEVENTEEN

Moments before Gentry had dropped exhaustedly to his sleeping bag for the night, he'd slid the large wall of rusty mesh to its position two feet inside the front door. The seven-foot-high contraption weighed over two hundred pounds and slid along a three-foot track on the floor. On each end of the fence there was a hinged wing, and each wing locked to a clasp on either side of the door. This effectively created a barricade capable of slowing down a breaching team, forcing them to bottleneck at the most dangerous point of any breach, the doorway. The mantrap was here when Court inherited the cache, and he had not placed much value in its capabilities due to the fact that it could easily be blown apart with explosives or knocked over with a battering ram or even a few serious blows from a boot heel, but as he leapt out of his sleeping bag to a crouch after the grenade went off out the front door, he immediately knew the rusty old barricade had just saved his soundly sleeping ass.

Frantically he kicked the two duffels of gear by his sleeping bag back down the hole to the tiny basement. He grabbed the Brügger & Thomet and fired a full magazine at the front door with one hand before sliding down into the hole. Once in the six-foot-deep cellar, he reached above and pulled the floorboard lid over himself.

Number Three knelt over bloody snow to the left of the shack's entrance. The grenade fragment had hit him squarely in the elbow and passed through both meat and bone. But he was a disciplined soldier; he made little noise and quickly packed a handful of snow on the wound, wincing only with the shock of cold on skin, because he could not yet feel the pain he knew was soon to come.

Number One ignored his injured man as he ordered Two to set the fuse on his entire stock of breaching explosives and toss them through the doorway. A few seconds later a tissue-box-sized block of Semtex came to rest at the edge of the mantrap's slide rail on the floor. The three uninjured Libyans at the front of the shack turned to run, and numbers Two and Four each grabbed Three under an arm and lifted him off the ground as they scrambled for cover.

It was quiet in the black forest for a few seconds. The only sounds to be heard were the gentle hiss of snowflakes striking pine needles and their fallen brethren already on the ground, and the panting of the kill squad from Tripoli, now tucked tightly behind a fallen oak.

The black night and the soft sounds were replaced with a white flash and an earsplitting explosion that made the earlier hand grenade blast sound like the pop of a champagne cork. The doorway to the cabin, from the floor below to the slat roof above, blew to pieces, and lumber and fresh pine trees blew forward, landing as far away as one hundred feet from the building.

Bits of burning debris floated down with the snowfall through the pines as One, Two, and Four penetrated the wreckage of the cabin. Each man fired a burst or two as they entered the torn hole in the front wall. One went to the right, Two to the left, and Four moved straight through the small building. They used the light from burning fabric and paper to negotiate their footfalls over a blown-down metal fence, a smashed bookcase and table, several boxes and cooking utensils, and myriad unrecognizable objects.

Once the three were sure there was no one alive in either the main room or in the little bathroom, they began kicking over and through the debris on the floor, searching for the scorched and shredded body that surely must lie among the ruins. Five checked in to confirm all was quiet at the back of the cabin as the three Libyans inside began to worry. It was a small shack. Even in the deep shadows from the fires, it took less than ten seconds to verify there was no body to be found.

One looked to the ceiling. In a second he determined there was neither a loft nor an attic. Slowly he looked down to his feet.

"There's a trapdoor here. Find it."

Two did find it, next to the overturned furnace, after kicking a few coal bricks away. The fires were burning themselves out, so One turned on an electric lantern that had fallen from a shelf but had miraculously survived the explosion. He placed it on the floor next to the trapdoor.

"Careful. He may have set a surprise for us. Unless there is a tunnel through this mountain, he is trapped."

Two and Four nodded; their confidence grew. The Gray Man was hiding like a rat below them.

Number Five stood behind a thick pine at the back of the structure. Twenty feet in front of him was the padlocked storage shed. It stood five feet high, alongside the cabin, but it was clearly not attached to it. He checked in with the men inside. They were about to lift the trapdoor with a long metal pole. Then they would toss grenades in, follow that with rifle fire, and then finally climb down to cut off their target's head.

Five was missing all the action. He cursed aloud at the snow around him. His Skorpion waited at the low ready.

Suddenly he heard the coughing of an engine coming to life inside the cabin. No, not inside the cabin. In the storage shed. Just as his eyes moved down to the doors of the shed, a loud boom barked through the forest, the padlock blew forward and off, and the doors flew open wide. Number Five had just begun to lift his submachine gun to his eye when the motor noise screamed, and a large figure launched into the air from the darkened recesses of the small shed.

The young Libyan soldier had never before seen a snowmobile.

The bullet-shaped vehicle crashed back to the ground a few feet in front of him, and he dove to the side, rolling in the snow and slamming his back hard into a fallen stump. He looked up in time to see a human form on the back of the vehicle, leaning forward with a mask on his face and a large pack on his back. The image in his night vision goggles was a blur, and the blur was gone in a single second.

The Libyan scrambled for his submachine gun, but he'd lost it in the fallen needles and accumulating snow. By the time he'd gripped his weapon and lifted it to his face, the black shadow was disappearing over a tiny rise, tearing through snow and shrubbery and small saplings and flinging everything in its path to the left and right of its skids.

"Five! Report!" came One's scream through the earpiece.

"He's here! He's back here! He's heading up the mountain!"

"Shoot him!"

Five began running up the hill. "Come help me! He's on a motorcycle with skis!"

The Gray Man knew he had to turn the snowmobile around and go right back down past the hit squad. The forest ended abruptly at a huge rocky wall on the top of the hill. He could perhaps find a place to hide in the woods for a while, but he knew all of Guarda was awake and calling the local constabulary a few kilometers away in Chur. It would take them a while to get there and most of an hour to get a real force in all the way from Davos, but Court had no intention of waiting around for minutes, much less hours.

"Shit!" he screamed into the icy air. He'd already left one of the two packs of gear behind. He could not fit it through the three-foot-long upward-sloping, dirt-walled tunnel from the dirt basement to the toolshed where he kept the snowmobile. He'd grabbed a sawed-off twelve-gauge shotgun from the cache to use to blow open the padlock from the inside, and now the powerful weapon rested in front of him between the handlebars of the snowmobile.

He was also furious because he knew there was only one other person alive who knew of the existence of this cache. Donald fucking Fitzroy. Sir Don had offered Court the established cache's location soon after the Gray Man joined his stable. The venerable English handler had admitted at the time that the availability of the cache was due to the fact that the man who'd erected and used the hidden cabin no longer needed it, as he'd been found dismembered in a shallow grave somewhere just outside of Vladivostok.

Gentry hadn't worried about the bad omen, and he'd accepted the gift of the shed from Fitzroy. He liked the central location, the seclusion of the village and the valley, and the fact that any approaching vehicle could be heard for hundreds of yards if it was on wheels or for miles if it was under propeller power.

It had been a good cache. It would have remained so, Gentry was certain, had Don Fitzroy not given up its location to the men trying to kill him.

The snowmobile ran out of snow forty seconds after heading up the mountain away from the killers. Gentry turned hard to avoid the granite wall a dozen feet high that ran both left and right. He used his feet and the throttle to turn the machine back around, facing towards the forest and cabin below and then the village beyond. For now, Court was protected by the lip of a hillock. He could not see down to the men with the guns and the bombs, and they could not see up to him. But they were surely at this moment negotiating their way up the icy, unpaved road. He had no idea if there were two men or five or fifteen or fifty. He only caught a brief glimpse of one at the rear of the shack, but he was hardly certain he hadn't passed more men in the woods and, anyway, the bulk of the action had seemed to be at the front door.

Court considered his options for a moment. He looked around at his predicament and immediately pronounced himself trapped. He could fight a few of them, maybe, but the wide expanse in front of him over which they would surely come was a disadvantage. If they spread across the frozen meadow and approached simultaneously in a wide line, he would not be able to engage targets at his left, right, and center before they could gun him down.

The high ground was supposed to be a tactical advantage but, Gentry saw, *this* high ground sucked.

Off to his right there was another way down the hillside. A sheep trail, not more than four feet wide and incredibly steep, dropped more or less in a straight line through the forest towards the meadow on the other side. But the grade was far too sheer for the snowmobile to negotiate.

Even trying it would be suicide.

Now Court heard voices below him. Shouts of men, wild in the frenzy of the hunt.

They were moving up the road to him, closing on his cornered position.

"He's got nowhere to run!" shouted number One. He didn't bother with his radio. The noise from the explosion and the gunfire had withered his and his men's hearing for the rest of the night. He just shouted out to the three men around him jogging up the slippery road. Number Three had been left behind at the cabin. He'd wrapped bandages over his injury, and he was lucid and ambulatory, even if out of the fight.

The four Libyans nearing the crest of the rise above them quickly dropped their magazines from their Skorpions and checked them for sufficient ammo. Professionally they reseated the clips and clicked them back into place. Their night vision goggles covered their eyes. The steady snowfall gave movement to the green view ahead. They slowed as they neared the top, spread quietly across the road without waiting for instructions to do so.

Suddenly the engine noise of the snowmobile screamed again. It revved higher and grew louder and then in front and above the four Libyans a single headlight appeared, glowed like a green specter in their night vision optics as it barreled down towards them.

"Open fire!" screamed number One with a shriek. The four assassins knelt into crouches and poured rounds at the oncoming vehicle. Twenty rounds a second of hollow-point ammunition sprayed from each of the four braying guns. Tracer rounds arced and struck and bounced into the sky like rocket-powered fireflies.

At thirty meters distance the vehicle left the ground. It floated to twenty-five meters and then came down hard, bounced again into the air, and then landed on its side. The light stayed on as the machine slid down the hill past the four Libyans and came to a stop twenty meters behind them.

The engine idled.

Hot gases poured from the motor and hazed the men's optics.

Number One ran to the snowmobile after reloading his weapon. He slipped on ice and fell to his knees. Number Two passed him as he got back up. A quick scan around the road by all four men confirmed their suspicions.

"He's not here!"

There was a moment when Court thought he might have been sliding at fifty miles an hour. Everything seemed faster at ground level, of course, and the snow and ice and crunchy bits of stick and grass that flew into his face no doubt added to the perception of speed.

But whatever the actual velocity, Gentry knew he was descending the sheep trail way too fast.

It was hard to part with the second duffel worth of gear, but he'd seen no alternative. He'd dumped the weapons and the grenades and the binoculars up there on the ice. He lashed the sawed-off shotgun to the handlebars to keep them straight and then used a length of cord to tie the throttle open. He watched the machine leap over the ledge and down the road, then he ran as fast as possible across the snow along the shelf, along the granite wall, to where the sheep trail began and led down at nearly twenty degrees through the forest, through the lower meadow, and then to the little village, still dark, still an hour from the first hues of dawn over the mountains to the east.

At a full sprint, Gentry leapt through the air, his injured feet first, holding the big canvas duffel bag behind his backside, and landed on the snow. The grade was especially sheer at the beginning. He'd lost control almost immediately but found his position again at a slightly less severe stretch of trail that proved to be all too short.

On the hillside to his left he could hear the gunfire and sense the flashes of light, but he did not turn his head away from his feet and what was in front of him.

For nearly a hundred yards he'd been happy with his plan. He sledded quickly out of the kill zone. And in truth, it wasn't a bad plan really, but, as it turned out, its execution was wanting. When he skidded into the woods, the pine roots crossed the sheep trail, and he was sliding too fast to stop.

He went airborne at an ice patch over a root knob, and his body flung ninety degrees in the air. He landed on his side, perpendicular to the direction in which he was traveling, and this sent him spinning, rolling over and over. His bandaged knees took his body weight in a glancing blow as he spun, his feet caught a snowdrift, and this jerked his body around ninety degrees more. He found himself headfirst, his duffel bag sled was long lost behind him now, and he shot out of the forest and into the meadow above the old village of Guarda with his hands out in front of him like Superman and with absolutely no control over his momentum.

The slide, in its entirety, lasted just over forty-five seconds. To Gentry it seemed like a lifetime.

When it was over, he lay on his back in the snow. After taking a few seconds to control his vertigo, he sat up, checked his body for functionality, and then stood unsteadily in the black morning. He took stock of his pain. The bullet wound in his right thigh throbbed more than usual; he was certain he'd reopened any flesh that had rejoined in the last two days. His knees stung; they were likely bleeding. His ankles hurt but seemed to be operational. His rib cage on the right side flared with ache when he sucked in a breath of the cold mountain air. He thought it likely he'd cracked one of his floating ribs, which would be painful but not particularly burdensome. His left elbow seemed to have hit something, or a series of somethings, or every goddamn something on the mountainside, and the area along his funny bone was stiff and swelling.

With all that taken into account, the Gray Man knew he was fortunate to find himself in such good condition. Sliding, rolling, and bouncing down a steep hillside in the dark could have gone much worse, even without the gunmen firing machine guns at him.

Then he took stock of his belongings. His buoyed spirits sank anew. He'd lost everything but the small Walther handgun in his ankle holster, his wallet snapped shut in his back pocket, and a folding knife in his front pocket. Everything else—sat phone, medical equipment, extra ammo, guns, grenades, binoculars—all gone.

It took him another twenty minutes to get to the bottom of the valley, down to the one road and the one railroad track, to the one-room train station. The snow had turned to sleet, and he shivered, his ungloved hands buried deep in his pockets.

He saw a minivan, the only vehicle parked in the tiny lot. He took this as the kill squad's vehicle. He broke the driver's-side window and climbed in quickly, then smashed the steering column apart with two kicks of his boot heel. In seconds he had the ignition barrel out, and in under a minute he'd sparked the ignition wires. But the van would not start. Hurriedly he felt around under the dash for a kill switch. Finding none, he climbed back out of the van, slammed the door shut, and jabbed his knife into each of the tires. He knew sabotaging it would show the gunners he'd made it down this far and was certainly on the road by now but, he decided, they would have to leave Guarda immediately anyway. The police would be arriving within minutes. The kill team wouldn't be able to search the forest for him all morning, so there was little use in trying to mislead them that he was still on the mountain.

As it stood, he figured they were no more than ten to twenty minutes behind him now, depending on how concerned they were about being detected by the villagers or how nervous they were about bumping into the first police cars coming up the hillside.

Court broke a small windowpane in the door to the train station, reached around, and opened the latch. First he checked a schedule on a wall, a timetable for all the trains in the country. Then he pulled a heavy brown coat off a coat stand. Gentry slipped it on. It was a little tight at the shoulders, but it would keep him alive. A woman's bicycle with thick tires leaned against a wall, and Gentry took it, closed the door behind him, and winced along with the flare-up of pain in his lower rib cage when he kicked a leg over to mount it.

It was after six, and he knew the trains would not begin running through the valley until seven. He needed to make it to a larger village to get the first express train of the morning to Zurich.

So he biked west on the Engadine Road away from the hint of a faint orange daybreak behind him. His lower back, right thigh, and left knee burned with each revolution of the pedals. His face stung in the cold. He leaned into the snowfall, dead tired and wounded and disheartened. He'd wasted an entire day going after documents and weapons, and he'd acquired nothing but injuries. Still, there were few men on earth who could summon determination in the face of adversity as well as the haggard and bloody man in the ill-fitting coat on the woman's bike. He had no plan, no gear, no help, and now he was certain he had no friends. Fitzroy had lied to him, had set him up. Court knew he had every right to disappear and leave Don to whatever had hold of him, whatever made him burn his number one asset.

But Court decided to continue to the west, if only for now. He knew he needed a better understanding of what was going on, and he only knew one way to get it.

EIGHTEEN

Shortly before six a.m. London time, Sir Donald Fitzroy looked out the portside window of the Sikorsky and down at a green meadow. As the helicopter raced at an altitude of just a few hundred feet, the landscape dropped away, and whitecaps and dark water appeared a thousand feet down. Below him were the white cliffs of Dover, the end of the British Isles and the beginning of the English Channel. He and Lloyd and Mr. Felix, the representative of President Abubaker, along with the Tech and the four LaurentGroup henchmen, flew south towards Normandy. The sixty-eight-year-old Englishman did not know why. "Additional incentive," Lloyd had said an hour earlier. "On the off chance the Libyans botch the job in Switzerland and Court changes his mind, tells you that for all he cares your family can go to hell, then I have another lure I will use to reel him in."

Before Fitzroy could question further, Lloyd was on the phone ordering a helicopter fueled for a flight across the channel to be sent immediately to the Battersea Heliport.

Sir Donald traveled to the Continent often, occasionally by aircraft from Gatwick or Heathrow, sometimes by the Eurostar high-speed train through the channel, but he much preferred the overland and over-sea route. A train south through Chatham and then to Dover, onto a ferry to Calais in France or Oestende or Zebrugge in Belgium. This was the old way, the way of his youth, and neither the quick and easy airlines nor the modern expediency of the tunnel under the North Sea could compare with the feeling of pride and love that he felt when he returned to England on the ferry and, in the distant haze over the water, he could see the white cliffs of Dover in all their majesty.

Was there anything so beautiful in the world to an Englishman?

And above the cliffs, white birds soared, welcoming travelers over the channel much as they had the returning aircraft of the Royal Air Force seventy years before, the thin airframes pocked with holes and filled with young boys who had just killed and died and risked all for His Majesty in the air war against fascism.

Now Donald gazed with melancholy out the portside window, watched the beauty of Dover slip away behind him in the moonlit predawn, and knew he would likely never see this view again.

"I just got the word from Riegel. The Libyans have failed." It was Lloyd speaking over the intercom, his voice bleating through the earphones of the headset that pinched the tufts of white hair on either side of Sir Donald's head.

Fitzroy looked around the cabin and found Lloyd on the other side, facing back to him. Their eyes met in the dim red glow of the cabin lights. Fitzroy noticed the young American's suit had wrinkled in the past twenty-four hours, his necktie now hung loose around an open collar.

"How many lives lost?" asked the Englishman.

"Zero, surprisingly. One man injured. They are saying the Gray Man is a ghost."

"The comparison is not without merit," said Fitzroy into his microphone.

"Sadly, no. Ghosts are *already* dead." Lloyd sniffed. "I'm sending the Libyans to Bayeux to supplement the coverage there on the outside chance Gentry makes it through our gauntlet."

Fitzroy shook his head. "Forget it. I was the only one who knew about the cache in Switzerland. He will know it was I who tipped the assassins off. Knowing that I've been double-crossing him all along, he will not be so inclined to save my family."

Lloyd just smiled. "I've prepared for this contingency."

"Are you bloody daft? He won't come to my rescue. Can't you understand that?"

"That is no longer my plan." Lloyd turned away, conferred with the Tech.

The helicopter raced over the channel, and the moonshine flickered on the water below like a tray of loose diamonds. At seven in the morning, the Sikorsky crossed directly over Omaha Beach, the site of the bloodiest of the D-day landings. Nearly three thousand young American men died in the water and on the sand and in the bluffs off the beach below them. Lloyd did not look out the window. He was talking to the Tech over the helicopter's intercom radio; Sir Donald listened in but said nothing. Lloyd authoritatively barked orders, orchestrating the movements of the surveillance experts like chess pieces on a board. He ordered the Tech to send all kill teams now east of Guarda to the west of Guarda: Zurich, Lucerne, Bern, Basel. As the road between Gentry's starting point and objective shortened, the ten hunter-killer units still in the fight had less territory to cover.

"Let's move the Venezuelans from Frankfurt to Zurich. Have the South Africans head to Bern on the off chance he turns south. Who's in Munich? Then Gentry has already bypassed the Botswanans. Let's pull them all the way back to Paris; they can support the Sri Lankans on site there. The Kazaks are in Lyon. Right? Lyon is too far south, but we'll stage them there till we get more intel. Make sure they're near the highway and ready to head north. Send another detail of surveillance to Zurich and double-check Gentry's known associates list. Who else is in Paris? Well, I don't care how good he is, one man is not enough. Gentry has lots of history there; I want three teams in Paris *plus* the Korean. The Korean hasn't checked in? Don't worry about it. Just keep sending him updates. He's a singleton operator. He won't be calling in lonely."

Claire sat on the edge of her bed and worried. It was seven thirty a.m. The full shine of the morning was still a half hour off.

She'd slept, only because last night her mother had made her drink some awful green cough syrup. When she woke, it was still dark. She'd wondered where she was at first, then one by one, she remembered the terrible events of the day before, culminating in the short drive from the family villa in Bayeux to the large old château with the huge gate and the long driveway and the green lawn. She remembered the big men in the leather coats speaking the strange language and the scared looks of Daddy and Mummy, despite their continued assurance that everything was just fine.

Claire checked to make sure her sister was sleeping next to her. Kate was there; she'd choked down a mouthful of cough syrup, too.

Claire sat on the edge of the bed and looked out the window. The only movement was the huge man below her in the gravel car park at the side of the castle. A big gun hung around his neck, and he fished one cigarette after another out of his coat, smoking constantly.

Now and then he talked into a walkie-talkie. Claire knew what the radio was; she remembered the American, Jim, who'd stayed with her family when she was little. He'd had a radio, and he'd showed her and her sister how to press the button and talk into it like a telephone, with her mum answering on the other end in the back garden.

These men around her were nothing like Jim the American. Although she could not remember everything about his time in her house, she remembered he was nice and friendly, where these men had angry and unhappy faces.

Last night before Mummy made the girls drink the cough syrup, Kate had wanted to go exploring throughout the castle. Claire went along, but she was not playing like her silly sister. The angry men all but ignored them as they walked through the kitchen. Kate beat on pots and pans with a spoon because they echoed wildly in the massive château. They wandered down endless wooden-floored corridors and turned back from some because they were too dark and spooky. They found a cellar full of dusty wine bottles and they found a big library full of huge leather books and they found room after room where the walls were lined with the heads of large, scary animals with fur and horns and huge teeth. An orange cat ran down the hall, and they followed it down into the basement, watched it push open a little window high on a wall above a shelf and let itself outside and into the back garden.

Next the girls discovered a spiral staircase that wound up and up and up, and they climbed to the top of a tower. There they turned on a light, saw a man at a table sitting in a chair and looking out one of the open windows into the dark. He had a radio next to him, and he had a big gun in front of him. He'd yelled at the girls in that ugly foreign language, and Kate laughed and ran back down the stairs. Claire followed her sister, but her heart pounded in her chest. The man had barked into his radio, and soon men came and got the girls and took them by their arms to their parents' room. In English one of the big men told Daddy to put his girls to bed, and Daddy had yelled back at the man, told him to keep his hands off, and then stormed out on the balcony while Mummy brought Kate and Claire into the bathroom to drink the medicine.

It had been an awful day and an awful night, and now that Claire had awakened, she knew it had been no bad dream, and today would likely be just as horrid.

As Claire sat at the edge of her bed in the low light and worried, she thought she heard a funny noise in the distance. Soon it was louder, came closer to the château. The skies above her home in London were filled with helicopters, so it didn't take her long to identify the distinctive sound of a propeller.

She stood with her face to the window. The helicopter came over the woods on the far side of the big fountain in the big back garden. Its black rotors spun above its white body as it approached the far edge of the gravel car park, then it turned to the side, landed on its wheels, and sank down. The door on the side opened, and four men in suits climbed out.

The whipping wind of the helicopter blew open one man's suit coat, and even from sixty meters Claire could see the pistol holster against the man's white shirt.

More men with guns.

As the blades whipped above them, four more men stepped out of the chopper. The first man was black and wore a brown suit. The next man hauled two suitcases. He had a long ponytail and ran forward towards the château. Then came a man carrying a briefcase. He was thin and wore a black suit with a raincoat over it. His shiny black hair was short and messy in the wind, and Claire could tell, even in the distance, that he was someone important. The way he looked about, stormed forward on the balls of his feet, and gestured to those around him.

The next man who exited the helicopter was larger, older, bald except long white hair around his ears that lashed around below the spinning propellers. Claire pressed her face to the glass, squinted to get a better look.

Then she shouted out loud, waking Kate behind her with a start, though she'd somehow managed to sleep through the helicopter's approach and landing.

"Grandpa!"

Fitzroy was allowed a minute with his son and daughter-in-law in the kitchen on the ground floor of the château. Phillip and Elise were subdued and confused and a little too scared to be angry.

From there he was shuffled up to the third floor to a large room that was set up similar to the conference room at the LaurentGroup subsidiary in London. There was a seat for him, a big Louis XV armchair. Lloyd had his own chair, a sleek, black, modern model. The Tech was already on station, setting up equipment on a long bank of tables that had been hauled in from other rooms and pushed together to suit his needs. He was just now flipping switches on laptops and radio sets, bringing the new operation's center online.

The room had three doors leading from it. One was to an adjoining bathroom, the second was to the main hall, and the third, Fitzroy noted when one of the Belarusian guard force came through it to speak privately with Lloyd, was the entrance to a small spiral staircase that surely went both up towards the tower above them and continued down to the lower floors.

The new arrivals from London were still just settling in when Sir Donald's phone vibrated on the table next to his chair. A wire ran from it to a speaker box on the table. As Lloyd pushed the button to answer, the Tech shouted to the room that he was not yet ready to trace the call.

"Cheltenham Security," said Sir Donald. His voice was tiring, scratched.

"It's me," said the Gray Man.

"How are you, lad?"

There was a long pause. Finally, "You told them about Guarda."

Fitzroy did not deny it. He said softly, wearily, "Yes, I did. I am truly sorry."

"Not as sorry as you're gonna be when your family dies. Goodbye and good luck, Don."

Lloyd stood in the middle of the room. Quickly he walked to the table, leaned over the phone, and spoke. "Good morning, Courtland."

There was no reply on the line for so long that Lloyd picked up the little phone and looked at it to see if the call was still open.

"Who the hell is this?"

"Court, you may not want to be so hard on the good knight here. I am afraid I put him in an utterly untenable position."

"Who are you?"

"You don't recognize my voice?"

"No."

"We used to work together. It's Lloyd."

There was nothing.

Lloyd continued, "From Langley. Back in the halcyon days, you know."

"Lloyd?"

"That's right. How have you been?"

"I don't remember a Lloyd."

"Come now, Mr. Gentry. It hasn't been that long. I worked for Hanley, helped run you and some of the other assets on the sharp end back in the Goon Squad days."

"I remember Hanley. Don't remember you."

Fitzroy could see that Lloyd was genuinely offended. "Well, you knuckle draggers and door kickers never were known for your social IQ." He looked over at Sir Donald. Embarrassed, perhaps? He waved a dismissive hand. "Doesn't matter. What does matter is, even though you may feel disinclined to come here to Normandy to help your fearless leader, you might consider keeping your current travel itinerary for now. Because, let me assure you, there *is* still something here you *do* want."

"There's nothing I want bad enough to knowingly walk into a trap. Good-bye, Floyd."

"It's Lloyd, no *F*, double *L*, and you might want to stay on the line to hear my sales pitch."

"Were you the one who put out the burn notice on me four years ago?" asked Gentry. His voice was measured and sounded dispassionate over the phone, but Fitzroy knew a question like that must come filled with emotion and intensity.

"No. I didn't burn you. At the time I disagreed with the decision. I thought you still could have been useful to us."

"So who burned me? Hanley?"

"That's a discussion for another day. Maybe we'll talk it over when you get here."

"It's a date. Bye."

"At the moment you should be less worried about who burned you in '06, and more worried about who will burn you tomorrow if you don't drop in for a visit."

Gentry snorted into the phone. "Can't be burned twice."

"Sure you can. When I left the agency, I took out a little insurance policy. I saw what happened to you and a few other men. I knew what barbarity the politicians who run the company were capable of when a heretofore successful operation falls out of favor with the men and women who have to testify before Congress. I told myself, 'Lloyd, you're too smart to go down like dumb old Court Gentry and the others.' So I did what I had to do to ensure my survival."

"You stole secrets."

"Like I said, I'm a survivor."

"You're a traitor."

"Same thing. I copied documents detailing operations, sources and methods, personnel files."

"Personnel files?"

"Yes. I have them with me right now."

"Bullshit."

"Just a moment." Fitzroy watched Lloyd thumb through some papers in a gold folder on the table. There was a stack of similar folders alongside the one the young American picked up. "Gentry, Courtland A. Born 4/18/74 in Jacksonville, Florida. Parents Jim and Lyla Gentry. One brother, deceased. Entered grammar school in—"

"That's enough."

"I've got more. I've got it all. Your agency history with the Special Activities Division and the Autonomous Asset Development Program. Your Golf Sierra exploits. Your known associates. Photos, fingerprints, dental records, et cetera, et cetera."

"What do you want?"

"I want you to come to Normandy."

"Why?"

"That will be discussed when you arrive."

The pause lasted long enough for Fitzroy to hear snippets from the second floor of the château below him. Elise was yelling at Phillip. Sir Donald knew the marriage was rocky, knew this pressure was the last thing they needed.

Finally Gentry spoke. "Do what you have to do, Lloyd. Put my documents out there; I don't give a shit. I'm done with this."

"Very well. I'll spray your data to the world. Within a week, every mobster you've wronged, every enemy agency you've run against, every grumpy assassin you've beat out for a contract, they all will be after you. It will make the last forty-eight hours look like a vacation in a day spa."

"I can handle it."

"And Fitzroy dies. His family dies. Can you handle that?"

A slight hesitation. "He shouldn't have screwed me."

"Okay. You are a hard man, Court, I get it. But there is just one other thing I forgot to mention. Yours were not the only personnel files I filched from the agency. If you do not come to Normandy, I will distribute the names, photographs, and known associates files of all the operators in the Special Activities Division, active, inactive, retired, or otherwise indisposed. Every company triggerman will become just like you: burned, hunted, left hung out to dry because their services have been rendered useless and their names are popping up on every search engine on the Internet."

It was a long time before Gentry spoke. "What the fuck is all this about? Why would you do that, just to get to me?"

"This isn't just about you, you arrogant shit! You are insignificant in the scope of the real objective. But I need you here. I need you here, or I will scorch the earth clean of America's best covert operators. I'll see that every SAD asset and all their known associates are hunted dogs!"

Court Gentry said nothing. Fitzroy cocked his head, thought he could hear the clacking cadence of a train over tracks in the background of the connection.

Lloyd next said, "Of course, it will take a few days to dump all the personnel files of you and the SAD boys onto the net. There's so damn much of it. I'll have to start with something else. If you're not here bright and early tomorrow morning, the first to check out will be the Fitzroy family downstairs. I figure I'll begin with the little ones. The first-in, first-out principle. Know what I mean? I'll kill the babies, kill the parents, and then top off my morning by killing old man Fitzroy here."

Gentry spoke up finally. "If you touch Claire or Kate, I will find you, and I will torture you so slowly that the only prayer on your lips will be for a quick death."

Lloyd clapped his hands. "That's what I like to hear! Emotion! Passion! Well, you'd better get here in time for eggs and biscuits tomorrow, because snapping the necks of those pretty little girls will be the first order of business after breakfast!"

Fitzroy had been silent, sullen. He'd sat to the side during the conversation like a forgotten dog. But when Lloyd spoke his last piece, Sir Donald launched from his Louis XV chair and onto the American and grabbed at the young man's throat. Freshly led wires to the computers and speakers became caught up in their legs, and equipment was ripped from the table. Lloyd's swivel chair flipped up as the two crashed to the ground. Sir Donald tore off Lloyd's wire-rimmed glasses and smashed his fists into the taut cheekbones of his adversary's face.

It took almost ten seconds for the two Northern Irish guards to enter the room and pull the heavy Englishman off the young American solicitor. When finally they were separated, Fitzroy was shoved back in his chair. The two Scottish guards next rushed in and held his head and his arms. Shouts and screaming echoed all over the third floor as one of the Belarusians came up with chains found in the garage alongside the greenhouse. Fitzroy was strapped roughly into his chair, but he still fought against them all as chains were run over the arms and legs of the Louis XV and tightly around the arms and legs of Sir Donald. The cold steel links were strung around his neck, another loop at his forehead. Everything was secured with a huge padlock.

All the while Lloyd remained on the floor. He'd sat up, breathing heavily, pushed his hair back in place, and retightened his necktie. He found his glasses on the floor, bent the arms a bit to approximate their original shape, and put them back on. His face was scratched slightly, his arms and chin and neck were bruised, but he was otherwise uninjured.

Finally he climbed back into his chair and rolled back up to the desk near the telephone.

"Sorry, Court. Some technical difficulties there. We're back with you. You still there?"

But Gentry had hung up.

Lloyd looked to Fitzroy. Fitzroy looked to Lloyd, basically because he could look nowhere else with his head immobilized with chains.

"He'd better stay on track, Don. He'd better stay on track, or you and your family are going to die slow and miserable fucking deaths! You take me for some Ivy League lightweight? So did the CIA. I was shuffling policy papers while the door kickers got all the glory. Well, fuck them, and fuck you! I can play as dirty as the best of the dirty tricks boys. I can and I will do what I need to do to see this through. Abubaker will sign the contract, and we'll be readying our natural gas operation by noon tomorrow. You and yours will be forgotten by me. Between now and then you can live or you can die, I could not give a rat's ass which. It's your decision, Donny boy. Pull that shit again, and see if I give you a third chance."

"Court *will* stay on track. He will come. And he will kill you."

"He won't make it here. But even if he does, the Gray Man who makes it here will be a very different man than the one you know. He'll be hurt, short on time, short on sleep, short on gear."

"Gear?"

"Yes. These types are lost without their gear."

Sir Donald chuckled angrily. "You haven't a clue what you're talking about. Court's most valuable piece of kit is between his ears. The only weapon he needs is his mind. Everything else: guns, knives, bombs . . . they're all just accessories."

"Ridiculous. You've bought into the fairy tale of tactical operators. A glorified goon is all he is."

"It's no fairy tale, and there is no glory in what he does. He's a man at work and as cold and as brutal and as efficient as a corner butcher going about his business. Get in his way, and you'll see."

"Oh, I have every intention of getting in his way."

Fitzroy's corpulent face was beet red and covered in sweat after struggling with five men. He was chained like a beast to the chair with the thick links covering a third of his head. Still, he smiled.

"I've dealt with talkers before, little wankers who move their mouths when their backs are to the wall. Pricks with power. I have seen many a chap like you come and go in my day. You will have your moment, and then your moment will pass. You don't scare me."

Lloyd's face twitched as he leaned close to Fitzroy. "No? How 'bout I walk downstairs, say, 'Eenie, meenie, minie, moe,' come back up here with a little pigtailed prize? How 'bout I—"

"You little sod. Scared of the man in chains, so you threaten a child? The more you try to show me how dangerous you are, the more you fit into the mold of exactly what I took you for the first time I saw you. A weak little nancy boy. A pathetic prat. You can't sort out an old man lashed to a chair, so you have to go after a weaker target. Bloody fucking wanker."

Lloyd's eyes narrowed with fury, and his breath was heavy in Fitzroy's face. Slowly, the American sat up, smiled a little. He lifted a strand of hair away from where it had drooped on his forehead, pressed it back along his scratched scalp.

"I'll show you what I can do to you. Just you and me." He reached a hand out behind him, back to one of the security men from Minsk by the door. "Somebody give me a goddamned knife."

NINETEEN

Song Park Kim awoke at dawn in his suite at the swank Plaza Athénée. His quarters surrounded him with opulence, but he did not sleep on the bed, did not drink from the minibar, did not partake of the room service. He'd slept in a back closet on the floor after rigging tripwires and telltales all around him.

He left his room at six in the morning and began walking through the streets of Paris, memorizing the roads that led from the Right Bank, over bridges, to the Left Bank: taking in the looks and mannerisms of the westerners and memorizing the natural choke points of both automobile and pedestrian traffic.

He'd received a list of names and addresses on his GPS: the Gray Man's known associates in Paris: a former CIA coworker who now headed a market intelligence firm in a skyscraper in La Defense, to the west of the city; an Afghani interpreter used by the Special Activities Division in Kabul in 2001, who now ran a swank Middle Eastern restaurant in the Left Bank on the Boulevard Saint Germaine; an informant in Fitzroy's Network who was also a federal pen pusher at the Ministry of the Interior in an office near the Place de la Concorde; a pilot of renowned skill who had flown for the SAD in Europe and now lived semiretired in the Latin Quarter.

The Korean used public transportation to take a quick look at each site, checking them all out: access to the buildings, locations of nearby parking, and public transportation routes to and from each area. He knew there were local watchers hired by the people who had hired his government to send him, and in fact he'd seen men and women at every site on his list, men and women unable to remain undetected by an exceedingly well-trained operator. He had no doubt the Gray Man would see them, too. Kim knew he would have to supplant their support with his own tracking skills.

Afterwards, Kim patrolled the city center, still studying the map. He was prepared to rush back to any of the known associates' locations if there was a Gray Man sighting, but he did not expect his adversary to use an associate on his current mission. If he could, Kim was certain, the Gray Man would bypass Paris altogether. It was too congested an area, with too many police and too many cameras and too many old acquaintances that would invariably be under surveillance. If the American assassin was forced to go into the city for some reason, Kim knew, he'd do his utmost to get what he needed from sources other than those who could be traced back to him.

Kim knew this because he himself was a lone assassin. A singleton. He himself had been hunted down like a dog, and he himself had been forced to avoid all those who might have been inclined to help him.

But Kim also knew that isolation, exhaustion, injury, necessity, and desperation all led to mistakes, and he knew that if his target somehow made it as far as Paris and had some need in the city, the

Gray Man would be a desperate animal indeed, and all bets were off as to how he would act and react. This operator was perhaps already the most dangerous man in the world. Throwing in wild-eyed fear and a frantic race against time might make him slip up, but it would also make him even more dangerous to those around him. Kim knew that if the call came that the Gray Man was here, then blood would flow like a river through the streets of the City of Lights.

Gentry had ridden his stolen bike through the snowy dawn, then pulled up to the train station at the village of Ardez. A few locals milled about, waiting for the first morning trains west to Zurich or east to the Italian or Austrian borders. The American borrowed a cell phone from a kid waiting for the eastbound train and paid the teenage boy the equivalent of forty dollars to call Fitzroy for five minutes to confront his handler about selling him out. He walked twenty yards down the cement platform for privacy and stood in the snow as a train to Interlaken rolled by. He'd finally hung up the phone when a fight broke out on the other end of the line, erased the number in the phone's memory, and handed it back to the kid with the cash. A few minutes later, Court climbed aboard the first train of the morning to Zurich. It was a Saturday, so he was the only passenger in his car for the majority of the hour-and-forty-five-minute travel time through the narrow valley. One after another, the bright red train chugged on past the railroad stations of the villages along its tracks.

Gentry warmed up on the train, checked his wounds by dropping his pants in the empty car and poking at the sores on his knees and at the entrance and exit wounds on his stinging thigh with his fingertips. He was afraid he might have contracted an infection in the gunshot wound. Certainly, swimming in Szabo's cistern hadn't helped.

Otherwise, he was okay. He'd put miles on the lacerations on his feet, and they did little more than throb, just like his broken rib.

He knew he had to continue on to Normandy, though he felt his odds for success were lessening with each mile nearer he came to the trap waiting for him. Fitzroy was a bastard for tricking him as he had, but, Court had to admit, Lloyd had put Sir Donald into one hell of a difficult position. Court wondered what lengths he himself would have gone to, who he would have sold out, if the twins were his family and their lives were jeopardized by some motherfucker with a mob of gun monkeys and no compunction about killing innocent children.

Thinking about Lloyd made Gentry's blood boil. He honestly didn't remember the guy, but the CIA had never gone wanting for lightweight desk-riding a-holes who worked way back in the rear of covert operations, while the Gray Man and those like him operated on the sharp edge. Court couldn't picture any faces, but once in a while his superiors had cause to introduce him to some Langley suit. Lloyd must have been one of these, before taking top secret SAD personnel records and leaving the company for the private sector.

What a prick.

Court wanted to recall Lloyd, find something back in his memory banks that could somehow help him out of his current predicament, but the rhythm of the train along the tracks began to carry him off to sleep. With all his cuts, bruises, pulled muscles, and extra holes, it was a chore to relax at all, but it was almost as if he was too tired to hurt. He fell asleep a few minutes before arriving in Zurich, was jarred awake by the slowing of the train and the recorded announcement of the impending stop. As he stood and made his way to the exit, he cussed himself for his lack of discipline, for dozing with hunters so close on his tail.

In the Zurich Hauptbahnhof, he bought a ticket for Geneva. It would mean another two hours on the rails, so he made his way over to a sausage counter and bought a large bratwurst and a cup of coffee. It was a grotesque combination, but he hoped the jolt of caffeine and the half pound of solid protein would keep his body alert.

With twenty minutes until his train's departure, he descended the escalator to a large shopping center two levels below the station, found a pay bathroom, and commandeered a stall. Here he sat, fully dressed, on the porcelain, leaned his head back on the cold wall behind him. He drew his pistol and held it at the ready in his lap. Train stations were obvious places for his enemies to hunt him. He didn't like the scarcity of escape routes in a bathroom stall, but still, he knew he was better off hiding in the toilet than he would be standing at his track for a quarter hour just begging to be identified by the opposing force. If Lloyd's goons found him here, then he'd just empty a couple of magazines into the door of the stall in front of him and try to bust his way out.

It wasn't a good plan, but, Court admitted to himself, by taking on this operation in the first place he had forgone any pretense of wisdom. Now it was just about making his way through the shit in the hopes he would live to, and maybe even through, eight o'clock on Sunday morning.

With less than a minute to departure, Gentry walked up the platform alongside Track Seventeen and slipped silently on the train to Geneva just as it began to roll.

Riegel's phone rang at nine forty in the morning. He was in his office, putting in a full day on Saturday, having reluctantly canceled a weekend grouse-hunting trip in Scotland.

"Riegel."

"Sir. Kruger speaking." Kruger was a Swiss security chief for LaurentGroup based in Zurich. "I have information on the target. I had been instructed to contact Mr. Lloyd, but I thought I would let you know."

"Fine, Kruger. I'll pass the information. What do you have?"

"I have *him*, sir. He's just boarded the 9:40 for Geneva. Second-class ticket, no seat reservation."

"Geneva? Why is he going south? He should be headed west."

"He could be running away. Giving up, I mean."

"Maybe. Maybe not. It's out of his way, but he does have associations there."

"I can have surveillance in Geneva ready to intercept him at the station."

"No. We'll arrange a different welcoming party for him there if that is his actual destination. This could be a misdirection. He might get off along the way, take another train to France. I need you to organize coverage at every station where that train stops between Zurich and Geneva. Also make sure he doesn't get off before the train leaves."

"I'm on the train myself now. I'll babysit him along the route and update you as we get closer."

"*Alles klar.* Good work."

Riegel next called the Tech at the château in Normandy. "Get the Venezuelans heading south to catch up with the 9:40 from Zurich to Geneva. The Gray Man is on board, but he may try to get off along the way. The Venezuelans need to be ready to take him down at a moment's notice."

"Understood."

Riegel consulted a large map of Switzerland on his desk. "Get the South Africans in Basel to Geneva. If Gentry makes it alive to the station, they'll need to follow him out and do him in the street. There will be too many cameras and cops in the station."

Court didn't last fifteen minutes. He'd found a window seat on the top level at the back of the last car in second class. He had taken off his coat and draped it over his body. Under it, he pulled his pistol and laid it in his lap with his hand on the grip.

And then he drifted off to sleep.

"*—weis.*"

He woke slowly, his head leaning against the window. Though his vision was blurred by his bloodshot eyes, he watched snow flurries beating the window next to his face. He wanted to stick his tongue out and taste a fat flake through the glass. The countryside was covered in white, only the sheerest stony mountains shone gray and brown where the snowfall found the grade too steep for a foothold. The sky hung low and gray, and a village streaked by before him. It was a beautiful winter morning.

"*Ausweis!*" a voice said, close on his right. Court turned and looked quickly; he recognized the authority to the command.

Four uniformed Swiss police officers stood in the aisle above him. They wore gray pants and two-tone gray jackets. They were Municipaux, city cops. Not the highly trained feds. Big Beretta 92's hung off their hips. An outstretched hand at the end of the outstretched arm of the oldest cop.

"*Ausweis, bitte.*"

Court understood travel German. The white-haired police sergeant wanted to see some ID. Not a train ticket.

Not good.

Gentry moved the gun hidden under his coat, crammed it between the plastic cushion and the wall of the train car as he sat up.

Gentry had no identification, only a ticket. Once the weapon was out of view, he fished through his coat, pulled out the ticket, and handed it over.

The cop didn't even look at it. Instead he switched to English. "Identification, please."

"I lost my passport. I'm heading to the embassy in Geneva to get another."

All four policemen obviously understood English, because all four policemen looked at Court like he was full of shit.

"You are American?" asked the older officer.

"Canadian." Court knew he was in trouble. He may have dumped the pistol, but there was a leather holster Velcroed around his ankle. These guys looked sharp enough; there was no chance they would *not* frisk him. When they found the empty rig on his leg, the cops would just check his seat and find his gun.

"Where is your luggage?"

"Stolen. I told you." There was no sense in making friends. Court knew he'd probably have to kick these guys' asses before it was all over. He didn't feel great about knocking a bunch of innocent policemen's heads together, but he saw no way around it. Although it would be a four-on-one fight, the American operator knew that with surprise, speed, and violence of action, he could get the upper hand in such a small space like a train aisle.

He'd done it before.

Just then, the door to the car opened, and three more policemen filed in. They stayed at the door, far back from the rest of the scrum.

Shit. Seven on one. They were taking no chances. Gentry had no illusions about disabling four men, then advancing twenty-five feet and taking down three more, before being riddled with gunfire.

"Please stand," said the silver-haired policeman in front of him.

"Why? What did I do?"

"Please stand, and I will explain."

"I'm just heading to—"

"I will not ask you again."

Court dropped his shoulders, stood, and took one step into the aisle. A young cop approached and spun him around. Quickly, his hands were cuffed behind his back. The other passengers in the car watched with fascination. Camera phones appeared, and Gentry did his best to turn away from them.

He was frisked by the young officer, who almost immediately discovered the folding knife in his pocket and the ankle holster on his leg. His seat was searched, and the pistol lifted high into the air like a trophy for all on the car to see.

"I am a United States federal agent." Court said this because he didn't really have much else. He did not expect them to just hand him back his gun and pat him on the ass, but he hoped they might relax a little and give him some opportunity to escape.

"With no identification?" asked the officer in charge.

"I lost it."

"So you said. Have you been this morning in Guarda?" asked one of the cops.

The Gray Man, who, surrounded by camera phones and wide-eyed stares, did not feel much like a gray man, did not answer. One of the new policemen back at the entrance spoke into his walkie-talkie. A moment later, the train began to slow.

TWENTY

Riegel took the call at eleven thirty-eight in the morning.

"Sir, Kruger again. Gentry has been taken off the train at a little village called Marnand. Not a scheduled stop."

"Taken off by who?"

"Municipaux. He's cuffed and just sitting on the platform, surrounded by the police. I heard one of the cops calling for a transport wagon to be sent up from Lausanne. It should take no more than thirty minutes."

"Did you get off the train as well?"

"No other passengers were allowed off. I'll disembark in Lausanne and go directly to the police station, wait for him to arrive."

Riegel stared at a map on his computer as he hung up and called Lloyd. "Tell the Venezuelans Gentry's in Marnand, about thirty kilometers north of Lausanne. The police have him."

The American answered back immediately. "They can't have him! We need him!"

Riegel looked across his desk. The heads of a dozen brilliant animals, trophies of his hunts, stared back at him. He said, "I know that. Tell the Venezuelans they are weapons free. They can destroy whoever gets in their way."

"Now we're talking! Are they any good?"

"They are from the General Intelligence Office, Hugo Chávez's secret police. They are the best Caracas has to offer."

"Right. Are they any good?"

"We'll know soon enough, won't we?"

Gentry sat shivering on a wooden bench on the one platform of the small train station. His left hand had been cuffed to the bench's iron armrest. Five municipal cops stood around him in the light snowfall; the rest had stayed on the train.

He'd gotten the idea that his description had been distributed after the morning ruckus in Guarda. He guessed the stolen bike showing up at the train station in Ardez earned the ticket girl a questioning by the police. She would have remembered a foreigner on the first train to Zurich that morning. Zurich being the main transportation hub in the tiny nation, it was just a matter of alerting every cop to check every train, bus, and aircraft out of Zurich for a brown-haired male in his thirties traveling alone.

The sign on the platform said Marnand. He had no idea where this burg was on the map, but his body felt like he may have gotten a couple of hours of sleep, so he suspected he was not far from Geneva. He had to find a way to get free from these guys and get back on the road. In the back of his head a clock was ticking.

The lead policeman sat down next to him. His hair was white like a snow-capped mountain peak, and he smelled of fresh aftershave.

"We wait for a car from Lausanne. They take you to the station. Detectives come and talk to you about the fight in Guarda and the gun you have on train."

"Yes, sir." Gentry was trying on the friendly approach now, his strategy blowing around like a summer wind because he did not know what else to do. It wouldn't win him release, but it easily could help him get the upper hand with the police, cause them to lower their guard just enough for him to find a window of opportunity to exploit. Still, carrying a gun in your pants in Switzerland was an outrage with nearly the gravitas of mass murder in America.

"Can I go to the bathroom?"

"No. Hold your piss."

The younger cops around laughed.

Court sighed. It was worth a shot.

Off to his left, down the platform, a two-lane road twisted up and over a rise. The road was wet and clean and black like licorice, bisecting the white snowfall on the hill. A dark green panel truck was parked high up on the hill, fifty yards from the station's edge and a hundred yards or so from where Court sat and his police guards stood on the station's single platform. Exhaust vapors blew out from the muffler, rose into the air behind the vehicle.

Court looked to his right now, still trying to find a way to gain the advantage before more cops showed up. To his right was the edge of the village proper. Gingerbread homes were sprinkled in among more modern structures. Plumes of woodsmoke floated into the air above the homes and dissipated in the gray sky above.

A green truck, identical to the one on his right, rolled slowly out of the village and pulled into a gas station thirty yards from where Court sat. It jolted to a stop in the parking lot, away from the pumps.

The Gray Man decided in seconds that he had just been surrounded.

"Sergeant!" he called quickly to the cop in charge.

The older man was speaking with his subordinates, but he walked over towards Court on the bench.

"Please listen carefully. We have a problem. On both sides of us are green trucks. In or near those vehicles are men who have been sent to kill me. They will not hesitate to kill you and your men to get to me."

The policeman looked to his left and right at both of the vehicles, then back to Gentry.

"What is this shit you are saying?"

"They will be well-trained killers. You need to move us all inside the station. Hurry!"

Slowly, the policeman pulled his walkie-talkie from his belt and brought it to his mouth. His eyes did not leave Gentry's. In German he instructed his men behind him to come over.

He switched to English. "Two green vehicles. One to the north, one to the south. This man tells me they are men here to rescue him."

"Not rescue! Kill!"

All five looked up and down the platform at the vans. There was still no movement from either.

"It's a trick," said a young blond officer as he unfastened the retention restraint over the tang of his pistol.

"Who are you?" asked another man.

Court didn't answer. Instead he said, "We need to go inside. Quickly."

The lead policeman told his officers, "Watch him. I'll check this out." He turned and began walking up the platform towards the van to the south at the gas station.

"Sergeant! You really do not want to do that." Court called out but was ignored by the silver-headed policeman in the heavy coat.

The cop descended the platform steps and onto the property of the little gas station. The green van had tinted windows. It sat at idle, steam pouring from its exhaust and drifting away in the air behind.

As the Municipaux officer approached the truck, Gentry spoke to the four remaining men.

"He's going to die. Don't freak out; we will all have to work together. If you try to run, they will just gun you down. If you want to live, just do what I say."

"Shut up," said one, and all four were looking at their sergeant as he approached the driver's-side window. He used his walkie-talkie to tap on the tinted glass.

"Don't forget about the other van!" Court pleaded to the uniformed men standing over him.

"Shut up," repeated the policeman. Gentry could see their growing concern as their heads swiveled back and forth between the north and south.

The sergeant tapped harder on the glass. As Gentry and the others watched, the silver-haired man seemed to peer closely through the heavy tint. He must have seen something, some movement or other indicator of danger, because quickly the Swiss policeman stepped back and reached down to the pistol on his hip.

The driver's-side window shattered with the crack of gunfire. The cop backpedaled away quickly, and the door opened. A man in a black jumpsuit and a ski mask slid out from behind the wheel and onto the pavement, a short-barreled machine pistol in his hand. He fired another three-round burst into the sergeant's stumbling body, and the Swiss officer dropped dead on his back.

All four Swiss cops around Court drew their pistols with technique hampered by panic. At thirty yards an accurate shot would be difficult, but the young men fired rounds downrange as they shouted in shock and dropped for cover.

"The other truck! The other fucking truck!" Court screamed as he himself dropped to the cement. He lay on the cold pavement next to the bench, his left arm above him in the seat, shackled to the armrest.

The cops looked behind them and saw four masked men walking down the blacktop road towards their position. They all held rifles similar to the man at the gas station, who was now joined by three confederates. All eight moved closer with confidence, like they had all the time in the world.

"Uncuff me! We've got to get inside!" Court yelled, but the policemen just pressed lower into the cement platform, squatted and ducked behind a wooden pushcart or lay flat in the open, and they fired inaccurate rounds at the gunmen as the men in black approached menacingly through the swirling snowfall from opposite directions.

A bald-headed young policeman shouted into the radio affixed to the epaulets of his jacket. He crouched fifteen feet from Gentry behind a luggage cart that provided him poor shielding from the men on the hill to the north and no cover whatsoever from the men fanned out at the gas station to his south.

Court watched bursts of concrete stitch up the platform, race towards the young cop as he looked the other way and screamed into his microphone, unaware. Each explosion of cement and dust tracked closer to him, until finally supersonic machine pistol rounds burrowed into his legs and back. He spun onto his side and twitched on the concrete. The death throes ceased as quickly as they began.

"Somebody give me a gun!" Gentry shouted. The three remaining policemen ignored him. They fired inaccurately and reloaded slowly with jittering hands.

Court swiveled around on the cold concrete. He put his boots against the iron legs of the bench and kicked as hard as he could. He desperately tried to break the large iron end piece to which he was manacled free from the rest of the twelve-foot wooden bench. The metal handcuff bit into his left wrist as he kicked and pulled. Soon he created a rhythm to his work. A kick with his feet, cracks of the old wood, and searing pain in his wrist and hand.

A salvo of automatic fire hit the window above him, sending broken glass over the bench and onto the ground all around. As he kicked he looked back over to his right. A second policeman had been hit in the shoulder and hip. He dropped his gun and writhed on the cement in agony.

It took over thirty simultaneous strikes with both feet to break the iron end piece away from the wooden bench. On the last drive down with his boot heels, he yanked back with his arm. The pain in his left wrist was excruciating, but the bench broke apart. Gentry crawled to his knees, knelt over the heavy piece of ornamental metal, and lifted it. It was easily thirty pounds and still attached to his scraped and swelling wrist. He hooked his handcuffed arm over the metalwork and hefted it off the platform. Then, in the line of fire from both directions, he ran towards the injured cop writhing in agony in the middle of the platform. When he was still a dozen feet away, he flung the iron out in front of him, down next to the man, and fell with it in a slide. The piece clanged on the cement with nearly as much noise as the gunshots barking all around. His swelling wrist tightened inside the metal cuff.

Kneeling over the Swiss officer, he reached to the man's midsection.

The cop cried out to his rescuer. "My hip! I'm hit bad in the—"

"Sorry," Court said as he pulled the handcuff key off the chain on the cop's utility belt. It was smeared with the young man's blood. Crouching lower in response to a supersonic whine just inches from his right ear, the American assassin pushed the ornamental iron armrest out in front of him, towards the platform's edge. He crawled along as he pushed it again.

The injured policeman reached up and grabbed Court's leg as the American moved away, a pitiable attempt to both seek help from a rescuer and to regain control of his prisoner, as if that were somehow still an issue. Gentry kicked off the dying man's hand, picked the cop's Beretta off the platform, and kept crawling. A spray of sub gun rounds chased Court all the way to the edge of the platform, just missing him as he and his iron anchor rolled off. Gentry dropped four feet down to the ground and behind the cover of the platform's edge. His adrenaline-tinged brain nearly panicked when he lost the key for a moment in the snow, but he quickly dug it out. Rising to his knees, he kept his frozen red fingers steady as he unhooked the handcuff on his left wrist.

Of the five policemen who pulled him off the train, only two were still in the fight. Both crouched behind poor cover on the platform. Not wanting to place his head in the gun sights of anyone who'd watched him drop off the platform, Court moved down a few feet before he peered back over the top. He shouted to the cops, told them to break cover and come to him. One yelled back that he was out of ammunition. The other had a wounded right hand and was firing over a stone planter with his left. From the look of his technique Gentry determined the man to be right-hand dominant.

Movement in the train station caught Gentry's eye. The few civilians at the station had long since hit the road or hit the deck, so when he saw two men running towards the platform inside the building, Court knew some of the attackers had managed to flank his position.

The door to the platform flew open, and two black-masked men appeared over the policeman with the injured hand.

Court raised the Beretta in his right hand; his left was useless with its new injury. At twelve yards' distance, Gentry shot both masked men in the face. Their forward momentum coupled with the bullets' impact caused them to stumble into each other and fall out the door together to the cold platform.

Court's borrowed Beretta 92 locked open with the second shot. Empty.

"Hey! Slide me that rifle!"

This was the third time he'd called for a weapon. The difference this time, of course, was that the first two times were before the two surviving policemen had seen him at work. The young cop with the bloody hand quickly skidded one of the gunmen's small black rifles across the platform to Gentry. Court grabbed it and ducked back down.

It was an HK MP5, the most ubiquitous submachine gun in the world. It felt comfortable in the Gray Man's hands. The American pulled the mag and found it full, with thirty rounds of nine-millimeter ball ammo. He shouted to the injured cop to slide the other rifle to the uninjured man. When the transfer was made, Court said, "Put it on semiauto! Fire one round at a time in each direction! Do that until it's empty! Do you understand?"

"*Oui!*" shouted the cop.

"*Go!*"

In a crouch, Court hurried along the platform's edge, moving north, closing the distance between himself and the four who'd come from the truck on the hill.

A train was approaching in the distance from the north. Court heard sirens from the direction of the village. He tried to push everything from his mind as he crawled forward alongside the track through the snow. Everything but the men he knew would now be closing on the platform, just around the corner of the cement ahead. His wrist throbbed, and his knees stung from the window glass lacerations he received escaping from Laszlo Szabo in Budapest the afternoon before. The ever-present pain in his thigh from Thursday's gunshot wound was the least of his maladies at the moment.

Ten feet from the corner of the cement platform, he heard them: men speaking Spanish. *Spanish?* Was the entire fucking planet trying to kill him? They were tucked down by the steps up to the platform. Though Gentry's ears rang, he was able to make out the clicking and spring-tightening sounds made by the magazine change of an MP5.

When he stood, he encountered two masked men, also just standing up. Court fired the HK one-handed, fully automatic, at a distance of less than ten feet. Both attackers dropped, and Court fired another short bust into each twitching body. He dropped the submachine gun from his hands and hefted a new one off a dead gunman, then spun around and ran back up onto the platform.

He never even considered making a run for it, though he had the perfect opportunity to escape both the Spanish-speaking kill squad and the Swiss police. But there was a fight going on, Court was already in it, and disengaging at this point did not seem right. A couple of innocent cops were still alive, and they would not last long on their own. As the sirens approached, flashing lights beat off the few remaining panes of glass in the train station. Court Gentry ran back to the aid of the two policemen, his one good arm holding the HK out in front of him, searching for fresh targets.

TWENTY-ONE

Claire Fitzroy sat on her bed and looked out the window at the lawn and the thick forest beyond. The sky had been drab and gray since they'd arrived at the château the previous afternoon, but during the morning the low cloud cover had scattered, and now she could see a great distance.

Her lunch was beside her, all but untouched. Her sister was downstairs in the kitchen with Mummy and Daddy and the men in leather coats who followed around wherever her father went, but Claire had been excused from the table. She told her parents about her tummy ache, asked permission to go back to her room.

The tummy ache was real. It came from the worry that had sat heavily inside her for over a day now. The hurried shuffle out of school, the worried faces of Mummy and Daddy, the argument on the phone between her father and grandfather, the arrival of the men with guns, and the trip in the big black cars to the château in the countryside.

Something outside caught her attention. She leaned closer to the bedroom window, squinted. Then she stood excitedly. In the distance she could see the steeples. She knew those steeples! The steeples were from the huge Notre Dame Cathedral in Bayeux, and she knew Bayeux had a police station. It was near the big water wheel her Daddy had taken her and her sister to. She remembered the policemen in their smart uniforms smiling at her the previous summer.

If she could just get out of the house, maybe she could run across the huge back lawn, through the apple orchard, make her way through the woods and to Bayeux in the cold distance. Once there, she could find the police station and tell them what was happening. They could come help, make the men with the leather coats and the ugly foreign language let her family go.

Mummy and Daddy would be so happy.

It was a long way away, but she knew she could make it. She was the fastest winger on her football team. She could slip down to the cellar and out the little open window she and her sister chased the cat through the previous evening.

Resolute, eight-year-old Claire Fitzroy buttoned up her coat, pulled on her mittens, and cracked open the door to the bedroom. As soon as she stepped into the long and dimly lit hallway, she heard voices at the stairwell, but they came from upstairs. She scurried down the corridor and onto the staircase. Lowering her weight on each step, her little feet moved delicately to avoid making noise.

She heard a sudden cry above her. She stopped dead in her tracks and looked up. There was another shout. It came from the third floor. She started to descend again but looked back up to the source of the noise and heard a low, guttural sound.

It was Grandpa Donald. He sounded as if he was sobbing.

Quickly now she made her way to the first floor, bypassing the kitchen and the dining hall carefully, because her parents and sister were having lunch just now. If they saw her, her father would be angry, and he would just tell her to return to her room.

The hall turned ahead to the right on the way to the stone steps that led down to the wine cellar. Claire moved quickly but took care to avoid any noise that would give her away.

She turned the corner at a run and nearly crashed into the rear of a huge guard.

Claire stopped cold. The man wore a brown turtleneck, and from behind she could see the black strap of the rifle that hung in front of him on his chest. A handgun and a radio were attached to his belt. He patrolled down the hall, away from her, perfectly silent in his movements. Little Claire did not dare back up or turn and run away. She just stood there, silently, in the middle of the hallway behind him. He walked slowly. Five feet away at first. Then ten. Then twenty.

The guard opened a door to his left. Claire knew from her explorations with her sister the evening before that it was a small bathroom.

He pulled the door shut behind him.

Behind her she heard more men talking to one another. Quickly she hurried past the bathroom door and to the stone steps of the cellar.

One minute later she climbed up onto the shelf, pushed her little body through the window, and squeezed out onto the back lawn. She rose to a crouch, looked to her left and right, and saw a man walking a big dog on a leash in the distance. Just like the man in the hallway, he was moving in the opposite direction. Claire looked out past the white stone fountain, past the apple trees to the horizon line.

There they were: the steeples of Bayeux Cathedral.

One more look around satisfied her, and then she was off. She rose and sprinted as fast as her little legs would take her. It was cold, and her breath steamed as she tore past the fountain, reached the other side, and then ran as she had never run in her life.

Just weeks ago she scored a goal in a match against Walnut Tree Walk Primary School. She was on the left flank when the ball popped free from a bad clearance. She scooped it back towards the goal mouth at a dead run, dribbled close, and fired low, her first goal of the season.

Daddy had been so happy he'd taken the girls out for pizza on the way home. He'd spoken of it every day since.

Claire ran across the green grass of the manicured lawn like she was running for the ball in front of the goal. She just had to ignore the burning cold air in her chest and the little daggers of pain in her legs. She just had to make it into the orchard where the bad men could not catch her. She just *had* to get to the steeple so she could find the police station. She just *had* to tell someone what was going on at the château. She just *had* to rescue her family.

She was only a few yards from the start of the orchard, could already smell the sweet apples, when the earsplitting crack of a rifle snapped across the huge lawn from behind her, echoed off the tree line in front of her, and she stumbled and fell head over heels into the low shrubbery at the orchard's edge.

"What the fuck was that?" shouted Lloyd in surprise, but he knew a rifle shot when he heard one. He poked his head out of the command center. The guard at the end of the hall on the third floor was clearly as clueless as the questioner.

Lloyd rushed past him down the stairs. The young American's suit coat was off, his tie was untied and draped around his neck, and his collar hung wide open. His sleeves had been rolled up, and his armpits, face, and hair were covered in sweat. A mixture of perspiration and blood had streaked across his shirt where he'd recently brushed across a fresh wound.

At the second-floor landing he nearly crashed into a Belarusian coming up to get him.

"What's happening? Who's shooting?" Lloyd asked.

"Come, please to hurry!"

Lloyd followed the man down to the first floor. There was screaming from the living area. It was Elise Fitzroy's voice, coming from the kitchen. Men from Minsk yelled back at her. Mr. Felix appeared, asked Lloyd what had happened, and was curtly instructed to return to the library and shut the door. Lloyd started to enter the kitchen, but the guard who'd been leading the way turned back and took him by the arm. He said something, but his English was poor. Lloyd brushed the man's hand off him but followed him out the back door.

At first the American lawyer saw nothing but the white stone fountain, the green lawn, the distant apple orchard, and the clear blue sky. He followed the guard, moved sideways around the fountain, and found three Belarusians and a dog standing over a form on the grass.

"Gentry?" Lloyd could not believe it. How had he made it so quickly to—

The man with the dog stepped aside, giving Lloyd a clean view of the body facedown on the lawn.

Lloyd's jaw tensed. "Shit. Shit! This is the last thing I needed today!"

Just then another security man appeared from the orchard, another one hundred fifty yards away. He held the leash of a large black hunting dog in his right hand, across his chest was a shotgun, and the firm grip of his left hand was cinched around the wrist of a little girl with brown hair.

One of the twins. Lloyd hadn't taken the time to learn their names, much less tell them apart.

Lloyd yanked the radio off the hip of the Belarusian who had led him out to the yard. He pressed the transmit button. "You. Take her around to the front entrance. We don't need a hysterical brat on our hands."

"Yes, sir," said the man in the distance through his walkie-talkie. He yanked hard on the girl, pulled her along the edge of the orchard, well out of view of the body of her father that lay facedown in the thick grass, a small hole drilled into the back of his head and his face blown off.

Gentry pulled out onto the highway, heading south to Lausanne and then past to round Lake Geneva to the west. His green panel truck had a few nine-millimeter holes in it, but the oil pressure and gas needles remained steady in the center of each gauge. Behind him at the train station at least four South Americans lay dead in the snow. The rest were pinned down by the eight men from the four police cruisers that had just arrived on the scene. Court had made it across the tracks just as the large intercity train passed. He'd then doubled back up the hill and climbed into the green truck with the keys in it and the engine running.

And now he was hauling ass. Fifteen minutes earlier, he'd been the most wanted man in Switzerland. Though that mantle had surely been handed off to the Latin gunners shooting it out back at the train station, Court knew he was still in second place, and the local authorities would soon enough put the word out that a highly wanted man was driving around in a bullet-pocked green panel truck.

TWENTY-TWO

No one told the Belarusians at Château Laurent about the helicopter. Consequently, pandemonium ensued when a Sikorsky S76 appeared over the woods to the south, banked hard, and landed at the helipad next to the gravel car park.

Lloyd alone had been informed of the impending arrival of the helicopter from Paris. He sat in the control room, listened to the rotor wash beat against the leaded glass window next to him. He'd sent the Tech downstairs for a lunch break, and he'd pushed Fitzroy's chair, with Sir Donald chained to it, into an adjoining bathroom.

Lloyd just sat there alone and stared at the stone wall in front of him.

Three minutes later, the door behind him opened. Lloyd did not turn around immediately.

"Lloyd? Lloyd?"

Slowly, the American attorney rotated his swivel chair to face the newest guest to the château. Riegel was a big man, six five at least. He had swept-back blond hair with flecks of gray and bushy blond eyebrows. He wore thick khaki pants and a casual suede sport coat. His shirt was open at the collar. He was twenty years or so older than Lloyd, but he'd not let his body soften, and already his powerful voice and overbearing countenance told Lloyd the afternoon would be difficult and taxing.

Lloyd did not get up. "Mr. Riegel. Welcome to Château Laurent."

Riegel was angry. "Did it not occur to you to mention to the guards I would be arriving? I've had three Belarusians just tell me they almost fired on my transport."

"That would have been unfortunate."

Riegel looked like he was going to continue the argument, but instead he let it go.

"Where is Abubaker's representative?"

"Mr. Felix is downstairs. We've put him up in a room adjacent to the library. I told him I'd call down if I had news."

"You heard Gentry slipped through the noose again."

"I heard."

"We have Geneva covered, though. If he turns up there, we will get him."

"So you continue to say."

"We may not have dropped him dead in a street with one shot, but we are beating him down with simple wear and tear. He will run out of weapons, ammunition, escape routes, time, and blood before long."

"Hope you're right. *I'm* running out of hostages."

Riegel sat down in the Tech's chair. "As I told you on the phone en route, Marc Laurent has ordered me here to provide on-site consultation. Don't look at me like that. I don't want to be here any more than you want me. This fucking mess you've created and exacerbated will not help my career, regardless of the outcome. I am just the cleaner, the man to keep a terrible situation from becoming even worse. When Laurent heard about the hostage being shot by a guard . . . well, he just said, 'Kurt, get over there. Do what you have to do.'"

Lloyd's response was tinged with tired sarcasm. "Monsieur Laurent needn't worry. I doubt it will happen again. No more daddies to die here."

"Where is the Fitzroy family now?"

"Locked in a room downstairs on the second floor."

"Do they know about the shooting?"

"Kids don't. Mom does."

"What is her demeanor?"

"One of my close-protection detail injected her with enough sedative to keep her docile for a while."

Riegel just nodded. "And where is Sir Donald?"

Lloyd motioned to a door across the room. "In there."

"How did the shooting occur?"

Lloyd shrugged. He seemed momentarily disinterested in the entire operation. "One of the little shits made a run for it. Sniper on the roof saw her and radioed down. I was busy at the time; my radio was off. When the guards took off after her, Phil went nuts, thought they were going to hurt her, I guess. He barreled over two armed Minsk boys in the hallway, shot out the back door to get his daughter."

"And?"

"And the sniper took him out."

Riegel looked out the window to the back lawn. "The poor son of a bitch was just trying to protect his family. He'd have brought her back; he wouldn't have run out on the others. No father would ever leave his family behind."

"I don't suppose our sniper is much of a family man."

"Sir Donald knows?"

"Yeah. I told him."

"How'd he take it?"

"No emotion at all. Just sat there."

"All right. I am going to speak to him, try to explain this was an accident."

"Lots of luck."

"Why don't you take a break, Lloyd? You look like shit."

Lloyd stood up. Riegel saw the blood on his dress shirt but said nothing.

Lloyd said, "I am still in charge."

Kurt Riegel shook his head in disbelief. "Fine by me. I don't want responsibility for any more of this disaster than I have to take on. I am just here to consult. Maybe offer helpful suggestions. Like not losing track of eight-year-old girls, and not shooting hostages who pose no danger nor threat of escape, and not forgetting to tell your security that a friendly helicopter will be landing in their midst. Suggestions of that sort."

Lloyd stood and headed for the staircase to the kitchen without a word.

Riegel crossed the room and opened the door behind which Lloyd said he'd find Sir Donald. The German was surprised to be looking into a large, tiled bathroom. Fitzroy was seated in a chair in the middle of the candlelit chamber. He looked up at Riegel with wet and bloodshot eyes. His head and hands and ankles were secured to the chair with thick iron chains, his dress shirt was shredded on the floor next to him, he sat in a sweat- and bloodstained undershirt. His face had been beaten, and there were fat splotches of blood on his torn tweed trousers. Kurt Riegel took them for puncture marks.

"Scheisse," Riegel said. He stepped out of the room, leaned out into the hall, and called out to the two Scottish guards near the stairs. "I

want the prisoner's bindings removed; I want him cleaned up. Bandage his legs. And someone find him fresh clothing! Dammit, man, move!"

Fifteen minutes later, Riegel sat on a stool by the edge of a canopied bed in the master quarters on the second floor. Sir Donald lay on the bed and stared back at him. The Englishman had been unshackled and cleaned up and dressed in fresh clothes. A wet bandage hung on his left temple where an ineffective blow had cut his skin. The bruises on his chin and eyes had received little attention.

Neither man spoke at first, although Fitzroy had declined coffee with a shake of his head. His eyes hung low and malevolent.

Finally Riegel found a starting place. "Sir Donald. My name is Herr Riegel. First allow me to sincerely apologize for your treatment. I had no idea Lloyd was going to . . . Well, no excuses. I take responsibility for this. I will make it right."

Fitzroy said nothing, though his glare indicated no show of appreciation would be forthcoming.

"I have food and water on the way to you. Something heavier perhaps? A brandy, maybe? You Englishmen often enjoy an afternoon nip. Am I right?"

Still no response from the aged prisoner.

"Further. My deepest condolences for your son. Nothing I can say or do can—"

"Then don't bloody bother." Don's voice was sandpaper, gravel.

"Understood. I just want you to know . . . no one intended for this to happen. Again, no excuses. I should have been here on site all along. As soon as I heard about the accident, I was on the way. Your son did what any father would have done. He should not have been shot." Then he said again, "He only did what any father would have done in such circumstances."

Fitzroy seemed to think about this, but he did not respond.

"From now on I will be overseeing your care and the care of your family. Mr. Lloyd will coordinate the initiative to find and neutralize the Gray Man. I will also be in charge of the defenses here, to make things ready in the unlikely event Mr. Gentry manages to slip past the hunters we have out in the field looking for him."

"He'll be here soon enough, Fritz."

Riegel smiled a little and sat up. "He has managed to neutralize or effect the neutralization of the Albanians, the Indonesians, and the Venezuelans, and the Libyans suffered one inadvertent casualty during his escape from them. Meaning he has brought about the complete destruction of three kill squads and depleted the manpower of a fourth. Still, there are nine teams between him and ourselves. Forty men or so. Plus one hundred pavement artists searching for him. Plus a fourteen-man security detail in cordon here around the château. Plus a technician here monitoring the phones and computers of all Gentry's known associates along his probable route. And there is word he is injured. Surely he is tired. His resources are thinning."

"He'll be here." Fitzroy's voice was matter-of-fact.

The German smiled obligingly. "We'll see." Then his eyes turned darker. "Sir Donald, you are a professional. Surely you understand your situation. I would only insult your intelligence by telling you we will let you go when this matter with the Gray Man is resolved. You know as well as I that we cannot merely open the gates and let you walk out. Not to be dramatic but . . . as they say in the movies, you simply know too much. No. Regardless of the outcome with Gentry and the Lagos contract, you will not be leaving Château Laurent with your life. Ah, you knew that; I am glad to see this in your eyes.

"But I will make this promise between two professionals. The twins and your daughter-in-law will not be harmed. They have gone through enough. I just need to keep them here until Mr. Gentry's arrival. Then they are free. As long as the Gray Man does not contact others, bring police or military down upon our little château here, there will be no danger to the woman and her daughters, regardless of whether or not President Abubaker signs the contract.

"I also promise you will suffer no more indignities at the hands of Mr. Lloyd."

Fitzroy nodded and lifted his chin. "I want my son's body respected."

"It goes without saying. I'll see a proper casket is brought in. We'll ferry Phillip back to Britain via helicopter. He will be delivered to the place of his wife's choosing as soon as she returns home."

Fitzroy nodded slowly. "You do that, and you find a way to keep the girls out of the line of fire when the Gray Man shows up tonight, and I will be in your debt and be no trouble to your mission."

When the Gray Man shows up tonight. Riegel fought a little smile and won. "You have my word as a gentleman. Anything else I can do for you to make you more comfortable until the battle for the castle?" He could not help a little sarcasm.

"I would very much like to speak with Claire if I could. A bit of a worrier, she is. I hate to think what is going on in her head right now. Just a little chat between a grandfather and his granddaughter in private."

"Claire is one of the twins? I am sure I can see to that."

"That would be lovely, thank you."

Ten minutes later, Riegel stood across from Lloyd in the kitchen. They both drank coffee and ignored sandwiches on a platter on the large stone island in front of them.

"Why did you torture Fitzroy?"

"He wasn't taking the situation seriously."

"You are insane, Lloyd. I presume this insanity has been formally diagnosed, maybe back in your childhood, and you managed to hide that detail of your psyche from the CIA and Marc Laurent."

"Sticks and stones, Riegel."

"Leave Fitzroy alone."

"You have a bigger problem than me, Kurt. We need an asset in Switzerland to clean up the mess Gentry created."

"Meaning?"

"The Tech just got word from a watcher in Lausanne. He tells us two of the Venezuelan operators were taken alive by the Swiss. We need assurances that they won't talk."

"So you want them killed?"

"How else can we be certain of their silence?"

Riegel shrugged. "Without LaurentGroup, Venezuela's oil stops flowing. Without LaurentGroup, what oil they have for export doesn't make it across the sea to the refineries. Chávez needs us as much as we need him. A couple of shooters who could neither manage to succeed in their mission nor die trying will not jeopardize the good relationship we have with that lunatic. I'll make a call to the director of the General Intelligence Office in Caracas, let him know that even though they failed in their mission, I'll send him a consolation prize if he sees that his agents keep their mouths shut. When the Swiss allow officials from the Venezuelan embassy to meet with the two surviving operators in jail, I have no doubt the message those two bastards get will be very descriptive in what will happen to their families back home if they don't take the fall for the operation. One mention by them to the police of a multinational corporation's recruitment of several third-world intelligence agencies' hit squads to kill a man traversing Europe and . . . well, those men's wives, kids, parents, and neighbors will be tossed into the Venezuelan version of a gulag."

Lloyd was impressed. "That's one reason you didn't use mercenaries, isn't it?"

"Mercenaries don't have anyone to answer to but themselves. I much prefer using men who are subject to other avenues of influence that I can manipulate."

Lloyd nodded. "So now we just have to find Gentry."

"We have LaurentGroup assets at every choke point in Geneva, every location of a known associate, every hospital. We have phones and police radios monitored by the Tech here. We have the South Africans in the city center, ready for deployment. If one of my watchers sees the Gray Man, we will have a hit squad on him in fifteen minutes."

Fitzroy had not eaten, though he'd sucked down two brandies and some bottled water. The treatment he'd received from Lloyd had left him worse for wear but unbroken. Knife jabs to the thigh, open-handed strikes to the head. They were the actions of a desperate man, nothing more.

As a young intelligence officer working in Ulster in the seventies, Don was kidnapped from a taxi stand by a carload of hooded Provos. They took him to a warehouse, spent ninety minutes beating him with lengths of pipe. By the time the SAS quick reaction force fast-roped down from the helicopter, killed three of the five IRA men in the ensuing gunfight, and the other two execution-style against the warehouse wall, the twenty-six-year-old spy had suffered six broken bones and permanent reduction in vision in his left eye.

The work-over he'd received from Lloyd was nothing like that. The American had the zeal but not the talent for administering pain.

Plus he had no big cause or belief. Just one part personal dementia and two parts anxiety brought on by the desperation of his predicament. In this entire enterprise, Fitzroy decided, perhaps only Court Gentry was more imperiled than young Lloyd. Fitzroy presumed Laurent would likely order this Riegel fellow to kill the American lawyer if the contract was not signed by Julius Abubaker tomorrow morning at eight a.m.

Sir Donald, for his part, was beaten up but certainly not beaten down. He had a plan of sorts; he intended to use his wits and his tradecraft and a lifetime of experience manipulating those around him to achieve that which he could not accomplish alone. Though confined to a bed, Sir Donald Fitzroy planned cruel revenge on those who dared cross him, his family, and his top assassin.

The door to the master bedroom opened slowly. Fitzroy downed the last of his brandy and placed the snifter on the bedside table next to him quickly.

Claire entered warily, unsure. Then she saw him and ran across the room to her grandfather. She hugged him tightly around his thick neck.

"Hullo, darling. How are you?"

"I'm all right, Grandpa Donald. You're hurt!"

"A little spill on the stairs, love. No worries. How is your sister?"

"Kate's fine. She likes it here."

"You don't like it here?"

"No. I am afraid."

"Afraid of what?"

"Of all the men. They are mean to us. Mean to Mummy and Daddy."

"Are you behaving yourself?"

"Yes, Grandpa Donald."

"That's a good girl." Fitzroy looked out the window for a moment.

Then he said, "Claire, my dear, I'd like to play a little game. Would you like that?"

"A game?"

"Yes. One of the men here . . . watching over us. He came with me in the helicopter this morning. I've heard his mates call him by the name Leary. An Irishman. Do you know which one I am talking about?"

"With the red hair?"

"That's my girl."

"Yes, Grandpa. He sits in a chair down at the bottom of the stairs."

"Does he now? Well, Claire, I noticed Mr. Leary has a telephone clipped onto the pocket of his big blue jacket. I don't suppose he wears his jacket in the house. It's probably in a closet, on a floor, maybe lying on a sofa downstairs. I was thinking that maybe we can have a bit of fun with Mr. Red Hair, and you can sneak around like a little kitty cat and slip the phone out of his jacket. Do you think you can do that?"

"I saw his jacket on the coatrack. I saw the phone. When he goes into the kitchen for tea, maybe I can take it."

"That's a good girl. Please try to do that for Grandpa Donald. After you get it, I want you to hide it in your pocket or in your sweater, and then tell the guards you want to come see me."

"What if they won't let me?"

"You could tell them you are Kate. Can you pretend to be Kate? Tell them your sister got to come see me, so it's only fair."

"I don't look like Kate, Grandpa."

"Trust me, my dear, to these men you look exactly alike. Just change your clothes, tell them you're Kate, and you'd fancy a chat with your dear old grandpa."

"All right. I will try to steal a phone for you and sneak it back."

"It's not stealing. It's just a game, love."

"No, it isn't. It's not a game. I'm not a little kid. I know what is going on."

"Yes, of course you do. I thought you might. Please don't worry. Everything will be fine."

"Where's Daddy?"

Fitzroy's pause was short, his countenance unfazed. Sir Donald had been lying to his agents for nearly a half century. He found it no big trick to lie to his kin. "He's in London, love. You'll be home soon, as well. Run along now, and go carefully."

TWENTY-THREE

Court parked the van at the main train station in Geneva, the Gare de Cornavin, located on the seedier north side of the city. Parking at train stations was simple tradecraft. When the vehicle was found, which Court had little doubt would take no time at all, his followers would have to entertain the possibility that he'd just jumped on the first set of wheels rolling out of town, causing them time and manpower to investigate where he might have gone.

It wasn't much, but parking at the train station at least avoided the obvious "tell" of pulling his stolen vehicle up to the front door of his true objective.

The weather was cold but bright, and the last of the late autumn leaves blew across the wide streets of the city. From the station he walked south, past the afternoon street whores and the sex shops of the red-light district, over the bridge crossing the canal into huge Lake Geneva, passing middle-aged bankers and diplomats heading towards all those street whores and sex shops behind him. Five minutes south of the bridge the wide and modern streets gave way to uneven cobblestone passageways and the chic shops lining the roads morphed suddenly into medieval stone walls as a steep hill rose away from the modernity and towards the ancient, picturesque buildings of the Old Town.

Gentry consulted a tourist map hanging on the wall of a hotel lobby, hid his scraped and swollen left wrist from the Japanese couple next to him, and then returned to the chilly street. Another minute or two of climbing an alley brought him to the square in front of the Cathédrale St-Pierre. There Saturday afternoon tourists stood, heads and eyes and cameras all pointed to the thousand-year-old cathedral's impressive facade. Court walked behind the two dozen or so sightseers, then melted down a side street that ran along the south side of the church. On his left was a white wall six feet high with a large iron gate in the center. As he walked past the gate, he glanced inside. There was a white house with a small front garden, a large chestnut tree on either side of a narrow walkway to the front door. The trees strained for light in the shadow of the Cathédrale St-Pierre that loomed high in front of them. Court walked on down a cobblestone passage that ran off the little one-lane street, followed the winding footpath through a narrow tunnel that led him down and around to the back of the white house.

Here the wall was two stories high. Modern structures stood alongside it: an apartment building with a nail salon on one side, a nursery school on the other. A few tourists wandered towards a narrow shopping street that ran farther down the hill behind.

Gentry saw the watcher immediately. An attractive woman with long, braided blond hair, she sat at a picnic table in a little playground alongside the shopping street. Court was twenty-five yards from her, but her eyes were on the white house to his right.

Gentry turned, walked back through the foot tunnel, followed it up and around towards the white wall of the white house. There was an iron handrail built into the wall to aid pedestrians with the steep incline of the passageway. Court stepped up on this and, with his good right arm, pulled himself up on the top of the wall. He kicked one leg and then the other over and dropped down, letting his good left leg take the majority of the impact with the ground.

Still, the one-handed climb and the drop hurt like hell.

Inside the small garden, Gentry saw the security system through the glass. He knew how to circumvent all sorts of countermeasures, but this looked too sophisticated for him. He'd need schematics and tools and time.

Court moved low below a window, rose again at a side door. He drew a Beretta pistol he'd picked up on the platform shortly before fleeing the scene, left there by a dead Swiss municipal policeman. He held it low by his side as he tried a side door.

It was unlocked.

He entered a hallway and then a well-appointed kitchen. The lights were off, and he could easily make out the sounds of a television in the next room. The glowing set reflected off a mirror in a hallway on the other side of the kitchen, and Court used the flickering light to make his way.

He saw a pistol sitting on the kitchen counter: a full-sized 1911 forty-five caliber.

An American's gun.

Gentry crossed the long kitchen carefully. He hefted the weapon and slid it into the back of his pants. His swollen wrist rewarded the movement with a hot jolt of electricity up to his elbow. Court moved into the hallway, rose confidently now, and entered a wide living room.

A plasma screen hung above a large fireplace that crackled with pine logs.

A lone man sat on a leather sofa with his back to Court. His eyes were trained on the television. The language coming from the TV was French, but the images were clear enough to Gentry. Less than two hours earlier he'd stood on that same train platform. He'd spoken to that young policeman who now lay facedown and dead on the snowy cement, the video images catching the moment when a yellow tarp was draped over his still form.

Court holstered his gun. There was no one else around.

"Hello, Maurice."

The man stood and turned. He was pale and wrinkled, easily seventy and unhealthy-looking. If Gentry's appearance in his flat was a surprise to the old man, he made no sign of it. He stood on thin legs.

"Hello, Court." American English.

"Don't waste your time looking around," Gentry said. "I have your gun."

Maurice smiled. "No. You have *one* of my guns." The old man pulled a small revolver from under his shirt and leveled it at Gentry's chest. "You don't have this one."

"I didn't figure you for the paranoid type. You weren't so careful in the old days."

"Even so, you should have kept your weapon trained on me till you knew I was unarmed."

"Apparently so."

The old man hesitated several seconds. The revolver did not waver. "Damn, boy. I taught you better."

"You did. I'm sorry, sir," Gentry said sheepishly.

"You look like shit."

"I've had a rough couple of days."

"I've seen you after rough days. You've never looked this bad."

Court shrugged. "I'm not a kid anymore."

The old man regarded Gentry for a long moment. "You never were."

Maurice turned his revolver around in his hand, tossed it underhanded across the room to the younger American. Court caught it, looked it over.

"Thirty-eight police special snubby. The other one's a 1911. You *do* know, Maurice, that there is no law that says that just because *you* are old, your guns have to be, too."

"Kiss my ass. Want a beer?"

Gentry tossed the revolver underhanded onto the leather sofa. "More than anything else in the world."

Two minutes later Court sat on the kitchen counter. He held a fat bag of frozen blueberries over his left wrist. The cold burned his skin, but it reduced the swelling. He could still move his fingers, though, so the hand was functional, if barely.

His host was Maurice, just Maurice. Court didn't know his real name, could only be certain that it was *not* Maurice. He was an old agency man, Gentry's primary instructor at the Special Activities Division's Autonomous Asset Development Program training center at Harvey Point, North Carolina. Court only knew tidbits about the man and his history. He knew he'd cut his teeth in Vietnam, performed targeted killings in the Phoenix Program, then spent the next twenty years as a Cold War spook in Moscow and Berlin.

He'd been demobilized for years, working as a trainer for the CIA when a twenty-year-old convicted murderer was brought into his prefabricated aluminum classroom within sight of the Atlantic Ocean. Gentry was both cocky and quiet, raw beyond belief, but in possession of intelligence, discipline, and zeal. Maurice turned him out in under two years and announced to Operation's leadership that this kid was the best hard asset he'd ever built.

That was fourteen years ago, and their paths had seldom crossed since. Maurice had been lured back into the game after 9/11, as were most high-level retired assets still in possession of a pulse. Because of his age and uncertain health, he was sent to Geneva to work in the finance end of the CIA's Directorate of Clandestine Services. His knowledge of Swiss banking and bankers, accrued through forty years of utilizing numbered accounts for CIA shell corporations in his operations, made him an effective paymaster for operatives and operations around the globe.

It was easy work—clean, compared to some of the jobs he'd done as a younger man—but it was not without danger or controversy. Shortly after Court had been drummed out of the agency, Maurice himself was cashiered by the brass. Something about misappropriated funds, though Court did not believe the official story for a minute.

The word from Langley was that Maurice was now completely retired from the CIA. Court did not know that for sure, wasn't 100 percent certain Maurice wouldn't turn on him, which explained the pupil's initial suspicion of his teacher.

Maurice handed Gentry a bottle of French beer, so the younger man cradled the frozen bag of blueberries in his lap and let his wrist rest upon it. The stinging cold slowly numbed the ache. The old man asked, "You hurt bad?"

"Not really."

"You always were a tough bastard."

"I learned from the best not to whine. It never worked around you."

"I haven't seen you in six years. Cyprus, was it?"

"Yes, sir."

"You saw the watcher outside?"

"Yeah. Girl with the braids."

"Good boy. She's pretty good, dressed like a tourist. We get a lot of tourists here in the Old Town. I hate tourists."

"Transitory faces."

"That's right. Do yourself a favor, Court. If you make it to retirement, move someplace so damn godforsaken no tourist would set foot there."

"Will do."

Maurice coughed. Cleared his throat. "There's news floating about. Not connected yet, just bouncing around in the ether, waiting for dots to be connected. Prague, Budapest, and then this morning up by the Austrian border. I knew something big was going down, didn't figure I knew any of the players until the coverage on my house started about eleven thirty. 'Bout an hour after she showed up, all the local stations began broadcasting the news of the gunfight just north of Lausanne. At that point, I knew you were heading this way."

"How did you know it was me?"

"I connected the dots. A hunted man who just kept on living. Death and destruction in his wake. As the bodies got closer, I told myself, 'Here comes Court.' "

"Here I am," Gentry confirmed distantly, looking at the bottle in his hand.

"Tell me you didn't shoot those poor cops."

"You know me. I wouldn't kill a cop."

"I *knew* you. People change."

"*I* didn't change. The police were holding me when a wet team showed up. I tried to convince them *I* was no longer their biggest problem. They wouldn't listen."

"A lot of people want you dead, Court."

"You aren't exactly the flavor of the month yourself. The CIA burned you, too."

"There's no shoot-on-sight directive against me. You were the one they really fucked over."

"Still, how they framed you was wrong, Maurice. You were one of the honest ones. They should have left your reputation intact."

Maurice said nothing.

"What are you doing these days?" Court asked.

"Finance. Private sector stuff. No more spook work."

Court's eyes scanned the expensive real estate around him. "You look like you are doing okay."

"There is money in money, or haven't you heard?"

Court detected a little defensiveness. He swigged his beer and rotated his arm to spread the cold around his swollen wrist. "You remember a guy at Langley named Lloyd?"

"Sure. Sharp-dressed little fag, law degree from London. King's College, I think. He got in the way of a finance operation I worked in the Caymans not long before I got shit-canned. Smart kid, but a prick."

"He's at the center of all this stuff I'm dealing with now."

"No kidding? He was like twenty-eight at the time. Must be only thirty-two or so now. He left Langley about a year ago, I heard."

"What happened to all the good guys?" asked Court rhetorically.

"Before 9/11, we were a basket with a few bad apples. After 9/11, we grew into an orchard. Now there are enough bad apples to fill baskets. Same shit, different scale. No surprise."

They both sipped beer for a minute in silence, relaxing in each other's company, as if they spent every Saturday afternoon together. Maurice started to cough, and his coughing morphed into a violent hack.

When it ended, Gentry asked, "What's wrong with you?"

Maurice looked away a moment, answered without emotion. "Lungs and liver, take your pick."

"Bad?"

"The good news is I may not die from the lung cancer because the liver disease may get me first. Conversely, I may be buried with a working liver if I can only die from lung cancer. Drinking and smoking fifty-some-odd years."

"Sorry."

"Don't be. If I had it to do over again, I wouldn't change a thing." He laughed, and this turned into a raspy coughing fit as well.

"How much time do you have?"

"There's an old Henny Youngman bit. Doc says I've got six months to live. I tell him, 'I can't pay your bill.' He tells me he'll give me another six months." Maurice's laugh turned into a wheeze and then a violent hack.

"So six months, then?"

"That's what they said. Seven months ago."

"Don't pay 'em," quipped Court. It was gallows humor, though Gentry wasn't comfortable joking with his mentor about impending death.

"Let's get back to you. What have you gotten yourself mixed up in?"

"It's related to a job I did last week. I pissed someone off, I guess."

"The colored guy who got it in Syria. Ali Baba, whatever his name was. That was you, wasn't it?"

"Abubaker," Court corrected, but he neither confirmed nor denied his involvement.

Maurice just shrugged. "He needed to go. I've followed your career as a private. Your ops are always white on black. Not just nicely performed, but moral, just."

"Tell that to Lloyd."

"A lot of people say that thing in Kiev was you."

"That's what they say."

"So?"

Maurice's phone rang. The old man reached a reed-thin hand to the handset on the wall and answered it. His gray eyes widened slightly as he looked up at his young guest.

"It's for you."

TWENTY-FOUR

"Shit." Gentry took it. "Yeah?"

"Court? It's Don."

"What do you want?"

"They don't know I'm calling. I got Claire to pinch a phone from one of the chaps guarding the château. She's a right chip off the old block, is she not?"

Gentry gritted his teeth. Maurice handed him a fresh bottle of cold beer. "What the fuck is your problem, Don? Claire is not some Belfast tout! You can't run her like one of your agents! She's a little girl! She's your family!"

"Desperate measures for desperate times, mate. She was brilliant."

"I don't like it."

"Do you want the intel I have, or not?"

"How can I use anything you've got? How do I know you still don't—"

"They killed Phillip, Court. Claire did a runner. The bastards shot my boy as he went to look after his child."

"Jesus Christ."

"We can only hope."

"I'm sorry." Court paused. "How did you know I was here?"

"Lloyd knows you're in Geneva."

"Figured the shoot-out on the way from Zurich might tip him off."

"Quite. I racked my brain as to what you were doing there. Knew you were too smart to approach somebody in my Network. Then I remembered there was an old agency banker in Geneva, used to be SAD, ran hard asset training. Figured you must have had dealings with him in your former life. I called a few contacts and got a number."

"How are you able to make phone calls without them knowing about it?"

"They think I've given up. I'm lying in a bed with stab wounds and busted teeth from that fucking poof Lloyd. He tried to rough me up, did a cock-up job of it. Can't even torture a man respectably. They have me pegged as a half vegetable, a compliant old shell-shocked nutter in bed upstairs. But I haven't given up, Court. When I thought the only hope for my family was to make you dead, that was my intent. I'll admit that to you. Now I know bloody well the only hope for my family is to get you here. To help you in any way I can to hit this place as hard as you can with everything you've got."

"Just keep the girls out of it from now on. Can you do that? They're just kids."

"You have my word."

"Lloyd really does have the documents he says he does?"

"He has your CIA personnel file, a couple dozen others, too. Papers and computer disks. He brought us down from London to add another enticement, to make sure you'd come."

"Why is he doing this?"

Fitzroy told Court all about LaurentGroup. About Abubaker's demands. About Riegel and the Minsk guard force and the pavement artists. About the gauntlet of a dozen hit squads from a dozen intelligence agencies in a dozen third-world countries, all sent after him for the twenty-million-dollar bounty.

As Sir Donald relayed all the information he had about the operation against Gentry, Maurice pulled a blue box from a cabinet and brought it to the kitchen table where Court was seated. The aged financier and former Clandestine Services operator cleaned the cuts on his young protégé's wrist with antiseptic, then squeezed bags of cold gel to force a chemical reaction, turning the compresses frosty white in seconds. These he wrapped around Gentry's swollen left wrist, followed by a compression bandage to hold everything in place and prevent further swelling. It was a tight, neat job, executed by someone who had obviously been trained to tend to the wounded.

When Fitzroy finished his report, Court said, "I can't believe they'd go through all this just for the contract. I get it, ten billion dollars is a lot of cheese, but for Abubaker to confidently make a demand like this, I've got to think there is some other motive in play here."

"I agree. The shoot-out with the Swiss cops—that's an incredible risk for a company like LaurentGroup to take, even if they did it by proxy with Venezuelan shooters."

Gentry said, "There is more than just a contract at stake. Look into that, okay, Don?"

"I'll talk to Riegel. He's a bit more lucid than Lloyd."

"Good. Keep that phone with you. Ringer off."

"Any way I can contact you while you're on the move?"

Gentry looked up to Maurice. "You wouldn't have a spare sat phone just lying around I could buy off of you?" The older man laughed, disappeared down a long hallway, a fresh coughing fit almost doubling him over at one point. Moments later he returned with a satellite phone; it was a high-tech Motorola Iridium, a model Gentry knew well. Used by spies and soldiers and high-risk adventurers, it was not much larger than a regular cell phone, housed in a clear plastic case that was shockproof, waterproof, practically bombproof. Court nodded appreciatively as he took it. The number was written on tape on the back, and Court read it off to Donald before slipping the device into his front pocket.

After he recited the number back, Fitzroy paused a moment, then said, "Court, my boy, one other thing. When this is all over, when you've killed every last living thing that is a threat to you, I am going to contact you and give you an address. It will be a tiny out-of-the-way place that will be easy for you to slip into and out of without worry. You will find a little one-room cottage, and I will be in that cottage, sitting in a chair, stripped to my undershirt with my hands flat on a table, and I will be waiting for you. My neck will be bare. For what I have put you through, for what you have done for me, I will give you my life in recompense. It will give you little comfort, but maybe it will help you. I am sorry for what I have done to you in the last forty-eight hours. I was desperate. I didn't do it for me; I did it for my family. Save them, and I will go to my death to give you a measure of peace.

"Court? You still there?"

"Keep the girls safe, Don. Do that one thing for me. We'll settle up the rest when this is over." Gentry hung up.

After Court handed the phone back to Maurice, he finished his second beer. Wiping his fingerprints from the bottle with a rag from the counter, he walked to the rear of the home and looked through the long curtains.

"When I leave, can you handle the watcher?"

"She's just sitting there. I think I can manage that. I'm not dead yet."

"You'll outlive us all."

"Coming from you, son, that's not particularly comforting." He changed his tone. More fatherly now, he asked, "How can I help you?"

"I've got to do a . . . 'thing' in northern France. Have to get up there and engage by first thing tomorrow morning."

"You're in no condition to—"

"It doesn't matter. I have to go."

"You need some money?"

"A little, if you can spare it."

"Of course, I can float you some cash. What else do you need?"

"I'll take the forty-five, if you've got a few more mags."

Maurice chuckled, hacked. The sickness in his lungs seemed to grow with the conversation. "You'd probably just hurt yourself with a big manly weapon like that. They don't make them like they used to. That's my baby. I'll get you something a little more contemporary."

"I was hoping you might have a bug-out bag that you'd staged for a rainy day. I've got nothing, so any gear you could spare would be much appreciated."

"I've got a SHTF cache a couple of blocks from here. In case the shit ever hit the fan. From what you're telling me, I'd say your situation qualifies."

"I really appreciate it."

"Anything for my best student." Maurice disappeared down a back hallway. He returned a minute later with a sheaf of euros in an envelope and a key on a chain. He wrote an address down on the envelope and handed it to his protégé. "I think you'll be pleased with the gear."

Court pocketed the items.

"Another beer?"

"I'd love one, but I'd better get moving."

"Understood." Maurice poured several anti-inflammatory pain pills from a bottle in a cabinet into Gentry's hand. Court downed them with the last swig from his bottle. Then they walked together towards the back door.

Court said, "I wish I could say I'd see you again. If I make it through tomorrow, I'll have to drop off the face of the earth for a while. Maybe if you don't pay your doctor's bill, we can have another beer someday."

Maurice smiled, but this time he did not laugh. "I'm dying, Court. No sense in putting lipstick on a pig. I can't make it any prettier than it is."

"Is there anything I can do for you? Anybody you need me to see? Look in on after you're gone?"

"There's nobody. No family. No friends. There was just the Agency."

"I know the feeling," Court said. Spending time with his mentor was good in that Gentry had so few opportunities to talk to someone who'd gone through some of the same things in life as he had. But it was also bad. Depressing, because Court saw a measure of himself in the tired old cynical eyes of the man facing him in the living room and knew that, though no one likes to get old, in Gentry's profession, mere survival was the absolute best one could hope for.

And this was success?

"You can do one thing for me." Maurice smiled as he spoke. "When you get yourself extracted from this mess you're in, I want you to get away to some tropical island somewhere. When you read in the paper about an older-than-dirt disgraced American banker dying in Switzerland, I want you to go out to your favorite cantina, find yourself a pretty girl, and drink the night away with her. I'm serious. Get through this and get out of this life. There are still corners of the world where no one gives a shit what you've done. Go there. Meet somebody. Live like a human. Do that for me, kid."

"I'll try."

"Someday you will learn. All the things you've done, all the things in the past you thought were dead and buried—you think you've put them behind you, but you haven't. You've just stored them away. Stored for the time when there is only you and a quiet room and your memories and the goddamned demons of those you killed."

"I've got to go, Maurice."

"I know I can't stop you from doing what you have to do. But think about what I am saying. All the shit I taught you back at Harvey Point. Sooner you forget what I taught you then, sooner you follow what I'm telling you now, the sooner the killing and the death will be dealt with. End of sermon, kid."

They shook hands.

Court's game face reappeared in a flash. He crammed the wad of cash into his pants pocket and the sat phone into his jacket and headed for the back door. He peered through the blinds out the front window, into the medieval passageway.

Instantly he sensed that something wasn't right.

"What is it?" asked Maurice, picking up on his protégé's unease.

"Check the back. See if the girl is still there."

Maurice walked down the hall to the back living room and called out to Court, "She's gone."

"They pulled her."

"Who pulled her?"

"Hitters."

"Because they want her out of the way when it goes loud?"

"Exactly."

"They're here?" asked Maurice as he returned to Gentry's side.

"Not here, but close," confirmed the Gray Man. "I can fucking smell them." Gentry's eyes narrowed. "Tell me you didn't set me up, Maurice."

"Not on your life, Court."

A moment's pause. "I believe you. Sorry."

"Who's out there? Any idea?"

Court and Maurice barricaded the doors with an armoire and a bookcase. "God only knows. In the past three days I've had everyone but killer Martians on my ass."

"This must be the killer Martians, then. I hear they're real bastards. You can get out through the ceiling. There are boards in the crawl space laid out to a vent. Push the vent out, and you should just about fit through. This will drop you into the attic of the preschool behind my house. They are closed on Saturdays. They have a basement that leads into the nail salon next door. You look like you could do with a manicure, but try to fight the urge. Slip out their front door to the Rue du Purgatoire, then down the little alleyway, Rue d'Enfer. That should get you clear."

"What about cops?"

"The closest station is at the Palais de Justice, but we aren't talking frontline troops. Better we don't call them at all lest a bloodbath ensues."

Gentry stood motionless and just stared at Maurice.

The elderly man laughed heartily, fought his wheezing. "I set the escape route up long ago. For me, back when I could have managed. I had a neighborhood boy test the crawl space just a few months back. No problem. Go on then."

"Come with me."

"You aren't getting my feeble ass into that crawl space. I'm not running from anyone. Now go."

"Maurice, in a few seconds an alpha team is coming through those doors. They will know you helped me. They'll do whatever it takes to get intel from you."

Maurice smiled, shrugged. "I've never been afraid of dying, Court. But the thought of dying for nothing really chaps my ass. If I'd taken a bullet back in Nam like every goddamn friend I had back there, then it would have been worthwhile. If I'd died on the job with the company, that would have been honorable. I mean, depending on what we were doing at the time, you know what I'm saying. But sitting here in my house in Geneva, flipping channels on the television and waiting for the moment my lungs cough up or my liver pisses out . . . there's just no nobility in that."

"What are you saying?"

"I'm saying I'll die for you, kid. You've done more righteous hits than the entire damn agency in the past four years. You deserve someone to help you when you're down."

Gentry did not know what to say, so he said nothing.

"Don't fuck it up, boy. Get out of here. I'll slow them down, maybe bloody a nose or two in the process. No promises, but I'll try to thin their ranks a bit."

"I'll never forget you."

Maurice smiled and pointed upwards. "If I get past security and make it up there to heaven, I'll put in a good word for you with the Man. See if I can't save your scrawny ass in the afterlife, too."

An awkward hug between two men whose minds were tightening for impending action. Maurice said, "One more thing. I hope you will remember me in a positive light. Not think bad things about me if . . . if you should learn that I made a mistake or two along the way."

"You are my hero. That's never going to change."

"Thanks, kid."

There was the sound of a truck's brakes out front. "Go!"

Gentry nodded. He squeezed the frail man on the shoulder and leapt to the rafter overhead without another word. Quickly he pulled himself up and into the attic, his broken rib and his swollen wrist both shrieking with pain. He had just replaced the tile when a crash at the front door knocked the armoire a foot into the room.

Maurice spun around and moved into the kitchen as quickly as his old legs and scarred lungs would take him. Another impact cracked the door behind him. He grabbed hold of the huge commercial stove, yanked the old gas appliance back a few inches with a jerk. Desperately he reached behind the stove, stretched his aged body to its limit, but he could not take hold of his objective. He looked around the room for something to extend his reach.

The South Africans were commandos from their nation's National Intelligence Agency. The leader of the six-man squad stood in the front yard of the white house, his Benelli shotgun resting on his shoulder, as the rest of his team finally made entry on the barricaded door. They moved in a well-practiced tactical train throughout the two-story building. They split into two units in the middle of the first room. One team went into the kitchen and found an old man sitting at a table, hands on top of his head, fingers laced, facing the far wall, the image of submission. The first man in the train pulled him down to the floor roughly and searched him in the narrow breakfast nook. He found a pistol in the old guy's waistband and threw it up and into the sink.

"That gun is an antique, idiot!" said the elderly man as two South Africans shoved him roughly back into his chair. They dragged him and his chair into the main room and waited until the other four members of the unit pronounced the rest of the house clear.

When the entire team re-formed around their prisoner, the old American looked at all the faces.

"South Africans," he said, obviously having heard their accents.

The leader asked, "Where is the Gray Man?"

"Look at you guys." Maurice ignored the leader's question. "Three black, three white. Ebony and ivory. Back in the old days you whiteys would be beating down on you darkeys, wouldn't you?"

There was no response.

"You white boys must miss those apartheid days, huh?"

The leader repeated himself. "Where is the Gray Man?"

"Ah, but the head of the operation is white. You boys still roll like that? The plantation owners put the slaves in the big house, but they still give the orders. Am I right?"

One of the black operators unhooked his Uzi from his chest rig and raised it to smash its butt into Maurice's jaw.

"Stop!" shouted the leader. "He's just tryin' to slow us down so his lover boy can get clear. Won't work, old man. Now . . . where is the Gray Man?"

Maurice smiled. "This is the part where I say, 'Who is that?' "

The leader's eyebrows furrowed. He spoke in a thick Afrikaans accent. "And this is the part where my man hits you across the face for giving us an attitude instead of an answer." He nodded to the black operator still poised above him, and the Uzi's squat butt smashed into the old American's jaw, sending his head snapping back.

"Now, fooker. Let's try again. Where did he go?"

Maurice spat blood and a bit of his bottom lip on the floor in front of him. "I don't remember. I have reached the advanced age where the memory starts to falter. Very forgetful, you understand. Getting old sucks."

After several seconds of waiting, the leader shouted into the man's face, "I will not ask again. The Gray Man was here. Where is he now?"

"Sorry, young man. I'm unwell. You mind terribly if I use the restroom?"

The leader of the assassins looked to his subordinate. "Hit the fooker again."

Maurice said immediately ,"He is gone. And you will not find him."

The South African sneered at the thin man. "I'll find him. I'll find him, and I'll kill him. The Gray Man's reputation is nothing but a load of hype."

Maurice laughed and coughed. "Do you have any idea how many men who said that very thing are now rotting away eternity in a pine box?"

"That ain't gonna be me, mate."

Maurice nodded appreciatively. "I will have to concede that point to you. There's not going to be enough of you left for a pine box. But not to worry, I hear mortuary services here in Geneva are exceedingly diligent. With a little luck they may salvage a blob of you big enough to half fill an urn on your mother's mantel."

The South African cocked his head. "What the hell are you talking about, you nutter?"

"I'm just saying, your future looks bleak, pal, but there is good news."

The South African looked around to his men. He was clearly speaking to a crazy old buzzard. "I'll play along, chief. What is the good news?"

"Your bleak future will be short-lived." Then Maurice smiled. He softly began a prayer asking forgiveness for his sins.

Just then the Tech's voice came over the radio. The six men put their hands to their earpieces to aid their hearing.

"Watcher Forty-three reports the subject just came out of the nail salon a block behind the house. He's on foot, heading west."

The leader of the South Africans nodded, turned his attention back to Maurice.

"Good news all around, Granddad. We won't have to torture you to find out where he's going."

Maurice did not look up from his prayer. The South African team leader shrugged his shoulders, lowered his shotgun to the seated man's chest, and fired one-handed.

As the slug left the barrel in a shower of fire, the South African lifted into the air and flew backwards into the kitchen. His neck snapped, and the skin burned from his face and hands. The other five suffered similar fates, though in the confines of the living room there was less open distance for the men to fly.

Maurice died instantly from the twelve-gauge blast to the chest at close range.

Firefighters on the scene minutes later would recognize the telltale devastation of a massive gas leak, probably from the connection between the wall and the big industrial oven. This was an unfortunate but all too common occurrence in old homes like this one, and was hardly a surprise. Only hours later, when the fire had been doused and the water and foam levels lowered to where the bodies could be examined, were the investigators scratching their heads. The seven bodies soaked and burned beyond recognition gave them little information. But the massive amount of firearms surrounding all the victims save one was highly irregular in peaceful Geneva, to say the least.

TWENTY-FIVE

Five minutes after exiting the nail salon, the Gray Man walked west on Rue du Marché, searching for the address on the note card in his hand. A light rain began, blurring his view of the numbers on the buildings. He'd just turned north on Rue du Commerce when an explosion roared behind him.

He stopped in his tracks as did the pedestrians around him on the pavement. Unlike them, however, Gentry did not turn around. After a few seconds standing motionless in the rain, he took a step forward. The momentum returned to his body, and he continued on, his head and shoulders slumped a little lower.

He spotted a watcher, so he dodged into the Rue du Rhône, a small, covered passageway, where he lost his tail in the foot traffic near the McDonald's.

Minutes later, he found the single-car garage in the back of an underground parking lot below the Rue de la Confédération. It was a Saturday afternoon, no one was around, and the key Maurice gave him unlocked the sliding door.

It opened with a creak, and the dust from inside the unit mixed in his nose with the scent of motor oil. He felt the walls for a light for a half minute before bumping into a large object in the middle of the floor. Above it was a cord attached to a lightbulb hanging over the middle of the room.

Gentry found himself dazzled by the brilliance of the bare bulb. Quickly he pulled down the garage door to seal himself into the room, turned back to find that the object in the center of the garage was some sort of automobile covered by a large tarp.

Maurice had said nothing about loaning him a car. For a second Court wondered if he'd somehow gained entry into the wrong unit.

He pulled back the tarp and let it fall to the pavement.

Before him sat a large black sedan, a Mercedes S-class four-door with a black, all-leather interior.

Court figured the vehicle must have cost over one hundred thousand dollars.

"Thanks, Maurice," he mumbled.

Opening the unlocked driver's door, the Gray Man saw the keys were in the ignition. Looking at the dash, he noticed the car had fewer than four thousand miles on it. She was a beauty, and it would certainly make his eight-hour drive to Normandy quicker and more comfortable, but there were other ways to travel. No, what he really needed were weapons. In Europe they were far more difficult to come by than efficient means of transportation.

With anticipation, he popped the trunk of the Mercedes and walked to the back.

Four large aluminum cases stood side by side. Court pulled the first one on top of the others and flipped it open.

The corners of his mouth twitched upwards.

Heavy metal.

"My hero, Maurice," he said.

An HK MP5, well-oiled and stored in a foam encasement; four magazines with thirty preloaded nine-millimeter rounds in each lay side by side in the foam; and two fragmentation hand grenades, one resting on either side of the MP5.

He loaded the submachine gun, chambered a round, and tossed it in the front seat of the Mercedes with all the spare magazines.

The second case contained two fragmentation and two flash-bang stun grenades, two door-breaching charges, and a small cube of Semtex plastic explosive with a remote detonating device. Court left this equipment in the trunk for now.

Brushed aluminum case number three housed a handheld GPS unit, two matched walkie-talkies, and a laptop computer. All this gear went into the backseat of the car.

In the final case Court found two Glock-19 nine-millimeter pistols and four loaded magazines.

Also in this container Court found a utility belt and two thigh rigs. One was for carrying a Glock on his right hip, and the other would hang on his left leg and hold magazines for the submachine gun and the pistol.

On a hunch he lifted the carpet up in the trunk of the Mercedes. There he discovered one more weapon, an AR-15 carbine assault rifle. Alongside the spare tire was a plastic container with three loaded magazines full of .223 ammunition, ninety rounds in all.

Court spent a few minutes powering up the sat phone and

familiarizing himself with the GPS. All the while the police, fire department, and ambulance sirens continued to wail a quarter mile away at Maurice's house.

This massive weapons cache told Gentry two things about his former mentor. One, though he was out of the CIA and living in the open, he still had some reason to believe he might need to blast his way out of a sticky situation.

And two, from the look of the top-notch automobile and the insane quantity and quality of the gear, it was apparent to Gentry that the rumors about his mentor had been true.

He *had* likely embezzled from the accounts he maintained for the CIA.

Maurice had surely known Gentry would come to this conclusion, yet still he offered up his cache to his young protégé. It was the dying man's last wish that Court use the hoard to get away and succeed in his mission, and not to judge him too harshly for it.

As Gentry pulled out of the garage, looked straight ahead through the tinted windows, and passed more first responders on their way to the crime scene on Rue de l'Evêché, his emotions were conflicted. Court had never misappropriated a dime in his life. He had never even run up per diem charges when working hits and black bag jobs for mobsters and drug dealers. No, he was a killer, but he was no thief. That Maurice had stolen from the company was disappointing, but in the end a great bit of those stolen funds Gentry planned to put to use. Court was at once both idealistic and pragmatic. Maurice's thievery was wrong but, he told himself, he would not judge his old instructor too harshly. Instead, he'd redeem the old man's honor, use every last goddamn bullet and gun to save the three innocents in Normandy and retrieve the personnel histories of all the assets in the Special Activities Division.

Riegel stood behind the Tech. Lloyd stood on his left. The young ponytailed man sat at his desk in front of computer monitors, headphones pressed to his ears.

From the expression on the young Brit's face, the two men in charge of the operation could tell the news was not good.

The Tech said, "We have confirmation from our local sources that all of the South Africans are dead. There was a large explosion at the target location. Looks like it may have been a gas leak. No doubt brought on by gunfire or some other use of ordnance. The fire department is still working on the blaze; they don't have a body count just yet, they only confirm there were no survivors. Multiple fatalities."

Lloyd said, "Gentry?"

The Tech shook his head. "He was seen leaving the building minutes before the explosion."

"Seen by?"

"A watcher who lost him in the crowd."

"Come on!" screamed Lloyd. "Do I have to kill him myself?"

Riegel pulled his phone from his pocket and made a call. Waited a moment. "Yes, it's me. I need a helicopter. Pick up the following items and get here before dark. Write all this down. Thermal imaging units, motion detectors, remote sensors, monitors, and cabling. You have all that?

"Also find Serge and Alain and get them on that helicopter. Tell them to grab anything else they need to put a three-hundred-sixty-degree electronic wall around Château Laurent." Riegel hung up.

Lloyd stared at him. "What was all that about?"

"Electronic surveillance gear. Men to install and monitor it."

"What's it for?"

"It's for Gentry. It's for tonight."

"There are still three hundred miles and thirty-five shooters between him and here. You don't seriously think he's going to make it through to the château, do you?"

"It's my responsibility to ensure he dies. Whether he dies in Geneva, on a road in the French Alps, or out here on the lawn, it is my job to salvage your operation. I am going to use every instrument, every technical advantage, every warm body, and every gun I can put between his current location and his destination."

The Tech looked up to the two men behind him. For the first time, the young Englishman showed emotion: fear. "Nobody said anything about him actually coming here. I'm not a field man, for Christ's sake."

Riegel looked down at him sternly. "Consider yourself promoted."

The Tech turned back to his terminal.

Next Riegel called up to the tower and had the Belarusian sniper join him and Lloyd out in the back garden. The sniper met them by the fountain, his large Dragunov rifle cradled across his chest. Together they walked slowly past the bloodstained grass, towards the apple orchard that started at the end of the backyard and continued on for several hundred yards to the high stone wall that ringed the entire property. Riegel and the sniper sniffed the air, then knelt to the grass and put their hands in it. They looked at everything in their environment carefully. Lloyd just looked bored and annoyed.

Riegel spoke to the sniper in Russian. Lloyd stared off towards the orchard. "You understand the rules of engagement?"

"If it moves towards the château, shoot it."

"That's right."

"Simple enough."

Riegel's hiking boots sank in the well-manicured lawn. He sniffed the air again. "Did you have fog this morning?"

"Yes. Visibility not more than two hundred yards. Couldn't see as far as the apple trees until almost ten a.m."

"Shouldn't be an issue. If he makes it here at all, it will be before sunrise." The Belarusian just nodded as he scanned the orchard through his scope. Riegel said, "You should not have shot the father."

The sniper just shrugged as he scanned the near distance. "If you were on the scene, I would not have. As it was, I did not have leadership. I made the decision to shoot. That is what I do unless told otherwise."

Riegel nodded. He regarded his sniper for a moment. "I saw the body. The entry wound. Good decision or not . . . it was a magnificent shot."

The Belarusian lowered his eye from the scope of his Dragunov but continued his survey of the orchard. He betrayed not a speck of emotion. "*Da*. It was."

Lloyd was tired of being ignored. "Look, Riegel. You're wasting time. Even if Gentry does make it here, which he won't, do you really think he's going to come running straight up the middle of the yard?"

"It's a possibility. He will do whatever he considers his best option."

"That's insane. He's not going to storm the castle by himself."

"I have to prepare as if he will. His options will be limited."

"Well then, why don't you line the fucking garden with land mines?" Lloyd's sarcasm was delivered with utter derision.

Riegel looked at him a long moment. "Would you know where I can get some land mines?"

Just then, Lloyd's phone chirped in his pocket.

"Yeah?"

"It's the Tech here. Gentry is calling on Sir Donald's phone. I can forward the call to you."

Lloyd hit the speakerphone on his unit. "Do it."

"Hello, Lloyd." Gentry's voice was tired.

"So you slipped the noose again. I was hoping to be standing over your charred remains sometime this evening."

"No. Instead, your rented thugs just killed a seventy-five-year-old American hero."

"Right. A terminally ill, out-to-pasture spy on the take. Excuse me while I dab the tears from my eyes."

"Fuck you, Lloyd."

"You're in Geneva?"

"You know that I am."

"Do you need me to fax you a goddamned map? Northern France is in *northern fucking France*, not southern Switzerland. I don't know why you went to see Maurice. Money, documentation, weapons, another gunman, whatever. None of that shit is going to make a damn bit of difference in the long run. The only thing you need to be worried about right now is time, because tomorrow morning when the little hand reaches the eight and the big hand reaches the twelve, it is open fucking season on little British girlies up here!"

"Don't worry, Lloyd. I'll be there soon."

"Why are you calling?"

"I was sitting here worrying that you may begin to relax, you may think that I died in the explosion. The possibility that you might be having a comfortable afternoon was really beginning to chap my ass, so I thought I'd give you a ring, let you know to leave a light on for me tonight."

Lloyd sniffed into the phone. "You just wanted to make sure I didn't give the mission up for lost. Didn't go downstairs and kill the Fitzroys because I don't need them anymore."

"That, too. I don't know how many more hit teams you have between you and me, but all the goons on earth won't stop me from getting my hand around your throat in just a few hours."

The Tech ran up to the three men in the back garden. Out of breath, he held up a sheet of paper on which he'd hurriedly scrawled the words, "Sat Phone—no trace."

Lloyd frowned. He said, "Court, your death is an inevitability. Why don't you save us all some time, make things easier on everyone, and kill yourself, then put your head in a cooler and ship it up to me."

"I'll make you a deal. I'll supply the head. You get the ice chest ready. Soon enough, I'll give you the opportunity to put the two together."

"Sounds like a plan, buddy."

"Come tomorrow morning, Julius Abubaker is going to have to find himself a new bitch to bargain with, because when you fail, and you *will* fail, either I will kill you, or someone else will."

Lloyd's face twitched in anger. "I'm nobody's bitch, you knuckle-dragging bastard. I've seen a lot of smug scalp hunters come and go in my days. You're no different. You'd do well to remember that even with your reputation and your spooky nickname, you are just a glorified door kicker. You'll be dead in a few hours, and I'll have forgotten about you before the maggots finish you off."

There was a short pause. "Let me guess, Lloyd. Your dad was somebody."

"As a matter of fact, my father *is* somebody."

"Figures. See you soon." Gentry hung up the phone.

Riegel hid his smile from Lloyd. The Tech still stood with his hands on his knees, breathless from the run. He said, "Gentry sounds like he really thinks he'll make it here." There was palpable terror in his voice between his gasps for air.

Lloyd snapped at him, "Get back to work. I want helicopters in the air, I want men on the trains, and I want him dead before he gets to Paris!"

An hour later, Riegel stood on a flat rampart lining the rear of the château's roof. He looked out through the decorative battlements at the cold but sunny afternoon. Three teams of Belarusians, each consisting of two men with assault rifles and radios, walked the grounds in a crisscrossing pattern. The sniper and his spotter were on Riegel's left, high in the tower with a near-perfect 360-degree view of the lawn in the back and the lawn in the front. The helicopter with the thermal imaging equipment had just radioed in that they were on their way back from Paris with all the gear and the two-man team of engineers that could set it up in under an hour.

The Tech had put a hit team on the TGV from Geneva, the high-speed train to Paris. They'd reported no sign of Gentry. Three more teams and most of the available watchers were taking up positions on the highways through the French Alps that the Gray Man would have to traverse if he was traveling by car or motorcycle. Three more kill squads were in Paris. It was a natural staging area, a city full of his known associates and a city in which he might well stop for supplies or support.

There was not much left for Kurt Riegel to do at the moment but wait.

Still, something was bothering him.

It started out as a nagging irritation in the back of his mind and grew by the minute as he reconciled himself to the fact that he'd tidied up all the ends of the operation that he could at the moment. But it somehow remained after he could think of no other preparations to make.

Finally he closed in on the origin of his ill ease: something the Gray Man had said to Lloyd. Sure, Gentry would have figured out this op against him had to do with his assassination of Isaac Abubaker. But what did he mean by Lloyd being Abubaker's bitch? How could Gentry have known that Lloyd wasn't just an employee of Abubaker, or of the CIA, doing a job? That he did his job for some other reason. Some sort of bargain. Riegel had read the Tech's handwritten transcripts of Gentry's phone conversation with Lloyd earlier in the day, before Riegel was on site. There was no mention by Lloyd or Fitzroy of LaurentGroup or the true reasons behind this endeavor. Why on earth would the Gray Man assume this operation involved some sort of deal between the parties, which clearly the term *bargain* implied? Why on earth would the Gray Man assume Lloyd's life hung in the balance of his success?

It was another full minute of speculation, and when the answer came to Riegel, the sign came to him like it would were he hunting prey on safari. When tracking an animal, a skilled hunter can find indication in the animal's tracks, indications that it knows it is being pursued. It had picked up a scent. It had seen movement. The gait changes when prey senses trouble, and only a uniquely adept hunter can pick up this subtle alteration in his quarry's tracks.

Kurt Riegel was such a hunter.

Gentry had more than a scent of the real operation against him. He had specific details that he only could have gotten one way.

Kurt Riegel spun on the rampart and entered the château. He passed Lloyd, who was stepping out of the bathroom, continued down the corridor with the bearing of a storm trooper.

Lloyd saw the hunter's determination. "What is it? What's wrong?"

Riegel said nothing. He marched down the hall and descended the wide, carpeted staircase to the second floor. He stormed down this hallway, past the sconces and the paintings, past the door to Elise Fitzroy's room, past the bedroom where the kids were locked up. With Lloyd close on his heels, he passed Leary, one of the Northern Irish thugs Lloyd had brought along from LaurentGroup London. The fifty-two-year-old German threw his shoulder into the heavy door Leary was guarding, and it flew open. In the large room beyond, lying on his back in the bed, covered in white linen and facing the door, Sir Donald Fitzroy stared back at the procession of men filing into the room.

Riegel stomped across the room to Sir Donald's bed. He showed none of the courtesy he had displayed in their earlier meeting. His face was that of a man who'd been played for a fool and was out for blood in recompense.

In a hushed voice that was incongruous to his mannerisms, Riegel asked a one-word question. "Where?"

Lloyd and Leary stood back in the center of the room. They looked at one another, searching for some clue as to what was happening.

"What are you talking about?" asked Donald.

Riegel drew his Steyr pistol, pressed it hard to the bald forehead of Sir Donald. "Your *very* last chance." His voice was still a whisper. "Where is it?"

After a brief pause, Sir Donald Fitzroy's arms moved slowly under the covers. Soon a mobile phone appeared. He handed it to the big German.

Riegel did not even look at it. He slipped it into his pocket. "Who?" he asked now, still in a hushed and angry voice.

Sir Donald said nothing.

"It will take me seconds to determine the owner of this phone. You can save yourself some measure of misery by giving me the answer yourself."

Sir Donald looked away from Riegel, across the room to Lloyd, then his eyes drifted to the Northern Irish guard.

"Padric Leary worked for me back in the old days, back in Belfast. You were one of my best touts, Paddy." He looked back to Kurt Riegel. "Still, the wanker shook me down for a king's ransom to make a couple of lousy calls."

As Riegel's fury turned from the Englishman to the Irishman, Fitzroy called out to the stupefied guard, "Sorry, old boy. Don't guess I can come through with the ten thousand quid, after all. You'll just have to take solace in the fact you remain a loyal servant to a nobleman of the Crown."

Leary looked to Riegel. "A bloody lie! There's a right bleedin' Brit for ya! He's bloody lying! Before two days ago I'd never laid eyes on the fooking old bastard!"

"Is this your phone?" Riegel pulled it from his pocket and held it out.

Leary looked at it for several seconds, then began walking towards Fitzroy in his bed.

"How the fook did you get your wrinkled old hands on my—"

A gunshot cracked in the small room. Leary's head snapped forward, and he crashed face-first at Riegel's feet. The German dropped to a knee in a blur of action, raised his weapon in a flash as he went down.

Lloyd stood in the middle of the room, his arm outstretched and a small silver automatic at the end of it. It was still pointed to where the back of the Irishman's head was before the .380 hollow-point round sent it lurching forward.

"Nein!" shouted Riegel in a Germanic scream.

As Lloyd spoke, he waved the gun around the room, used it as a pointer, swung it with his gesticulations. "We have enough problems out there without having to worry about enemies in our midst." He then motioned to Riegel, who was still in a low crouch, eyes on the handgun dancing about the room at the end of Lloyd's arm. "You wanted to treat Donnie boy like a gentleman, and this is how he repays you. You were too soft, and he used that against you. He's been manipulating people since before I was born. That's what he does! Find out who he called and what he said. You do it right now, or I will call Marc Laurent and tell him you are getting in the way of my mission!"

Lloyd lowered the gun and turned. He left the room. After a few more seconds on his knee with his gun raised, still scanning for targets, Riegel holstered his weapon, looked back to Fitzroy, and said, "I'm disappointed."

Fitzroy's voice was surprisingly strong. "I see the desperation, Riegel. I see it in your eyes as well as Lloyd's. This is not only about a contract to siphon and ship natural gas. Abubaker has something else he's holding over LaurentGroup. Some dirt about your past, your practices. Something that, should it see the bright light of day, would blow your organization to pieces."

Riegel looked in a mirror hanging above a large armoire. He fixed his graying blond hair with his fingertips. "Yes, Sir Donald. We've allowed ourselves to be caught up in quite an unenviable predicament. My father used to say, 'If you lie down with dogs, you will wake up with fleas.' Well, we have lain down with many, many a dog for many, many years. Abubaker is one of the worst, and he knows much about what Marc Laurent will do for money and power. Since the decolonization of Africa, the continent's resources have been ripe for exploitation for anyone prepared to dance with a despot. We have had Abubaker in our back pocket for years . . . and now we are in his. He's threatening to talk about the length to which Marc Laurent has gone to take resources from Africa. It's not a pretty story. We'd very much prefer the outgoing president held his tongue."

With that, Riegel started to the door. Without a backward glance, he called out to his prisoner, "I'll send someone to clean up the body."

"Don't bother. When Court gets here, there will be corpses all over the house."

TWENTY-SIX

Five soldiers of Saudi Arabia's Al Mukhabarat Al A'amah, or General Intelligence Directorate, flew west over the Alps in a stolen Eurocopter EC145. The chopper was the property of a local owner-operator who'd made a good living ferrying snowboarders and extreme skiers to otherwise inaccessible peaks on Mont Blanc and other mountains in the area.

Now the sleek black Eurocopter's owner, a former French army major, was dead in his hangar, shot once through the heart with a silenced pistol, and the Saudis flew his craft north over the highway. The road below them rose and fell, weaved and disappeared into alpine tunnels and rushed past bright green forests and lakes so blue the bright sky around them looked positively dull in comparison.

Only the Saudi pilot spoke English. He stayed in sporadic contact with the Tech, an open two-way communication between his headset and the command center that came and went with the jagged peaks on either side of the aircraft. The Tech simultaneously ran other hit teams in the area and relayed reports from the watchers at bus stations and taxi stands. No sign of the Gray Man had been reported since he slipped his coverage just after leaving the financier's home in Geneva.

The A40 is the obvious highway for a traveler to take from Geneva, Switzerland, through southwestern France, into the French heartland. There, at the city of Viriat, one could stay on the A40 to the A6, or one could go northeast on the A39 into Dijon. Either way it is roughly a five-hour drive to Paris, as compared with six or more hours by avoiding these routes.

The Saudis in the helicopter knew where to look for their target. If he came over the roads, they knew he would pass below them on the A40.

They just did not know what type of vehicle they were looking for.

Thirty watchers positioned themselves at overpasses, rest stops, along the highway's shoulders with the hoods up on their vehicles. Others drove along with the traffic. Each pavement artist watched the road, scanned the occupants of as many cars as possible for the most basic profile. It was a large operation to remain concealed to the police, and for that reason and others, Riegel had been against the enterprise entirely. When it became clear Gentry had not boarded a train or taken a bus, Riegel wanted all watchers, all kill teams, and all resources to be pulled back to Paris. He was certain the Gray Man would not bypass Paris altogether. Riegel presumed, and Lloyd did not dispute, that the CIA financier Court met in Geneva had probably supplied him with some equipment, weaponry, a vehicle, medical attention, and likely cash. Also, Riegel supposed that if the Gray Man had time to field a call from Sir Donald Fitzroy, then he had time to get other contacts from the well-connected ex-CIA banker. If Court had made arrangements to pick up men or matériel, he would have no time to go anywhere other than locations already on the way.

Paris was the last major city on his route, and it was chock-full of shooters, document forgers, black-market gun dealers, former CIA pilots, and all other manner of ne'er-do-wells the Gray Man could employ to help him rescue the Fitzroys and take back the personnel files Lloyd stole from American intelligence.

Riegel wanted all the operation's resources to concentrate on Paris, but Lloyd demanded one final choke point ambush set up on the main highway to the north to stop Gentry before he made it any closer to the château.

But Gentry did not take the A40 to the A6, nor did he take the A40 to the A39. These were, by far, the most efficient routes but, Court reasoned, they were only efficient to those travelers not targeted for termination by dozens of killers along these roads.

No, Court decided the operation against him warranted his adding an extra two or so hours' driving time on his tired and hurting body. It would suck, seven full hours behind the wheel just to make it to Paris, but he saw no alternative. Buses and trains were out of the question with all the gear in the trunk he had to transport. He had to drive.

At least he was driving in style. The Mercedes S550 was sleek and solid, and the nearly new interior filled his nostrils with the luxurious scent of fine leather. The 382-horsepower engine purred at eighty-five miles an hour, and the satellite sound system kept Court company. From time to time Gentry put on local radio, struggled with the French to pick up tidbits of information about gun battles in Budapest, Guarda, and Lausanne, and something about a house explosion in the Old Town section of Geneva.

By five in the afternoon, Gentry's exhaustion threatened to run him off the road. He pulled into a rest stop just shy of the town of Saint-Dizier. He filled his tank and bought a ubiquitous French ham and cheese sandwich in a large baguette. He downed two sodas and bought a huge bottle of water after a bathroom visit. In fifteen minutes he was back on the road. His GPS resting on his dashboard told him he would not make it into Paris until nine p.m. Calculating all he needed to do before heading on to Normandy, Gentry determined he'd arrive at the château about two thirty in the morning.

That was, he admitted to himself, only if he did not have any problems in Paris.

"It's time to pull everyone back to the capital," said Riegel. He stood behind Lloyd and the Tech, having just returned to the command center after working for two hours with the two French security engineers on the electronic cordon around the château.

Lloyd just nodded, repeated the German's words to the Tech sitting next to him. He then turned back to the VP of Security Risk Management Operations.

"Where the hell is he?"

"We knew there was the possibility he would take another route. There are a hundred ways he could have gone. A drive through the countryside will delay his arrival to Paris, but it will still get him there."

"*If* he goes to Paris."

"We assume he is not going to attack a defended fortress full of gunmen and hostages by himself. He's going to have to get some help before he comes here, and he has more known associates in Paris than anywhere else. If he stops at all, he stops in Paris. We have all the associates covered. Plus, since he's injured, I've got men at all the hospitals in Paris to keep watch."

"He won't go to a hospital."

"I agree. Probably not. He won't expose himself like that."

"A doctor in Fitzroy's Network, perhaps?"

"Possibly. But the pavement artists are all over the place, staked out at every known contact."

"I don't want him getting out of Paris alive."

"I gathered as much, Lloyd."

TWENTY-SEVEN

Gentry hit the eastern edge of Paris just after nine o'clock on Saturday night. His pains in his feet and knees and thigh and wrist and ribs were only exceeded by his overwhelming fatigue, but still he pushed into town, found an overpriced parking space in an underground garage next to the Gare Saint-Lazare train station. He put all the guns in the backseat, locked the vehicle, and headed up to street level.

He'd had plenty of time to work out his Paris plan of action on the drive and had used the GPS to find a couple of shops in the area. After a few minutes on foot through the cold and misty evening, he hit a McDonald's, pushed through the crowd of kids of all nationalities, and made his way to the bathroom. Here he spent a minute and a half washing his tired face, slicking back his messy hair, using the bathroom, and wiping his clothing with a small gel air freshener.

It was a feeble attempt to clean up, but it was better than nothing.

Five minutes later, he stepped into a men's store on the Rue de

Rome just as the salesman was turning the sign at the door to *Fermé*. Court picked up a high-priced off-the-rack pinstripe suit, black, a white shirt, a muted blue tie, a belt, and shoes. He paid for these at the clothing counter, then headed across the street to a sporting goods shop with his suit bag over his shoulder. Here he bought a full wardrobe of rugged outdoor clothing in subdued browns.

He made his way back out into the street just as the last of the late-night clothing shops shut for the evening, found a pharmacy across from the station, and purchased an electric razor and a straight razor, scissors, shaving cream, and a few candy bars. He took a pair of black-framed costume glasses out of a rack and tried them on, decided they would suit his needs. Just as he stepped up to the counter to pay, he spotted a distinguished-looking long black umbrella hanging off a shelf by its hooked handle. The well-made accessory had caught his eye. Fumbling with his new wares and his other bags, he snatched up the umbrella and paid the bored Asian man at the register.

Just after ten, Gentry hauled all his loot back to the train station, stayed close to the walls, and kept his head down and away from the security cameras around the long, open hall. He ignored a half dozen Bosnian women begging for change and entered an empty bathroom down a hallway from a platform that had accommodated its last train of the evening. He stowed all his bags in a stall and went to work.

Quickly, he stripped to his undershirt and cut his hair. He tried to get as much in the toilet as possible but also laid plastic bags from his clothing purchases on the floor to catch the rest.

Next he used the electric razor to shave his head down to the absolute stubble. The straight razor and cream finished the job. He popped out of the stall twice to check his work in the mirror but retreated back to privacy quickly to avoid arousing suspicion, should someone walk in.

When he finished, he carefully pushed the bags of clippings into the waste bin and then flushed the toilet of hair. With his head cleanly shaved, he washed it again in the sink, quickly put on the suit and the shirt and the tie and the shoes. He slipped on his costume glasses, hefted his distinguished-looking umbrella, and collected the rest of his bags.

Eighteen minutes after Gentry walked into the bathroom, a different man walked out.

The hair and clothing had changed, of course, but also his gait was longer, his posture more erect. Court fought against his desire to limp off his right leg. The suited gentleman descended the stairs back to the parking garage and deposited his bags, retrieved one of the Glock pistols, then returned to the street, just a well-dressed Parisian strolling alone on his way home from a nice restaurant, his umbrella swinging along beside him as he moved with the pedestrians in the November mist. He climbed into a cab on the Rue Saint-Lazare at eleven thirty and instructed the driver in halting French to take him to the Saint-Germain-des-Prés neighborhood of the Left Bank.

Song Park Kim had spotted the Kazakhs by the Notre Dame Cathedral. He had no doubt they were hunters after the same target as he. From his sharp eye they could not hide, and the Korean had no doubt the Gray Man would ID them just as easily. He also passed three or four static surveillance operatives; his training picked them out in the Saturday-evening crowds, but he determined them to be adequately skilled, nonetheless.

Kim knew his target. If the Gray Man were to make a stop-off in Paris at all, he should have arrived by now. His already supersharp senses prickled a bit more as he listened to each dead-end report from the Tech over his earpiece, and the Korean walked from boulevard to boulevard, appearing nonchalant but remaining carefully equidistant to the known associate locations.

Kim walked in complete silence on an empty street. A single Irish pub lit the cobblestones ahead of him; otherwise it was dark, and the Korean used the night as his confederate, moving quickly and comfortably like a nocturnal hunter. At the corner of Boulevard Saint-Michel and Rue du Sommerard he ducked down an alley, found a fire escape he'd spotted earlier in his full day of wandering the city, and leapt high to grab hold. The rucksack on his back swung, the HK machine pistol and the extra magazines causing the olive green bag to hang down as the Korean assassin pulled himself up the rungs. He climbed onto the metal staircase without a sound and scaled up to the sixth floor. Another heave with his strong arms, and he was over the top and on the roof. From here he could see the Eiffel Tower more than a mile away in front of him, the Seine was on his right, and the Latin Quarter all around him, stretching off to his left. The rooftops continued along the Boulevard Saint-Michel, touched one another, and made a path high above the streets below.

This would be Kim's starting point for the evening. If Gentry ventured anywhere on the Left Bank, Kim could move quickly and quietly over this row of buildings or others like it. If the Gray Man showed on the Right Bank, Kim could be there within minutes by dropping down and running across any one of the bridges a few blocks to the north that spanned the cold, swift river, its surface shimmering as it flowed through the City of Lights.

Court Gentry climbed out of his taxi at an Internet café on the Boulevard Saint Germaine. He ordered an hour's Web time and a double espresso from the bar, paid, and then politely nudged his way through the throngs of students towards an open computer at the back. His glasses low on his nose, his cup and saucer in his hands, his fancy umbrella hooked over his arm.

Once online, he opened a search engine and typed in "Laurent-Group properties in France." He clicked on a Web site that showed off the real estate holdings of the huge firm: ports, offices, truck farms, and a Web page for corporate retreats. Here he found Château Laurent, a family property used by the corporation northeast of the tiny village of Maisons in Lower Normandy. Once he had the name, he searched the Web for more information about the property, found a site showing private châteaus of Europe, looked over the glamour shots of the squat seventeenth-century manor house. He committed many of the facts to memory, ignored others that didn't seem so important, like the fact that Mitterrand had shot rabbits on the grounds or that some of Rommel's senior officers had billeted their wives there when in town to make final preparations to the Atlantic Wall.

He wrote the address down with a pen borrowed from a dark-skinned boy sitting next to him, then he surfed to LaurentGroup's corporate Web site. It took him a few minutes to find the address in its corporate holdings—the château was listed just as a satellite office and not a company retreat—but from here Court found the listed phone number to the building. He wrote this on his forearm while the young kid who loaned him the pen laughed and offered him a sheet of paper, which Gentry declined.

Next the American took a few minutes to look at a satellite map of the area around the castle. The layout of the forest, streams running nearby, the orchards behind the 300-year-old stone building, and the graveled country roads outside the encircling wall.

He took one more look at the shots of the structure. A large turret was the high point of the building. Court knew a marksman would lurk there. He also knew there were 200 yards of open ground between Château Laurent and the apple orchard in the back. There was a shorter distance in front of the building, but a higher stone wall and better lighting. He imagined there would be patrolling men with dogs, watchers in the village, and maybe even a helicopter in the air.

Lloyd clearly had the resources at his disposal to protect a mansion from one lousy, limping attacker.

The fortification was not impenetrable; few places were impenetrable to Gentry. But if he left Paris right this very minute, he would not get to Bayeux before two in the morning. He had until eight to rescue the Fitzroys before Lloyd's deadline, but this was false comfort. He knew if he was to have any chance for success, he'd have to make his move in the dead of night when the guard force would be groggy, and reaction times would suffer.

So, even though there were surely ways to breach Château Laurent, Court knew it would be tough to breach without laying up for hours and hours to get a feel for the security measures.

He would not have hours and hours. A couple hours' watch at most before daylight.

And again, that was only if he left Paris right now, and that was not his plan.

At one a.m., Gentry sat in the Café le Luxembourg and drank his second double espresso of the evening among the young and the beautiful on the Rue Soufflot. A small ham sandwich sat untouched on a plate in front of him. The coffee was bitter, but he knew the caffeine would help him through the next few hours. That and good hydration, so he chugged his second five-euro bottle of mineral water while he pretended to read a day-old copy of *Le Monde*. His eyes darted around, but they kept returning to a building across the street, number 23.

Really, Court just wanted to get up and go, get out of town without pursuing his objective in Paris. He knew he would be taking a tremendous risk to pay a visit to the man in the apartment building across the little street, but he needed help, not just for himself but also a way to get the Fitzroys clear. The man across the street was named Van Zan; he was Dutch, a former CIA contracted ferryman, and an awesome pilot of small prop planes. Court had planned to pay him a surprise visit, wave some cash under his nose, grossly underplay the danger in making a five a.m. trip up to Bayeux to pick up a family of four and Court himself, and then fly them low over the channel to the UK. Van Zan was a known associate, so Lloyd would have had his phone tapped within minutes of beginning this operation and would have planted surveillance outside his door. Court knew he couldn't call Van Zan, but he figured he could duck past a watcher or two and drop in for a personal visit.

Yeah, it was a good plan, Court told himself as he gulped bitter espresso and pointed his unfocused eyes at the newspaper in front of his face.

But slowly he realized it wasn't going to happen.

Sure, Court knew he could slip a couple of surveillance goons and make it in to see Van Zan.

A couple, yes.

But not a half dozen.

While sipping his espresso, he'd compromised five definite watchers, and there was another person in the crowd who did not belong.

Shit, thought Court. Not only did he now know there was no way he could get into Van Zan's place to make him an offer, but he was beginning to feel extremely hemmed in and vulnerable, surrounded by a half dozen eagle eyes.

There were two, a young couple hanging out in the Quality Burger across the street. They checked out each white male passerby, then jacked their heads back towards the doorway to the alcove to Van Zan's place. Then there was the man alone in his parked car. He was Middle Eastern, strummed his fingers on the dash like he was listening to music, watched the crowd as they passed. Number four stood at the bus stop in front of the Luxembourg Gardens, like he was waiting for a bus, but he never even glanced at the front of any of the buses that pulled up to see where they were going.

Five stood on a second-floor balcony, held a camera with a lens the size of a baguette, and pretended to take photos of the vibrant intersection, but Court wasn't buying it for a second. His "shots" were up and down the pavement below him and across the street at the alcove. Nothing of the well-lit Panthéon up the road to his left. Nothing of the typically French produce stands and the beautiful iron fencing around the Luxembourg Gardens.

And number six was a woman, alone, in the café just a few tables ahead of Gentry. He'd made sure to get a table towards the back but near the window that ran along the side of the eatery. From here he could keep an eye on everyone in the room with him while covering his face with the paper, and yet still look to his right to Van Zan's place and those around it. She had done the same thing, sitting just ahead.

Number six was slick. She spent 80 percent of her time looking down to her big, foamy mocha, not bouncing every glance out the window. But her mistake was her dress and her attitude. She was French—he could tell by clothes and countenance—but she was alone and did not seem to know anyone in the café. A pretty French girl in her twenties who spent Saturday night alone, away from friends but still out in the crowd, in a café unfamiliar to her, in a part of town she did not know.

No, Court determined, she was a pavement artist, a watcher, a follower, paid to sit there and keep her big doughy eyes peeled.

After eating his little sandwich and finishing his coffee, after giving up on his great plan to set up a foolproof escape route after saving the Fitzroys, he decided he needed to get away, get out of town, get up to Bayeux and work something out. His spirits had ebbed to their lowest point since yesterday morning—he was even more dejected than he'd been when sitting in the moldy pit in Laszlo's laboratory—but Gentry knew the absolute worst thing he could do right now was sit and sulk. He dropped a wad of euro notes on his table and slipped down a back hall to the bathroom. After relieving himself, he continued down the hall, ducked into the kitchen like he belonged, walked straight to a back door and then through it onto the Rue Monsieur le Prince.

No one in the kitchen looked up at the man in the black suit.

The Gray Man had that ability.

Five minutes later, Riegel stood again on the walkway on the roof and stared through the crenellations at the moonlit gardens. The scent of the apple orchard in the distance mixed with the cold darkness. Riegel hoped to clear his head a bit, to get away from Lloyd and the Tech and the Belarusians and the incessant radio reports from the watchers in Paris who had yet to see anyone and the kill squads who had yet to kill anyone. His phone chirped in his pocket. His first inclination was to ignore the call. It was probably one of the foreign intelligence service chieftains wondering why their team hadn't checked in and how the fuck they could have all been wiped out working on a commercial job. Riegel knew he'd spend months or years smoothing over this catastrophe, and that was only if the Lagos contract *did* get signed by eight a.m. If not, and Riegel did not want to even think of this, but if not, he'd likely lose his job or at least his position. Laurent had too much riding on this to not put every possible pressure to bear.

Riegel felt like his head was on the chopping block much like Lloyd's. Not literally like Lloyd. Riegel was certain Laurent would eventually order Riegel to have Lloyd killed if the operation failed. Riegel would not die for this fiasco like the young American, but still, his career would be ruined if his corporation's excesses in Africa were brought to light by that shameless son of a bitch, Julius Abubaker.

The phone rang again. With a sigh that blew vapor into the night, he pulled the phone from his pocket.

"Riegel."

"Sir, it's the Tech. There's a call for you on the landline. I can send it to your mobile."

"The landline? You mean the château's phone?"

"Yes, sir. Wouldn't say who he was. He's speaking English."

"Thank you." A click. Riegel asked, "Who is speaking, please?"

"I am the guy you just can't quite seem to kill."

A chill ran up Kurt Riegel's spine. He did not know Fitzroy had given his name to the Gray Man.

After a moment to collect himself, he said, "Mr. Gentry. It is an honor to speak with you. I have followed your career and consider you a very formidable adversary."

"Flattery will get you nowhere."

"I've been looking over your file."

"Interesting?"

"Very."

"Well, read up, Kurt, because I intend to pull my file out of your cold, dead hands."

Kurt Riegel chuckled aloud. "What can I do for you?"

"I just wanted to make a social call."

"I have hunted all manner of quarry in my life, big and small, including quite a few humans. This is the first time I have had a social conversation with my prey shortly before the kill."

"Same here."

There was a short pause. Then Riegel laughed. His laughter carried across the dark expanse of the château's rear garden. "Oh, *I* am *your* prey now?"

"You know I am coming for you."

"You won't make it, and if you somehow do make it to Normandy, you certainly won't make it to me."

"We'll see."

"We know you are in Paris."

"Paris? What are you talking about? I'm standing right behind you."

"You are a funny man. That surprises me." Riegel said it with a chuckle, but he could not help himself from looking back over his shoulder and at the empty walkway around the château's roof. "We have all your known associates covered with literally dozens of watchers."

"Really? I wouldn't know."

"Yes. You must be going from one old friend to the next. You are identifying my surveillance teams because you are good, but you are not good enough to become invisible. So you must turn away from your potential source of aid. Water, water everywhere, but not a drop to drink."

"Proud of yourself, aren't you?"

"As soon as we see you, we will swoop down. I have nearly as many guns in Paris as I do sets of eyes."

"Lucky for me, I'm not in Paris."

Riegel paused. When he spoke again, his tone had changed. "I want you to know, Phillip Fitzroy's death was a regrettable accident. I was away at the time. It should not have happened."

"Don't bother to try to charm me with professionalism. That won't save you when I come. You and Lloyd both are dead men."

"So you continue to say. You should know, I recovered the telephone Sir Donald took from the guard. Your intelligence source from inside the château has been eliminated."

Court said nothing.

"It's looking bleak for your side, my friend."

"It is. Maybe I'll just walk away. Give up."

Riegel considered this. "I don't think so. When you went south to Geneva, I thought perhaps you were leaving the chase. But no. You are a hunter, as am I. It is in your blood, isn't it? You can't turn away. You have your quarry, your objective, your raison d'être. Without men like Lloyd and me to target, you would be a sorry soul, indeed. You will not walk off into the morning. You will come for us, and you will die along the way. You must know this, but you would rather be killed by your prey than give up the hunt."

"Perhaps we can make an alternate arrangement."

Riegel smiled. "Ah. Now we come to the reason for your call. Not just being social, then. I am listening with interest, Mr. Gentry."

"You will lose the contract. When I am still alive in seven hours, Abubaker will give your natural gas deal to your competitor, and he will use whatever it is he has on LaurentGroup against you. You cannot avoid that. But if you let the girls and their mother go, just get them to a safe place, when I come tomorrow, after the deadline, I will kill Lloyd, do your job for you, but I will spare you."

"Spare me?"

"You have my word."

"In my mind's eye I always pictured you as a two-dimensional predator. A gunman, nothing more. But you are actually a clever fellow, aren't you? You and I could be friends under other circumstances."

"Are you flirting with me?"

"You make me smile, Gentry. But you will make me smile even more when I am standing over your body, another trophy for my case."

"You really should consider my offer."

"You overestimate your negotiating leverage, sir. We will have you within the hour."

A pause. "You'd better hope so. Sleep well, Mr. Riegel."

"I might stay up awhile. I am expecting some good news from my associates in Paris. *Bon soir*, Court."

"*À bientôt*, Kurt. See you soon."

"Just one more thing, Mr. Gentry. Call it professional curiosity on my part. Kiev . . . Not you, was it?"

The line went dead, and Riegel shook in the cold that seemed to have just blown down from the coast, four kilometers to the north.

TWENTY-EIGHT

The watcher was bored, but he was accustomed to boredom. He'd spent twelve hours on the same street corner, sipped espressos in three different cafés, the first two at tables outside in the bright morning and the graying and chilly afternoon, and then lastly inside at a window table as the air filled with vapor and the last of the day's warmth left the street and sidewalk.

At nine he'd moved to his car, a small Citroën parked at an hourly meter that he'd been feeding all day like a hungry pet.

But the watcher was good, and his boredom did not affect his tradecraft. He had the engine running for warmth but did not play the radio; he knew his ears were nearly as likely to pick up any hint of his quarry as were his eyes. The radio would rob from his senses the sharpness needed to pick a man he'd never seen out of a passing crowd of thousands.

He did not know the larger picture of this mission, only knew his role. He was static surveillance. Unlike other watchers on this detail, he was not assigned to a known associate location. Instead, his detail was a general choke point overwatch. He had a photograph of a man, and he was to spend the day trying to match the two-dimensional, years-old, five-by-seven picture to a living, breathing, moving target who would likely be trained in surveillance countermeasures and no doubt flow along in a crowd who would obstruct the watcher's view.

But the watcher stayed optimistic; there was no other way to work. He knew if he doubted he'd see the man, this would detract from the acute senses he needed to bring to bear on his little operation.

The watcher was no killer, just a well-trained pair of eyes. A long time ago he'd been a cop in Nice, then he worked awhile in French counterintelligence as a pavement artist, following Russians or whomever around in leapfrogging details of surveillance, the bottom rung of the espionage ladder. More recently he'd practiced as a private investigator in Léon, but now he was principally an odd-job man for Riegel in Paris. There was always a need for the surveillance of someone on the Continent, and this watcher was usually one of the team. Though he was older than most of the rest, he was no leader. He was better than the rest when he was sharp, but he was a once and future drunk, could not be relied on long-term, though tonight he stayed off the wine and on the mission.

The watcher looked back again, for the thousandth time, to the photo in his hand. It was of no concern to him what the face had done or what fate awaited the face after he'd been spotted.

The face was not a man, just a target.

The face was not alive, did not breathe or think or feel or hurt or need or love.

The face was just a target, not a man.

Identifying a target in the field brought a bonus from Riegel. It did *not* bring even a shred of regret or guilt to the watcher.

Just after one thirty, the watcher pissed into a plastic bottle without missing a drop, also without batting an eyelash at the ignobility of his action among the beautiful people passing by unawares within feet of him on the Boulevard Saint Germaine. He screwed the cap on tightly and tossed the warm bottle to the floorboard and just looked up when a man appeared in the half-light of a streetlamp. He walked along with another group of passersby, but he stuck out somehow to the watcher. He was younger than the others, was not coupled as were they, and his suit was slightly incongruous to their less formal attire. The man was twenty-five meters away when first noticed by the man in the Citroën. As he came closer, the eyeglasses and the shaved head and general facial features sharpened.

The watcher did not move a muscle, only glanced down to the photo clenched and moist and wrinkled in his hand, then back up to the three-dimensional figure closing in the evening fog.

Maybe. At fifteen meters, the watcher squinted, thought he detected a slight limp in the stride. Yes, this man was favoring his right leg. The French-speaking Brit who'd been sending out the updates throughout the day had said the target might have an injury to one thigh.

Yes. When the target moved to his closest point to the Citroën, not more than five meters away, the watcher saw two things about the man's face that clinched his certainty that his choice of choke point and his twelve-hour-long vigil had paid off. There was a wince in the man's cheeks with each step, just a touch, when his right foot touched down.

That and his eyes. The watcher was good, was well-trained; he saw the darting movement of the younger man's eyes as he strolled. Where his body language portrayed a man sashaying through the Left Bank without a care in the world, the eyes were a flutter of constant movement. This man was watching out for watchers, and as soon as the pavement artist in the Citroën noticed this, he broke off surveillance, looked down to his hands until the man had fully passed. With a suddenly ferocious heartbeat, he waited several seconds to glance into his rearview, did not turn his head or lift his shoulders or even flex his neck to do so. Just his eyes flitted up and caught the man in the suit as he moved on, west on the Boulevard Saint Germaine.

The watcher put his car into gear as he pressed a single button on his earpiece.

After a beep indicating his call had been put through, he heard, "Tech, go ahead."

The watcher was trained, was good, but he could not hide the excitement in his voice. This, even more than the money earned from the jobs, was what he lived for.

He said, "Tech, this is Sixty-three." A very slight pause. "I have him. He's moving east on foot." He needn't say more. The Tech would have his location on the GPS.

Moments like this fueled the watcher, kept him off the drink for long enough to see the mission through. He'd done well, he knew it, and now he would go home and celebrate with a jug of wine. And he would celebrate in the same manner in which he worked.

Alone.

The call was broadcast over a net that ensured all five kill teams in Paris would hear the news simultaneously. This was a mistake on the Tech's part; it all but assured discord among the competitors, did not allow for fallback teams and coverage of escape routes. But the young Brit could not help himself; they'd been a half day without a positive sighting of the target, and it was only an educated guess that he would go to Paris at all, so when the ID came through, he just sent every man with a gun towards his location.

He would never admit it to Lloyd or Riegel, but since the target had disappeared in Geneva, the Tech had been fighting a growing wave of panic. He'd run operations, black operations, wet operations, had overseen logistics of hard assets, but never at any jeopardy to himself. This was the first time his superiors had purposefully set up a scenario where the hunted man, an überkiller, had known good and goddamn well where the operation's control center was and how to get there. The bad guy had been given a golden-engraved invitation to come to the Tech's physical location, and that was just fucking stupid. Still, the ponytailed man amid the huge table of technology had to admit, it did have the effect of focusing his skills acutely on the matter at hand.

The Tech had a personal incentive in getting this son of a bitch before he got to the château, and for that reason he'd just broadcast the target's current coordinates as soon as the confirmation had come through.

Lloyd appeared behind him suddenly, just as he was admitting to himself he'd made a stupid move. His superior's proximity made him jump a little. This entire operation made him jumpy.

"Riegel heard on the radio! We've got him?"

"A watcher on Boulevard Saint Germaine, a first-rate veteran, spotted him at a choke point. It was a low-probability sighting, to tell you the truth. Can't tell from his known-associates list where the hell he's going."

"We aren't going to lose him, are we?"

"I'm sending a couple more watchers into the area. Not too many. The Gray Man would surely spot anyone who isn't topflight."

"Understood. Which kill team are you sending to go after him?"

The Tech hesitated, cringed. Surely Lloyd would be furious when he learned they all were on their way. But before the Tech could answer, Lloyd said, "Fuck it. This ends now. Send every goddamned gun you have after this bastard. Who gives a shit if it gets messy? We've got to get his ass right there."

The Tech breathed a sigh of relief that deflated his lungs. "Yes, sir."

The Botswanans and the Kazakhs were closest; they ran from different ends of the Latin Quarter, arms down by their sides to keep their coats from flapping open as they jogged and revealing their weapons, their eyes fixed to the next obstacle in front of them and ears tuned to the radio headsets in their ears. The Tech relayed the last known whereabouts of the target. He was out of the initial watcher's field of view now, but pavement artists were moving closer, and their intel would be relayed.

The Botswanans, five men, each carried sidearms, caliber .32, a relatively weak bullet, but they augmented their marginal firepower with their tactics. These men were trained to execute three-round strings of fire called a Mozambique Drill: a pair of rapid shots to the chest and then a third, coup de grâce, to the forehead. The term and the tactic came from fighting in Mozambique, when a Rhodesian soldier found his small-caliber handgun had trouble downing an African with shots only to the chest, so he added a headshot for added effect.

The four Kazakhs wore small Ingram machine pistols with folding wire stocks under their winter coats. Their running stood out to a policeman, and he called out to them as they sprinted across the street. He took them for foreigners up to no good and made a few hand motions to tell them to slow down.

One member of each kill squad also carried a digital video

camera attached via Bluetooth connection to their mobile phones. This way they could prove to those at the command center that they were the unit responsible for the termination of the subject and the team who warranted the top prize.

This was, after all, still a contest.

Each team knew from their earpieces that the other was approaching the last known whereabouts of the target from the opposite direction; this rushed them as much as the need to close on the target before he disappeared. This was more than a hunt—it was a competition, and to these teams, professional pride meant as much to them as did winning the money.

"All elements, this is the Tech. We have two watchers three blocks east of the last target sighting. Neither watcher has reported any signs of the target. He may have stepped into a hotel or café on the street, turned south into the Latin Quarter, or north towards the Pont Neuf to cross the river."

Both teams, closing from opposite directions, slowed and conferred after getting this last intel from the Tech. Then both teams continued on. The Botswanans ran east on the Saint Germaine, the Kazakhs west on the Saint Germaine. They spread out to cover both sides of the street in groups of two or three, each small team of hunters looking in doorways, alleyways, cafés, and hotels along the way.

Song Park Kim ran along the roofs of the buildings, got ahead of his quarry's last sighting. His earpiece came to life. From the distinctive beeps, the Korean could tell the transmission was not open to the other teams and watchers. He was the only one receiving.

"Tech to Banshee 1, do you read?"

"I read."

"Find a way down to street level, and I will guide you to him. He'll ID the other teams and the watchers and try to get away. They will force him to flee, and he won't be expecting a single assassin. I'll put you in position to stop him."

"Yes."

Kim stepped over the edge of a six-story apartment building's roof, fluidly found footing on a windowsill, lowered himself down, reached across to a drainpipe, and swung his legs over. The pipe was poorly attached to the wall, so he used it only to make his way to a fire escape, followed it down, and dropped the final few feet to the ground, six floors of descent in under a minute.

"Banshee 1 is on the street, Tech. Guide me to the target."

"There are two teams closer than you, Banshee 1. We think he's turned onto the Rue de Buci, sticking with the crowds for security. You can move two blocks north and be in position to cut him off if they don't spot him."

"Yes," said Kim, but he had no intention of following this direction. The Korean felt he could read the Gray Man's thoughts. Kim had been hunted many times, and from this experience, he felt he could divine this hunted man's every move. If teams of foreign agents were following him through central Paris on a Saturday night, Kim would notice, and so would the Gray Man. If dozens of static watchers were placed in his path, Kim would be immediately aware of it, and so would the Gray Man. He might not identify every single adversary, but the Tech had thrown so many bodies into the operation, it would have to be obvious to an operator as skilled as the Gray Man that he was facing a full-on wet operation, that all the stops had been pulled and all normal rules of engagement and restraint were out the window. There would be no safety in a crowd. The gunmen that the Gray Man surely had spotted by now were going to take the first opportunity to destroy their target, and bright lights and passersby would be more hindrance than security blanket to the hunted man.

Yes, Kim could feel what the Gray Man was feeling just now, and he allowed this symbiosis to guide him, not the directives of the Tech. This melding of the minds between Kim the hunter and the Gray Man the hunted steered the Korean assassin through the misty night, three blocks to the east, to a darkened alleyway just a half block off the noise and lights and swarms of diners and revelers. He knew the river Seine was just a hundred meters to the north, meaning if the Gray Man detected the heavy surveillance, he would need to turn south to melt into the night; the north would afford him nothing but a bridge or two, natural choke points that he would avoid at all costs.

Song Park Kim found the darkest spot in the little alleyway, twenty-five meters north of the Boulevard Saint Germaine and twenty meters south of the Rue de Buci. He could move off in either direction in seconds if the watchers spotted the target nearby. But Kim had a feeling this little alley would be the site of his final confrontation with his adversary. There were restaurants and nightclubs brimming with patrons just yards from his darkened hiding space. Plus there were competing kill teams close by. He did not want to draw attention to his act by using a firearm, so he left the MP7 in the backpack on his shoulders. Instead, he pulled his folding knife from his front pocket, flicked open the matte black blade, and tucked his body deeper into the dark to await his prey.

Court Gentry felt his black suit moistening from the sweat running down his back as he walked east on the Rue de Buci. In his right hand his umbrella swung by his side with each step; he fought the urge to use it as a cane because his feet were hurting from the lacerations he'd picked up in Budapest the day before.

But it wasn't the walk that caused him to sweat, it was the eyes scanning the street in front of him. Thirty yards distant he saw a young couple huddled together on a bench, talking to one another but actively checking the male passersby. Court had found a bald-headed man about his own age to follow behind; he kept his eyes ahead of the man to see if he was garnering attention that seemed out of place. This would indicate to Gentry he'd been spotted and identified via radio to other surveillance teams in the area.

Immediately the young lovers fixed on the bald man for a few seconds, one seemed to speak to the other about the man, and then their eyes moved on, satisfied he was not the subject of their surveillance. Court knew immediately he had been compromised. He'd seen at least ten watchers so far and was reasonably sure he'd slipped every one of them, but there must have been someone he missed, some asset static in a dark window or a car on the street or somewhere Gentry could not get a fix on him, and this asset had broadcast Court's appearance and direction to every watcher and hunter in the city.

Quickly, Court chanced a glance back over his shoulder. Three dark-skinned men were moving quickly, looking in a shop window, not twenty meters behind. Across the street there were two more. These guys were part of the same squad, and they were scanning the north side of the street, looking over tables full of diners in front of a café.

Shit. Court turned left down a little passageway off the Rue de l'Ancienne Comédie and followed it in the dark. At its end was dim light from a quiet passage twenty yards on. The watchers would be sparse off the main drag of the Left Bank as long as they didn't know he'd spotted the surveillance on him.

Court walked into the dark, his eyes on the light ahead, the tip of his umbrella scuffing the wet cobblestones. The noise echoed in the black, covered passageway.

Court needed to catch a cab back to the Gare Saint-Lazare, pick up his Mercedes, and head on to Bayeux. This stop in Paris, like the stop in Budapest yesterday afternoon and the one in Guarda last night, had been all but useless. At least this time he had gotten away without being hurt, and that was something, though he really needed more help before—

From the close dark, there was a flash of movement. Quickly from his left came the figure of a man. Before Court's lightning reflexes could react, he sensed further movement low, an arm swinging towards him. Gentry moved his own right arm to parry it, but he was too slow.

He was never too slow.

Court Gentry felt the knife stab into his belly and shear through soft flesh just above his left hip bone.

TWENTY-NINE

At two a.m., a shaft of light poured into the blackened second-floor bedroom. Sir Donald lay awake. The rest of the family had been moved into his room so that they could all be watched over by just one guard. Claire slept fitfully on her grandfather's left; Kate snored on his right. Elise was so medicated it was hard to tell if she was with it or not. She lay sprawled across a chair and ottoman on the other side of the room.

Donald saw the silhouette of the Scottish guard, the one named McSpadden. He figured he was in for a covert beating and wondered if he could take much more.

McSpadden walked up to the bed, ignored the little girls, and whispered to Fitzroy, "I'll do you a deal, old man. Here's a phone. Snuck it out of one of the Ivan's kit bags. They're all at battle stations now; I'm the only one on the floor."

"Bugger off. I'm trying to sleep," said Fitzroy.

"Plenty of time for that come the morning if you're dead."

"You don't think I can smell a trap? Why would a tosser like you just hand me a bloody phone?"

"Because . . . because I want some . . . consideration when this is through."

Fitzroy cocked his corpulent head and pressed it deeper into the pillow to focus on the man standing above him. "What sort of consideration?"

"The Gray Man . . . Heard he did Kiev. If he did Kiev and he did half the other ops they say he did, if he did the team in Prague and Budapest and the teams in Switzerland . . . Hell, he just might make it here. He makes it here, and my gun's going in the dirt, I'm doing a runner. I'm not fighting it out with that cold bastard. Got a couple of things to live for, I do. You understand me? Yeah, he shows up, and I'm doing a runner, and I don't want Donald bleeding Fitzroy or his crazy attack dog coming after me, you see?"

The Scot held out the phone to Fitzroy, and he took it.

"On the level?" asked Fitzroy.

"You're probably dead as dust come the morning, Sir Donald. I'm not sticking my neck out too far. But if you do make it, remember Ewan McSpadden was the one who helped you."

"I'll do that, Ewan."

"Call your dog, tell him if he makes it . . . I'm the bloke with the green shirt and the black trousers. My gun will be in the dirt; he needn't worry about that."

"Good lad, McSpadden."

The Scot receded into the dark; the shaft of light reappeared and then narrowed and extinguished behind him.

The knife dug deeper into Gentry's stomach. The pain was horrific. Knee weakening. Bowel loosening. Something was happening that Gentry didn't understand, so he looked down, saw he'd somehow caught the attacker's wrist with the hook of the umbrella. Gentry pulled down and away on the umbrella's shaft, did not have the strength to pull the knife out of his body, but at least his effort kept the blade from sinking in more than a couple of inches. Painful, excruciatingly painful, but much better than the knife digging in hilt deep or worse, cutting up into his gut like a fish filleted.

With all his might Court pulled down on the umbrella with his right hand. With his left, he reached out at the attacker. He fisted him in the chest weakly, because there was little strength in reserve after the exertion from his right arm and the pain deep in his belly. The assassin punched back, tried a head butt, but Court leaned away from it in time.

Court reached across his body to his waistband, took poor hold of the Glock pistol with his left hand but drew it anyway, just pulled it free of his belt as the assassin knocked it away.

The steel and polymer weapon clanged to the cobblestones, rattled off in the dark.

Their free hands fought one another, the attacker in the dark warding off an attempted eye gouge and Gentry deflecting an open-handed blow to his Adam's apple that would have surely killed him, the tempered steel shaft stabbing into him notwithstanding.

The attacker gave up on trying to yank the knife up to the sternum or push it in deeper; the umbrella's hook on his arm prevented him from accomplishing either task. Instead, the blade cut down, came to rest against the hip bone and gouged into it.

Gentry stifled a scream. He was nearly out of his mind from pain but knew more killers were yards away. Any slim chance he had at survival against the blade in him and the man manipulating it would disappear if more men intent on his demise heard his cries.

Court changed tactics himself. He pushed forward with his legs and shoved his chest into the smaller man, an Asian he could clearly now see. He slammed him into the wall, which only served to jab the knife in him a fraction of an inch deeper.

Court followed this with a head butt that slammed the two men's foreheads together with a crack louder than any other sound in the alleyway since the fight began. The umbrella still held the Asian's right hand down. Court pushed again with his body, and the Asian stumbled backwards all the way across the alley and slammed into the other wall. Court was still attached by the knife's blade, so he moved along with his attacker. The light was better over here and, through the agony that threatened to cloud his mind to mush, Court saw the straps of the backpack and realized the man was now trying to take hold of something behind him in the bag with his free hand.

Court grabbed the Korean's wrist with his own free hand and slammed it back into the brick wall.

"What'cha got?" Court asked, his voice quavering with pain and exertion. "What's in the bag?" There was enough light for eye contact on this side of the covered alley, and their eye contact did not waver, though both men's lids twitched with the expenditure of effort. One pushed forward, the other pushed back. "What's in the bag?"

Gentry yanked sideways with the umbrella, pulled the Asian quickly off balance, used the moment to reach behind the man to the pack pressed against the wall. The American had to tighten his abdominals to do so, and his voice cracked as he groaned in agony.

The Asian turned the knife; the two-inch-deep wound opened

with the twist and Gentry felt blood run freely across his crotch and down the insides of both legs.

"Ahhh." It was quieter than a scream, but it echoed in the alleyway nonetheless. Court had the bag now and got a hand on a zipper. Kim knocked the hand away with the side of his head. Another head butt from Gentry stunned the assassin, and Court quickly opened the top of the backpack and reached inside with his left hand.

"What's this? What's this?" he asked as tears began streaming down his face. The tears dripped into the spit that sprayed from his sobbing mouth as he spoke. The discharge flew into his attacker's face with his words. "This what you want? This what you're after? Huh?" Court pulled the end of a small black sub gun from the bag, stared into the new fear in the eyes of his adversary. Kim reached back and got his hand around the squat suppressor of the weapon, then pushed harder on the knife hilt. Court tried to back off of the blade but could not, and the shaft sank another millimeter into his gut.

Court slid his finger into the trigger guard and fired the MP7. Kim had left the fire selector switch on semiauto, just as Gentry would have. The barrel was pointed at the brick wall behind Kim, and rounds exploded off the masonry and debris whizzed around them both. As fast as he could, Gentry pulled the trigger. Each ignition of a cartridge in the breach caused recoil, which made Court's body jerk, which allowed the knife in his gut to bite into a new morsel of flesh and bone. Three rounds, five rounds, ten rounds, twenty rounds. Kim screamed in agony and let go of the weapon's silencer, nearly white-hot now from the gunfire. He wrapped his burned hand around the hand that held the knife, and now with both clenched fists and all his might, he tried to force one last, fast, massive thrust of the blade through to the Gray Man's spine.

The American's blood pumped over his scorched fingers.

Gentry brought the empty HK down in one quick action, smashed the hot barrel into Kim's face, breaking his nose.

Both men fell to the cobblestones, their connection finally broken. Kim lay on his back, head against the bullet-pocked wall, blood gushing out his nose, and his burned hand cradled in his lap. His chest heaved from exertion. Gentry lay on his side in the center of the alley, his chest also heaving, the black hilt of the black knife jutting obscenely from his lower abdomen.

Court tried to pull the knife free, cried out as he did so. The Asian, exhausted and stunned from the concussion, clambered to his knees and frantically crawled across the cold stones to close the distance between them.

At five feet he leapt into the air, desperate to get his hand on the knife before the Gray Man pulled it out of his stomach.

An instant before he landed on his target, the full length of the black knife's blade appeared in the low light, slick, wet with blood. Court slashed it backhanded across the wide-eyed Asian's throat as he came down. Arterial blood spewed forth.

Song Park Kim thrashed in the alleyway and died in seconds, his lower torso ending up across the Gray Man's body.

Gentry dropped the knife on the cobblestones and pushed the dead man's still-spasming legs off him. The body rolled unceremoniously onto its back, and all movement ceased. Court unfastened his tie with one hand and wadded it into a ball. He took a couple of deep breaths to steady himself and then pressed the ball down into the hole in his abdomen. Blood ran down his white shirt onto the pavement.

"Jesus!" he screamed, tears and spit and snot covering a face contorted with pain. He felt the nausea brought on by abject agony but quelled it by focusing on his work.

Normally he was careful about his DNA, but now he didn't bother.

It would take a bathtub of bleach, a five-man cleaning crew, and a full day to sanitize this scene, and Court had nothing of the sort.

The pressure of the wadded necktie actually reduced the pain when he flexed his abs; without it, he would not have been able to stand. But he did stand, stumbled, steadied himself on the alley's wall, and shuffled on. He heard voices behind him. Passersby had been alerted by the noise of the scuffle. Police and killers would be here in seconds. He stumbled around the corner to a shopping passage. The stores were closed for the night, and there were no window shoppers. With his body slumped over, his face white, he staggered away from the orgy of blood behind him.

He moved north off into the cold night, his life's blood draining down his leg and dripping onto the paving stones at his feet.

Thirty seconds later, one of the Botswanans shoved his way through a panicking crowd and found the Korean's body, the dark alley a blood-dripping horror show in the beam of light from the African assassin's tactical flashlight. He called it in to the Tech.

"There is a dead man here. He is Asian. Nearly decapitated."

Lloyd and Riegel stood behind the Tech as the Botswanan assassin's accented English came over the speakers.

Mr. Felix entered the room, stood back in the shadows, and watched intently.

The Tech flipped a switch on his bank of electronics in front of him. "Banshee 1. Do you read? Banshee 1, how do you copy?"

There was a shuffling sound on the speaker. Lloyd and Riegel looked up in hope.

"He can't come to the phone right now, don't bother to leave a message," said a mocking African voice. The Botswanan had obviously pulled the radio set off the dead Korean and was speaking into it.

Riegel said, "The Korean was probably the best man we had on this job. His organization is going to be furious he was lost on this operation."

"Fuck 'em," snapped Lloyd. "They should've sent us someone who could complete the task. When they gave us only one man, I knew their heart wasn't in this game."

"You are an idiot, Lloyd. Do you have any idea what that assassin has done in his career?"

"Sure do. He left a greasy stain in a Paris alleyway. The rest I couldn't give a flying fuck about."

Just then the Botswanan hunter came back over the speakers. "There is a blood trail leading north. We'll follow it; we'll find him."

"You see," said Riegel. "Banshee 1 served his purpose."

Three minutes later, a watcher came over the net. "Fifty-four to Tech."

"Go ahead, Fifty-four."

"I'm in a fourth-floor window near the Place Saint-Michel. I believe I am tracking the subject on my camera. I can send it to you for verification."

It took ten seconds to make the connection. When the plasma monitor in the control room sparked to life, the lights of Paris shone brightly, silhouetting the Notre Dame Cathedral. The Seine was a glimmering ribbon bisecting the city. The camera did not seem to be centered on anything in particular.

"Where is he?" shouted Riegel the hunter, wild from the chase now, frantically searching for his quarry. "Fifty-four, tighten up on the subject!"

"Oui, monsieur." The image zoomed to the Pont Neuf bridge that ran over the river to the cathedral. A lone figure in a dark suit hobbled, stumbled, stopped, and stooped in the middle of the bridge. Clearly the man was wounded, fleeing, trying to cross from the Left Bank to the Île de la Cité, the tiny island in the middle of the Seine upon which the cathedral of Notre Dame stands.

"Look at him. He's toast!" shouted Lloyd with excitement. "Who do we have close by?"

The Tech answered before Lloyd finished posing the question. "The Kazakhs are thirty seconds out. You'll see them coming up the bridge from the south. The Botswanans are close behind them, and the Bolivians are to the north of the Seine. The Sri Lankans are still ten minutes west."

The video image widened enough to see the buildings on the Quai des Grands Augustins, the Left Bank road that rimmed the Seine. Several men sprinted along the road and turned right onto the bridge. One of them slipped on the wet cobblestones and fell, but the others held their footing and raced up the incline of the Pont Neuf.

"This is it!" Riegel proclaimed victoriously. "Tell them to finish him, get the body into a car and on the way to the heliport. We'll have it ferried here for Mr. Felix to see up close."

"That would be satisfactory, Mr. Riegel, thank you," said Felix, standing like a statue behind the animated men in front of the bank of monitors.

The watcher's camera tightened back in on Gentry. He'd turned around and was facing the Kazakhs, who were not more than forty yards away now. The injured American stood upright, though it obviously pained him to do so. He looked back over his shoulder to the other end of the bridge.

Lloyd said, "You won't make it, Court. You can't run anymore. You are so fucked." There was mirth in his voice.

But Riegel muttered, "Shit."

"What's wrong?" asked Lloyd.

"*Scheisse,*" Riegel repeated himself in German.

"What's wrong with you? We've got him!"

Just then, the Gray Man stepped to the cement railing. He looked back up to the men closing on him, twenty-five yards off.

"No!" said Lloyd, understanding Riegel's worry. "No, no, no, no—"

Kurt Riegel pulled the microphone off the Tech's table, jammed the button down, and shouted, "*Schiest ihn sofort!*" He caught himself speaking German in his excitement. He screamed, "Shoot him now!"

But it was too late. Court Gentry tipped himself over the railing, fell thirty feet to the shimmering water, its crystalline surface exploding as his body crashed through it, his dark form disappearing as the current re-formed into a swiftly flowing mirror.

Lloyd spun away from the monitor. He put his hands on his head in shock. Then he turned to Felix, who remained silently behind.

"You saw that! You saw him! He's dead!"

"Falling into water does not kill a man, my friend. I'm sorry. I need confirmation for my president."

Lloyd turned back to the Tech and screamed loud enough to be heard all over the château, "Goddammit! Tell them to get their asses in the water! We need his corpse!"

The image on the plasma screen showed the Kazakhs converging on the portion of the Pont Neuf just vacated by the target not five seconds earlier. They all looked over the side. Five men were on the bridge. Two jumped over the railing and dropped into the cold, black water, while three ran back to the Left Bank.

Riegel belted out instructions to the Tech. "He's injured badly, and that fall didn't help him. Get the Botswanans there; move the Bolivians and the Sri Lankans, too. Put somebody in a boat in case his body doesn't wash up immediately. Brief everyone to search both banks. Move all the watchers downstream to hunt for where he washes up. We need his body, and we need it now!"

THIRTY

At two thirty a soft rain began to fall. Five hundred yards east-southeast of the cathedral of Notre Dame, on the Left Bank of the Seine, the Jardin Tino Rossi was barren in the dark. Fifty feet from the cobblestone quay, a grassy embankment ran along next to a low stone wall. There, between a tree and the wall, a figure lay on its back, knees raised slightly and arms askew. Anyone who walked up to the water-logged body would see it had obviously come from the river. Perhaps a defiant final jolt of strength had allowed its weak arms to crawl clear of the river's edge into the soft, wet grass; maybe it even found its feet for a moment, but then those arms and legs must have given out wholly, and the body had collapsed on the cold ground.

There was no movement at all from the body, no sound either, until an electronic noise began peeping, muffled by soaked clothing.

The body did not stir at once. Finally a twitch in the shoulders, a slight turn of the head in new recognition of its surroundings. After another ring, the form slowly reached into a coat pocket, pulled out a plastic case, and fumbled with it with one hand. It popped open, and the satellite phone dropped into the grass. The body's eyes remained on the sky.

After jumping from the bridge, Gentry had hit the water hard. The cold took away what breath remained in his lungs after the impact. He sank deep. When he found the surface, he had already been carried downstream, under the Pont Neuf and towards the west. He sucked air and water as he bobbed for a minute or so before seeing a small house barge churning upstream towards him. Though Court was weak, on the verge of losing consciousness, he hooked an arm around the bottom rung of a ladder hanging off the side of the slow-moving black boat as it passed him. He held on with one hand, kept his head low in the boat's foamy wake as the craft towed him back under the bridge from which he had just fallen. He heard the shouts of men in the water around him as they dove down, looking for a body, or trained their flashlights around the spans of the bridge.

Ten minutes later, Court was free of immediate detection. With nearly his last ounce of strength, he tried to climb the ladder to get on board the boat, but he fell. His weak legs, the pain in his gut, his wet shoes, the numbing cold all worked against him, and he dropped back into the frigid current. He reached out for the barge, took nothing but a fistful of the river, while the black ship chugged away upstream.

Fortunately for Gentry, he was not far from the water's edge. He made it to the Left Bank, struggled up onto the pavement, climbed to his feet, but fell again in the wet grass next to a tree in the Jardin Tino Rossi.

And here he lay for twenty minutes, eyes open but unfixed, the soft drops of rain falling and beating and exploding against his pupils.

The phone rang again, and he lifted it off the grass, his eyes still on the impossibly low rain clouds illuminated by city lights around him.

His voice was weak and distant. "Yeah?"

"Good evening. This is Claire Fitzroy calling. May I please speak with Mr. Jim?"

Gentry blinked away the rain. His eyes instead filled with tears. He controlled his voice as best as possible, did what he could to mask the pain and the exhaustion and the despair and the utter sense of failure. "It's past your bedtime."

"Yes, sir. But Grandpa Donald said I could call you."

"You remember me?"

"Oh, yes, sir. I remember how you drove us to school. Slept on the little cot in the hall, but Mummy said you didn't really sleep, you watched out for us all night. You drank coffee, and you liked my mummy's eggs."

"That's right. Extra cheese." Court's pelvic bone had been gored, his abdominal wall punctured. He did not think the knife made it deep enough to slice through his intestines, but the pain burning into the center of his being was indescribable, nonetheless. He assumed he was still bleeding. He'd done nothing to stanch the flow since he'd dropped into the river nearly an hour earlier.

The sirens of emergency vehicles screeched past on Gentry's right. He was hidden from their view by the stone wall and the darkness.

"Mr. Jim, Grandpa Donald said you are coming to save us."

Tears streamed down the American's face. He wasn't dead, but this felt a lot like dying. He knew he could not make it to Bayeux, and even if he somehow could, what could he do but bleed to death on the castle's doorstep?

"Where is your grandfather?"

"He's in the bedroom. He can't walk right now. He said he fell down the stairs, but that is not true. The men here hurt him. He gave me the phone and told me to go into the bathroom closet and call you." She paused. "That's why I have to whisper. You are coming, right? Please tell me you are coming. If you don't come . . . You are our only chance, since Daddy's gone to London. Mr. Jim . . . are you there?"

Typical of Fitzroy. If Sir Donald himself had made this call, Court would have told him all was lost. But the cagey bastard had known Gentry would be in dire straits right about now, so who better to entice him to keep up the fight than one of the twins?

"I'll do my best."

"Do you promise?"

Court lay there in the dark, his freezing, soaked suit askew on his body, the cold mud pressed into the back of his neck and his shaved head. Slowly, with a weak voice, he said, "I'll be there very soon."

"Do you promise?"

Court looked down at the wound in his belly. He pressed hard upon it now. "I promise," he said, and he seemed to muster a little power in his voice. "And when I get there, I need you to promise you will do something for me."

"Yes, sir?"

"When you hear a lot of noise, I want you to go to your room, crawl under your bed, and stay there. Can you do that for me?"

"Noise? What kind of noise? Do you mean guns?"

"I *do* mean guns."

"Okay."

"Stay there until I come to get you. Get your sister to do the same, okay?"

"Thank you, Jim. I just knew you would come."

"Claire." There was a shred of new strength in Gentry's voice now.

"I need you to sneak the phone back to your grandfather. I have to ask him a very important question."

"All right, Jim."

"And Claire? Thank you for calling. It was nice to hear from you."

Sixteen minutes later, Gentry staggered along the Rue du Cardinal Lemoine. The rain had picked up, and there was no one around, which was lucky for the Gray Man, because he walked with both hands pressed to the left side of his abdomen, his left leg ramrod straight as he kicked it forward. Every twenty-five yards or so he stopped, leaned against a wall or a car or a lamppost, bent forward from pain, recovered after a few seconds to push off and cover a few more steps before again seeking refuge from the exhaustion of the blood loss.

He found the address Fitzroy gave him. The door was closed and bolted as he knew it would be, so he found a dark alcove a few doorways down and tucked into it, sat on a piece of cardboard like a bum, and leaned his head on the stoop to rest. Singsong police sirens wailed in the distance, maybe a mile away now. Surely the cops and the hitters and the watchers were all along the Seine looking for him, though hopefully they were concentrating their search not upstream but down, and hopefully they were all hindering one another with their respective presence.

He was just on the verge of dozing, his fist pressed into his bloody stomach, when he heard a noise back by the address Fitzroy gave him. He peered out of the alcove and saw the locked door open slowly. He'd expected someone to come by car, but apparently whoever worked at the location lived in a flat above in the same building.

A woman appeared on the pavement, barely visible from a streetlamp twenty meters on. Court rose to his feet and staggered forward.

"Allez!" she shouted in a whisper. "Hurry."

He passed her, staggering still, and found himself in a long hall. Steadying his weak and swaying body on the corridor's walls, he saw immediately he was smearing his own blood with his hands as he walked. The woman quickly tucked her head under his arm and hefted him. She was tall and thin but strong. After each step he felt himself giving in to her more and more.

They went through a doorway and into a darkened room. Before she could flip on the light, encumbered by the 170-pound man, Court was startled by a barking dog, close. Then another, then ten or more dogs barking at once, all around him.

When the bright overhead snapped on, he realized immediately that the emergency clinic Donald had sent him to was, in actuality, a veterinarian's office. His knees gave out, and his weight dropped on the girl by his side. With a boyish grunt she pushed him forward and down to a small chair.

"Parlez vous français?" she asked, looking down to him. He looked up and saw, apropos of nothing, that she was rather pretty.

"Parlez vous anglais?" he asked.

"Yes, some. You are English?"

"Yeah," he lied, but he had no intention of trying to fake an accent.

"Monsieur. I tried to tell Monsieur Fitzroy. Zee doctor is out of town, but I called him; he's on his way here now. He will arrive in a few hours. I am sorry, I did not know how badly you were hurt. I cannot help you. I will call an ambulance. You need a hospital."

"No. You are in Fitzroy's Network. You at least have medicine and blood and bandages."

"Not here, I am sorry. Dr. LePen has access to a clinic nearby, but I do not. I only work here with zee animals. You need a hospital. You need emergency aid. *Mon Dieu*, you are cold. I will find you a blanket."

She turned from him and left the room, returned with a thick wool blanket that smelled like cat piss. She draped it over his shoulders.

"What is your name?" Court asked, his voice at its weakest point yet.

"Justine."

"Look, Justine. You're a vet. That's close enough. I just need some blood and—"

"I am a veterinary's assistant."

"Well, that's *close* to close enough. We can make this work. Please help me."

"I give baths! I hold zee dogs down for zee doctor! I can't help you. Zee doctor is on his way, but you cannot wait for him. You are completely white. You need blood. Fluids."

"I don't have time to wait. Look, I know battlefield medicine. I can talk you through what I need. We'll have to get some blood, just a couple units of O positive, some antibiotics, and your hands. When the weakness and pain get to be too much, I won't be able to do what needs to be done."

"Battlefield medicine? This is no battlefield. This is Paris!"

Court grunted. "Tell that to the guy who did this." He opened the blanket and took his hand from his knife wound. His blood pressure was low enough now to where the blood no longer pumped from his waist, but it oozed and glistened in the harsh light of the treatment room.

Justine gasped. "That looks bad."

"Could be worse. It's through the muscle, bloody, but I'll be okay if I can get some O positive. If you can help me, I'll be on my way. Fitzroy will pay you and your doctor for the trouble."

"Monsieur. Are you not listening? I work with zee dogs!"

He shut his eyes, seemed to drift off a bit, but he said, "Just picture me with fur."

"How can you joke? You are bleeding to death."

"Only because we're arguing. Where is this clinic? We can go there, get what I need. I can't go to a hospital. Have to do it this way."

She breathed out a long sigh, nodded, and tied her brown hair in a ponytail behind her head.

"Let me put a bandage on that so you do not lose more blood."

The barking of the dogs began to subside.

The small surgical center in the vet's office was filthy. It had not been well cleaned after the close of business on Friday.

"I am sorry, monsieur. If I knew you were coming—"

"It's fine." Court made to pull himself onto the metal stand in the middle of the room, but Justine stopped him, grabbed a spray bottle, and perfunctorily wet and wiped down the brushed aluminum surface while her patient leaned against a shelf of bandages. She ran out through the door and came back with a cushion from the sofa in the waiting room.

"You must let your legs hang off zee side. It is not made for persons."

"Okay."

He used his last bit of strength to rip open his shirt. Buttons flew and bounced over the tiled room. Justine pulled off his rain-soaked shoes and used shears to cut his pants off, left him in his shorts.

"I . . . I am not so experienced with humans," she said.

"You're doing great."

She fought her timidity and looked Gentry over from head to toe.

"What happened to you?"

"I got shot in the leg. A couple of days back."

"With a gun?" She looked down at the open three-day-old wound in his thigh, then back up to the bloody hip. She quickly pulled rubber gloves on over her small hands. "*Mon Dieu.*"

"And then my legs and feet got cut with broken glass."

"I see that."

"Then I snapped a rib rolling down a mountain in Switzerland."

"A mountain?"

"Yes. Then I fucked up my wrist busting out of some handcuffs."

Justine was silent. Her jaw had dropped open slightly.

"And your stomach?"

"Knife wound."

"Where?"

"Here in Paris. About an hour ago, I guess. And then I fell into the Seine."

She shook her head. "Monsieur, I do not know what you do for a living, and I do not want to know. But whatever it is, I think you should find some other type of job."

Court laughed a little, setting fire to the stab wound. "My skill set is not conducive to honest work."

"I'm sorry. I do not understand these words."

"Never mind. Justine, we can stanch the knife wound with this bandage, more or less, but if I don't get some blood in me, I'll pass out."

"The clinic is close by, but it is closed."

"We're going to open it," Court said. "Let's go. I need to be on the move in under an hour."

Justine had been wrapping a compression bandage tight around Court's waist to hold the thick square of gauze she'd placed over the knife wound. "Move? You don't need to move at all! For days. Do you not understand how badly injured you are?"

"*You* don't understand. I have someplace I have to be! I just have to get patched up so I can leave!"

She clenched her teeth, and her eyes widened. "Monsieur, I am no doctor, but I can promise you there is no place you need to be right now other than in medical care. You could die within zee hour."

"I'll be okay. I have to be."

Justine knelt down, unlocked a low cabinet, and began pulling equipment from it. "That is impossible! If we give you a transfusion, zee blood will just leak out of your stomach if you move. You need stitches. When you get the stitches they will just break if you try to move."

Court thought it over. He looked down to his wristwatch to find it was three a.m. "I . . . I need to get to Bayeux, up in Normandy."

"Tonight? Are you crazy?"

"It's life or death, Justine."

"Yes, *your* death, monsieur."

Court pulled Maurice's envelope of cash from his pocket. It was soaked, but it was a miracle it had survived the river, as had his car keys. He handed the soggy envelope to Justine. "How much is it?" he asked as she looked through it.

Her eyes returned to his. "It's a lot."

"It's all yours. Just help me get to Bayeux before eight a.m."

"If you can't even drive a car, what do you expect to do when you get there?"

"I can drive the car, but I need you to stitch me up and bandage me while I drive. We can do the transfusion on the way."

She stood slowly. Said each word alone. "Sutures? In, zee, car?"

Court nodded.

"While you drive zee car?"

"Yes."

She muttered something in French that Court did not understand. He picked up the word for *dogs* and figured she was saying it was due to moments like these that she preferred her patients to be the four-legged variety.

She tied the bandages around his waist and helped him put his wet dress shirt back over his shoulders. She did not look up from her work as she spoke. "What is going on in Bayeux early on a Sunday morning that you absolutely cannot miss?"

"Would you believe me if I told you I was singing in the church choir?"

She shook her head without smiling. "No."

"Okay. Then I will tell you." And he told her. He told her with holes in his story jumbo jets could fly through about what had happened and what he had to do by eight a.m. He told her about the kidnapped girls and the father who died trying to protect them. He told her about the teams of foreign operatives after him, and as the blood loss and fatigue addled his brain, he told her again about the phone call from Claire and again about the little kids he just had to protect.

She reacted with horror when he talked of the killers and the killing, the mortal peril of two little girls for the sake of the reputation of some thuggish corporation. Yes, Justine worked for a doctor of veterinary medicine who occasionally kept some strange hours and dealt with some highly suspicious patients, and the doctor had told her enough about Fitzroy and the Network to where she knew to ask no further questions, but she never imagined in a million years that men were as brutal and as callous as those in the stranger's story.

"So . . . what do you think?" asked Court.

"Why are you trusting me?"

"Desperation. I was dead on the riverbank forty-five minutes ago. Since that moment, you have become my only hope. If you double-cross me, I am no worse off than I was lying there."

"What about the police?"

"Lloyd says he will kill the hostages if anyone but me shows up at the house. I know men like this. They will do exactly what they threaten to do. I have to go alone, with your help. I'll leave you in Bayeux. My destination is a few kilometers north of the village. You can be on the morning's first train back to Paris. You'll be miles from any danger, I promise you."

"What do I call you?" she asked.

"Jim."

"Okay, Jim. We will go on one condition."

"What's that?"

"Let me give you a little pain medicine, just for the procedure. We'll find something at zee clinic that we can give you once the transfusion brings your blood pressure back up. We will take my car. I will drive to Gare Saint-Lazare to get your car. Then we can go. There will be no traffic on zee road once we leave town. I will work on your injury as you drive."

Court thought about it. Every fiber of his being was against taking any medication that would cloud his mind and dull his senses, leave him less than completely focused on the task at hand. He felt he could handle the pain.

No, he did not like Justine's plan, but for some reason he *did* trust her. And as he looked at the cute, gangly girl standing over him, still pretty with her ponytailed hair messy from her bed and no makeup on her face and sweat forming above her lip from the work she was doing to keep some scary stranger alive, he conceded he was in absolutely no position to argue.

Justine helped Court back to his feet, and the two of them staggered together slowly out of the treatment room and down the hall towards the back of the clinic. Gentry winced with each step. Once his head bobbed low as if he would pass out.

Justine propped him against the wall in the courtyard while she fumbled with her keys.

"What the hell is this?" Gentry asked.

"It's my car."

"That's a car?"

"What's wrong with it?"

"It's small."

"When I bought it, I didn't know I would be transporting patients in the passenger seat."

"Fair enough. It's fine. It sure as hell won't draw much attention."

They both smiled a little, but the smiles drifted away as she tried to help lower him into the seat. Court cried out in pain, a cry that culminated with shallow panting.

It took her nearly a minute to fire the little engine. By then Court was asleep. She'd dropped his seat to where he could lie almost flat. With considerable effort, she was able to get his legs up on the dashboard to help keep him from going into shock. As she turned north on Rue Monge, she saw helicopters in the air in the distance over the river.

Justine parked her car a few doors down from the clinic off the Rue des Ecoles. At half past three, there was not a soul around. Court stirred, looked around for a moment, and then asked her for a pen and a piece of paper. She dug through her purse a moment and then passed him an envelope and a pencil.

"There's another med I need you to find. Should be with the pediatric drugs."

"One of the twins needs medicine?"

"No. It's for me." He jotted something down and handed the envelope back to Justine. She looked at it.

"DextroStat? What does it do?"

"It will help. It's very important. Find it."

She shrugged, promised to look for it. Without another word to Court, she climbed out of her tiny Uno and went back to the trunk. Gentry did not, could not, turn around to see what she was doing. A few seconds later she walked to the glass door of the building and looked quickly in both directions. A tire iron in her right hand crashed through the glass, and she reached through the sharp shards to open the door from the inside. As Court watched, completely helpless, she disappeared into the dark clinic as a piercing alarm filled the street.

Even with the impending danger, Court fell asleep again in the car. He awoke with the jolt of the tiny two-door as it lurched forward. In the glow from the streetlamps flickering above them as they moved away from the alarm bells, he caught a glimpse of the young woman's face: intensity and determination.

"What did you get?" he asked.

"Three units of O positive, two bags of dextrose, morphine, Vicodin, transfusion equipment, antiseptics, and a suture kit."

"And?"

"And the medicine you asked about."

"Well done."

"Yes," she said with a little smile. "That was fun."

In the parking garage below the Gare Saint-Lazare, Justine and Court climbed into the big Mercedes. Gentry took the wheel and sat there, woozy and grimacing from agony. Justine began the transfusion of blood and a bag of nutrients as they sat together in the dark and empty garage. She hooked the bags on the dome light above them to keep the drip going and the supple black leather interior gave way to the French girl's movements as she knelt over Court, poured antiseptic freely on his waist to let it soak into his bandages and his wounds.

Justine instructed Court to just lie there and relax, and she left the car. She disappeared from his view while he sat alone and tried to think about the task still at hand. He knew these delays meant he would not make it to the château before six in the morning. He would have virtually no time to lay up and get a feel for the territory. No, as it now stood, he'd only have time to drive up to the front door and begin his attack if he wanted to do so under cover of darkness. Shit. Court realized his chances for success were never good, but after the stabbing in Paris, they had now become incalculably small.

Just then Justine returned with a bag of pastries and two large servings of coffee. Court pulled one foam cup from her hand and swigged it until his mouth burned.

"*Arrêt! Stop,*" she demanded. "Sip it slowly."

Court took a croissant and ripped into it with abandon. She tried to butter it for him while he ate, but he just took the little pat of butter from her hands and gobbled it down, too.

Justine lectured him. "Your mother would not be proud. Relax. You are getting the fluids and nutrition you need from the IV. Too much food with the morphine, and you will throw up. Drink the coffee slowly. Can you drive?"

"We're about to find out," Court said with a look of grim determination, and he backed the Mercedes out of the space, exited the underground garage slowly, and rolled out into the night.

They took the A15 north out of the city, and just as Justine had promised, there was virtually no traffic at four on a Sunday morning. She cursed loudly when she noticed the blood bag empty just a few minutes out of town; she switched it out with a second full liter bag and switched out the dextrose just to keep the fluids dripping into the IV at the fastest rate possible.

The A13 was the most direct route to Bayeux, but Court avoided it. He knew surveillance could easily be set up on the main route to the château. Instead, Court took a series of back roads that would add a half hour or so to his journey.

For an hour they delayed the inevitable. Justine talked about her family and friends and her six cats. Her nervousness was evident to Court from her random conversation. With less than an hour to go till the château, Justine grew quiet, carefully injected a tiny dose of morphine into Gentry's IV. If his blood pressure was too low, as it surely had been back at the vet clinic, the morphine could have stopped his heart. But after two and a half units of blood, she determined a small shot of the strong painkiller was worth the risk, considering what he was about to endure.

As they drove through the dark, Court began feeling better, the pain medicine and the blood and the sugar water boosting his strength and spirits. They discussed the procedure, and Justine took several minutes to ready her sutures and bandages on the dashboard in front of her. She cringed as she threaded the razor-sharp hooked needle and dipped it in a bottle of antiseptic, laid it down on sterile gauze. She opened his shirt and cut off his bandages and poured half the contents of the bottle on his stomach, and he recoiled from the sting.

They both unfastened their seat belts, and she rose to her knees in the passenger seat. Gentry put his hands high on the wheel to allow her access to his belly. He gulped down the last few swigs of cold coffee and tossed the cup over his shoulder into the back. Justine then used adhesive tape to fasten Court's small flashlight to the bottom of the steering wheel, lighting the area of her focus perfectly as long as she was careful to keep her hands from casting shadows over the stab wound.

"I have never done this before on a human, even in the correct conditions, but I have sutured cats before."

"You will do fine," Court said. He realized they were both trying to steady the nerves of the other.

But Justine's resolve faltered first. She looked up at the American and asked, "Are you sure? I will have to go deep into the muscle to close the wound. If I just pierce the skin it will tear as soon as you move."

Court nodded, his eyes already watering in anticipation of the agony. "Justine," he said, softly. "Whatever I say or do . . . do *not* stop."

She nodded, steeled herself. "Are you ready?"

He nodded shortly, pulled his seat belt off his chest and placed it in his mouth. He bit down hard.

The roadway ran flat and straight, and the headlamps showed the way.

Justine pierced her patient's flesh a half inch from the bloody knife wound. The hooked needle found its own path deep through his abdominal muscle. It passed through the slit, and fresh blood bubbled into the flashlight's beam. The curvature of the sharp spike sent it back out of his skin, a half inch on the other side of the stab wound.

Court screamed into the seat belt wedged in his mouth.

Justine took the thread with her gloved hand, pulled the instrument backwards the way it came, and rethreaded the needle. Even with a quarter dose of morphine going through her patient, she felt his teardrops on her arms as she made her second suture, close to the first.

For ten kilometers she continued. She did not look away from her work as she sewed him up, but she spoke to him in soothing French throughout, just as she would an injured dog. Above her, her patient winced and groaned. Miraculously, to her way of thinking, he continued to drive, execute gentle turns as needed, once even braking slightly. Justine assumed the road ahead and his need to concentrate on it was the only thing keeping him coherent.

She used gauze to swab away the blood as she worked, poured antiseptic from the bottle she'd staged between his legs to get a better view of the pumping wound.

Finally she said, "Almost done. I only have to pull it tight and tie it off. Just a few more seconds now." Above her she heard him panting and sobbing. There was a rhythm to his sounds that distressed her; she knew he could go into shock at any time. "Here we go . . . I will be as gentle as possible." She pulled on the thread, the wound closed beautifully, and the last of the bleeding stopped immediately. "Yes, perfect. Now I just tie it and—"

The tires below her ran over a series of bumps. The Mercedes's suspension was awesome; she barely felt the rough surface. But when the bumps did not stop after several seconds, she looked up to check on her patient.

She was horrified to see his head hanging down just above her, his eyes closed.

Jim had passed out.

The black Mercedes ran off the road and crashed at five thirty a.m.

THIRTY-ONE

All ten Belarusian guards were on station around the property: six outside, two at ground-floor windows, and two in the tower above. Serge and Alain, the two electronic security engineers, sat in the ground-floor library, their bloodshot eyes scanning back and forth across the screens, watching the infrared images around the perimeter of the building. Every five minutes, they used walkie-talkies to communicate with the patrols.

The Libyans were the only hunter-killer squad still in the area. They fought exhaustion as their van patrolled Bayeux. They were certain by now they were out of the big money. The other teams who had been in the area had since been sent to Paris to search for the target, as had every pavement artist within 300 miles. The Libyans had been given a clear chance at the target back on the hillside in Switzerland, and they had failed, so now they were ordered to sit tight and wait, were facing a hundred-to-one odds at best they would get another crack at the Gray Man.

No one expected Gentry to make it to Bayeux now.

Riegel, Lloyd, the Tech, and Felix sat in the control room in low light, sipped coffee, and watched computer monitors displaying the rocking and bouncing images broadcast from digital video cameras held by the watchers and kill teams in Paris. The Tech was still organizing the search around the Seine. By now Riegel and Lloyd both conceded Gentry must have made it out of the water downstream and staggered off, so the net was widened and then widened again on both sides of the river.

By five thirty a.m., there was fresh news in Paris that generated a flurry of activity around the château. A watcher listening to police radio had learned about a break-in at a minor emergency clinic in the Fifth Arrondissement. This was upstream from where the target went into the river, but the Tech had sent a watcher over to find out what he could. The owners of the clinic had arrived and announced the medicines and blood and equipment stolen were all items necessary for wound management.

Riegel stood behind the Tech. "We'll have to split the search. Keep the Bolivians and the Sri Lankans in Paris. Tell the Botswanans to come here via the highway, see if they can spot him on the way. Send a helicopter up to pick up the Kazakhs. They are the most skilled gunners; I want them here. They can patrol the back roads around the property, checking anything that moves. And alert the Libyans in Bayeux! They need to stay there to watch the train station and the routes through town. If the Gray Man is somehow still in the fight, he'll be here before daybreak."

The Tech muttered to himself, "We bloody saw him. We bloody well saw him hurt. We bloody well saw him fall into the water."

Lloyd slapped him on the back of the head as he stormed out of the room, heading downstairs to tell the men monitoring the infrared cameras that their target may be on the way.

"Please! Please, Jim! You must wake!"

Court Gentry opened his eyes. Above him, a figure loomed close in the dark. Instinctively, he reached out and took the figure's neck and grabbed it tight and slammed it to the ground next to him as he tried to roll on top of it.

Court fell on Justine in the tall, wet grass.

"Sorry," was all he could say as he climbed off of the French girl. He moved sluggishly, his body clearly impeded by drugs.

She was slow to get up as well. It was dark, and he could make out her wide eyes best of all. She sat up next to him finally, and he looked away uncomfortably. He took stock of his surroundings.

He was seated in wet grass, both of their backs leaned against the Mercedes. They were in a field, the black sedan four-fifths through a thicket. Gentry assumed the road was on the other side. The glow of the moon was diffused by the mist above him, but he could make out the lumbering movement of cows in the muddy field near the car.

The air was cold.

"What . . . what is . . . Where are we?"

"I could not wake you. We are west of Caen, still thirty minutes from Bayeux."

"Shit. What time is it?" The American slowly remembered his mission, as if it appeared from out of the fog of his drug-addled brain.

"It is almost seven. The sun will be up in under an hour."

"We crashed, didn't we?"

"No, monsieur, *we* did not crash. *You* crashed."

It was coming back to him, but slowly. He put his hand down to his injured belly, though it was barely hurting at the moment. He wore a clean brown shirt. Through it he could feel bandages cinched tight.

He looked down at his new pants. "You dressed me?"

Justine looked away, out to the dark field. "I found the clothes in a bag in the car. After the wreck."

"Are you hurt?" he asked.

"Not bad. Some bruises. We were lucky. You ran off the road onto a cow path through the hedgerow. We crashed through these trees. The car is stuck. After the wreck I gave you a little medicine, bandaged you, and dressed you. We have been here ever since. A little while ago a helicopter flew over. It scared me. I thought maybe they are looking for us."

Court's head was clearing by the second; he was back with it now. "I'll never make it in time."

"You told me eight a.m. We can still make it before then."

"I needed to be in position before the sun came up." Gentry sighed, let it go. He stood slowly, found it less difficult than he expected. "What did you give me?"

"I gave you some painkillers, and I put bandages very tight around your waist to lower the pain."

Gentry was checking the wrappings through the shirt as she spoke. "Good. I don't feel too bad."

"It won't last. The pain will return soon. I did not give you the other drug. Zee DextroStat. I read zee bottle. It is a very strong amphetamine. If you take one of those pills, your blood pressure will increase. If my stitches are not perfect, you will bleed very badly. You could bleed internally, as well. It would be crazy for you to swallow one of those pills."

"I'm not going to swallow one of the pills. I am going to break open three of them, pour the contents into a cup of hot coffee. That will break down the time-release coating, so I will get all of the effect instantly."

"That is suicide!" she said. "I am not a doctor, but I know what that will do to your body."

"This will help me stay sharp for a half hour or so. If I bleed out after that, well, that's okay. I just have to do my job first."

She began to protest, but he interrupted her. "We need new transport. Something local, something that will not draw attention."

Justine shook her head in frustration. "There is a farmhouse just over there. Maybe you can borrow their vehicle."

Court looked around the side of the hedgerow to the farmhouse, seventy-five yards away. Already a light was on in the window. An old, white four-door, splattered waist-high with mud and manure, sat outside glowing in the window's light. "Yeah, I'll go *borrow* their vehicle." He reached slowly into the trunk of the Mercedes and retrieved the second Glock pistol. The first he had lost in the Paris passageway. Without looking, he pulled back the slide an inch and used a fingertip to make sure the gun was loaded. "I'll be right back."

In the last hour before dawn, Riegel had the entire force at the château at full battle stations, because he fully expected the Gray Man to come then, if he was to come at all. The ten gunmen from Minsk were divided into three groups of two, patrolling the garden and driveway to the main gate, their Kalashnikov battle rifles in hand. Two more manned AK-47s on the first floor of the château; one watched out a window to the drive and the other a window towards the garden in the back.

The final two Belarusians were in the château's turret above: one sniper with a Dragunov scoped rifle, the same man and the same weapon used to end the life of Phillip Fitzroy, and one spotter who wore an AR-15 on his back and looked out in all directions into the night with binoculars.

In addition to the ten Belarusians there were Lloyd's three men from London, the Northern Irishman and the two Scots. The other Northern Irishman now lay discarded in the basement next to Phillip's body. Two were in the kitchen, radios in their ears and submachine guns in their laps, waiting in reserve to be sent by Riegel himself to wherever the Gray Man appeared. The third, McSpadden, was in the hall outside of the second-floor bedroom covering the Fitzroy family.

There were also the two French engineers in the first-floor library, watching over the monitors of the infrared cameras positioned around the yard. These were both ex-infantrymen in their forties; they wore pistols on their hips and knew how to use them.

Finally there was the Tech, Lloyd, Felix, and Riegel in the control room. Of the four, only Riegel could be considered a real gunfighter. He wore his pistol in a shoulder holster underneath his suede jacket. Dangerous to others or not, Lloyd was armed with his small automatic, and a charged Uzi had been placed on the Tech's computer desk, though the ponytailed Brit had never before been so close to a loaded weapon.

This made the odds nineteen defenders versus one attacker, but this was merely the inner line of coverage around the château. The four Libyan Jamahiriya Security Organization operators were in constant radio contact with the Tech, ten kilometers away in Bayeux. They watched the road from town to the château and the soon-to-open train station, the only reasonable route from Paris. The sleek, black Eurocopter flew lazy eights at high altitude, carrying the five Saudis. The chopper watched the roads down from Caen to the east and even along the coast to the north in case the Gray Man magically appeared on a Normandy beach like a one-man replay of the D-day invasion.

And the four Kazakhs, just in from Paris, patrolled in a small blue Citroën, their Kalashnikovs in their laps with the stocks folded. They drove through the countryside, pulled up behind early-rising drivers and checked their plates, shone bright lights into cars to scan the vehicle's occupants.

The Kazakhs did not use their radios. Yes, they listened in to the Tech's communication with the other teams, but they never acknowledged or responded to the Tech's calls for them to check in. They were there to kill the Gray Man and make the money and go home. They would communicate with the men in the château only when they dumped Gentry's body at the front gate and demanded their money.

Riegel oversaw the entire operation from the third-floor control room. He'd be the first to admit it was no fair fight, more than thirty armed men against one horribly wounded adversary who was operating with limited resources and little sleep.

But Riegel was a hunter, and a fair fight was not his game.

THIRTY-TWO

The early morning glow shone off the English Channel, and a hint of the morning's first hues brushed the back of Justine's shoulders as she drove the dirty white four-door west along the coastal road. She kept to the marked speed limit, read the signs carefully.

Her passenger seat and her backseat were empty except for several aluminum suitcases.

She motored alone, made a left in the coastal village of Longues-sur-Mer, did not speed up or slow down when a black helicopter swooped a couple hundred feet above her. It made a second pass and then a third before disappearing from her view, heading to the southwest.

She had the road all to herself for a while, but not long after the helicopter's departure, a blue Citroën pulled behind her from a gravel lane to her left, dust and exhaust rising behind it. She chanced a glance into her rearview and saw nothing but bright headlights. They stayed close behind her for several hundred meters, and then the car pulled alongside. Justine gripped the thin steering column so hard she thought it would break off in her hands as a flashlight beam illuminated her, then scanned around behind her in the backseat. Then the light turned off, the Citroën pulled ahead of her, and she was certain she would see its brake lights come on, forcing her to stop. But the car sped away. Its taillights disappeared in the mist ahead after another minute.

After heading south for a few kilometers, she looked down at the map in her lap, noted the pencil marks Jim had put there for her. There was a left turn ahead, and she took it after flipping off her lights. The narrow road ran straight; thick hedgerows reached high on each side of her. After three minutes of driving through the darkness, the road turned to the south, but she slowed, bumped the little car off the pavement, and revved the engine just enough to send it into a deep thicket.

A large stone wall rose from the ground on the other side of the thicket, three meters high. From her view, it filled the windshield and seemed to reach up into the infinite sky. She bumped the sedan's front bumper against it and turned off the engine.

It was nearly pitch-dark here with the high trees on either side of the narrow road. Quickly, she climbed from the driver's seat. She was careful not to slam the door behind her. She knocked four times slowly on the trunk of the Fiat, a prearranged signal that all was well.

A moment later, the trunk lid lifted. Jim looked up at her from his tight squeeze inside, an empty paper coffee cup by his side and a black rifle in his arms.

"No problems?" he asked as he slowly climbed out. She could see the pain on his face that came with the movement's effect on his injuries. He left the rifle in the trunk of the car, walked around to the side, stretching out after suffering the cramped confines of the trunk.

"There are men around. In a car and in a helicopter. I am sure there are more inside the property. They must think you are a very dangerous man to have so many people waiting for you," Justine said as she stood behind the car in the road.

The American had pushed through the tall bushes on the passenger side to pull open the door to the backseat. "My reputation is exaggerated."

"What?"

"Never mind. I want to thank you for all you've done. You've earned every cent of that money. I could not have done this without you."

Justine smiled in the low light. "You haven't really done anything yet, Jim."

"That's a fair point."

"How do you feel?" she asked.

"Like I just downed a triple dose of speed with a double espresso. Your stitches are holding fine."

Without warning, a car's headlights raked over Justine's body. She turned to look to the light, then quickly she spun back to look to Jim for guidance, but he was gone.

Seconds later, the blue Citroën pulled to a stop behind her, and four men quickly climbed out.

Justine stood in the bright light and raised a hand up to shield her eyes. The light washed over her, and she felt naked in the bright beams. The four men moved in front of the lights and were silhouetted in them. She saw the profiles of long guns in the men's arms. Someone shouted at her, but she did not understand, and she could not speak. Instead, she looked to her left and to her right, into the predawn's dimness all around.

Somewhere in the safety away from the shafts of light, she knew Jim had run away and gotten free from the men in front of her. She thought he must have somehow made it over the stone wall. He'd left her here to explain the trunks of equipment in the car and to come up with some plausible reason she should be right here right now.

The terror in her body threatened to burst her heart open inside her chest.

"Bonjour," she said to the four silhouettes, her meek voice little more than a whimper.

The figures moved closer to her as one, guns still pointed forward.

Fifteen meters, ten meters, the shadows converged as they closed.

Then the steady movement forward of the silhouettes changed suddenly, a fast shadow from the left, a profile turned towards the movement, the shape of a long gun beginning to rise and then a cry of surprise from the specters in front of her as one tall figure crumpled into a ball.

Quickly she backed up, bumped into the trunk of the car, watched the dancing movement of light and dark in front of her. Through the confusion on the road she distinguished the outlines of arms and legs as punches rained down and kicks flew, guns spun free through the air and clanked to the dusty gravel amid the shouts and cracks of fists on flesh and bone on bone.

A second figure dropped and stilled, this one flat under the headlights' beams. She saw that it was not Jim. More convergence of shadows in the rising dust cloud, and a man's outline wrapped its dark appendages around the head and neck of another profile and spun, lifted the silhouette off the pavement, and Justine heard the snap of a neck as cervical vertebrae shattered from obscene torsion.

Justine had seen fistfights on television action shows. This was nothing of that. The movements were faster, more brutal, crueler. There was no ballet or poetry in the relationship between the adversaries, no choreography. No, it was unyielding surface on unyielding surface, the jerking reactions and the grunts and cries of wild beasts, labored breathing from exertion and panic. The sounds of cracking impacts and the frenzy of a combat so pitiless, she was sure all the men would tear to pieces in the street in front of her.

Three men were down now, and a fourth ran out of the shafts of light to go for a rifle that had fallen and skidded free of the fight. Justine saw Jim now as he pursued in the dusty street and knocked the other man down from behind. Blows were exchanged by each, and Jim was thrown flat on his back in the cold road. Quickly the Frenchwoman turned to the trunk to lift the rifle the American had left there, though she had no idea how to turn it on so that she could use it. As she looked away from the fight, she heard a sick cry of pain. She hefted the big gun and turned back to find Jim up on his knees and the fourth man rolling away from him, hands over his eyes. Jim regained his feet, bringing a long gun up with him and then over his head. While Justine watched, Jim beat the writhing man with the butt end of the gun. One after another, like an axe chopping wood, the blows fell onto the struggling man's back. His hands raised in defense, but the rifle's butt beat its way to the horror-stricken eyes. The eyes erupted in blood and his jaw broke and hung open sickeningly. It must have taken a dozen merciless blows to the crushed head to still the man on his back in the cold road, and Justine could not look away.

Slowly, when it all was over, the Frenchwoman slid down the bumper of the car to the ground. She laid the rifle in front of her, and her empty hands shook as she covered her face and cried.

Court fought hyperventilation as he cleared the four bodies from the road. He heard a helicopter above in the lightening morning. With the hedgerows on both sides and the high wall surrounding Château

Laurent, the chopper would have to fly directly above to spot his position, but Gentry knew every second he stayed exposed on the dusty road was a gamble.

Quickly he checked the trunk of the car for any equipment he could put to use. Immediately he found four sets of level 3A body armor. All but worthless against a rifle-caliber bullet, but damn effective stopping pistol fire. Quickly he pushed his head through a vest and Velcroed the side panels tightly around his waist. Also in the back were hard-shell tactical knee and elbow pads. He put these on as well, figured a scuffed elbow would be the absolute least of his many worries in the next few minutes, but there was no sense leaving an ounce of protective gear behind.

Then he sat down in the driver's seat of the little Citroën, shoved it in gear to drive into the thick hedgerow in an attempt to conceal it from the air. Looking down, he realized he'd popped some if not all of the sutures Justine had used to tie his stomach back together. His knife wound bled and wet his bandages and his shirt under the bulletproof vest. Blood trickled out of his stomach, down his pants, and onto the car seat. "Shit," he said aloud. Once again he was operating on borrowed time.

After hiding the bodies and the car and tossing the AKs into the bushes, he went to Justine, who was still kneeling by the car. She wiped tears and strands of tousled hair from her eyes. Slowly she rose to her feet.

She looked towards the bodies poorly concealed in the bushes. Discarded. Arms and legs splayed unnaturally. "They were bad men, yes?"

"Very bad. I had to do it, and now I have to go over that wall and do it some more."

Justine did not respond.

Court began opening the aluminum cases, cinching a utility belt tightly around his waist, hooking the drop-leg pistol holster on his right thigh and the sub-load magazine carrier on his left. "I'm out of time. I have to go." He slung the M4 assault rifle over his neck and left arm and fastened the small HK MP5 submachine gun, muzzle down, to the vest on the chest rig he'd taken from the blue Citroën. He slid the Glock 19 pistol into the thigh holster and Velcroed the two fragmentation grenades into place on the vest. From the front seat of the car he took the satellite phone and jammed it into his hip pocket.

In just under three minutes he was ready. He turned back to Justine, who stood silently behind him, still looking at the exposed legs of the four shattered corpses. "I'll need to use the hood of the car to climb over the fence. Once I clear the top, I want you to back up, turn around, drive back up the coast. Go west, not east. Park this car at the next train station you see, get on the first morning train to Paris, and go home. Thank you again for everything you've done for me."

Justine's eyes were distant. Gentry knew killing the four men in hand-to-hand combat right in front of her had shaken her badly. It would upset anyone, he thought, at least any normal person who did not live his life.

"Are you going to be okay?" he asked gently.

"Are you a bad man, Jim?" she asked, her pupils still wide from the fight.

He put his hand on her arm, held it gently if uncomfortably. "I don't think so. I've been taught some bad things. I do some . . . some bad things. But only to bad people."

"Yes," she said. She seemed to clear a little. "Yes." She looked up at him. "I wish you luck."

"Maybe, when I'm done with this, we can talk—"

"No," she interrupted. Looked away. "No. It's better I try to forget."

"I understand."

She hugged him briefly, but to Gentry she felt distracted, as if she took him as some sort of animal now after his brutal display of violence. She clearly just wanted to get away from him and all this madness. Without another word, she climbed into the driver's seat of the car, and he got up onto the hood. The painkillers she'd given him while he slept provided some relief. Even so, climbing the wall was pure agony for a man with such a savage wound in his abdomen, to say nothing of his wrist, leg, and rib cage.

Gentry slid over the top of the stone wall, hung his feet down, dropped into soft grass, and heard the little four-door back away and turn around in the road. Court looked down at his watch. It was seven forty a.m.

The heavy fog totally obscured the château. All he could see was the beginning of an apple orchard in front of him. Bright red fruit lay on the ground under row after row of small trees with narrow trunks.

Court checked his gear one last time, took a deep breath to control his aches and pains, and began running through the orchard and into the deep gray mist.

THIRTY-THREE

"Shut it down," Riegel said.

The two Frenchmen who'd been staring at the bank of monitors in the library for twelve hours straight did as they were told. They began flipping switches from left to right, turning off the images from the infrared cameras around the property.

Lloyd appeared behind them all in the library's doorway and asked, "What are you doing?"

Riegel answered, "Infrared cameras are for the night, Lloyd. It is no longer night."

"You said he'd come at night."

"I did, yes."

"But he's still coming, right?"

"It does not appear so," answered Riegel the hunter, his voice tinged with both confusion and dejection.

"We've got fifteen minutes to get a body for Felix. What the fuck are we going to do?"

Riegel turned to the younger American. "We have a helicopter overhead and over one hundred men and women looking for him. We have thirty guns right here at the château, waiting on him. We've shot him. We've stabbed him. We've sent him down a mountain, off a bridge. We've killed his friends, we've bled him dry. What else can we do?"

Just then the Tech's voice chirped over the walkie-talkie feature of both men's phones. "We have a couple of problems."

"What is it?" asked Riegel.

"The Bolivians have left the contest. They just called from Paris to tell us they quit."

"Good riddance," snapped Lloyd.

"And the Kazakhs are not checking in."

Riegel lifted his phone from his belt. "They never check in."

"The Saudis' chopper can't find them on the road."

Lloyd spoke into his phone now. "We would have heard gunshots if they were in battle with the Gray Man. Don't worry about it. The bastards probably ran off like the Bolivians."

Lloyd and Riegel walked back up the two flights of stairs to the third floor. Both men were dead tired, but neither would allow the other to see any sign of weakness. Instead they argued over what could have been done differently and what last-minute actions could still be taken.

They entered the control room and immediately noticed Felix standing by the window, his mobile to his ear. After a few seconds, the thin black man in the suit disconnected his call and turned to face the room. He had not spoken a word in hours. "Gentlemen, I am sorry to say your time is up."

Lloyd stormed up to him, wild-eyed. "No! We've got ten minutes.

You've got to give us a little more time. You saw him fall into the water. We've fucking killed him. We just need time to find whatever ditch he crawled into to die. Tell Abubaker you saw him fall—"

"Your instructions were to produce a body. You have failed in this undertaking. I have reported this to my president. I am sorry. It is my duty. You understand."

Riegel's broad shoulders dropped, and he looked away. He could not believe the Gray Man, if alive, had not come to save the kids.

Lloyd said, "Any second he'll turn up. Abubaker doesn't have to sign over the contract until he leaves office in another hour."

"It is now a moot point. I notified the president of your progress . . . or should I say, lack of progress. He signed your competitor's contract while we were on the phone together. I've been instructed to return to Paris to await further instruction."

Riegel nodded slowly. He said to Felix, "You can fly back with the French engineers. They will be leaving for Paris within the hour."

Felix nodded in polite appreciation. "I am sorry this endeavor did not work out for you. I appreciate your professionalism and hope our interests will coincide again someday." The German and the Nigerian bowed to one another. Ignoring the American, Felix left the room to ready himself for departure.

Riegel looked to the Tech. "Notify the teams. It's over. They have failed. Let them know I will contact their agency heads this afternoon to discuss some sort of . . . consolation."

The Tech did as he was told. Then he flipped off the monitors in front of him. He pulled off his headphones and laid them on the table slowly. He ran his hands through his long hair.

The three men remaining in the control room each sat alone with their own thoughts for a few minutes. The morning light shone through the window, seemed to crawl across the floor towards them, taunting them with their failure. They were to have their man by sunrise, and sunrise now mocked them.

Lloyd looked down to his watch. "It's five till eight. No sense in putting it off any longer."

Kurt Riegel was looking into the bottom of his coffee cup. He was exhausted. Distractedly he asked, "Putting what off?"

"The obligations on the second floor."

"Sir Donald, you mean?" Riegel straightened. "I'll handle it. You'd take all day."

Lloyd shook his head. "Not just Don. All of them. All four."

Riegel looked up from his chair. "What are you talking about? You want to kill the woman? The children?"

"I told Gentry if he didn't show, they would die. He didn't show. Don't look so goddamn surprised."

"He didn't show. That means he's dead. Why punish a dead man, you idiot?"

"He should have tried harder." Lloyd pulled the silver automatic from his hip and let it hang in his hand by his side. "Get out of the way, Riegel. This is still my operation."

"Not for much longer." There was menace in the big German's voice.

"Be that as it may," Lloyd said, "I still have a job to do, and I don't see you stopping me. You can act all sanctimonious about that family, but you know they could identify us. Identify this place. They've got to die." He pushed past Riegel and stepped into the hallway.

On the Tech's desk, Sir Donald Fitzroy's phone rang. Lloyd reappeared in the doorway instantly. The young technician quickly sat back down and slipped his headphones back over his ears. Felix stepped back into the room, curious, his attaché in his hand and a camel-colored raincoat over his arm.

The Tech put the call through the overhead speakers. Lloyd said, "Yes?"

"Good morning, Lloyd. How are things?"

"You are too late, Court. We lost the contract, which means you have failed. I don't need the leverage of the Fitzroys anymore. I was just heading downstairs to put some bullets into them. Want to listen in?"

"You need them alive more than ever now."

Lloyd smiled. "Oh really, and why is that?"

"Life insurance."

"Yeah, Court? I watched you fall off that bridge last night. I don't know where the hell you are, but you are in no position to—"

"Forget about the contract with Abubaker. Don't worry about your boss firing you. Put out of your mind Riegel's henchmen showing up at your door some cold night. Ignore all your future troubles. Right now, the only danger in your world is me."

"How are you a danger to—"

"Because I'm heavily armed, I'm royally pissed, and I'm right outside."

In the control room there was a silent flurry of activity. Riegel moved to the window quickly, pushed the lace curtains aside with a fingertip. He scanned the heavy mist over the back lawn. The Tech lurched across the desk to his handheld radio and frantically began whispering the news to the guards on the property. Felix pulled out his mobile and charged into the hallway, thumbing buttons as he moved.

Only Lloyd did not flinch. He stood as if his feet were stuck to the floor. "You're bluffing. You just expect me to let the Fitzroys go because you say you are outside? What kind of an idiot do you take me for?"

"An idiot with an expiration date. And I assume LaurentGroup's grim reaper is listening in. Riegel, the same goes for you. You brush a hair on the heads of those kids or Mrs. Fitzroy, and you will die in that house."

Riegel spoke up. "Good morning, Mr. Gentry. If you are outside, why don't you come to the front door? The Lagos contract is lost; our incentive to kill you has vanished. We've just called off the wet squads. The game is over. If you are really here, why not drop in for coffee?"

"If you doubt that I'm in the neighborhood, maybe you should try checking in with the four smelly guys in the blue Citroën."

That sank in a moment. Riegel did not know what car the Kazakhs drove, but the Tech anxiously began trying to raise them again. As he did so, receiving no reply, he looked up to his two superiors with eyes of terror.

Finally Riegel said, "Most impressive. A man in your condition still able to dispatch four tier-one operators without a shot fired. As I said, we have no quarrel with you any longer. Please come in and we'll—"

"You free the Fitzroys and hand over the SAD files, or I swear to God I will murder every last living thing in that house!"

Lloyd had been quiet, his hands on his hips and his sweat-stained shirtsleeves rolled up to his elbows. But now he moved. Storming across the room to the Tech's desk, he leaned into the mobile phone's microphone. "Fucking bring it, you gimpy piece of shit! In the meantime, I'm going to take a straight razor to those two stupid little bitches downstairs—"

Riegel pulled the American lawyer away from the phone, shoved him hard against the stone wall. He leaned in himself, cleared his throat. "Yes, Court? Could you allow us a few moments to discuss your proposal? You know how corporations are; we must call a meeting for everything."

"Sure, Riegel. I'll check back in a bit. Take your time, no rush." The phone went dead.

Lloyd screamed to the Tech, "Get all the teams here, now!"

Riegel held up his hand to stay the Tech. When he spoke, his voice was more reasoned. "For what purpose, Lloyd? The contract is not at stake anymore. The game is over."

"But the Gray Man is still out there!"

"That's our problem, not LaurentGroup's. Marc Laurent will not spend a dime for the foreign kill squads to protect us. There is no more twenty-million-dollar bounty to be paid out."

Clearly, Lloyd had not thought of that. He shrugged his shoulders. "We don't have to tell the hitters that."

Riegel shook his head. "So instead of fighting one wounded man now, you want to piss off Marc Laurent and a half dozen nations' security services, fight our corporation and six countries later? I know you are insane, Lloyd; that's been established. But are you suicidal, too?"

The Tech was looking back at his two bosses, waiting for instruction. Then he cocked his head to the side, put his hand to his headset. "Wait! All the teams are coming here anyway!"

"Good," Lloyd said, glad the matter was settled.

"Why?" asked Riegel.

"Felix contacted them. He's offering twenty million dollars cash from Abubaker to the team that kills the Gray Man."

"Perfect!" shouted Lloyd. "How soon till they—"

"Not perfect!" said the Tech. "He's told them to kill anyone who gets in their way. Including the other teams! Including us. They are going to fight each other for Gentry's head right here at the château!"

Kurt Riegel did not hesitate. "Pull all the Minsk guards inside the building! Alert Serge and Alain, and the three UK guards. We must defend these walls against all threats! The Gray Man or the kill squads."

The Tech looked up at Riegel. "The Libyans will be here in moments! The Saudis are overhead now!"

Riegel looked out the window a final time. "Call LaurentGroup Paris. Have an evacuation chopper scrambled to get us out of here! Then raise the kill teams, tell them we can still work together. Tell them Court is outside. Tell them we won't let anyone in the castle. They need to kill him before he gets in."

The Tech spun in his chair and placed the call to the home office.

Gentry had no intention of calling Riegel back. Every second he delayed his attack on the château was another second the defenders could ready themselves, search the grounds for him, bring in more reinforcements. And it was more time they could use to kill the girls.

No, he had to move now. The grounds were awash in the morning's light as he lay in the apple orchard at the back of the property. Through the gray mist he could just make out a faint outline of a large, looming structure on a rise ahead of him. He'd covered a quarter mile since he'd dropped over the wall, and he was still easily two hundred yards from Château Laurent.

The open ground in front of him was his biggest concern. Once he broke free from the coverage of the tree line and the thick fog hanging in the air, he would be completely exposed. Also, there was a helicopter flying circles high in the air. He could not see it, but its beating rotors announced its presence above the property.

This would be hard enough even without his multitude of injuries, but regardless of his poor personal circumstance, he knew there was no more time to waste. Court rose to his kneepads, then slowly up to a crouch. He felt blood on his left leg and knew it was again draining freely from the knife wound. The heavy dose of speed he'd introduced to his bloodstream would increase his blood loss significantly.

"Fuck it," he said aloud. He unslung the M4 and hefted it in his arms.

He stood.

Then ran forward with every ounce of strength he possessed.

As soon as the Tech alerted the security cordon around the château that the Gray Man was outside, Serge rushed from the kitchen into the library and flipped the monitors back on. He knew the infrared cameras would pick up anyone hidden in the vapor. Intently he stared at one display and then the next. Back and forth he scanned. Soon his eyes locked on an image. His hand lunged for the radio on his desk. He broadcast to all elements in the château.

"Movement in zee back! Movement in zee back! One man, and he's coming fast!"

Lloyd came over the radio. "Where? Where the fuck is he?"

"Coming through zee orchard. *Mon Dieu*, he can run!"

"Where in the orchard?" screamed Lloyd over the radio.

"He's running right up zee middle!"

The spotter in the tower broke in over the same channel. His thick Belarusian-accented voice was calm, the antithesis of Lloyd's shriek. "I do not have a target. We do not see any . . . Wait. Yes. One man, coming fast! We'll take him!"

Maurice had left Gentry an impressive array of equipment, but Maurice was decidedly old school, and the gear Court was forced to use was not ideal to his needs. The Colt rifle in his hands wore iron sights; there was no scope or holographic sight like the high-tech wizardry Gentry preferred on his weapons. As he broke through the mist, the château forming clearer in front of him with each labored footfall of his sprint, he made out the turret of the tower above. He knew this would be a sniper's hide, and he knew this man would have the best skill and the best scope and the best rifle and the best chance to put a stop to Court's ridiculous one-man assault.

So the Gray Man raised his rifle to his shoulder, still at a dead run. Targeted fire with the iron sights while running was impossible; his goal was to simply pour as much lead as he could at the tower to keep his enemies' heads down until he could make it to the building's wall. Court knew there was no one in the house with as much close quarters battle training or experience as he. He just had to survive long enough to make it to close quarters to have any sort of chance of success.

The sniper saw the target shoot out of the fog in front of him. Wisps of vapor swirled in a vortex behind him as he ran. The thirty-year-old Belarusian adjusted his aim and placed his crosshairs on the sprinting man's chest. He brought his finger to the trigger for a quick center-mass shot. He noticed body armor under the tactical vest and lowered the buttstock of the big Dragunov a millimeter to move the crosshairs up to the sprinting man's forehead. As his fingertip began to press on the tight trigger, he sensed more than saw his target's primary weapon rise in front of him. Flashes from the muzzle of the weapon and the cracks of rifle fire. The sniper heard pops and explosions in the stone and wood of the turret and smoky dust filled the air around him as high-speed metal jacketed rounds collided with hundreds-year-old masonry. His spotter cried out to his left, but the sniper was disciplined. He did not remove his cheek from the rifle; he did not remove his eye from his scope.

Confidently he pulled the trigger at the man storming towards him.

THIRTY-FOUR

Gentry had fired almost an entire thirty-round magazine at the tower looming above him as he closed on it as fast as possible. He wanted to finish the magazine with a couple of more accurately placed shots towards the tower, so he brought the black rifle up to eye level in front of him to make an attempt to get some sort of a sight picture through the round ghost ring sight on the gun's carry handle. Just as he did so, the rifle slammed back into his face, ripped out of his hands, and flipped up through the air.

Court ran on, empty-handed.

After no more than four or five steps across the wet lawn, his face burning from the blow of his buttstock below his eye, he realized his M4 must have been hit by a round from a high-powered rifle. Though he'd lost his primary weapon behind him, he understood the gun had saved his life, deflecting a sniper's bullet to his head. Without a loss of stride, he reached down and pulled the squat MP5 submachine gun from its resting place on his chest. He fired again at the tower, now no more than one hundred yards away. The MP5 was about as effective as a fly swatter for a sprinting man covering open ground and engaging a tiny, distant window without a sight picture, but he hoped it would at least keep some heads down.

The sniper had seen the running man reel from the impact of his shot, and then he lifted his head away from the scope to attend to his partner. The spotter had taken a piece of stone masonry to his face. His glasses were broken, and he was bleeding from the forehead, but he was coherent and not badly hurt. Just then, more gunfire erupted from the back garden. With surprise, the Belarusian sniper looked back down and saw the man he was sure he'd just put a bullet through continue his charge. From the reports of the gun in his hand, the man in the tower knew the Gray Man had switched to a nine-millimeter submachine gun. Quickly he sat back at the table behind the Dragunov. Took up his position behind the scope in under two seconds. Suddenly new cracks of rifle fire erupted, this time from behind him on the other side of the château. For a moment he did not understand what was going on, until the voice of one of his countrymen below came over the radio on the table.

"It's the Libyans! They're at the front gate! Tower, take them out!"

Reluctantly the sniper lifted the big Dragunov from the table and took it to the front portal of the tower. The Gray Man was someone else's problem now; he needed to engage the distant targets, the Libyans.

The Gray Man was no longer distant. He was close.

Just outside the sniper's tower, the black Eurocopter hovered low above the roof's walkway. Four heavily armed Saudi operators in tactical gear poured out and dropped the six feet to the flat eastern roof. They ignored the gunfight now raging at the front of the building. Instead, they all took up positions behind the decorative battlements overlooking the back garden and the lone man running towards them over open ground.

As Gentry closed on his objective, he redirected his fire from the tower above the château to a first-floor window where bright muzzle flashes flickered. Gentry emptied his first magazine at the window in front of him. The walls around the window pocked, granite snapped off in dusty chunks, glass shattered, and the lace draperies whipped left and right as a few lucky shots from Court's rifle found their mark though the space. It was difficult firing at a full sprint, impossible to accurately aim. Court saw no more muzzle flashes from the window but instead noticed the sleek, black Eurocopter above and in front of him, and the men who leapt from it.

"Fuck!" He was still seventy yards from cover. He pushed his legs even harder to get as close to the château as possible before the men now exiting the black chopper could get in position to open up on him. Here on the flat lawn he'd be a sitting duck to aimed fire.

Gentry pulled a fragmentation grenade off his vest as he ran, yanked the pin out with his teeth, and let the spoon fly. A large, blond-haired figure appeared in a window on the third floor directly in front of him, raised a handgun, and shot through the glass. Court dove forward at the wet, green grass to avoid the fire, landed on his right shoulder, and executed a forward roll. As he came out of the roll, he rose to his feet. His running and his somersault had given his body an incredible amount of momentum, momentum he used to throw the grenade as high and as far as he could. From forty-five yards away the potato-sized bomb whizzed through the air in an arc, rose over the edge of the parapets, and exploded, just missing the Eurocopter, which escaped into the sky, fleeing from the fight as fast as possible. The blast above the Saudis' heads killed one man outright and injured one more in the neck and back. The other two had found cover in time, but they'd missed their opportunity to get an open shot on their target on the lawn.

At the front of the house, two Belarusians and two Libyans were already dead. The guards from Minsk were killed not far from the front gate. They'd been running back to the safety of the château when the vanload of operators from Tripoli busted through the ironwork, the Middle Eastern men firing their Skorpion machine pistols from the moving vehicle. The two Libyans were felled as the van screeched to a stop in the gravel drive. The sniper in the tower took out the operator in the front passenger seat with a round to the face, and the first man out the sliding back took three AK rounds from the only pair of Belarusians still outside the château.

The two remaining Libyans killed the men on the driveway and closed on the front door to the château. They poured automatic fire from their Skorpions into the windows on either side, kept disciplined distance between one another, and shouted calls for cover as they reloaded and repositioned.

Number Two fired half a magazine at each of the two hinges of the heavy oaken door, and then kicked it open. As he reloaded, it crashed into the building in front of him, and he caught a double-tap from a Northern Irish guard in the foyer, spinning the Libyan dead to the ground. The last living Libyan answered the Ulsterman with his Skorpion; blood and tissue splattered across the white wall behind the man in the foyer as he went down.

Riegel had never seen anything like it. The Gray Man had been in his sights; he wore a dark brown shirt with bloodstains on the waist, a drop-leg pistol holster on his right hip, and a magazine sub-load on his left. A black vest and a submachine gun adorned his chest. His head was shaved, and even at fifty yards, Kurt thought he could discern a fierceness in the eyes.

When Riegel drew his handgun and aimed it at the running man, he knew it was a long-distance shot for a pistol, but for a trained target shooter like the German, he should not have missed. But the running man had dropped just below his rounds at exactly the right time, rolled, risen back to his feet, and hurled a grenade into the air. Instinctively, Riegel dove to the ground next to the Tech's desk, presuming the bomb was meant for him. The detonation blasted just above him on the roof. He heard shouts and screaming through the window now, and he quickly regained his position to get a few more shots off at Gentry as he closed.

But when he looked back out the window, the Gray Man was gone, and now there was no way to stop him from entering the building.

Incredible.

Just as Gentry had promised over the phone the evening before, the prey had become the predator.

Court slammed his back against the wall of the château and reloaded his weapon with a fresh magazine from his thigh rig. Two stories directly above him was the big blond man with the pistol. Above that man would be the shooters from the helicopter. He was reasonably certain he'd thinned their ranks some, but he held no illusions that he'd eliminated the threat on the roof.

To his left and right there were windows waist-high. Glass shattered from Gentry's HK made them dangerous to enter without prepping them first. To his left were steps up to the main back door, around the corner to his left was the front drive and some sort of battle raging, and to his right was the long back wall lined with windows and then a small set of doors. In a crouch he rushed along the wall, shoulder scraping the stone to stay out of view of the shooters above him.

He was near the door when it opened outwards. As it swung open, he raised his weapon to fire a burst through the wood but hesitated at the last second. What if it was one of the Fitzroys? Court recognized he was not the best man to undertake a rescue operation. He had a tendency to shoot anything that moved in a combat situation; now he had to take that extra moment to ID his target.

A head peered around the edge of the door to him. It was big and Slavic, and when he saw the barrel of a rifle pass the door's edge, Gentry satisfied himself of the validity of his target. He sent eight rounds through the door as he ran towards it. It was set to lock when it closed, but the doorstop of freshly dead goon kept it open for Gentry as he entered a darkened hallway.

At the first sound of gunfire on the back lawn, Claire and Kate Fitzroy ran to their sleeping Mummy and shook and screamed at her to wake. Once on her feet, Elise stumbled; the girls steadied her with both hands as they led her to the other side of the bedroom where

Grandpa Donald sat upright on the four-poster bed. Claire relayed to all that Jim wanted them under the bed, and Grandpa Donald agreed. Mummy fell back asleep facedown on the hardwood. Claire and Kate huddled together in fear, peeking under the bed runner towards the door to the hallway, while Grandpa Donald remained above them.

After a loud explosion on the roof two stories above, Grandpa Donald called out to the guard, "McSpadden! McSpadden!"

Claire saw the boots of the Scottish guard move into the room. She heard the conversation above her, though she didn't understand all of the words.

"Lad, best you do your runner now, but be a good chap and leave us a gun."

"Fuck you, Fitzroy. It's too late to run. I'll need my guns to fight off your attack dog. Over the radio they say he's already in the house."

"McSpadden, if you *see* my attack dog, the last bloody thing that will save you will be a gun in your hand. You might take off your white underpants and swing them in surrender if you haven't managed to soil them yet. Come now, lad. You understand what you're up against. You can only save yourself by helping us."

Claire saw the man shuffle his boots like he was going to run away, but instead he moved back to her grandpa. A hand reached down, lifted one of his trouser legs, and yanked a shiny silver gun from it.

Claire put her hand over Kate's mouth to squelch a scream.

"I'll leave you my backup. Just a little six-shooter."

"It's a fine one, laddie. Now, off you go, back out the door to guard us in case Riegel or that psycho Lloyd come to check. You see the Gray Man, tell him you're with me."

"Right, that'll work just fine as long as he wants to chat me up first. I'm fucked, Fitzroy."

The guard's feet turned away and left the room. A few seconds later, Grandpa Donald slid off the bed and crawled under with them, the shiny gun clenched in his meaty hand.

"It's all right, ladies. Won't be long now. Jimmy boy is on the way."

Riegel, Lloyd, and the Tech remained in the third-floor control room. Lloyd stood near the open door out to the hallway, his pistol dangling in his right hand, his dusky blue shirt collar open, and the knot of his tie hanging below it.

Kurt and the Tech were at the computers, near the shattered window and midway between the room's two exits. They used radios to communicate with the remaining Belarusians throughout the building and the two French engineers on the first floor. One of the Scots was missing, but the other Scot and an Irishman were still on station.

Gunfire erupted suddenly on the roof. The big German presumed these would be the Saudis from the Eurocopter engaging the sniper team through the turret windows. He called the Scottish security officer and ordered him up to the third floor to cover the hall outside the room's main exit.

Just then, one of the Belarusians announced that the Sri Lankans were here, coming up the front drive. A call went out to the sniper team on the roof, but there was no reply.

And no one knew where the Gray Man had gone.

Riegel knew his only mission now was his own survival. He did not need the Gray Man dead; that mission had expired. That said, if Gentry came through either the door to the hall on his right, or the doorway to the circular staircase to his left, if anyone came in from anywhere, he would put three rounds from his big Steyr into their face before he bothered to identify them.

He just had to hold out until the rescue ship arrived from the home office.

Court wanted to crouch low as he moved through the house, but the pain in his abdomen prevented it. If push came to shove, which surely it would, he could drop, roll, crawl, whatever he had to do. But he was afraid that if he had to squat low or dive to the floor, he might not be able to get back up. So he walked fully upright, nearly dragging his numb left leg behind him.

Into the huge kitchen now, he heard gunfire above him, on the third floor or the roof perhaps. On the first floor, near the foyer, it sounded to the Gray Man's practiced ear like a one-versus-many battle had just ended, and now a new threat had arrived, maybe four-on-four. He recognized the distinctive reports of AK-47s and twelve-gauge shotguns, and shouts in what sounded like Russian on one side of the fight.

Court crossed the kitchen. He'd almost made it to a door towards the rear of the château, away from the shooting, when a black man in a brown suit appeared in the doorway in front of him.

Court trained his MP5 on the wide-eyed man. "Who are you?"

"Only the butler, sir. I have no part in this."

Gentry grabbed the man by the throat and turned him up against the wall. With the hot muzzle of his weapon pressed against the thin man's neck, the American frisked his prisoner quickly and found not a single weapon. Court tossed the man's cell phone into a pot of water sitting on the stove next to him. He found no identification.

"What's your name?"

"Felix."

"Let me guess. Felix the Nigerian butler?"

"No, sir. I am from Cameroon."

"Sure you are, buddy."

Court pushed the man towards the door out of the back of the kitchen. The black man kept his hands in the air as he walked, Gentry several feet behind him. They crossed an ornate dining room with a fireplace with gilded trim and rounded the huge, oaken table. Tapestries and portraits lined the walls. Stepping into a small hallway with a door immediately on their left, Gentry whispered again to the man in front of him, "What's in there?"

A hesitation. "It's . . . it's a bedroom."

"Not sure? A butler who doesn't know the rooms of the house?"

"I told you . . . a bedroom. I am new here, sir. I am scared."

"Open it. Let's see if you're right." Court drew his Glock and held it down the hallway behind him with his left hand, while he held the MP5 at Felix's head with his right.

The suited man opened the door and turned back to the Gray Man. Court looked in over his shoulder. There were stacked sheets and blankets in shelves from floor to ceiling. It was not a bedroom; it was a large linen closet.

"If you *are* a butler, you suck."

Felix said nothing. The gunfire at the front of the house continued without pause.

Court holstered the Glock on his hip and took his last fragmentation grenade off his vest. He pulled the pin and put it in his pocket, held the spoon down, and placed it in Felix's sweaty hand. When the American assassin was certain his prisoner had a good hold, he said, "Don't drop that. And don't think you can use it against me. There is a six-second fuse. Plenty of time for me to shoot you dead and duck into a room to get clear of the blast."

Felix's voice cracked. "What am I to do with—"

"Just keep walking ahead of me. I'll take it back from you and let you leave once I get to my objective. Don't worry, you'll be back home in Cameroon in no time."

The corridor turned to the left and ended at a large set of double doors. Court shoved the confused man forward. Twice the man tried to speak, and both times Gentry hushed the strong African accent. "Open those doors," Court demanded, still behind at the turn in the passageway.

"But I—"

Gentry pointed his submachine gun at his prisoner's head.

Slowly, Felix turned back around, opened the door on the right, the grenade hidden behind his back in his left hand.

Almost immediately cracks of handgun fire echoed out of the room ahead, and oak splinters snapped off the heavy doors. Felix spun where he stood, fell facedown in the doorway.

Court spun out of the line of fire, dropped onto his kneepads with a grunt, and counted to six.

Serge and Alain moved towards the door to the library in a combat stance, their Berettas in front of them in outstretched hands.

Alain ID'd the man they just killed. "It's zee Nigerian."

"Merde," said Serge, and he depressed the button on his walkie-talkie just as the grenade on the floor by the dead man's body exploded.

Lloyd and the Tech both jumped at the sound of the hand grenade two floors directly below them. The noise came not from the raging gunfight in the foyer but instead back towards the rear of the building. The sound also came through the speakers of their radios. Kurt Riegel chanced a quick look out the window again. He saw the black Eurocopter drift in and out of the morning mist as it flew off to the south. Below, near the marble fountain in the garden, two men moved low in a crouch. They were black, small, they carried machine pistols, and they wore black ski jackets.

"The kill squad from Botswana has arrived, or maybe these are the Liberians." Riegel said it to the room without emotion.

"It's a virtual United Nations of assholes around here," said Lloyd from behind.

The German watched the two Africans as they crossed the grass towards the steps up to the back door. He did not shoot at them. With the Gray Man in the building, Kurt felt there was a better chance these Botswanans would be more help than hindrance.

Riegel said, "Let's barricade this room. The three of us will have to hold everyone off until the helicopter arrives from Paris."

"Even if I survive this, you are going to kill me, aren't you?" Lloyd asked.

Riegel answered as he slipped his pistol back into its shoulder holster underneath his jacket. "Gentry was right; you've got more to worry about than me right now. Come and help me." He lifted a chair to put it in front of the door to the spiral staircase.

"Be that as it may," said Lloyd, "I prefer dealing with any threat at the most advantageous opportunity."

Riegel's back was to Lloyd. He stopped, put the chair down, squared his shoulders, and turned slowly. The American attorney's silver automatic was leveled at Kurt's chest. They were twenty feet apart.

"Put down that damn gun. Come on, man! We don't have time for this. There will be time enough for the aftermath of the operation after we get out of here."

The Tech sat at the desk and watched the two men intently. He said not a word.

Lloyd said, "I could've had the bastard. I could've saved the contract. *Your* operation failed, not mine."

"If you say so, Lloyd."

"No . . . I want *you* to say so. Take out your phone slowly. Call Mr. Laurent and tell him *your* plan was fucked up. Take responsibility for this."

"And then you will shoot me? Think, Lloyd! He'll know I was speaking under duress." For the first time, they heard gunshots on the third floor, far down the corridor from their position. "We need to seal off the room now! We'll talk after that."

"Take out your phone. Make the call. No tricks."

Kurt sighed and slowly reached into his jacket with his right hand. His eyes narrowed on Lloyd. Instead of the phone, Riegel put his hand around the butt of his Steyr. As he began to draw the gun from its concealment, prepared to dive to the side to duck the lawyer's inevitable gunfire, he noticed Lloyd's eyes had turned away from him and focused on something behind. Kurt took the opportunity to pull the Steyr, and he leveled it at the American's chest. Just as he was about to fire at the distracted Lloyd, a voice called out from behind.

"Did I come at a bad time?"

THIRTY-FIVE

"You're bleeding bad, Court," said Lloyd. His pistol remained pointed at Riegel, his back remained to the open doorway to the third-floor corridor, but his eyes were on the bloody man in the tactical gear. The Gray Man had appeared silently through the door from the spiral staircase, and while Lloyd had been fixated on Kurt's hand inside his jacket, Gentry had gotten the drop on him. He held a squat, evil-looking submachine gun at eye level, its barrel centered on Lloyd's chest.

"Drop the gun," said Gentry.

"Who are you speaking to?" asked Kurt, his back to the Gray Man. To see Gentry, he would have to take his eyes off of Lloyd, and he was not about to do that.

Court replied, "If you have a gun in your hand, asshole, then I'm speaking to you."

Lloyd said, "You aren't going to make it much longer, Court, old buddy. Your face is white. You're weak. Your blood is staining the floor."

"I'll live long enough to kick your ass. Drop your weapons. You, at the table. Stand up slowly."

The Tech was the first to do as he was told. He stood with his hands high over his head, shaking from fear.

Lloyd began lowering his pistol. Kurt Riegel followed suit. The German turned his eyes from Lloyd to look at the Tech for an instant.

And in that instant, Lloyd put a bullet through Kurt Riegel's chest.

The big German grabbed the wound and then fell to his side. The Steyr bounced away on the hardwood floor.

The Tech screamed in fear.

The Gray Man fired a burst at Lloyd as he disappeared through the doorway to the hall.

Court fought a dizzy spell, an inevitable consequence of his dropping blood pressure. He wobbled on his knees, and his eyes glazed over. His brain seemed to reboot, and when his head cleared, he realized he'd lowered the MP5 to his side. Quickly he raised it at the man with the ponytail and the headphones who stood by the desk with the computers. The man had not moved a muscle apart from the quivering in his shaking hands over his head. Gentry realized he could have been knocked down with a feather there for a few seconds. He was glad the man in the ponytail was too terrified to try it.

"Who are you?" Court asked.

"Just . . . just a technician, sir. I run the comms and whatnot. I have no quarrel with you."

"At least you didn't try to tell me you're the butler."

"Sir?"

Court crossed the room to the man. On the way, he kept his weapon trained on the open door to the corridor, and he kicked the Steyr pistol farther away from Riegel's body as he passed. On the Tech's desk Court found the classified SAD files. "Is this everything?"

"As far as I know, sir."

"No backups? No copies?"

"I don't believe so."

Court scooped them up and tossed them into the fireplace. He ordered the Tech to set them alight.

Once the files began to burn, the Gray Man turned the technician around and pushed him back down to his seat, facing the equipment in front of him. "You're the one who communicates with the men hunting me?"

"Oh, no, sir! Not me! I just maintain the elect—"

"Then I guess I don't need your ass, do I?"

The Tech began nodding quickly. Changed his tune in a single note. "Yes, sir! I am in charge of all communication and coordination between the pavement artists and the government operatives."

"Good. Call them all. Tell them I just jumped out the window, and I'm escaping through the orchard in the back."

"Right, away, sir." The Tech's hands shook mightily as he flipped switches on his radio console to bring up every radio channel at the same time. "All elements, this is the Tech. Subject has exfiltrated the château. He's moving to the north, through the orchard on foot."

"Well done. Now, take off your belt."

The Tech did as he was told quickly and offered it to the Gray Man.

"Bite down on it hard."

"Sir?"

"Do it!"

Wide-eyed, the Tech put his belt in his mouth.

"You biting down?" asked Gentry.

The Tech nodded.

"Good." Court smashed his rifle's butt into the man's temple. The Tech started to fall from his chair, but Gentry caught his unconscious head and laid it facedown on the table in front of him. Gentry then fired a full magazine into the computers and radios on the desk.

Court reeled from another dizzy spell, but recovered and reloaded the rifle. He checked on the burning documents in the fireplace. Satisfied that this part of the operation had been successfully completed, he exited into the third-floor corridor, his small rifle out in front of him.

Claire Fitzroy was the first to hear the footfalls outside the door. There'd been some close shooting, right outside even, a few minutes earlier, but since then it had been quiet. But now someone else was coming. She squeezed Grandpa Donald's shoulder tightly from fear. Her little eyes blinked hard from the stress, but they stayed focused on the bottom of the door to the hallway.

She heard the clang of metal on wood, more shuffling, and then the rattling of the latch. The door opened slowly, and Claire felt her grandpa's thick arm squeeze tighter around the gun in his hand, now pointed at two sets of feet entering the room.

The left boot of the man in the back was wet and red.

"It's Ewan, Sir Donald. Don't fire."

Claire started to crawl out with Grandpa Donald, but he pushed her back. He'd no sooner stood up when she heard talking.

Grandpa said, "Bloody good to see you, my boy!"

"Where are the girls?"

Claire recognized Mr. Jim's voice, and now nothing could have stopped her from crawling out from under the bed. When she stood, she ran to him, crashed into his leg and waist, and hugged him tighter than she'd ever hugged anything in her life. It was a few seconds before she backed away and looked up at him. He wore a black vest on his chest and guns and bags on a belt and hanging off his legs. In his hand was a rifle, and his face and bald head were white as parchment paper and his brown pants were covered in blood.

His eyes were red and watery.

Sweat dripped from his face like rainwater.

Grandpa Donald noticed the stains on Jim's clothes, too.

"Is that your blood, lad?"

"No, it's not. But I *was* borrowing it."

"Bloody hell, man. You need a doctor."

"I'm good." Gentry motioned to the Scottish guard standing next to him. "This guy says he's with you."

"Ewan has been quite helpful."

"You trust him enough for me to hand him a weapon?"

There was a slight pause. "I do." And then, "Just watch yourself, McSpadden."

"Aye, sir."

Court unslung the MP5 from his neck and handed it to McSpadden. Gentry pulled his Glock from his hip rig, kept it in his hand at his side. "Where's Lloyd? I think I hit him, but he got away from me. I figured he'd be down here taking hostages."

"Haven't seen the cunt," said Grandpa Donald, and Gentry looked down to Claire and Kate.

"Don. The language."

"Sorry."

Court looked around. "And Elise?"

McSpadden and Sir Donald pulled Mrs. Fitzroy from under the bed by her arms. McSpadden hefted her onto his shoulder and held the Heckler & Koch submachine gun out in front of him as he moved. Ewan led the way, with Sir Donald limping from his wounds behind him, wielding the stainless steel revolver. The two girls followed on the heels of their grandfather, and Gentry brought up the rear, staggering behind slowly now, bracing himself on the corridor's walls and the railing of the stairs. Once Claire tried to hold him up, but he just smiled at her, said he was fine and that she should stay close to her grandfather.

The caravan moved slowly, as it was comprised chiefly of children, the injured, and the wholly unconscious. After a time, they made it down the stairs to the first-floor foyer. Gentry called out from behind, "Girls! Look right at your grandpa's back. Straight ahead, you understand? Don't look around the room." Around them in the huge hardwood and stone entry was utter carnage. Four bodies right inside the blasted-open doors, two more bloody corpses in the middle of the room, and another two on the staircase alongside them as they descended. Both of the little girls began to cry. Kate coughed in the thick stench of cordite and blasted stone dust and burnt wood. At the base of the stairs, a prostrate figure moved and writhed. It was a bearded Middle Eastern man. He was alive, on his side. McSpadden passed him, as did the rest. Court was the last one to the injured man. Their eyes met for a second, but Court did not slow to help him.

The Gray Man showed no mercy to his enemies.

They moved out of the foyer and into an open sitting room, untouched by battle. The walls were lined with large family portraits. McSpadden paused to get a better hold on the Fitzroy woman, and Gentry leaned against the wall for a moment's rest. Just then, a shirtless man entered from the far doorway. He was one of the Belarusian guards. He had a neck injury he'd wrapped with a towel, but his Kalashnikov remained in his right hand. Surprised by the entourage in front of him, he lifted his weapon quickly. Sir Donald opened fire with the revolver, blasting the shirtless man back through the doorway and onto his back.

The girls covered their eyes and shrieked.

Court lifted his head slowly when it was all over. He had not even been aware of the threat. Quickly, he spun his head back around him, certain Lloyd would be standing behind him, but there was no one there.

Court's knees weakened, and he fell backwards, stumbled into and over a narrow table, and smashed it to the floor. Fitzroy and the two girls ran to him and pulled him back to his feet. They steadied him while he regained his balance.

"I'm all right. Keep moving."

The six of them made it out a side door to a pathway that led around to the graveled parking circle in the back. Still, the Scotsman led the way, the unconscious woman over his shoulder. In the distance of the misty apple orchard, they could hear a smattering of gunfire. Apparently the kill squads were engaging one another in the fog. Sir Donald found a large, black BMW sedan, saw the keys in the ignition, and instructed everyone to climb in as fast as possible. Court had lagged behind; Claire turned and ran back to him, held him up, and this time he did not protest. Twice Gentry looked back over his shoulder for any sign of Lloyd. Both times his head spun and reeled with the movement. At a snail's pace, he staggered, only able to do so now with the nominal assistance of an eight-year-old girl.

Claire struggled to hold Jim up. It seemed as if with each step he put more weight on her shoulders. He grunted and winced as they moved along the gravel towards the big, black car. The guard from Scotland gave his gun to Grandpa Donald and put Mummy in the backseat, and Kate climbed in with her. The guard got behind the wheel, and Grandpa sat in the front passenger seat. The engine started, and Jim nudged Claire in front of him, urged her to run on ahead to the car. She did as she was told, climbed into the backseat, and turned to help pull her rescuer in behind her. Jim was a few steps back but nearing. He smiled weakly as their eyes met.

A single gunshot rang out from the château. Claire was looking at Jim as his eyes widened and his body lurched forward, nearly propelling him to the vehicle but not quite. The American dropped to his kneepads on the gravel, looked up to the Scotsman behind the wheel, and cried out, "Go!"

The big car lurched ahead. Claire's door slammed shut with the movement. She shrieked as she spun around to look out the back window. She banged her little hands against the glass.

On the gravel behind them, Jim teetered forward off his knees, then fell hard on his face.

A dust cloud from the car's wheels in the gravel whited out Claire's view of the man left behind.

THIRTY-SIX

Court pulled himself pitiably across the gravel drive with his arms. His legs barely moved, and pebbles stuck to the blood on his forearms and face and in the sweat on his scalp. It was five yards to the wet grass. From there it was two hundred yards to the edge of the apple orchard. At the pace he was moving, it would be nightfall before he reached any measure of cover.

It was hopeless, but he moved without rationale, only instinct. *Get out of the kill zone.* Destination unimportant.

"Yo! Tough guy? Where the hell you think you're going?" Lloyd's shout came from behind. It was followed by the crunching of shoes on gravel. The footfalls closed quickly.

"I have to admit . . . you've lived up to your hype. You torched the SAD files *and* you got the Fitzroys. Looks like you managed to save everyone's ass but your own."

Court kept crawling on his bloody forearms, into the cold, wet lawn. Lloyd finally stepped on his back to stop him. The Gray Man looked over his shoulder with a wince. The lawyer held a small Beretta pistol out in front of him. His left arm and shoulder were bloody and limp. Lloyd seemed unfazed by his wounds.

"I shot you in the back. Not terribly noble, I suppose. I didn't know you had a vest on. Bet that still hurt, huh?"

Court rolled slowly on his back. The morning sky had blued considerably since he'd entered the château, maybe fifteen minutes earlier. Lloyd stood over him and looked straight down. Court knew his Glock had skidded away somewhere when he fell. He had no strength to lift his head to look for it.

"I still don't remember you, Lloyd," Gentry said it through a raspy cough.

"Well, you'll remember me in hell, won't you? My face will be the last fucking thing you see."

Lloyd lifted the pistol to Court Gentry's face, and a shot rang out.

Lloyd cocked his head, a show of confusion. The young lawyer staggered forward a half step. Blood appeared on his lips and in his nostrils. His eyes remained on Court, though the lids narrowed. He steadied himself and again raised the gun to Court's chest.

From behind came another shot, then another. Lloyd spasmed with each crack. His Beretta fired, but it was low by his side now. The bullet kicked up a spray of white stones between Gentry's legs as the Gray Man just lay on his back and watched.

Lloyd dropped his pistol in the gravel, then crumpled down on top of it, dead.

For several seconds Court just stared at the sky. Finally he forced his head up, looked back to the château. Riegel was in a third-floor window, the glass shattered in front of him, his pistol now trained on Gentry.

Slowly, the German lowered his gun to his side.

The two men just looked at one another for a few seconds. They were both too weak for words, too far apart for eye contact. But the long acknowledgment showed a sense of mutual respect: two warriors, each recognizing the efforts of the other.

Kurt Riegel fell backwards and disappeared from view.

Court dropped his head back in the grass. Through the ringing in his ears he noticed the distinctive sound of a helicopter. It was not the black Eurocopter; it was a bigger ship, steadily approaching from the east.

His head did not rise back off the dewy grass, but he rolled it to the right in time to see the large white Sikorsky land seventy-five yards away. LaurentGroup was written in blue on the side. Armed men poured from the vehicle, a half dozen or so. They began moving towards the château carefully. Then the aircraft disgorged a trio of men in orange jackets carrying backpacks: doctors or EMTs or some other sort of emergency personnel. Lastly, three men in suits crouched low as they ducked under the rotor's wash. One carried a notebook of some sort, another hefted two large briefcases, and a third, who was much older, wore his suit coat across his back like a cape.

Like a Frenchman.

Court lost interest in the activity and went back to enjoying the beautiful sky. A minute later, or maybe it was ten, a rifleman stood over him, but he seemed to be more interested in Lloyd's body lying alongside. The Frenchman shouted into a radio.

Shortly thereafter, the three men in suits appeared. Court raised himself up to his elbows as they approached.

The older man with the coat for a cape was unfamiliar to Gentry, but Court figured from his bearing and his dominion over the other two that this could be none other than Marc Laurent.

"Monsieur Gentry, I presume?"

Court said nothing. The little man with the notepad on Laurent's right stepped forward and kicked him with an expensive-looking shoe. Court did not feel the blow; his entire body had gone numb. "When Monsieur Laurent asks you a question, you answer!"

"It's okay, Pierre. He's unwell." Laurent looked around him at the bodies and broken glass and smoke billowing from the roof of the château. "Pierre? Make a note. We'll need to move the board of directors' Christmas retreat this year. I don't believe we will have the property cleaned up in time."

"Oui, Monsieur Laurent."

"Mr. Gentry. I see young Mr. Lloyd there. He appears to be about as useful as ever. Would you happen to know where I could find Herr Riegel?"

Court spoke softly, sleepily. "Lloyd killed him. He killed Lloyd. There was some interdepartmental rivalry in your corporation shortly before you arrived."

"I see." Laurent shrugged, as if his people died all the time, and it was of no special concern to him.

"I knew nothing of what was going on here," said Laurent, and Gentry did not respond. The statement was made in the way a man of power says something manifestly untrue. He had no concern whether the Gray Man believed him or not, only that it was put out there, as if to fulfill legal obligations.

Implausible deniability.

The next words from Laurent's mouth surprised Court. "I am in need of a man." He looked around at the bright morning. "It's a problem, you see. A fellow with whom I've had a long-standing business relationship has outlived his usefulness. And if that wasn't bad enough, he's in possession of information that might prove embarrassing to myself and my pursuits. Allowing him to continue on in his present course of action would serve no one's interests."

Marc Laurent seemed almost bored. He looked at the fresh manicure of his fingernails. "And, as it happens, I understand you are the man to see about such problems. Might you be available?"

Court was up on his elbows in the wet grass. He turned his head to the left and to the right and took a moment to regard Lloyd's body.

Gentry said, "I am kind of in the middle of something at the moment."

Laurent waved his hand dismissively. "Oh, I can see to that."

"That would be good," Court replied with extreme understatement.

"And as I understand it, you might just have a personal interest in the demise of former president, and now regular citizen, Julius Abubaker. Rumor is you eliminated his brother, and now the former president is arranging attempts on your life."

Court blinked twice before answering. "I've heard that rumor, as well, Mr. Laurent."

Laurent nodded. "Abubaker has made certain claims about me. All lies, of course. I run a business based on integrity and impeccable core values of honesty."

Gentry's facial expression did not change. "No doubt."

"Still, sometimes sensational claims can take on a life of their own, raise unnecessary concerns, invite uncomfortable scrutiny. I'd like to avoid that if possible."

"So you want me to kill him."

Laurent nodded. "I'd pay handsomely for your services."

Court hesitated. "I just see one little problem with your proposal."

The Frenchman's eyebrows rose. "And what would that be?"

"I am bleeding to death."

Laurent chuckled, snapped his fingers, and the three men in orange jackets appeared with a stretcher.

"No problem, young man," said Laurent as Court dropped from his elbows and passed out. He relived the conversation in a dream, and thought it later to be one of the oddest and most fanciful dreams he'd ever had.

EPILOGUE

There were only four days left until the Christmas break, and Mummy had told the girls they could wait until after the new year to return to school. Kate had taken Mummy up on the offer, but Claire declined. Routine is important for a child; she wanted to get back into the swing of things.

Maybe it would help her forget.

She would love to forget Daddy's funeral, the château in France, the noise and the fear and the guns and the blood. She would love to forget leaving Mr. Jim behind. Grandpa Donald had promised her that Jim had gotten away, but she did not believe a thing Grandpa Donald told her anymore.

She knew that Jim, like Daddy, was dead.

She entered Hyde Park. She always cut through on her way to school, walked purposefully east on North Carriage Drive, turned down a foot-path that led over to North Row, and then shortly to her school on North

Audrey Street. Her mummy wanted to walk her to school, but Claire had said no. She wanted everything to be the same as when Daddy was around. She'd walk herself to school, walk herself home.

A man sat on a bench by the footpath. She paid him no attention until he called her name as she passed.

"Hello, Claire."

She stopped in her tracks and turned to face Jim. Her knees weakened from shock, and she dropped her schoolbooks to the footpath.

"I didn't mean to scare you. Your granddad told me you did not believe that I was okay. I just wanted to come and show you that I'm fine."

She hugged him, her mind not quite accepting that he was there.

"You . . . you were awfully hurt. Are you feeling better?" she asked in a sob of joy.

"I'm all better." He stood and smiled and took a few steps up the pavement and then back to her. "See, I don't even need you to help me walk anymore."

Claire laughed and hugged him again. Tears filled her eyes. "You must come to the house straightaway. Mummy would so love to see you. She doesn't even remember you being there in France."

Jim shook his head. "I'm sorry. I have to go. I only have a few minutes."

She frowned. "Are you still working for my grandpa?"

Jim looked off into the distance. "I am working for someone else right now. Maybe Don and I will patch things up someday."

"Jim?" She sat down on the bench, and he followed her lead. "The people who killed my father. You killed them, right?"

"They won't hurt anyone else, Claire. I promise."

"That's not what I asked. Did you kill them?"

"Many people died. Good and bad. But that is all over now. That's all I can really tell you. I can't help you make sense of it all. Maybe someone else can. I hope so. But not me. I'm sorry."

Claire looked across the park. "I am glad Grandpa Donald wasn't lying about you."

"Me, too."

It was quiet for a moment. Jim began to shuffle a little on the bench.

Claire said, "You have to go now, right?"

"I'm sorry. I have to catch a plane."

"That's okay. I have to go to school. Routine is important."

"Yeah." He paused. "I guess it is."

They both stood, hugged again. "Take care of your sister and your mother, Claire. You are a strong girl. You will be fine."

"I know, Jim. Merry Christmas," she said to him, and then they both said good-bye.

Court walked slowly out of the park and onto Upper Grosvenor Square. The limp he had managed to hide from Claire had returned, and he winced with each step. A black Peugeot sedan idled just outside the gate. He ducked into the backseat without a word to the occupants.

Two Frenchmen in suits turned to face him from the front. One handed him a satchel as the car pulled into traffic. Quietly, Court opened it, checked its contents, and zipped it shut.

The middle-aged Frenchman in the passenger seat said, "The jet is waiting at Stansted. Three hours' flying time. You should be in Madrid by early afternoon."

Court did not respond; he only looked out the window.

"Abubaker will arrive at his hotel at six. Are you sure you have enough time to prepare?"

Still nothing from the American.

"We have arranged a room on the floor directly below his suite."

Gentry just stared at the park as it passed. Children walked with their parents. Lovers arm in arm.

The Frenchman in the passenger seat rudely snapped his fingers in front of Gentry's face, as if admonishing an inattentive servant. "Monsieur, are you listening?"

The Gray Man turned slowly to the man. His eyes were clearer now. "Understood. No problem. Plenty of time."

The older Frenchman barked, "I don't need you fucking this up."

"And I don't need your advice. It's my show. *I* call the time and location."

"You are my property, monsieur. We have spent a lot of money on your recovery. You will do as you are told."

Court wanted to protest, wanted to reach into the front seat and break the passenger's neck, but he checked his urges. Kurt Riegel's successor was a bigger asshole than Kurt Riegel, but he was also Gentry's boss.

If only for the time being.

"Yes, sir," said Court, though he wanted to say more. He turned his head back to the window, caught a final glimpse of the southern tip of the park, the lovers and the children and the families and the lives of others so incredibly different from his own.

The Peugeot turned left on Piccadilly, left the park behind, and melted into the heavy traffic of London's morning commute.

PROLOGUE

The asset sensed trouble, both a threat to his operation and a threat to himself, and it immediately occurred to him that he was screwed.

The American had been trained through decades of fieldwork to miss nothing, to question everything. While most people lived in a world of black and white, he saw shades of gray, and he knew how to navigate his way through them. It had kept him alive thus far, but he did not yet know if he'd identified tonight's problem in time for his training to save him now.

It was a small thing, but to the asset it was unmistakable. Simply put: his target's mannerisms were all wrong for a wanted man.

This target had tradecraft. Just like the asset, both of them had spent most of their lives doing this shit. The target would know to have his head on a swivel; it would be second nature by now, and the fact that the fifty-five-year-old American moved through the market street stalls alone this warm Caracas evening, idly looking over handmade leather goods and wall art, without a care as to what was going on around him, meant to the asset that this just might be an attempt to lure him into a trap.

The asset did not overreact in the face of this danger. Instead he turned slightly to his left, ending the foot-follow, and strolled lazily into an alley, leaving the throngs of marketgoers behind. He feigned nonchalance, but all his senses were on fire, his mind racing, secure only in the knowledge that he needed to get the fuck out of here.

Now.

He only picked up his pace when he was out of sight of the market.

This was the time for action, not reflection, but as he moved quietly alone through the dark, the asset still couldn't help but wonder what had gone wrong. How the hell did he get made? He was new to Caracas; this wasn't his turf, but still he was confident in his abilities to blend in with the crowd, *any* crowd.

But clearly he *was* blown, nothing else made any sense, and his only objective now was to minimize the damage to the overall op by contacting his masters as soon as he was clear.

He was fifty yards away from his rented Toyota Hilux, just down Calle Cecillio Acosta, on the far side of the heavily trafficked street, and he knew that by climbing into his vehicle and pulling a U-turn he could be on the Francisco Fajardo Highway in just minutes.

The asset thought he was home free.

He was not.

Eight men, Venezuelans by the look of them, government goons by the smell. These weren't cops. No, from the weight of their bearing and their obvious confidence, the asset took them for state security. They had that air of authority, that posture of coordination, and their sharp eyes locked onto him as they closed the distance in the alleyway.

He didn't see guns, but there would be guns. The asset knew that no one in this situation would approach him without a firearm.

The American could have drawn his own weapon; he kept a 9-millimeter Walther PPQ inside his waistband, but this wasn't that kind of an op. He could throw some fists if things got rough, but he wasn't going to start shooting Venezuelan spooks.

Not because he gave a shit if any of them lived or died, really. These dudes were government thugs of a dirty regime. But he couldn't shoot them because he knew he'd be strung up by his masters if he turned this into a bloodbath. The gun was under his shirt to handle unavoidable street crime, not to create international incidents.

The asset didn't speak much Spanish, so his words were in English when he got close enough to the men, who were now blocking his path in the alley. "All right, boys, what's on tonight's agenda?"

One of the hard-eyed plainclothed men walked up to him, his hands empty and out to his sides, and when he got within striking distance, he threw a right cross.

The American asset read it all the way. He ducked under it and then came up behind the swing, pounding the man in the right kidney with a powerful left hook that dropped the Venezuelan to the ground like a sack of wet sand.

Another man had moved forward; he swung a stainless steel telescoping baton, but the American spun away from the movement, sidestepped the blow, and hammered this man with an uppercut into his jaw.

But the others had taken the opportunity to close in, and they were on him before he could reload for his next punch. They came with fists, feet, and knees, and then small saps and more batons. The asset gave as good as he got, for a moment anyway, dropping a third man and momentarily stunning a fourth with an elbow to an eye socket, but a metal truncheon from nowhere took him in the back of the neck. The American fell to the ground, covered his head, rolled into the fetal position, and did all he could to weather the blows.

They had him, he knew it, and as far as he was concerned, he deserved to get his ass kicked for somehow fucking this up.

The American never lost consciousness—he was a tough bastard—but he did lose track of time. After the pounding he was hooded and thrown into the back of a car, dragged and frogmarched and all but carried into a building with steel doors that clanged shut with a sound that told him he wasn't going anywhere for a while.

He was no longer an asset. Now he was a prisoner.

He was pushed into a room, another door shut behind him, and then his hood was removed. Four men forced him into a chair with iron cuffs built into the armrests, and they locked him down.

A tough-looking younger member of the roll-up crew grabbed a bottle of water from a shelf, opened it, and poured it over the top of the American's head, washing away a little sweat and blood but annoying the prisoner just the same.

His ribs hurt, the back of his head was cut, and both his eyes had been blackened, but his thick, muscular body seemed to remain intact, and for this he was glad.

The prisoner just sat there while the water and blood ran off him, and then a grizzled older man stepped in front of him and knelt down.

In English the man said, "You don't speak Spanish, do you?"

The asset shook his head.

"You have been detained by SEBIN. You will only insult me if you deny knowing who we are."

The prisoner *did* know SEBIN, but he had no problem insulting this guy, so he denied it. "Never heard of you. I'm a tourist. Is this how you treat visitors down here?" He was playing cool, but it was an act. SEBIN was Servicio Bolivariano de Inteligencia de Nacional, the Bolivarian National Intelligence Service, both the FBI and CIA of Venezuela, and if the American harbored any doubts about his predicament before, *now* he knew for certain he was fucked.

He spit blood on the floor and said, "Why don't you tell me why you arrested me for walking down the street of your lovely country?" He was playing dumb, and it occurred to him he'd probably be playing dumb for a very long time.

But before anyone replied to his question, the door across the room opened and a man entered from a dark hallway. As he stepped into the light over the chair, the prisoner recognized the figure.

Clark Drummond. The target he'd been tailing through the market.

Drummond was fifty-five, a computer scientist and software engineer at the National Security Agency. Or he had been, anyway, before he disappeared one year earlier. A boating accident, or that was the quite reasonable assumption made when his twenty-six-foot Sea Ray power craft was found bobbing capsized in the Chesapeake Bay after a thunderstorm.

But here he was. Low-profile in Venezuela, obviously supported by the local intelligence service, and brazen enough to walk right in here among them like he was running this whole damn country.

Drummond sat down in a chair in front of the prisoner and flashed a smug smile across his face. "You must be incredibly confused right now."

"You think?" the prisoner said. "Are you from the State Department? These assholes just came out of nowhere and started beating the shit out of—"

"Save it," Drummond said with a little smile. "You know I'm not consular affairs. You know who I am and . . . unfortunately for you, *I* know who *you* are."

The prisoner did not respond, but his mind was racing nonetheless. *Never change your story. No matter what, never change your story.*

"I also know who sent you," Drummond continued. "The Agency somehow found out I'm still alive, and I had been hoping to avoid that." He put his hands on his knees and sat upright. "They'll send another asset down here. Hell, they'll probably send a rendition team at this point. Whatever. SEBIN will roll up the next batch of CIA, just like you got rolled." He grinned even more broadly now; his confidence seemed genuine to the American in front of him. "Matthew Hanley can keep trying, but he will never drag me home in chains."

The prisoner cocked his head. *Play dumb, stay dumb.* "Who's Matthew Hanley?"

Clark Drummond rolled his eyes as his smile faded. "You're a bit of a bore, aren't you? Hanley runs CIA ops and . . . obviously . . . Hanley runs you. Or he did anyway. You won't be running anywhere any time soon."

Clark Drummond stood, then started for the door, but turned back. "He didn't tell you what I have, did he?"

The prisoner did not respond.

"He didn't tell you I left the U.S. last year with tools that made me all but rendition proof. When you showed up on cameras in my neighborhood, I saw you myself, and SEBIN was alerted. They were on your ass within hours."

The prisoner hid his anger well. He hadn't been told that the man he'd been sent to find was in possession of the means to easily identify him. That would have been useful information, to be sure, and he would have conducted his surveillance differently had he known.

But still, he said nothing, because nothing he could say would matter. He was destined for a dank and nasty Venezuelan prison cell; the rest was just noise.

Drummond continued to the exit, but he stopped in the doorway and again turned back around to the shackled American. "Hanley fucked you, Hightower. You never stood a chance."

The steel door slammed shut a moment later, and Zack Hightower's shoulders and head slumped forward. He was a beaten man. He had no idea how it had happened, but he was a beaten man.

ONE

Templeton 3 Annex is almost impossible to find if you don't already know about it. Nestled deep in a sterile office park in an unincorporated stretch of Prince George's County, Maryland, just a few minutes south of Joint Base Andrews, the front door simply reads: Palmer Holdings, LLC.

But there was no Palmer, there were no holdings, and the office space behind the door housed no limited liability company.

Templeton 3 Annex is the bland code name for a clandestine medical facility run for personnel of CIA black operations, those deemed too covert for regular medical care, and not only was Templeton 3 physically hard to find, even deep within CIA operations, only a very few knew about it at all.

No one had ever come through the door to Palmer Holdings accidentally, but if someone had they would have been turned away by the pair of men in nondescript security guard uniforms sitting behind the desk. A well-trained eye might be curious as to why men so obviously young and fit would be working the security D-list here in an out-of-the-way office park, but a visitor would get no farther into the building without passing the pair—and the Heckler & Koch MP7 Personal Defense Weapons they kept out of sight but within reach.

But at four fifty a.m. on a rainy Tuesday in August, someone with the right credentials *did* come through the door, and he stepped up in front of the two guards. Though surprised by both the time of the visit and the identity of the visitor himself, they disengaged the electronic lock to a door, which the large man in the dripping raincoat passed through. Here he encountered another pair of guards sitting in a snack room guarding yet a third door. After an okay radioed by the lobby crew, the lunchroom team asked the visitor to put a hand on a scanner, and then, when the locks popped open, the men escorted the visitor down a wide staircase and into the basement of the four-story building.

A short hallway led to more security, and the men here didn't bother to hide their weapons. Submachine guns dangled from their necks as they stood up from the table by door number four and again examined the visitor's credentials, even though, after two other checks, it was simply pro forma.

The fourth door opened, and the early-morning visitor finally stepped inside the heart of Templeton 3.

Visitors from Langley were not a particularly uncommon occurrence, but a visitor at four fifty in the morning was, so the doctor working the graveyard shift here was startled to his feet. Eugene Cathey stood at his desk, computer monitors all around him, stiffening a little in an attempt to hide the fact he'd been caught dozing.

And when he recognized the big man in the wet raincoat, he only stiffened more. As far as Dr. Cathey knew, Matthew Hanley, deputy director for operations for the Central Intelligence Agency, had never been here in person.

For this reason, and also due to the time of day, Cathey immediately sensed trouble, and he wasn't wrong.

In lieu of any greeting, Hanley asked, "How's the patient?"

Dr. Cathey looked to his nurse, also now standing nearby, and she excused herself into another room.

"Stable, but certainly not ready for operational status," the doctor replied.

Hanley heaved a sigh, then looked towards a closed door across the darkened and sterile space. There was a small window in the door, and through it he could just make out a hospital room, dark inside save for the glow of a few electronic monitors.

"Explain."

Cathey cleared his throat and came around his desk, standing in front of it now. "He took a knife just below the clavicle. Deep. Somehow, the blade missed the subclavian artery, so he survived, but by the time he was brought here he couldn't operate his upper left extremity. We identified the problem: the knife damaged the nerves of the brachial plexus. They have since healed to a large extent, although he does have some residual numbness and tingling in his left hand."

"He's right-handed," Hanley said.

Cathey cocked his head, paused a moment, then continued. "We're confident the nerves will completely heal in time; they aren't the problem. The problem is, the knife wound below the patient's clavicle developed an infection. A small piece of the blade broke off in his collarbone and held on to the bacteria even after a course of heavy antibiotics. I had to go in and clean it out, which I did, but he's got sixteen fresh stitches, he's got the pain from the procedure, and he's still fighting the infection. It's likely in the bone, and it will take a lot of IV antibiotics to diminish it. He'll be fine, but he needs time."

"How much time?"

"A few more weeks."

Hanley sighed again. Looked around at the machines and monitors and other equipment that lined the walls behind a small nurses' station. Several other hospital rooms ran down the hallway, but their doors were open and their lights off.

There was only one patient at Templeton 3.

Hanley said, "What if he doesn't get a few more weeks?"

"Why wouldn't he get—"

"If I take him out of here right now. What will happen?"

Dr. Cathey lifted his chin, a mild show of defiance. "In my professional opinion, your man will get very sick and die."

Hanley rubbed his wide face with a hand like a catcher's mitt. The doctor couldn't tell if he was worried or just annoyed. "How long until he gets sick, assuming the worst?"

And with that question it became clear to the doctor that the DDO wasn't concerned about the health of the man in the next room for any reason other than that he was impatient to get his asset back in the field.

Cathey did not hide his disdain now. "That requires speculation, and I don't—"

"I need you to speculate."

Cathey hesitated, then answered back with a twinge of anger. "Okay. You take him out of here, give him pills instead of the IV antibiotics. That will, *maybe*, suppress the infection somewhat, but it won't cure it. Within one week . . . two at the outside, he could be on his back, dangerously ill and in need of the nearest ICU."

Matt Hanley nodded, more to himself than to the doctor, then began moving for the door. "Plenty of time."

The doctor surprised both himself and the DDO by reaching out and taking Hanley by the arm. "I'm not sure I'm being clear enough about his condition."

The deputy director stopped. "I need him, Gene. I need him more than he needs to sit here. It's just as simple as that."

Cathey was emboldened by his anger. "Get someone else."

Hanley sighed again. "I *did* get someone else." He said nothing more, just let the comment hang in the low light, the sound drifting off over the noises of the computers and monitoring equipment outside the hospital room.

"Look," the doctor implored. "These assets. *Your* assets. You're running them too hard, not giving them enough time to recuperate after whatever the hell is done to them in the field." He continued, "You bring them in here broken, and you don't give me long enough to fix them. The woman last month. She wasn't cleared back into active status, but your people came and collected her anyway."

"I needed her. I need *him*," he said flatly. "He's tough. He'll be fine."

"Are you a medical doctor, Director Hanley?"

Hanley licked his lips, then ran a hand through his graying blond hair. "There's an old joke. A soccer player gets knocked unconscious in a game, the trainers drag him off the field and check him out when he comes to. The coach comes over, whispers to the trainer, asks if the player is okay. The trainer says, 'He can't remember his name.' The coach replies, 'Then tell him he's Pelé, and put his ass back on the field.'"

Dr. Eugene Cathey just stared at the DDO.

Hanley clarified. "The point I'm making is this. If we tell the asset he's fine, he'll be fine."

"With apologies, Director Hanley, that's not how medicine works."

"Well, in this case, it's how American national security works." He looked back to the door. The matter was settled, and both men knew it. Hanley asked, "Is he awake now?"

"I don't know. But when he *is* awake, he just stares into space. There's a TV in there. Internet. But I haven't seen him do anything in nearly three weeks other than sit and gaze at the wall, listening to music on the radio. I have concerns about his psychological cond—"

"This guy doesn't need a shrink," Hanley replied flatly, and then under his breath he said, "It's too late for that." He started forward again; the doctor had let go of his arm, but he called out to the DDO as he walked away, one final attempt to fulfill his Hippocratic oath.

"You brought me into this to give you my unvarnished opinion."

Hanley stopped again. "No, I brought you into this to keep my assets operational. Look, doc, I don't do this shit because I'm an asshole. I do it because I have crucial work that needs doing. Now, will you let me take him or not?"

The doctor, deflated, walked back over to his desk and sat down. "You can do whatever you want, and I can't stop you."

Hanley continued towards the door. "Just wanted to double-check that you understood our relationship."

Photo by Claudio Marinesco

ABOUT THE AUTHOR

Mark Greaney has a degree in international relations and political science. In his research for the Gray Man novels, including *Sierra Six, Relentless, One Minute Out, Mission Critical, Agent in Place, Gunmetal Gray, Back Blast, Dead Eye, Ballistic, On Target*, and *The Gray Man*, he traveled to more than thirty-five countries and trained alongside military and law enforcement in the use of firearms, battlefield medicine, and close-range combative tactics. He is also the author of the *New York Times* bestsellers *Tom Clancy Support and Defend, Tom Clancy Full Force and Effect, Tom Clancy Commander in Chief*, and *Tom Clancy True Faith and Allegiance.* With Tom Clancy, he co-authored *Locked On, Threat Vector*, and *Command Authority.*

CONNECT ONLINE

MarkGreaneyBooks.com

MarkGreaneyBooks

MarkGreaneyBook

#1 *NEW YORK TIMES* BESTSELLING AUTHOR

MARK GREANEY

"Mark Greaney reigns as one of the recognized masters of action and adventure."

—Steve Berry, *New York Times* and #1 international bestselling author

For a complete list of titles,
please visit prh.com/markgreaney